SUICIDE TANGO

My Year killin' it with a Shrink

TRIPSY SOUTH

Edited by New York Times Bestselling Ghostwriter & Editor
WILLIAM GARNER

ADAGIO

ADAGIO

AN INDEPENDENT PUBLISHING CRUISE
est. January 1, 2001

Katharine L. Petersen
Publisher
William Garner
Senior Editor

Copyright © 2005-∞ Tripsy South LLC
All rights reserved

Designed, built and published in America by Adagio Press

Adagio and colophon are Trademarks of Adagio Press

Library of Congress Control Number: 2017956432

ISBN: 978-1-944855-23-9

Interior illustrations: MarinaK
Cover design and photography: Erik Hollander
Book design and layout: Dino Garner

This book and its story contents are *realistic fiction*. Any resemblance to actual persons, cool cats, Australian Rainbow Velociraptors, places, events or concepts is coincidental and unintentional. There are no internet *challenges* in this novel, so don't be an idiot and off yourself. If you ever feel anxious, depressed or suicidal, please find a good, reputable help/suicide call line and reach out to a live human being. It may not be what you want in that moment, but it's a great start, connecting with a warm person who will listen to you without judging. The National Suicide Prevention Lifeline is a wonderful beginning: (800) 273-8255. Please and thank you.

P19610915
First Impression ~ 01 June 2019

for Kelly ~

Enjoy

for Every Beautiful Soul
who struggles with personal demons
and, on occasion, slays the fuck out of 'em

Dear Reader,

Tallulah's Laws of Bad Medicine was presented to me by one of my first suicide patients as a warm thank-you for listening so intently. TW later recovered and became a successful psychiatrist who worked with suicidal girls and women. Over the years, she compiled these details about psychiatrists, psychologists and other mental-health professionals who "treated" suicidal patients.

Shrinks claim to treat patients but most simply diagnose and (over)medicate them with prescription pharmaceuticals that do more harm than good.

Shrinks congratulate themselves and celebrate their "treatments" and "successes" at conferences, meetings and seminars, yet America is in a suicide epidemic . . . and it's only getting worse.

Shrinks are notorious for misdiagnosing patients, and end up killing thousands of innocent people every year.

Shrinks treat their profession as a "healing art" rather than science or medicine, because they can get away with murder and not be held accountable.

Shrinks are largely smart, but they are not necessarily good thinkers who can find satisfactory solutions to their patients' problems.

Shrinks are arrogant MDs who fully expect to be treated reverently by their patients. Further, they also expect deference from everyone, given they see themselves at the top of their profession.

Shrinks' patients typically have a shorter lifespan than the average healthy person in America today. Patients of shrinks die more than twenty years earlier than expected.

Shrinks still use electroshock therapy to treat some patients, although not one single shrink can explain how it works or even if it's actually efficacious for the patient. Still, they prescribe it.

Shrinks allow "pharmers" (BigPharma executives and reps) to dictate what medications to use on patients, and even accept bribes to do so.

Shrinks will tell patients they don't know their own minds and bodies, and will ignore what patients say.

Shrinks (and most doctors) practice "Wal-Mart" medicine, because Medicare/Medicaid and Obamacare pay so little: see as many patients as possible per day, collect as much money as possible.

Shrinks know they can prescribe medication that have a lot of side effects, and then to treat these additional health issues, shrinks will prescribe even more pharmaceuticals that do more harm than good to the patient.

Shrinks will shame patients, telling them their issues are their own fault, which causes the patient to experience even more detrimental affects.

Shrinks never admit to their mistakes, because their lawyers have told them not to. Forget that a shrink killed a patient because of over-medication.

Shrinks are poorly trained as General Practitioners, so they have little idea of how to treat organic diseases that may be the underlying cause of a patient's anxiety, depression, etc.

Shrinks ignore what many healthcare professionals have said: shrinks could cease and desist prescribing all psychotropic and psychodynamic drugs without any harm to patients.

Shrinks are the new confessors and are adept at extracting as much private, personal and sensitive information from patients as possible. Some shrinks use this information against patients, rather than helping them.

Shrinks are well shielded by the medical community. So are all doctors. It takes years for a shrink to lose his license, even after dozens of complaints from patients and family and loved ones. The medical community as a whole does not listen to patients and their needs.

Shrinks almost never discuss with their patients preventive health measures, because it is more lucrative for shrinks (and all doctors, hospitals, and BigPharma) to keep patients medicated and visiting their offices.

Shrinks rarely speak out against bad practices in their own profession, nor do they "rat" on their own peers, even if those other shrinks harm patients.

Shrinks from India are fuckn arrogant beyond description, self-entitled, and horribly condescending to patients. Indian shrinks silently wish for the caste system here in America, with them at the top and all Americans beneath them. Indian shrinks make therapy all about them, and how patients should hang on their every word. They release those who don't obey them, falsely labeling these patients uncooperative. Indian shrinks are the worst of all those from foreign countries, and do the most long-term damage to those in distress.

Shrinks don't know jack about suicide. That's why we kill ourselves more than ever before in the history of America, including during depressions, recessions and times of war and strife.

Shrinks suck.

Sincerely,
Jon Harley Moore, MD/PhD

Advance Praise for *Suicide Tango*

"A challenging black comedy that aims to entertain and save lives . . . Readers get a series of philosophical—though darkly comedic—discussions and a genuine primer on handling suicidal teens."

—*Kirkus Reviews*

"Illuminating, gallows humor look at teen suicide . . . Full of wry observations, and justifiable outrage, *Suicide Tango* is a must-read for everyone."

—*Seattle Book Review (4-Star Review)*

"An entertaining, edgy portrait of therapy . . . The author excels at capturing the intimate struggle between therapist and patient, the resistance that prevents them from understanding one another."

—*BlueInk Review*

"A well-written book that slaps the reader upside the head with the snark of a young woman."

—*Chanticleer Reviews (Best Book, 5-Star Review)*

"A provocative novel . . . the climax is emotionally draining, and getting there is a roller coaster."

—*Foreword Reviews*

"Unlike anything I have ever read before. All I can say is WOW!"

—*Deborah Carpenter (5 stars, NetGalley.com Reviews)*

"This book had me speared through the heart . . . Tight and raw writing, highly recommended."

—*Corinne Cambridge (5 stars, NetGalley.com Reviews)*

Haters Need Lovin', Too

"Ridiculous, arrogant, condescending, dull.. You might find humor in the extreme hubris, but then again you might just find the constant 'schooling' just grates on your nerves. This serious subject deserves better than this object-lesson in the dangers of self-publishing."
—*Amanda Clay (1 Star, NetGalley.com Reviews)*

"I don't think I have experienced such strong dislike for a book since required reading in high school. I imagine the narrator-type character is supposed to be disliked, but it was extremely difficult to make myself read this. It highlights everything that's wrong with psychiatry--the condescension, the self-importance. I will say that the tone they have is pretty accurately represented. If you at all have any experience with mental illness and/or therapy, this is probably not the book for you. If you want a sensationalized wild ride, then this will probably do it."
—*Stacie Taylor (1 Star, NetGalley.com Reviews)*

"This novel (also titled "WTF Dorkus") did elicit really strong emotions for me - unfortunately, they weren't positive ones. I had a whole host of issues with this book, but here are the main ones. The writer completely missed the mark on accurately describing mental illness, a working therapist-patient relationship, and how people actually experience suicidality. I get that the author was trying to write a satire, but that form has to be based in reality to work. Instead, this felt completely irresponsible. Now, anyone who reads this will think teenagers who are suicidal are merely acting out to get attention or that it's perfectly okay for a male medical professional to describe how intoxicated he is by his young female patient (and not in an intriguing, artistic Nabokov way). Additionally, I don't think the author has actually spent time around teenagers in order to write their dialogue (no, 2019 teenagers do not use the words 'rents, dorkus, hooter (smokes), etc.). And to top it off, casual racism was thrown in there about Mexican immigrants, Chinese people, and Muslims. I could not have been more offended by the tone and content of this piece. Not sure who this will be marketed to but it should not be read by YAs (or adults who can't discern the inaccuracies of the story)."
—*Erin Konrad (1 Star, NetGalley.com Reviews)*

"This is really just a girly novel in which the author flaunts her use of the English language. Filled with witty humor and sarcasm, the novel deliberately makes light of suicide by presenting the protagonist as some flippant, mischievous, teenage girl who would most likely grab a Starbucks and post memes about how terrible it must be to be single."
—*Ricardo Dutton (1 Star, NetGalley.com Reviews)*

"Probably should have kept the title WTF...because that's exactly what I think of this book! Maybe I need an IQ of 181 to appreciate this book? The shrink was clearly in love

with the patient, or at the very least completely infatuated with her...which was creepy!"
—*Andrea Schlimgen (2 Stars, NetGalley.com Reviews)*

"Written from the perspective of a psychiatrist, [*Suicide Tango*] explores the reasons that teens might commit suicide told through the voice of Tripsy, the patient. I didn't enjoy this book and I think its because it wasn't realistic to me. This psychiatrist borders on creepy pedophile at times as he appreciates the beauty of his teenage patient, he never acts on any of the feelings that he has but it just gave me the creeps that he would even express the things he expresses about Tripsy. It wasn't that this book was poorly written, it just wasn't my cup of tea."
—*Mindy Walski (2 Stars, NetGalley.com Reviews)*

"I thought that this book took a humorous approach to deal with teen suicide and I did enjoy that parts of the book rang true like when he talks about how children's minds work so differently from adults, especially their ability to tell time and see that there is a light at the end of all that pain. As someone who worked through cutting and depression as a teen and young adult, I could relate. However, I also found a lot of parts off-putting, such as when the author uses words like atavistic and ensconced without really anything to define them."
—*Jesse Presgraves (2 Stars, NetGalley.com Reviews)*

"Everything you think you know about suicidal patients in general and teenaged suicidal patients in particular— backwards . . . Although teenage suicide is a very serious subject, bear in mind that this book is both a parody and a satire and the opinions reflected therein should not be taken seriously . . . I rate this book 3 stars and don't recommend it to anyone with any serious mental health issues."
—*Colleen Louw (3 Stars, NetGalley.com Reviews)*

"To spend a great deal of time reading about a foul-mouthed, mostly stoned young person focus all her energy on discussing ways to kill herself and treating it in an off-hand, joking manner is pretty hard to get through . . . The dialogue seems largely unrealistic, especially for a teenager, albeit a very intelligent one. Likewise, the therapist is not very believable as, more often than not, he ignores his requirement to report the abuse that Tripsy talks about having been subject to nor her threats to harm herself and others. The writing style leaves much to be desired. Much of the book is badly overwritten . . . The author seems to be pushing for humor, but that tends to fall short."
—*Rosi Hollinbeck (3 Stars, Manhattan Book Review)*

"This book is a heavily camouflaged autobiography. The author, whose own longstanding psychological complexes have never been addressed and tinge every damn word, had a mid-life crisis that manifested as a face-to-face- meeting with his own anima. You know, the Jungian archetype of the feminine side of the psyche. Since he specialized in treating teen children in a wealthy suburb, that is how she appeared. As I read, and also viewed the very flattering line drawings probably done by the author himself, I could never find a single clue that he was speaking to anything but a projection on the cave wall of his own huge ego.

What is more, the distilled contempt in his descriptions of absolutely every other human being in the narrative with the exception of his 'Tripsy' reveals deep narcissism typical of thwarted artistic types.

I had terrible trouble feeling amused by this tale. In fact, only if I interpreted it as a hallucinatory journey akin to Castaneda could I bring myself to finish it.. This is an American who has never left California, I suspect, except in his dreams. That's okay. It may be that he and Tripsy speak to a certain Californian spirit and it need not be useful farther afield."

—Helgaleena Healingline (Katya Luomala) (3 Stars, NetGalley.com Reviews)

Jon Harley Moore, MD, PhD
Board Certified in Child and Adolescent Psychiatry / General Psychiatry
Director, Moore and Associates Psychiatry, LLC
Santa Barbara, California

A Brief Introduction

There was a time in my volatile, formative years when I wanted to be a musician. Not the guy who hustled small change and Canadian quarters from apathetic tourists and locals at State and De La Guerra.

What I had in mind was borderline maniacal: the in-your-face, frontline rock musician/singer, melding the sulfuric-acid guitar of Jimi Hendrix with the rock-smoke voice of AC/DC's Brian Johnson, the bane of every parent who had an out-of-control sixteen-year-old child, screaming at my feet for ninety solid minutes, then ripping off a few articles of clothing and offering them up to the Godda Baddass Rock.

Yup, that was the *me* I kept hidden from every molecule in the galaxy, especially those ecclesiastical atoms that comprised my parents.

When I told them one evening over dinner, they fell into an eerie silence. I still recall the horrified look on my mom's face, the nervous 10-Hz twitch in her left eye, the accidental clinking of her wine glass against her plate, as she raised it to inhale in a single woosh what was surely $50 dollars' worth of some French bordeaux.

Czechoslovak crystal met Danish porcelain in a distinctive high-C note, with a dozen small yet highly significant harmonics that reverberated off the peach-colored walls of the great dining room, always a gathering hole for high-end Palm Beach vultures. The molecular displacement of the surrounding air gently vibrated the silken walls; they shimmered in tiny waves that made me giddy. Those walls were my only ally.

I loved the otherworldly component frequencies and their rhythmic effects, all those beautiful, singing details. Secretly I wondered what mysteries they held.

After the mortifying silence that typically follows a carpet bombing, my father continued devouring his rare filet mignon and told me exactly where I would attend university and in which dorm I would reside. A quick swish of Dom Pérignon, chilled precisely to 45° Fahrenheit, chased with a decorous rinse of unfiltered Antarctic glacial water, and then he proudly told me he'd already ensured a place for me at his old medical school, bought with his deceased father's old money and seemingly endless power, even from the grave. Another dollop of Dom, then: "You'll study psychiatry, son."

While most kids back then were dreaming up their own futures as Captain America, James Bond, God and Farrah Fawcett's swimsuit, mine was served to me at dinner by the prick who designed and built the term bully, then wrote the how-to manual. Dessert went something like this: "You'll practice in Palm Beach. Be a millionaire at thirty," followed by a small dish of plain vanilla ice cream, no magically delicious topping in sight.

Back then I wanted to toss that man in the ocean. . . .

Some commotion in the outer office. Looked up at my door, which I always kept closed for privacy. Staring at it, I contemplated all the possible dangers: the Chinese weren't scheduled to launch their invasion of California until 2047 during the Year of the Rabbit, ISIS was running dangerously low on extramural funding, and North Korea's latest ICBM could barely do a drive-by over Japanese airspace . . . but not necessarily explode in a riot of fire as the owner's manual stated.

Maybe I should stop for just a moment and introduce myself: I'm Jon Harley Moore, MD, PhD, a psychiatrist specializing in treating anxious and depressed children and suicidal teens. I also do research on human and animal behavior, and write scientific papers on emerging subjects. One of my speculative works is in Appendix C, should you be the curious sort: *The Laws of Neurophysicochemistry and Correlative Behavior.*

While it is accurate to say that my father did indeed get his way, I prefer to state that I simply did not get exactly what I had dreamed.

Actually, that's not entirely true: far from a real dream, I know, but I did choose to treat children. His choice for me, of course, was listening to wealthy Palm Beach matrons whose primary complaint was the vapors, then billing their philandering husbands some unholy sum.

When I heard that, I almost took it, more to hear salacious stories about these resourceful, gold-digging bitches' Carlisle parties, where they plotted and schemed to fleece their men for millions, and then rendezvous twice a year for lesbian weekends in Cabo, each lady bedecked in a $50,000 ensemble.

Temptacious as it was, after about five seconds of careful thought, I summarily rejected my father's choice for me. In some unknown and otherworldly way, I was drawn to guiding kids through the wasteland of puberty and what I called the "teen streets," doubtless the worst years in the life of a human being. I had lost several junior high and high school friends through suicide. I knew it well.

Maybe I just wanted to hear stories that were surely worse than my own. Most of the time, though, my pathetic past took the checkered flag.

Bottom line: I didn't want to see any child do as some of my unfortunate young friends had done. . . .

Everyone knows I'm not the best psychiatrist in town: the guy who bills at $400 an hour, has high-end clients who don't mind a 30-minute hour, has a 22-year-old busty leggy blonde and beautiful trophy wife, lives in a 10,000-square-foot Tuscan villa in Montecito, and drives a Porsche TurboSomething with a pearlescent finish.

Nor am I considered the worst: the guy who is lucky to get low-end clients from the Santa Barbara County court system, works very long fourteen-hour days, lives with his mom in a double-wide in Lompoc, and routinely gets ambushed by former patients brandishing stolen paintball machine guns. The aftermath, I'm told, is always quite colorful and cathartic (for the patients, I'm certain).

Even my detractors would agree on this: I'm a middle-of-the-road shrink, safely ensconced in a popular practice, somewhat successful in spite of my continually punishing my deceased father. He knew exactly what I was doing, and admonished me for it by dropping my name to the end of his will, right after the six French poodles and inhabitants of the thousand-gallon seawater aquarium.

Lately, though, the blame for my current lot in life lay squarely on me and me alone. I had gotten tired, lazy, inconsiderate and downright unprofessional. Worst of all, it was beginning to manifest in peculiar behaviors that closely smacked of a tired, lazy, inconsiderate and downright unprofessional nature.

The better part of me felt I was a leader without followers.

That should be enough about me for now. Please allow me to tell you more about what happened on my 40th birthday. . . .

Remember those noises I mentioned before—all that commotion? Well, it all suddenly stopped, like an old clock that just decided—without permission from me, of course—not to tick-tock any longer. The silence was magnetic. I guess I'd grown up standing under one too many Palm Beach thunderstorms that always had that sudden period of calmness before unleashing a torrent of God-knows-what calamity.

As if back in Palm Beach, I just sat there dumbly, like an unknowing cow, chewing on my afternoon greens and staring at the first draft of a manuscript I'd written on teen suicide. It sat there as dumbly as I, gathering a lovely matte coating of particles that drifted over from the Gobi desert, dried-up Mongolian rivers and open-air Indonesian toilets, not to mention a few billion specks of pollen, fungi, bacteria and viruses, all on a host-hunting mission.

I reasoned that, in the very least, every time I inhaled the gathering miasma, it provided my immune system with a new source of protection from exotic and emerging diseases. That's the only reason I let my precious manuscript collect so prolifically. Honestly.

Besides, I had published a paper in a small, obscure and rather insignificant online medical journal on my recent findings about suicide in southern California teens. Only one person read it, and she had been one of my former patients. Tallulah had gone on to a successful career in psychiatry. She called "as a professional courtesy" to thank me for being brave to put it out there, even if no one else read it.

I still couldn't understand why people didn't appreciate my hypotheses and thoughts and recommendations about teen suicide and how best to treat it. Either they were all wrong . . . or I was all wrong. An old personality profile on me suggested that my ideas were twenty years ahead of their time. The profile failed to mention whether my ideas were actually applicable to anything. Even the most insecure part of me says my far-fetched ideas were indeed relevant, but only time would tell.

Recently, for some reason, things have changed: after fifteen years, I was quite exasperated listening to these kids vent about their miserable lives. My goodness, if only they knew what true misery was! According to my pharmaceutical rep's and their all-knowing literature, the best way to "cure" these children was to medicate them until their brains went the way of semi-intelligent mashed potatoes, and that's what I usually did, taking the path of least resistance.

My staff had been commenting lately that there seemed to be more pharm'ers passing through our doors than patients. I'm still assessing whether that was an insult to my increasing laziness and lack of interest in . . . everything, I guess.

There was nothing on my calendar for the next two hours, so I grabbed a small garlicky salad from the reefer and sat down to relax, if you can call it that. Rather than share a meal with friends or colleagues, I always chose to eat alone in my office in between seeing patients.

No one seemed to enjoy hearing my pet hypotheses about remaking an entire human being on all levels, so deceased organisms could be resurrected with 100% accuracy. Worse, I seemed to be equally if not more disinterested to hear about their hellish nights out with great friends, heli-ski vacations to the frozen wasteland of British Columbia, and bloated family gatherings at Thanksgiving and Christmas, and nights out with *Maxxim* models.

Besides, I could always lock my door and secretly jam with Brian Johnson and the boys of AC/DC, singing in perfect rhythm to Back in Black or his acidic rendition of *Route 66*. Today, I imagined myself as the mystery guest on stage with the boys, spicing up an already world-class act and sharing the mic with Brian, screaming and—

"Ya got some green shit stuck between your teeth, dorkus."

The very nanosecond she walked in, the normal flesh tone in my face descended into a deep crimson and hovered there. Some invisible hand, perhaps even my own, reached out and flipped off the music. I froze, and then willed every atom in my body to become transparent, allowing me a stealthy and hasty exit. Some deep unchartered river in my mind floated a morbid thought: I would be mercilessly and unceremoniously sucked into her vortex, flailing all the way.

She entered like she owned the place, assessed the decor and made a little smirk, then lifted her nose and sniffed at the air in front of my desk. "This an Asian kitchen or a shrink's office?"

"I'm sorry, uh, miss, but who are you?" I decorously placed my hand in front of my mouth and exhaled an invisible cloud of garlic, and silently admonished myself, not even once considering the various herbal scents wafting up and about the room. Was I blushing? Out of the corner of my eye, I noticed the bronze bust of my beloved Zxta, the Aztec warrior-poet. I swear she winked at me.

I immediately turned to the young woman, rose and offered my hand: "Hi, I'm Jon Moore, and you are?"

To her, I was just another inanimate something, blending in nicely with Zxta and the objet d'art I had collected from Japan, Russia and some antique shop in Kansas. She examined my books, especially the truly precious diaries lining the highest shelf, my autographed pictures of Jimi Hendrix and Brian Johnson, and then casually regarded my Zxta, making a barely audible sound that combined a derisive snort and an inquisitive hmmm. My eyes tracked her as she plopped down on my couch, adjusted the half-dozen or so pillows I had placed just so—well, because they looked good only in those perfect positions I put them in.

My disappointed unshaken hand slinked its way back and found something else to do: pushed my lunch aside and reached for some breath mints. Here's an important math equation for you, right up there with the quadratic equation and the Laws of Thermodynamics: Big Garlic + Tiny Mints = Big Garlic + Trace of Mint.

In seconds, she then shook out and spread the neatly folded blanket over herself, and appeared to settle in nicely. After a moment of silence, she pulled out her hairbrush and gently and lovingly brushed back her long strawberry-banana locks, and then draped her yard-long mane over her shoulder. Absently, she then cleaned her hairbrush. I watched in mute amusement—or was it horror?—as exactly seventeen long strands of her gorgeous tresses fell to my just-vacuumed, virtually dust-free carpet.

They gathered in a small delicate pile of what I could only describe as whole-wheat angel-hair pasta, self-assembling into a beautiful little nest. I wondered what otherworldly creature would inhabit such a cozy and inviting little home.

I must've looked like an idiot, let alone one with green shit stuck between his teeth, because she looked over at me and said, "Well?"

"Excuse me, but I have no idea who you are." Was she here to interview for a position we'd just posted in the local paper? With that kind of moxie, I would've hired her on the spot.

For what? I'd figure it out.

Even if I lost my head in some terrible car crash, I don't think I could ever forget the first sight of her: six feet tall, athletically built, horribly attractive. Is that contradictory: horribly attractive? My wish at that time was that she was my age and not a teenager. Oops. Now that I think about it, she was like a lie-in-wait predatorial cat, one of the big ones you see on the African savanna—on Animal Planet or a NatGeo special, at least.

Overall she resembled girls from eastern Euro, Czech, Belarus, Estonia, or maybe some Fill-in-the-blank-istan. Girls with skin like freshly stirred cream that only hours ago was flowing out of the udder of some milk cow. Her eyes were the deepest cobalt-blue, with a little padding over the top. Some called them double-Mongolian eyelids and you find them on only the most exotic people, eastern Euro runway models or girls from some undiscovered latitude.

Deceptively powerful hands like sculpted wood fingered her hair and just about every article of clothing on her. Long, well-muscled legs, like those of a world-class sprinter, peeked out teasingly from her skirt, something so flimsy and sheer that it resembled elegant toilet paper, probably Hecho en France. Just looking at it made me wish I could sneeze.

At first blush, I thought her bulemic, which meant I could break out that expensive, exotic chemistry set from BigPharma and play doctor. Her face was smooth and taut, held together by some unearthly character that allowed her age to slip only sporadically. I swear she morphed from a child into an elegant forty-something woman and back to a child again. Maybe it was just the way the filtered sunlight fell over her and played tricks with my vision. Anyway, she did this multiple times and it drove me up one notch, the one just below nuts.

Her clothes were sort of sprayed-on dirt grunge, the whole ensemble thrown together with pseudorandom laziness, it seemed. If it were the latest fashion, it probably took only seconds to apply, leaving her 23.99 hours each day to lie around and do nothing. The size eleven or so black jungle boots without laces spoke of a hard character, softened only slightly by the rainbow-colored socks. A hard-boiled Easter egg. Without the laces, the boots flopped about, making a characteristic PLOP PLOP PLOP when she walked over the Florentine porcelain-tiled floor.

I found it eerily musical, an atavistic African drum, calling in the cannibals whose marching orders were secretly encoded in those beautiful secondary and tertiary harmonics.

Believe me, please: I know some of my comments will come across as inappropriate. I know this. I feel it is important to this whole story to share a fair and balanced view of Tripsy. And of me and my behavior. Please know this, though: I never once thought of Tripsy in any salacious way whatsoever. Never. Quite the contrary: I admired her otherworldly nature, and was in awe of her. I secretly wished to discover a lovely woman just like her, except forty years old.

I wondered again if she were a new patient whose history I had failed to review beforehand. Could I have been so careless? Yes. After all, I had been slipping some: failing to check the calendar each day, not reviewing past notes, not signing paychecks on time, not returning phone calls to parents of my patients. Little things. Pesky details that my able staff took care of in my mind's absence. Wait a minute: wasn't my staff supposed to alert me to new patients? Were they now taking cues of laziness from me?

In spite of my obvious shortcomings and continual subtle attempts at self-sabotage, it was a well-trafficked practice, and all the parents loved me. After all, I was the magician who tamed their little monster with a single daily pill, patch or injection. Or two. In my own defense, I should add that I also treated each patient with love and care. Yes, genuine.

"My appointment, remember? Didn't my mother call you?"

The voice seemed to come from Zxta, so I glanced over at her, mumbled "Oh, my" or something. I can't even remember hearing myself. Normally I'm in reasonable control of my faculties and I sound like a pretty smart guy, especially when I'm talking about suicide in children. Really. Now, though, I found myself shaking and stuttering a bit, wondering how and why I got into this sorry state of affairs.

Was it this young woman? Maybe my reaction to her? Or was it the future she was about to visit upon me, something that would engulf me like invisible quicksand?

Some were probably true, because she had just short-circuited the entire electrical apparatus of my nervous system, leaving me utterly helpless.

All that control I thought I had over my mind, thoughts and actions vanished into the ether. I was back under my father's cathedral ceiling again, conjuring up ways to burn down his 12,500-square-foot industrial complex some called a home.

She pulled out a pack of what looked like organic cigarettes and lit one. It smelled sweetly of the same medicinal marijuana a former girlfriend used to take for what she claimed was a "chronic pain in her ass," caused by her parents' constant nagging. Then she took a long drag on her hand-rolled—what do you call these things nowadays? Hooters?—and then exhaled a plume of smoke that seemed to curl up like a huge python, diffuse slowly over to me, and then, with the deception of a ruthless predator, envelope me like a warm firm blanket.

Within minutes, I was high as a runaway satellite spinning way past the Van Allen belt into darkness that wasn't likely to be mapped anytime soon, let alone inspected for a lone survivor. My bad luck: I was deathly afraid of flying. Being lost in outer space was absurdly incalculable.

Slightly disoriented, I still couldn't determine whether it was the second-hand hooter-smoke or my just being intoxicated by her that lifted me free of my corporeal body.

Suddenly a soft voice spoke, summoning me back to reality. I swear it was the strong and sexy bronze bust to my right, but she was, well, bronzed and quite preoccupied just sitting there looking like some regal warrior/poet/high priestess, flash-frozen during an obviously high point in her life. My only wish for myself at that moment was that whatever captain was in charge of bronzing us, uh, scholars would mercifully pass me by on this day.

I could hear my father now: "No need to concern yourself there, son."

Oh, shut up, old man. "Miss, there's no smoking in this office. Please extinguish your—"

"Emma Tripsy South. Call me Tripsy. Don't ever call me Emma, you moron." She tossed her head back on the pillow, blew out another cloud, looked over at me and said, "Tell me when you're ready, stud. We have a lot to talk about and I've only got one year left in me."

I do recall walking over to her and, as an awesome show of force and authority, abruptly yanking the hooter out of her hand and extinguishing it in my salad dish. It sizzled like a plate of newly minted fajitas. When I returned to my chair, she coolly pulled the multicolored bubble gum from her beautiful mouth and gently let it fall to the floor, then lit another one.

When she left, something on the floor caught my eye: that little nest of her long hair? It had her bubble gum safely ensconced in its center and it resembled a beautiful robin's egg. Please excuse me while I consult my volume on the subconscious mind's interpretations of this phenomenon. I don't even recall her leaving after her short introduction. Did she schedule another appointment with me?

What follows is a partial transcript of our sessions together over exactly twelve months to the day, my birthday. At first, I included every session so you could see her from day one and follow her progress to the last session. Then when I read it, I realized how 10X Tripsy really was, so unbelievably concentrated in every way, much like drinking a quart of Tabasco in one sitting.

I knew she would scare off just about everyone, so I pared down the final version. Don't worry, it still contains enough of Tripsy for you to get blindsided, without actually having a heart attack or stroke, or committing mayhem and mass murder.

If I were you, I'd read this little gem several times to get the full flavor of Tripsy and her off-planet wisdom. Oh, and please don't forget all the Appendices.

When I first started meeting with her, I felt she was simply angry and antisocial, and not necessarily suffering from any known disease. I did a complete physical exam on her, including all labs known to modern Western medicine, but they revealed absolutely nothing remarkable.

Tripsy appeared to be a completely healthy young woman.

As we progressed, I then witnessed a remarkable shift from one behavior or disorder to another. My chief of staff would have remarked that she was like a seasoned Hollywood actress, acting out each and every known clinical psychiatric problem. Question was, why? Did she conjure up these stories about herself, her parents, her experiences, et cetera?

There are several psychiatric terms that describe these conditions, but I won't bother with them now as none of them could completely describe her behaviors anyway. This is what truly hooked me into this lengthy investigation: discovering what made Tripsy tick.

Simply put, her clock was unlike any other and played to it's own composition, color and texture. And those are just a few reasons that encouraged me to study her case so intently. Subconsciously, there were hidden motives that released small clues along the way—doodles, poems, musings—but I was slow to discern their underlying meanings.

Looked over at the bronze bust of my beloved Zxta. She wasn't much for words, but I swear she winked and blew me a big kiss for luck.

Tripsy South

1

Why Do You Want to Kill Yourself?

Being a textbook practitioner of the anal arts—please read: compulsively obsessive and obsessively compulsive—I often puzzle over the impossibly complex neural processes that lead a human being even to consider taking her own life. After all, they and their parents, for most people, have already invested at least fifteen years in that life, although for the average suicide—excuse me, suicidal person—this may not have been a particularly pleasant experience.

[Public Service Announcement: This is a long chapter, and completely relevant and necessary, so please bear with me.
Okay, game on again.]

Evolutionarily speaking, when an organism invests that much attention, time and energy into its own life, it is usually unlikely that the organism will destroy all it has worked for, slaved over, plus contributed to a community, helped raised siblings, etc. Yet, despite the strong and well-established evolutionary pressures that favor living, suicide somehow remains a significant killer of our young.

How does one explain this phenomenon to someone who has already begun that long, slow descent into upward mobility—an adult? Let's try this: have you ever sat down and thought about how long fifteen years really is? If you're now a middle-aged adult, say, about forty-five, please imagine life at thirty again. Then make your way forward to forty-five, considering the thousands of experiences along the way. Somewhat of a dense blur, wasn't it? Allow me to sum it up for you: there were probably some career changes, a marriage and divorce, one or two children, death of a parent, significant financial gain (or loss, heaven forbid!), or, perhaps, one or two discreet affairs with a member of any readily available sex.

Rather simple, wasn't it? Thing is, you handled that big blur with some measure of maturity, either as a grown-up or an adult. Yes, there is a difference between the two: the former is a big kid; the latter, a mature and reasonably adjusted person.

Now go back to age two, which is about the earliest age a normal human can recall anything of note, and repeat the process. Over the ensuing fifteen years, you underwent the most significant changes in your life: fantastic growth of brain and body, from zero to sixty in practically a nanosecond! You also underwent significant development of speech and language, and practiced using all those marvelous senses. And who could ever forget this one? You learned algebra. Through it all you remember the spirit of adolescence and that scourge of puberty, yes? That horrific moment when a fragile young body and brain suffer quantum leaps on countless levels, and time seems to slow to an imperceptible crawl, thus drawing out the pain and agony to impossible limits.

To cap it, Mother Evolution doesn't even provide a modest owner's manual for a young child, not that she would read it. Even though all parents experienced puberty in one form or another—and raced to forget the whole process—they're still at a loss with how to cope with it, with their own child. They, too, would just as soon forget that horror story.

Point is, the early years of a child are so unbelievably packed with highly compressed information that simply disallows the child any real comprehension of her own being at that time. It's as if the human body attempts to speed through the necessitous process of incredible growth, begging the child to close her eyes and just go along blithely for the ride.

My goodness. I encourage you to re-read the above paragraph, as it truly explains in general terms what a child goes through in her first fifteen years of life.

When I first began treating suicidal patients, I would often remind teenagers how young and malleable they truly were, and that they're really just starting their lives and will soon outgrow the pain. Hold on just a little longer, I would plead. It became a mantra that I hoped every child I saw would repeat to herself every time pain surfaced, and then share the lesson with others.

On more than one occasion, one of them retorted, "fifteen [Expletive deleted.] years was a long [Expletive deleted.] time to be [Expletive deleted; yes, again.] unhappy."

Even though we studied this phenomenon in medical school and during my residency and fellowship, it didn't hit home until I was practicing on my own.

Therefore, when I saw it in those terms described by more than one young patient, I took a different view of what kids go through when contemplating suicide. I also learned that a year to an adult or reasonable grownup is 365 days. To a child, especially a suicide, a year is "hellacious infinity," everywhere, every day. Period. And whatever pain inhabited a child at that time, it felt like it was in permanent residence.

What a frightening reality, the thought of living 24/7 in a completely helpless state, one that never dissipates, let alone disappears altogether.

That's what a child in pain feels and is encouraged to live with, struggle through, and come out the other end as a well-functioning adult.

For kids, time is compressed, much like a Slinky at rest. When life is going relatively well for a child, time marches on very quickly and the Slinky remains compressed and appears relatively short, although physically it still contains the same amount of "time" or experiences to us adults. The alternative is to consider that the Slinky really is several times longer stretched out, which corresponds to real time to an adult.

When things turn for the worse, a child's time-spring painfully *decompresses*, or elongates, into what feels like an interminable forever. What was previously short and sweet is now hours or weeks. That Slinky went from being a short spring to an impossibly long coiled wire that seemed to spin and kink out of control.

A year to a child, as I said, is an impossible infinity. Children in pain can't even fathom the concept of a week. It's only relative as it relates to a school week, a vacation or the coveted weekend.

What's often worse, too, is that a child's timeline can become syncopated, where small and large events are dropped from conscious memory. There's too much sensory input for children nowadays, and social evolution pressures them to inhale and store as much as possible during every gulp of life.

While adults tend to feel that much of what kids absorb is garbage, the kids themselves sense things differently. To kids, "garbage" is exciting and entertaining, and forms a great part of their foundation as they grow into adults. One adult's garbage is another child's useful and necessary fantasy. We can also look at how children play in the dirt, which adults see as, well, dirt. That so-called dirt contains all manner of bacteria, fungi and other creepy invisibles that contribute greatly to a child's healthy immune system.

I'd like to add one additional analogy that may help describe the vast differences between adult reality and kid reality, using my favorite subject: physics. Adults can be thought of in terms of large molecules, whose gross molecular behavior can be approximated using classical Newtonian mechanics, something we all learn in high school physics.

If you were one of those who, ah, shunned the sciences, then please skip the next several paragraphs.

Newtonian mechanics can describe gross behaviors, like the movement of individual atoms and molecules from one place to another via a process known as diffusion. Or the ionic or covalent bonding of one atom with another.

But classical mechanics seems to break down below the atomic level, where funky forces come into play.

How does this apply to a child? The behavior of children can adequately be described—analogously, of course—not by classical mechanics but by quantum mechanics, which govern the behaviors of subatomic particles, well below that of "adult" molecules.

At the subatomic level, all sorts of funny physics goes on: particles move in strange and unexplained ways, new and fascinating forces create actions never before seen at the much-larger molecular level. Only someone who understands the nuances of quantum physics can fully appreciate the myriad effects at that level. A traditional physicist who only studied classical mechanics and electrodynamics may have considerable difficulty understanding the behavior of particles at the subatomic level, or may not grasp anything at all.

Imagine that: an adult who cannot communicate with or understand a child on any level. Maddeningly frustrating, isn't it? Some parents pull their hair out.

Adults are like large molecules; children are like subatomic particles like electrons, protons, neutrons, quarks, gluons, etc. As one can imagine, the strange goings-on within an atom—analogously, a child's mind—are not governed by any "adult" laws. Therefore, kids should be seen as separate and distinct entities, and should never be viewed as "miniature adults," regardless of how mature a child may appear. The physical laws and rules that govern the life of each precious child are a complete mystery to most adults.

Armed with information like this may allow a child psychiatrist to view and work with kids on a level far different and often more fascinating than that of adults. In effect, a good child psychiatrist delves well beyond condensed-matter physics; he becomes a practitioner of the voodoo arts that appear to define quantum mechanics. Of late, I was neither. And this was beginning to concern my staff, not to mention what was left of my delicate psyche.

Pain often forces a child to ignore certain events and stimuli, which can make treatment very difficult. How do you ask a child to explain how or why they feel mentally dysfunctional? How do you expect a child to even begin to answer a question like that?

We adults are obligated on many levels to fully understand how a child sees reality, and learn to separate theirs from ours. We tend to want our children to face reality as if these kids actually understood adult reality. They don't. And, unfortunately, most parents don't understand the reality of their own kids, even though parents went through it themselves. Society has trained children to act as society expects, not as these children would act if their creative freedom and dignity were intact and continually nurtured.

Sometimes, I wonder if some parents were hatched from alien eggs. They often ask kids the most irrelevant questions. A good example: "Do you understand me?" The traditional answer kids give is a nod of the head or a simple yes. Do you honestly think those kids are telling us the truth? When was the last time you heard a parent ask the child to explain what the parent just said, but in the child's own words?

The second-stupidest question in the English language that adults and grownups ask children really kills me: "Why did you do that?" My goodness! Here's what parents need to know: children are great sponges of vast amounts of information, and they have very little, if any, time to analyze those incoming data, let alone how to respond to them in a way we can understand and act on.

Parents and people in general do not realize that our conscious self—a simple bus driver who gets us from Point A to Point B—is the one being interrogated and it has little access to the valuable information others seek from us.

That information is stored and processed in one's *subconscious*, the deep entity that communicates information from The Universe to our conscious self through dreams and dreaming and the occasional daydream or little mental itch you sometimes feel. Your subconscious talks to your bus driver by that "nagging little voice" in the background that reminds us not to do or say anything stupid. Unless we listen to those communications, we are sometimes at a loss to explain ourselves coherently. Things get worse when we are stressed.

And please don't tell me it was Freud who invented all this cool information. He was a manufactured fraud who was directed to "present" his so-called ideas to the world. Pure propaganda, so please do not believe his poop. You can believe mine, though, because it's accurate.

Anyway, where were we?

Oh, yes!

So how could we possibly expect a child to answer us accurately?

It's nearly impossible.

A child storing all that information is already like drinking water from a fire hose. Blasting on high. We adults and grownups should not ask children to evaluate, much less be responsible for, inbound information. The process of human physical growth has been honed by evolutionary pressures for millions of years, so we're obligated to let Mother Evolution take her course in the development of our children, with nurturing supervision.

Yes, children do learn to associate their parents' words and emotions with relevant actions and behaviors. But parents often expect too much too soon because parents don't understand it themselves.

What people fail to appreciate is that children must go through certain steps during early years, and must be allowed to act and behave like children. When those steps are removed or shortened to make room for more adult behaviors, the child loses an important part of their emotional growth, thus rendering them basket cases as adults.

There're countless cases of child prodigies who failed miserably as teens and adults because parents and society pushed too hard. Some stories ended well. Others, at the morgue.

What brings on thoughts and feelings of suicide? I can hear you now: "Information overload, you idiot. Get on with the story!"

Often, it's merely a chemical insult that begins with some form of trauma, be it physical or behavioral or externally chemical. Other times,

I've ascribed demonic intrusion as the root cause. I know it sounds silly, but demons do exist. I've seen them in parts of West Africa, where I studied briefly, and even a few in south Florida. While I don't think Tripsy is possessed in any way by a demon from a netherworld, I wished to include it as a prospective cause of suicidal thoughts, in general.

Over the years, I've often found it helpful to ask this simple question of my patients contemplating or threatening suicide—why do you want to kill yourself?—and then just encourage them to talk for the entire session. Often enough, they discover for themselves that suicide would not be in their best interest. And we both often find that they just needed someone to listen to their thoughts and beliefs, ideas and dreams, wants and wishes.

Recently, though—perhaps out of pure laziness—I've found it easier just to medicate patients and free them of the burden of abject pain, especially kids who may never have the mental faculties to understand their own self and behaviors.

It's true that some patients can be successfully treated using behavioral therapy, but many have to be medicated, sometimes for many years, if not a lifetime. Sadly, the cause is often some insult by family or society, including the poor quality of food, water, air and other chemicals. Behavioral trauma also adds to the mix in countless ways.

Of course, there's always the odd patient who believes that nothing short of killing themselves, and perhaps taking me with them, is the only recourse. At those times, I feel the need to be fully armed with a medium-size box of 10-mL syringes, each filled with 40 milligrams of diazepam. In case you're not sure what diazepam is, look up valium in the dictionary. Forty milligrams is enough to put a small horse into low-earth orbit for a week. Although I've yet to deploy it in combat against a child, I imagine an appropriate dose would cause immediate drowsiness and then put her into a deep, comfortable sleep. Hopefully, not too deep.

I have often thought of keeping on hand a small handgun for the truly odd patient whose chemistry resides to the far left of The Great Bell Curve, but I've found that merely brandishing a box of syringes with long hypodermic needles is more than enough to shock the patient back onto the couch and into her own head, however dangerously radioactive it may be at that time.

Did I also mention my 130-dB atavistic scream that follows the brandishing of the syringes?

One of my assistants, who happened to be present during one particular patient's rampage, quietly assured me that it was the scream that arrested that patient and welded her Converse All-Stars firmly to the floor.

Tripsy was quite—how to put it?—passionate about verbally expressing her beliefs, without being physically violent. Janice, my chief of staff, once referred to Tripsy as a "booming loudspeaker operating at full volume in an empty stadium and filling it with nothing but Tripsy."

I also recall her relating to me, "Tripsy didn't even have to be plugged in. She operated on her own power, and there seemed to be an endless supply of it, thus probably violating several important universal laws of physics. She's a true force of nature, probably not of this earth. With that said, Jon, you're probably in a lot of trouble."

I respectfully concur. In fact, I was fast developing a hypothesis that Tripsy was an Indigo child. I've studied this archetype over the years: very rare in number, personality, neurochemistry, behaviors. I've only come across one and he was someone else's patient who was referred to me for a second opinion. I was so in awe of him that I wanted to drop everything I was doing so I could study him for the rest of my life.

Sadly, though, he took his own life at just thirteen years old, shortly after he returned to his native Scotland, in Edinburgh. Didn't leave behind a letter or any indication that he was suicidal.

Liam knew that he couldn't possibly live in this world of such volatile intemperance and ignorance. Withdrawing into himself was his last refuge in the final months of his life, and that wasn't enough for him. I was heartbroken when I heard the news, yet I understood this boy's motive completely. I don't think he was suicidal at all, and I wanted to tell the world but I knew no one would listen let alone understand.

So much of his unusual chemistry was now right on front of me, and I wondered how I should approach this case. Would Tripsy slowly slip away from all of us like young Liam did?"

Session #1

Without my even noticing, Tripsy breezed in and took up what looked like permanent residence on my couch, screaming, "I'm sick o' my fuckin' life!"

I swear, a 120-dB rendition of Handel's *Zadok the Priest* accompanied her rocking intro, those off-planet arpeggios blasting out my eardrums. Jumped out of my pants, scrambled to put them back on again. All my senses were trained on her, awaiting her next fusillade and praying Handel had left the building. Along with his bloody fireworks. I do admit to being lazy and perhaps a little self-destructive at times, but I'm not normally shocked by a patient.

Was today supposed to be her first session? How did I miss that?

After a few seconds, I eased back down into my chair again, checked to see if I had wet my pants. No, thank goodness.

Tripsy seemed agitated, like her own skin didn't fit right. She pulled and tugged at every article of clothing on her, making me wonder just how disturbed she really was. After each of my senses proclaimed it reasonably safe, I fingered her medical record and accompanying case file, and opened it to some arbitrary page, hoping to read some encouraging news, something like, "Has terminal brain cancer . . . one day to live." Kidding.

Before I could say hello and without warning, she launched herself off the couch, sending me back against my chair, which rolled a few feet away from my desk. "Do I have to spell it out for you in the Queen's English, you moron!?" She pulled off the long multicolored scarf from her neck, fashioned it into what looked like a garrote and, without making eye contact with me, violently snapped it: CRACK!

All six feet of her towered over my oversized desk, not to mention the little guy sitting just behind it. "Since I treat suicidal teens, that's probably a good idea. Please elaborate for me." I was desperate to regain some sense of composure. After all, the girl was right in front of my desk, orchestrating the movements of every atom in my office.

After a few deep breaths, I moved forward and surreptitiously slid open the drawer that housed that box of valium-filled syringes. Valium!? Are you kidding!? Pull out your gun, you idiot! I decided against the military-grade hardware, because she probably would've responded by brandishing a .357 hand-cannon and blowing a hole in my face. At least her violent act would've razed my ridiculous expression of fear and embarrassment.

Worrying what she'd do next, I tried to compose myself further, while leafing through her file for signs of just how dangerous she may be. After finding the box of valium, I looked down at the small needles inside the sterile plastic containers. My nightmarish thought was that not even a 12-gauge hypodermic—a large-bore needle normally reserved for large animals—could penetrate her beautiful hide, even if I carried those monstrous arrows.

Dead silence for the longest four seconds I can recall. She seemed to inhale a roomful of air, much like dragons did immediately before spitting a river of lava.

Then she unleashed: "I AM SICK OF LIFE! Sick of my mother ragin' on me over stupid grades, sick of having to take the poodle out to pee. Why can't the butthead do it in the litter box like my cat?" With a few smooth twists of hand, she dismantled her garrote, wrapped the scarf around her neck again, making her look only slightly less menacing. Only slightly.

My eyes didn't leave her, not for a nanosecond. I took a few deep breaths—nothing of the order of Tripsy's dragon-like inhalation, mind you—then relaxed a bit, even though she was still right in front of my desk. "How was your stay at the hospital? And would you please take a seat, Tripsy? I'd like to discuss some things with you, including the results of your physical."

"Then they'd rag on me about emptying the litter box. I'm sick of thinkin' about it and it hasn't even happened! My teachers make me sick for making me read this worthless revisionist crap. Didn't anyone ever tell 'em that history's written by the dude on the winning team who could write at least semi-intelligently!?"

"What's your cat's name?" Hoped to shift her from this tirade. Heck, it worked on normal screwed-up teenagers.

Momentarily distracted, she stopped fidgeting and lay back down on the couch. "What!? My cat? Oh. Parks. His brother is Smootch the Australian Rainbow Velociraptor. Stop askin' dumb questions, dorkus! Where was I? Yeah! I'm sick of how the president gets in my face in my own living room and whines about how no one's supporting him, and he's gettin' laughed off the stage at the UN. Just nuke the guy and move on, dude! I'm sick of how so-called religious people treat each other: they preach bein' good Christians then go and bang the neighbor's wife and kids. Gimme a flippin' break. I'm sick of all this nonsense. Sick of it! If I knew how, I'd call in an asteroid strike on the whole planet. See Darwin in action." More fidgeting. "From scratch."

Velociraptor. That says a lot. "Uh, okay, would you like to tell me about the hospital? Thirty days inside must've felt like a prison." This kid could power Las Vegas for a week. Like many non-depressive suicides, she had boundless energy.

She went on like I wasn't there, the walls, ceiling and all non-breathing objects, all listening diligently: "Stop interrupting me, dorkus! I'd wipe out Microsoft, Tyco, *Wall Street Journal*, Walmart, the US Army, the stupid leaning tower of Pisa, the crumbling pyramids of Egypt, the Vatican, Hollywood, the Prince of Monaco and that idiot-asswipe Doctor Flippin' Jimmy. I'm sick of you creeps! If this is life, I'm sick of it, too! I wanna SCREAM for a year, until all the air inside me is sucked out forever!"

My mouth must've been wide open, because there was this little puddle of saliva on my desk under my chin. Again, I settled myself, wiped things up, and got back in the game. "Your mom told me that you spent the past thirty days in the psych ward. And I also spoke with Dr. Harrison who treated you there. He wasn't able to give me—"

"And I'm sooo sick o' you, too! Shrinks. Hha! I come here to get healed and end up monologuing with a dorkus."

Get healed?

Maybe there's a place for me after all. "Would you like a glass of water, Tripsy?" I also think I mumbled something like "and a few ounces of absinthe?" I was always careful to use her name as often as I could remind myself, to maintain our rapport.

"Drop dead, Fred. Drop flippin' dead, okay?"

"Tripsy, I think it might be helpful if we—" I sat there in disbelief as she walked right out the door and into the hallway. My eyes followed her, more because I'd never seen a woman move like that, one sent from the heavens or someplace else where they designed and built fiery angels like this one. Made me ponder the nest ecology within her home. Did she even have a nest to call her own? Had her parents created a safe ecosystem for this unusual girl?

Before she left the building, Tripsy stopped in the lounge area, in front of one of my younger patients, Tyra, who at ten years old was totally unresponsive to anyone. Tripsy bent down and reached out her hand to Tyra, who looked down and began to stroke it as if it were a kitten. Tripsy then leaned in to Tyra and whispered something to her, which made Tyra look up at her. I swear, the little girl smiled.

As Tripsy rose, she looked back at me, my jaw hanging loose in disbelief, then looked over at my fashion-conscious receptionist and launched: "And poo on you, too, Cosmo-girl!"

My chief of staff rushed in to check on me. I must have gone comatose for a few seconds, because when I awakened she was shaking me and calling my name. I turned my head a little and just looked at her for a moment, then said, "Please check on Tyra. She reacted to Tripsy." Janice had that look of utter disbelief on her face, same as me, so I confirmed, "Tyra Bailey just smiled." While she didn't say anything to me at that very moment, my normally calm and strictly professional chief of staff had that *holy crap* look on her face.

I ran to the window and caught a glimpse of her running to the bus stop down the street, soon melting into the afternoon throng of local government workers and tourons from Germany, Japan and Ojai.

Rather than wait, I immediately had my assistant call every physician and psychologist who treated her in any way whatsoever, and courier any and all notes, exam results, films, etc. that were not in her medical file. I wasn't simply intrigued; I was genuinely scared . . . about what I would learn, I guess. It immediately reminded me of how I felt when I tried to discern what lies over our galaxy, black and terrible mysteries beyond my comprehension. I felt like a seven-year-old boy all over again, yet strangely I wasn't as afraid of the cold, black unknown.

Though numb to just about everything in my life, I sat back and thought, *What the hell just happened?*

My skin tingled, an electric surge that screamed up and down my spine and all points above, below, fore and aft. The rolling, galvanizing thunder lasted all afternoon and evening. Couldn't sit in one place for longer than five seconds, nor could I concentrate on any one thing. Paced the floor of my office. Walked outside for some fresh Santa Barbara air, spiced up with Russian dust and Indonesian potty-soot. Only one thought in my mind, though: Who was this mysterious creature, Tripsy South?

One thing was certain: unless you had titanium skin, you didn't want to get into a conversation with this girl.

Session #2

"I can't take it any longer!"

How the blazes did this stealthy girl manage to sneak in here without my assistant or my own eyes seeing her? After her last outburst, I actually considered installing military-grade seat belts on my chair, the heavy-duty ones you find on fighter jets.

Heck, why not just get a whole ACES II ejection seat and aim for the back window? If I had to pull the handle, the worst that would happen was that I would launch out and become a permanent bas relief fixture on the east wall of our magnificent courthouse building.

Or, if I chose to subscribe to Occam's razor, I could just put a lock on the door.

"Hello, Tripsy, are we on a new topic here? I'd really like to hear about your recent hospital stay. Why don't you—"

It's as if she had never left after the previous session: she was in the exact same position as before, fiddling with her clothes, not looking at me or even in my general direction. She wore quite similar garb as before, although I do believe she changed her socks, now a rich tangerine with bright-blue polka dots.

Without looking at me: "Note to dorkus: new topic, new info. Now sit back, put your seat belt on, take your vitamin supplements, shut the heck up and just listen. You won't find this stuff in your shrink-school textbook."

Did she actually think she could educate a psychiatrist? Hmmm.

Closing her eyes, she pushed herself back into the couch, surrounded by her safety pillows. "I just wanna close my eyes and have all the noise and light and pain reverse back to zero. No mom yellin' at me to take the garbage out, no poodle pissin' in some far corner of the house 'cos I didn't come home in time to feed the little pooper, no tv tellin' me to run out and buy the latest Blahnik kicks at Bloomies, and then manipulate me into buying some cheap-ass accessories spawned in some sweatshop. It's all noise noise noise! I'm in endless info-techno-spirituo-mondo-flippin' overload!" She then tried to pull the silky locks off her skull.

Her voice trailed off: "My circuits are blown . . . fried to the core." Her eyes still closed, like she might be nodding off.

An opportunity to get a word in: "From where I sit, you have a lot to offer." I came off like an ineffective high-school guidance counselor.

Ineffective? No, make that stupid. Seems I must have been asleep during my own lecture about how children, including teens like Tripsy, are so unlike adults, because my only approach with her was a severely lame attempt to relate to her an adult level and it was going nowhere fast. Why would I even think of trying to do that, see her as an adult? Fact is, she had been diagnosed as suicidal and seemed to be obsessively preoccupied with it, although there was something strangely . . . normal about her overall demeanor.

Regardless of my initial assessment of her, I needed to reassure her, offer some measure of hope. Still there was a strange voice in my head, deep in my subconscious, screaming at me to shut up and just listen. Why?

A modest rotation of her head, slightly toward me, for effect: "My DNA ain't worth propagatin', dorkus. Pull me outta the gene pool before I pollute it with a billion mutations that'll take a gazillion years to filter out."

"Some mutations are worth saving. It's part of our continuing evolution. Without mutations, we don't get smarter, better, faster."

Looking directly at me: "I suppose now you're gonna tell me that I'm like Beethoven in some creepy way, and that if we'da pulled his Teutonic ass outta the pool because of all his imperfections we'da lost all that muzak!?"

"Something along those lines, yes."

"Look at me, dorkus: I'm nothin' but blonde locks, sexy legs and max altitude, plus three more inches in these boots."

I raised my eyebrows a bit, taking in what was painfully obvious and trying not to comment on it. "Tripsy, why don't you tell me about those thirty days in the hospital?"

I immediately heard my father's voice in my head: "You should have settled in Palm Beach and treated the vapors for $500 an hour."

Let's see . . . $500 times 2,000 hours a year equals . . . wow, a cool million dollars a year. I snapped out of my daydream and focused on Tripsy again.

More silence. She raised her eyes to meet mine. This kid thinks she invented the science and art of intimidation. Not seeing much of a reaction from me, she got up and strolled into the lobby, looked at the kids seated in the lounge area, and waved at Tyra who immediately reacted to Tripsy's attention: she waved back. Tripsy didn't turn around to see my reaction this time. She knew I needed CPR.

When I looked outside and scanned the area around the bus stop, I spotted Henry, a very old and decrepit musician who was Jimi Hendrix's chief roadie and "warmer," the guy who warmed up Jimi's guitars before The Man himself would play. Henry had long suffered from liver problems and diabetes, and had lost feeling in his feet. Poor Henry couldn't even walk on his own, now confined to a wheelchair.

The last we spoke, when I walked out to say hello some weeks back, he said he was "ready." I knew immediately what he meant, and had invited him to discuss it. He politely declined.

Before leaving the office this evening, I grabbed Tripsy's complete medical file and started for the door. As I reached it, I smacked myself for not calling Tyra's father about the good news, so I left a voicemail for him, explaining that a new psycho case of mine had somehow gotten his mute and unresponsive daughter to smile and wave. Actually, I left out the psycho part, although it seemed like the only accurate explanation.

Session #6

There I was, staring out the window like a little kid awaiting the descent of Santa's sleigh from the winter heights, wondering when she would appear across the expansive lawn. When I spotted her, I ran to my office door and stationed myself there, trying desperately to look like a heavily armed sentry. I prayed I wouldn't overdo it and give a snappy salute.

As soon as she entered the building, I yelled, "Stop!" I was standing in front of my office doorway. "Tripsy, when you come in here, I'd like you to come into my office first before we start our session."

She breezed past me like I was invisible, and then fired back: "I'm in despair over someone's death!"

Honestly, I don't think she heard a word I said. The others who treated her—if you wish to call it that—voiced similar concerns. Did they do anything about it? *Dropped her as an uncooperative patient* was the norm.

Now there's an idea.

Straight to the couch for her routine: lit the hooter and blew smoke rings at the ceiling. "Stop trying to sound like a DJ, dorkus. You don't do broadcast-voice well." She then looked at me blankly: "I almost killed myself when my brother died in a car accident when I was little. I was six flippin' years old and I went to father's closet and pulled out his old rifle.

Can you believe it!? Couldn't find the BBs, though."

Tried to hide a small laugh. "Hello, Tripsy, it's good to have you here. How was your day? Please recall our rule about no smoking in the building." I'd only smoked marijuana a few times before, with a former girlfriend who used to self-medicate with it, thanks to very liberal California laws. I actually liked the aroma of whatever Tripsy was smoking, but was deathly afraid of getting arrested for contributing to the delinquency of a minor. "Please extinguish your—"

Looking at me for briefest of moments, she said, "Oh, shut up." Back to her own little world: "When I heard about my friend in the school gym, I froze completely solid. She wasn't my best friend or anything, but she was my age and looked a little like me: wore the same jungle boots."

What the heck. I sat down and took it all in. Maybe some misdemeanor jail time for contributing to the delinquency of a kid who loved pot would do me some good, give me a new perspective on my less-than-average life, who knows? Made a note to suggest she vape her pot instead and apply for a medical marijuana card.

"Could've been you instead, you mean?" I said, hoping my staff didn't smell the illicit hooter-smoke. I jumped up, opened a back window and directed a fan to blow out the delicious offending aroma, and looked back at her. This troubled, messed-up kid needed a strong regimen of mind-numbing, body-melting pharmaceuticals, along with a stronger personality. Wait a minute. Was that last statement accurate? Did she need a different personality, or was I just a lousy shrink who didn't understand how to treat her?

Surrounding me were dozens of eager pamphlets from BigPharma, reminding me of an old advertisement I'd seen in a magazine: a glass of Coke sat next to a tray of ice cubes, several of which had tiny little arms and hands, frantically waving at the Coke to Pick me! Pick me! The tiny little arms and hands of BigPharma brochures didn't simply wave at me, they threw spears at me and screamed for my immediate attention, while Tripsy rambled on about something I let zoom past me.

Back to the breech: "So you thought about killing yourself because someone else did?"

"God, you're such an idiot . . . well, yeah I did think about it. But only once! It tore me up to think she killed herself because of bad grades. Jeezo-flip! Who the heck cares about grades!? Except maybe those Ivy-bound culture-nazis who went to all the right boarding schools and took ballet classes instead of MMA. It just made me think about what I think about myself: stuff like hanging with friends or with my Parks or Smootch. Made me so sad I felt like doing it to myself, too. And then it hit me: I do wanna do it. Just like she did. In some messed-up kindred way, I wanna go where she went. After feeling really bad over her death, I had that epiphany: I'd just do myself. Make a big mess, too. Let the 'rents clean it up."

"Your luck, Parks would probably get there first." I had absolutely no idea how that one slipped out. Was it was my frustration? Or maybe I was experimenting with meeting this kid on her level? Practicing modern-day psychiatry on this kid was clearly a bridge too far. For both of us.

Her mouth turned up in a wry smile. "Is that humor, doc?" She then turned away again, closed her eyes and launched a counter-strike: "Poo on you, dorkus. My Parks loves me. Smootch the Velociraptor might nibble on me, though, cuz he has no appreciation for how beautiful his prey really are, only how to dismantle the aesthetics right down to a few stray molecules."

"Sounds like Smootch is all fire and feathers."

That signature smirk. "Someday, Dorkus, a kind soul might accuse you of being cool."

And that was the end of that conversation, if you can call it that. She fell asleep on the floor in some yoga pose and didn't rouse until exactly fifty-four minutes later, when the session was officially over. Didn't see a watch or other type of timepiece on her, so I was stumped.

On a good note, I was grateful for several things: she'd stopped smoking that wonderful hooter, she wasn't yelling at me and calling me silly names, I could better study her file in peace, and I had the opportunity to observe her sleeping.

I've learned that you can tell a lot about a person by watching them sleep for hours at a time. Tripsy was peaceful, and it contradicted nearly every known observation about her and her behavior. There was so much more to this young woman than everyone realized. Except that one psychologist who tested her IQ and made a few other small observations. I think she mentioned *Indigo Child*, too. Something to follow up on.

Still, I had no idea where to start because I was overwhelmed by this off-planet child and her insoluble behaviors.

There is a wise saying: "If you're not sure where to start, start anywhere."

I pulled out all my mental maps and searched for "anywhere." Nothing obvious popped up. Again, I was at a total loss. At times like this, I've found it necessary to just let things happen, without too much planning or expectation. Since I had become somewhat lazy recently, this was an easy and familiar task. Besides, I could always put on the brakes or hit the accelerator, turn the wheel and find a new direction.

Or slam on the brakes.

Session #7

Today, I stood at the door and greeted her with a nice, genuine smile, certainly not one of those fake ones Dear Old Father tried to teach me early on. "Good morning, Tripsy!" Also tried the high-decibel approach, sans deep voice.

Didn't work, evidently: she breezed past me, just brushing my shoulder. A sign?

"I'm flippin' in despair over . . . something!"

Even after half a dozen sessions, watching her routine was anything but mundane. She kept rattling off all the reasons to commit suicide. One thing was quite clear to me at this point: each topic appeared only once. She hit upon one, then another and another. What the heck was going on here?

"Another person? Didn't we cover that last time? Oh, and thank you for starting our session inside my office." I looked outside in the long hallway where several of my staff were grouped together, smiling nervously. They gave me a thumbs-up. Tripsy wasn't the only wise guy in this place.

"Does it have to be over a person!? I'm dyin' here because I can't go to school with my best friend!"

I closed the door and gleefully pranced over to my chair. Why was I so gleeful today? Since I didn't know, I thought it best not to probe myself too deeply. Besides, I was getting paid to probe someone else. How convenient, that avoidance behavior.

"She's off to Columbia and I'm stuck at some crazy low-rent ghetto UC surfer school. Ever seen products of that system!?"

"Tripsy, didn't you apply to Columbia? I thought you looked down on those Ivy League types. And if you hate school so much, why bother with it?"

Daggers in those cobalt-blues: "Know something? There's a space for your head on that wall over there. Somethin' else, smartass: instead of offin' myself, I really need to take you out back by the woodpile and practice my dismemberment skills."

"If you really mean that, Tripsy, I'm obligated under law to call the police, as I'm sure you're well aware." With a 181 IQ, she was very creative, to be sure. Another part of me wondered whether she was actually violent at all.

Off in her own world again, she stared at the ceiling, then looked around at the walls, looking for a new target. She found one: a floor-to-ceiling bookshelf with my old college science books. "When I think about not going to a decent school, everything falls apart around me. I'll be a loser, stuck in this town forever, no one'll wanna be my friend. I'll go to the five-year reunion in torn jeans and an oil-stained shirt not even tucked in, from workin' at the gas station. Forget that. I'd rather be dead."

"You're right: pumping gas is worse than death." Her mediocre grades and near-perfect SATs suggested someone bored with school. But not dumb. No way. Plus, they didn't take her seriously, especially when she acted up and disrupted things. Still, how could her teachers not see beneath her exterior? Like the majority of teachers in America, they were overworked, underpaid and couldn't devote time to any one student. Saddened me, it did.

Took a long, hard look in my direction, sizing me up: "Is this your method with kids: sarcasm?"

She had me there. "I don't know, Tripsy. With you, I'm at a loss. Normally, I just listen and observe, then try different things. So far, you've ignored me and my questions, not to mention—"

She stood in front of me: "You actually went to school for this?

Dayum, the stuff I have to tolerate now, especially when I'm thinkin' of killing myself over not going to some decent college. Don't even think of talkin' me out of it. When you're this far down the rabbit hole, there's no goin' back. Trust me on that one. You just don't get it: this is everything to me. What's worst of all, my best friend isn't even smarter'n me. I got the highest SATs at school, waaay better than she did!"

How could this bright young woman be jealous of anyone else? I leaned back in my chair, exasperated: "Maybe you should waste her instead."

My father would've said, "Way to go, son, kill two chicks with one stone."

Big smile: "Not a bad idea, dorkus. Maybe her mom would give me her new Jeep."

Now that I was on a roll: "Tripsy, I'd really like to talk about your diary."

In one smooth, yet violent motion, she threw the blanket across the room and sat up, looking at me dead in the eye. "What the fu- fu- fu- fu- fuuuuuuuuu!?"

"And this means?" I have to admit this: at that very moment in time, I was actually frightened of this girl. I tried to act tough here, though. Heck, if she could, I could. Thing is, I couldn't pull it off as well, if at all. The passion just wasn't there.

"When I last looked it up, dorkus, 'what the fu- fu- fu- fu-' meant What The Fu- fu- fu- fuuuuuuuuuu-!"

"I still don't understand, Tripsy." Gathering up my composure in both arms, I got up and picked up the blanket, handed it to her. She ignored me, so I folded it and then placed it on the chair next to her, still within her reach. In the least, the exercise calmed me some, plus I got to move close to her, see if I could sense anything useful. Her body heat was amazing, even from a couple of feet away. There was also something else to it, other than heat, I mean. I've also heard that some people have incredibly huge electric fields, and they can even blow out light bulbs and street lamps. I wondered what they could do to a shrink's electric heart.

"Who told you about my diary?"

I turned around and faced her directly, just over a foot from her. "Your mother."

"Bitch." She grabbed the blanket again and threw it over herself in one perfect wave.

Moving away momentarily, I found my chair and sat down again, absently adjusting the various items on my desk, and said, "Lots of people have diaries, Tripsy."

Long pause, not looking at me, then: "Do you?"

"Yes."

Looking around the room, she saw unmarked books at the top of one of my bookshelves. My precious diaries. Her face softened imperceptibly; that much, I could tell.

"What's in it?" She feigned indifference, her voice then trailed off: "Not that I give a crap."

"Actually, there're dozens. I've been writing since I was thirteen. My thoughts about stuff. Family, friends . . . you know . . . stuff." The rows of my books stood high above her, a platoon of loyal subjects, resting easy. None was the same color or size.

"Thirteen?" She seemed to regard the number; was it somehow significant to her? "Why then? Why not ten or nine?" She slowly counted the number of diaries, her finger bouncing up and down, her lips moving silently to the count. "A hundred and forty-six. Pretty cool." With that, she looked around the room more, not even glancing at me, slowly pulled herself up from the couch, and started doing yoga stretches.

What was so attractive or inspiring about those diaries that held my deepest thoughts? Some advisors have cautioned that I shouldn't even have them here, if anywhere at all. Why? The unspoken rule is, never write anything down you don't want anyone to read. You can't count on "security," because it largely doesn't work.

One of my dearest friends tells me that the best security is anonymity. So why do I risk having mine there? Simple: in more than fifteen years of practicing, not a single person has dared touch any of my books. Not even my assistants or colleagues touch my belongings in my office. Never. They all think I'd have a hissy fit that would doubtless result in someone's bloody end. Other people's paranoid thoughts are my best security.

My father would edit one of my previous statements, explaining there was a huge difference between a risk and a gamble, according to the definitions set forth by Field Marshall Erwin Rommel: "Son, a risk is an action you take such that, if you fail, you can recover from it. A gamble is something you can't recover from if you fail. You're gambling with your past catching up with your future by having your diaries in your office, you moron."

"I see you do yoga, Tripsy."

"You still write?"

"Every day."

She perked up, caught herself not acting adult-cool: "You write about me?"

"Yes."

"Whatcha write about?"

"I can't answer that. It's. . . ."

Her left eyebrow arched up three millimeters: "Oh, not strictly professional? Naughty thoughts, then."

It was important that a forty-year-old professional healthcare provider respond appropriately to such a baited statement. But my fear was that if I always acted forty around this kid, I would surely lose her. Like most kids in her state, she simply did not respond well to authority, and that meant people like me—anyone over her age. "My thoughts about you are noble, Tripsy."

"You didn't answer my question." She bent over and touched her toes.

"What do you enjoy writing about, Tripsy?"

Now up again, she looked over at me, saw that I was looking away, and slowly adjusted her t-shirt and scarves, grabbed the blanket and tossed it on the couch, and walked to the door. "I hear you're writing a book." She looked over at my dust-covered first-draft tome, sitting forlornly on my desk, so eager to be disturbed in any meaningful way. Especially by me.

"Uhhh, yes, I am. Actually, I finished it recently." Another lie. I had completed the first draft eons ago—and, yes, I lied earlier about having just finished it—and now was at a loss for what to do with the thing. It just didn't flow right somehow. I almost pitched it in the trash a few weeks back, but a nagging voice in the back of my mind suggested I hold onto it a while longer. What's a little more dust on a ten-pound paperweight?

"Where is it?"

"On my desk." My head pitched over to the right to show her.

"You mean that dust magnet over there?" She pointed to my beloved manuscript that took fifteen years to think about, research and write.

"That would be the one."

"I hear California gets its dust from Asia?" She was actually looking at me.

"Yes, that's true."

"And who inherits our sloughed-off skin cells and other cooties?" Scratched some epidermal cells off her tanned and muscled forearm.

"The Mississippi delta."

Lifting a hand, she twirled a finger: "Explains the origin of the Blues."

I tried hard not to laugh, but couldn't hold it back. Something funky came shooting out of my nostrils. Serves me right, holding back something that would make me feel good. She looked over at me as I mopped up my mess and cleaned my nose.

Turned back to her and said, "Sometimes it's healthful to get thoughts out of one's head, which is a pretty polluted place. It's even better to share them with people in need. That's why I wrote my—"

Before my sentence was finished, she opened the door, turned briefly and said, "Isn't that what a soulmate's for, dorkus, sharing one's thoughts?" With that, she strode across the lounge area and found Tyra, who was clearly delighted to see her.

My chief of staff watched the encounter and then looked over at me and gave a little shrug. I wondered if she meant to say, "Look, Jon, this young woman is doing your job. You're clearly an imbecile and should take up golf or tennis full time." I hated both sports, so I figured it was a good idea to get back to work and learn how to be a proper shrink.

Looking down at my watch, I said to myself, "Woh, look at that: forty minutes left in this hour!" With all that extra time, I had two choices: go to Jack in the Box for a Bacon Ultimate Cheeseburger or . . . ahhh, heck, I sat back down and studied her file some more.

And after I finished reading it once, I read it again and again. Each time revealed something new, however small and seemingly insignificant. Also, I loved reading between the lines: all those singing details. If there was anything of use in those notes, it would be deep and well hidden.

The only way to discover would be to delve deeply into my subconscious. What might I discover? Was I hesitant or even frightened? Yes, but not about Tripsy. I was deathly afraid of my own demons, most of them designed and engineered by my dear old father in his dark basement laboratory.

This girl was more complex than anyone previously thought, and I was out to prove that hypothesis. My reasoning was this: if I prove to everyone, especially Tripsy, what a thinking genius she is, maybe it'll be enough to snap her out of this downward spiral she was digging for herself . . . or so it appeared.

Of course, the question about her possibly being an *Indigo Child* was an entirely different matter, and she did not need me or anyone else to alert her to the unique gifts she possessed. All we needed to do was sit back and listen to Tripsy enlighten us.

I knew this for certain: if no one intervened soon, Tripsy would fly into the ground. One of my fighter-pilot friends would put it another way: she's fixin' to make a smokin' hole in some forgotten swamp. What a shame it would be to lose someone so special, not unlike young Liam.

Didn't her parents know about her gifts? Apparently not, based on my conversations with them. Her mother, Sheila, was from Russia and was evidently a grand portrait artist until she had a total mental breakdown. The details are unclear and Sheila would not elaborate. The father, Russell, was an arrogant, elitist asshole who maintained his distance from Tripsy and her mother. I could characterize Russell as narcissistic and totally self-absorbed, but I'll just stick with *asshole*. Someday that term will make it into the *DSM*. Per my suggestion, of course.

How is it only I and that Dr. Kelley, the psychologist, could see Tripsy's extremely high thinking intelligence? It just didn't make sense. I wasn't even in Tripsy's intellectual league, much as I hate to admit that. Yet, no one else focused on her talents; they only fell victim to her caustic nature. With such an acidic persona, how could anyone dare venture past it? Was Tripsy some secret genetic experiment gone awry?

Session #10

She stopped in the middle of my office, dropped her bag, pulled off her sweater, kicked off her boots, and then went into a deep forward bend, touching the floor with both hands, mumbling, "This is beyond despair, dude. It's the abject realization that I'm a total idiot. I failed at school, my job, at having friendships with my family and people I was hoping would be my friends."

Pulling up, she arched over to the left, her left hand moving down her thigh. "I've failed to find a soulmate. Dude, I've failed at my hobbies! I can't even collect stamps right! I've failed to earn enough money to buy my own car. I've even failed at paying taxes." Now to the right.

"Most people would commend you on that last one." I closed a book, set it on my desk.

"Piss off. Taxes keep those missiles roaring into Afghanistan. I just wish I could afford to send one or two into Saudi Arabia, where they'd do the most good."

"You live at home with parents you don't care for, have a job that pays you enough so that you have to pay taxes like the rest of us, and you're in despair over having failed . . . what, exactly?"

She sat on the floor, spread her legs out 180 degrees, slowly dropped her arms and head onto the floor, then drew one leg in. "You're an idiot." Raised her head. "Despair is more of a chemically induced thing, right? That's all I hear these days: chemistry and genetics are the biggest bullies in our lives."

Without moving from my desk, I craned slightly forward to observe her. "Isn't everything about chemistry, including genetics?"

"I dunno. Is it?"

"Yes. In fact, nothing out there—behaviors, I mean—occurs without some sort of action by neurochemical means. You might say we're all just a nice little chemistry set on a scaffolding of bones and meat, and that nothing happens without, well, chemistry."

With that, she lifted her head and looked at me. Only for a second. "With all that undefined junk DNA and neuromushyware, there's no soul or spirit, you mean? That's a load o' poo, dorkus."

Seeing her reaction, I got up and walked around to the front of the desk, leaned against it, only a few feet from her. "Exactly. That's all part of humanity's way of coping with the fact we're just a bunch of squishy

creatures on this little flat plane, surrounded by other planes in a vast universe of dark matter that's moved about by dark energy. Religion, spirituality and the concept of the soul are mere distractions and control mechanisms."

She looked up: "Now I know why I feel so great all of a sudden! You paint such a rosy picture. One wonders how you manage to heal your patients."

"Maybe I don't."

"The hell good are you?"

My father used to tell me that. For years. "Maybe no good at all." I didn't bother telling my father this for two reasons: he already knew it, and I didn't want to appear to myself as—how did Tripsy put it?—a total screw-up.

"So, I'm in despair over failing like a miserable creep and all you can do is gimme two tentative maybes? Then you can't help me at all?"

"Yes. I just listen. You have all the answers. Just like your DNA stores all the necessary coding to make a complete human being—more or less—your mind has all the healing power you could ever want." On some level, she intrigued me. On another, she scared the poop out of me.

"But the default goes back to completely messed-up behaviors."

"That's chemistry."

"Dude, forget . . . this. Do you keep a loaded gun nearby?"

"Would you settle for diazepam instead?"

"Would it knock you out like, forever?"

"Use enough of it and you could stun a double-decker bus, replete with tourons."

She came out of the stretch, pulled her legs to her chest, looked up at me, smiled: "That's what I'm talkin', dorkus. Gimme the stuff." Back down again: "And what's a touron, dorkus?"

"A tourist, Tripsy. Someone who goes on vacation to some far-off place to have fun and look like a fool to the locals."

"Forget fun. I'm too busy being a screw-up." Still on the floor, she stretched some more, then drifted up like a ballerina and danced about for a second, picked up her bag and turned to me: "You're funny sometimes, dorkus. You come up with that one: touron?"

I shook my head and gave her a weak wave as she disappeared, noticing that today's session broke the forty-minute mark. I was now beginning to earn my hourly wage, pittance that it was. In only two and a half months, Tripsy had begun to open up, although I wouldn't call it any breakthrough just yet. She was still reluctant to discuss most topics, and always enjoyed controlling the conversation. In short, she normally just vented on me and I just took it. Sometimes that's the best therapy, although I don't think it was doing me much good.

This morning I paid several bills. Weeks early. And I asked my charge nurse to take a few extra days off to be with her kids.

My long-dead bastard father would have approved. Actually, the old prick would've said, " 'Bout time you got off your lazy ass, son."

Dear old father.

I decided it was time to look into the observations of that Dr. Kelley, so I looked over the results she had handwritten: "181 IQ ... her aura is Indigo/Lavender ... has all the characteristics of an *Indigo Child*."

She wrote further: "Parents rejected my observations about Tripsy. Dismissed me altogether, so I threw her out of my office because of her silly antics. I sensed she was going somewhere with them, but without the support of her parents, I could not continue with her. Mother was angry at me for throwing Tripsy out, so she withdrew payments to me, said they would place their daughter under psych eval when they returned to California. Both parents are flat wrong! Tripsy is NOT suicidal. She is gifted and has a definite agenda. She is manipulative in very clever ways. I believe she wants to help others but goes about it unconventionally. Her state of mind is due in no small part to her parents' lack of affection and understanding. A nagging thought is, who will inherit the duties of treating this extraordinary yet troubled girl? I wish I could assist further. Time for a vacation!"

As I watched Tripsy get in line for the bus, I noticed her looking intently down the street. When I scanned farther down, I saw Henry rolling up in an ancient wooden wheelchair. She cocked her head, seemed to regard him. My view was suddenly interrupted by the bus. When it pulled away, Tripsy was gone.

Henry was now at the bus stop, his head jamming in tune to a song only he would know. Jimi's list of songs flew through my head as I tried to imagine which one Henry'd be playing in his mind. Nothing readily came to mind.

I went home and popped the cork on a hundred-dollar bottle of Italian vino. Truth? I would've been happier with a two-dollar bottle of North Korean rice vinegar. After the third glass, her file and my notes were still on my lap, opened to that highlighted line: 181 IQ. There indeed was more to this young woman than anyone else thus far managed to conclude. Yeah, yeah, I've said that before but it's becoming all too apparent as time moved on.

Thing is, why should I take such an interest? After considering it, I wasn't sure whether I was more confounded by Tripsy herself or my keen interest in her case. And why was she faking every known disease in the *DSM*? Did she really have a boyfriend? I doubted it, plus something told me she wasn't interested in anyone at this point.

Not that she cared, but no boy or man could handle her. . . .

Session #13

At the door, she stood taller than her usual six feet, her new high-heel boots adding more inches. Plus, my ever-expanding opinion of her added another half a foot, as least. By the time she graduated from my little Academy for Dysfunctionals, she would be fifty feet tall and a master builder of the universe, right up there with BabyGroot.

"I got stoned one night and thought it was a cool idea to off myself!"

"So, nothing political here? No anger or feeling sick? Come in, Tripsy."

Still not moving, she said, "Can't it just be as simple as this? Does there have to be some hidden reason that's been lurking about for a century? No. I just got boned on some great hash last night and wanted to fly off a tall building." Under her breath, she mumbled, "I didn't, of course, or you'd have to report it."

"Without a parachute or some other flying aid or device?"

Off came the boots, which she carefully placed in front of my desk. Finally, a sign of respect? For the boots, probably.

"Yup. Smoked a few bowls and gradually evolved into a bird with these humongous wings. When I took my clothes off and saw myself in the mirror, I looked like some demonic winged creature, my long hair flowing behind me like white lava. Never looked cooler than that."

"That was an artificial, chemical-induced vision, Tripsy. Pink elephants."

"Duh. That's why I didn't do it. But I almost did." She sat on the couch, looked up at my Zxta.

"What kept you from it."

"Another hundred bucks."

"You ran out of money to buy more hash?"

"Saved by a lowly Benjamin." She looked over at me. "Can you believe it? If I'd had just one more, I'da morphed into a pterodactyl or something and done a swan dive off the top of the Golden Gate Bridge."

Why the Golden Gate Bridge? "And broken yourself into a dozen pieces. Why didn't you just chase the hash with alcohol?"

"Pay attention here, dorkus. I didn't have any cash left. Simple as that."

"So you would've killed yourself over a chemical high?"

"Beats the crap outta offin' myself over being depressed, doesn't it?"

"You get the same result, though. That warrants further discussion."

Sitting back now, her feet propped up, she looked over at me: "You're too smart for your own good, goober. Some things happen for simple reasons. There's no dark meaning behind it. You said so yourself that it's all just chemistry anyway, right? Well, then, this was just a chemically induced taking of one's life. Simple as that."

She hopped up, walked to the reefer, pulled out a soft drink, opened it and downed the whole can in one swallow. My mother could do that, too. It was one of several unladylike manners she unleashed behind the closed doors of my father's manse. And I loved her all the more for those peccadilloes.

"Are you glad you're still alive?"

BURRRRP! "Yeah, I guess. Now I get to come up with another reason, a better one this time, to kill myself. You up for that?"

Leaning back, staring at the ceiling, I felt exasperated. Told her, "All in a day's work, Tripsy. . . ."

The after-five crowd of county and city employees flooded the streets around the courthouse near my office. Tripsy walked out forty-two minutes after her arrival. Hey, at least she was staying a little longer, if only to abuse me as she wished. Did it make her feel better about herself?

I followed her out of my office and watched her stop and bend down to say something to little Tyra, who beamed at Tripsy and threw her arms around her, saying, "Tripsy! Tripsy!"

Tripsy turned to me and said, "Later, sport!" With that, she disappeared.

My goodness. I needed to trap whatever energy Tripsy had, bottle it and sell the stuff on the worldwide web for many worldwide bucks. Tyra would only say one word: Tripsy. Still, that was progress.

My executive assistant came in, beaming from having heard Tyra speak, and handed me a personal note from Tripsy's mother. I sat back and read the missive. Who handwrites letters these days? I'll share the snippets: Sheila said she read a few pages of Tripsy's notes on a book manuscript she had on her computer. Basically, it was all killing herself. Her mother asked what that meant.

I picked up the phone and called her, told her I had no idea what Tripsy was up to or what her agenda was. Of course, I lied. I opened my notes and started reading the summaries. Something began to take shape.

Why was she seemingly faking every known disease in the *DSM*? I stood up and looked around my office: all these books, all this knowledge, so much experience, and I was still a moron.

Started doodling . . . then scribbling . . . until this little ditty spilled out. Don't ask me where it came from; I'm just the bus driver. Hint: my subconscious was trying to talk to me but I was too stupid to understand.

```
        Trouble sashays in the door
            right up to the bar
        wearin' a little black dress
            two sizes too small,
            blood-red lipstick,
    and come-hither diaphanous blues
          under palm-tree lashes
        that swat my heart like a fly
```

Session #15

Though I was expecting Tripsy any moment, she still rattled me out of my chair, even from outside my window: "I lost my ghetto job!"

I motioned for her to please come in. She just stood there. This was getting ridiculous, I mumbled, walking to the window. "If you want to talk with me, you'll need to come inside, Tripsy." I then moved back to my desk, closed my eyes, waited.

Not a single molecule of air moved out of place as she walked in and lay on the couch. "Like I said, I lost my job." The whisper barely left her lips.

Feeling a little brave, which is uncharacteristic for me, I walked around my desk and pulled a chair up next to the couch. "Like getting disowned by your parents?"

"Duh. It's worse 'cos there's no one to blame." She fiddled with her skirt.

"Except yourself."

"I guess. Kids don't like to accept blame for things they do. We're incapable of accepting it. It's always best to blame the 'rents or someone else. Does anyone know how fragile a kid's sense of self really is? We can't handle this like you adults can! I know, I know, most of us are forced to deal with it, but you need to know that we can't. It's not in the cards. There should be some law that says kids can blame anyone else for all the grief we cause. When I walked into the store today, the manager just said I was fired for bein' late. I was five minutes late most days, and that's 'cos I ride the bus and he knows that! I told him that when I started! He just gives me crap 'cos I won't sex him. Plain and simple."

"You got fired because you wouldn't have sex with your manager?"

"Duh. When people are there, he's all syrupy. When no one's around, he tries stuff. His word against mine."

"Why not just file a report with those donut-eaters?"

"You know how the cops treat kids like me: they call us liars and thieves. They never believe a thing we say. That's what sucks so badly, that all these power-trippers like cops take sooo much advantage of underage kids. Weenies, all. I lost my crappy job and now I can't make money. My father cut me off completely, so there's no chance of having money for anything now!"

"With time, you can find another job and make more money, be self-sufficient."

"You're still not gettin' it, dummy!" She launched herself from the couch, moved to the bookshelf with the diaries, looked up at them. "Time to a kid is flippin' eternity because we make it so! Try tellin' a twelve year old that she'll be okay when she's done with puberty, oh, in about two years! For her it's a lifetime! We don't get time the way adults as old as God like you do. I know intellectually that, yeah, with time I can bounce back and feel happy and good again. The emotional concept of time doesn't exist to a kid! Do you get that!?"

Actually, this was déjà vu-ey, my hearing her explain my concept of time to a child. I was deeply impressed. "Why don't we talk about your diary, Tripsy. It appears to be very important in all this."

Silence.

"Why are you so curious about mine, Tripsy?"

Without turning her body, she rotated her head toward me, kind of like Linda Blair's Regan-thing in *The Exorcist*, and seemed to look through me. Then she smiled and looked back up at my diaries, moving her fingers up and down, up and down to some silent tune, counting all my memories again to ensure they were all there.

Was this her hidden comfort, being the guardian of my memories?

Honestly, I hadn't seen anyone move that quickly before. Tripsy was outside in less than a couple of seconds, running down the lawn to the bus stop. I looked through her file and my notes again, trying to ground myself in some reality, even if it weren't my own.

What the hell was reality anyway? I knew from experience that reading a patient's chart, old files, plus my own personal notes often revealed hidden discoveries that I had previously missed. It was also helpful to put aside all readings for a few weeks or months, then strike up again with a fresh perspective. Sometimes the subconscious needs a break, a clean washing, before it can communicate with me again.

With Tripsy's notes, though, I didn't trust the observations made by others. They were simply dull, boring, lacking insight and often just plain silly. She'd seen more than a dozen recognized psychiatrists over the years, and none longer than two sessions or examinations. This certainly wasn't long enough to formulate even the most meager of hypotheses, I reasoned. It was, however, fertile ground for labeling this young woman with twenty different, if not colorful, diseases and disorders, all of which I felt were inaccurate at best.

Then again, there were Dr. Kelley's unique observations about Tripsy: 181 IQ, *Indigo Child*, not suicidal, gifted.

Gifted, indeed.

My reverie broken by Dr. Kelley's thoughts, I shook my head and yelled at the ceiling and any wall that would listen, "What the heck is reality?"

More than one smart Italian physicist cautioned that we must look at all "reality" relativistically, because nothing in and of itself is true; it's always affected by something else, which makes its existence relative. And, of course, Heisenberg said that one cannot look at anything without disturbing its true behavior, although that was no longer true.

So where did that leave my discovering at least a working definition of my reality? As I tried to pinpoint it, I found myself rejecting every notion, mostly because they didn't fit any known definition or idea. Maybe I should just do what Tripsy does: blow it off and get on with life. And death.

But I couldn't do that, because I trained myself not to accept only the data at hand, then try to build a case based on it. The results of other doctors were useless. My own case notes showed a growing pattern of behavior that intrigued me, but I wasn't ready to form any working hypothesis just yet, only hunches. I sensed that Tripsy was guiding me along, and I was going to follow wherever it led.

Also, those crazy doodles of mine were revealing something new each time I read over and studied her case file and my session notes with her. Isn't it strange how our subconscious communicates with us in metaphors, symbols and other seemingly abstract ideas and images? It is our job to decipher them, but there is no manual on how to do it. Don't bother reading Freud. He was all wrong. To understand the meaning of my communications with my subconscious, I would have to become a six-year-old boy again.

Dear old father would say, "No problem there, son."

The subconscious speaks the language of a child, perhaps four to six years old, so you have to digress in language and lexicon to decipher what The Universe is relaying to our subconscious, and what our sub is telling us.

More scrawls, doodles and scribbles. Something tells me there's much more to this little story or poem, so I'll just have to wait for the next installment. Your interpretation is as good as mine so have at it.

We met back in October of
1936, you and I, during that
no-name typhoon that ravaged
the south seas, slapped
Tokyo on the ass, pinched
her nipples, and swept away
dozens of taxpayers, then got
bored and veered off deep into
Halloween.

You were a cold, lonely
molecule of two shivering
hydrogens and one weakened
oxygen atom, just barely
holding on, your bonding
energy sapped, with several
electrons threatening mutiny,
your nucleus on the verge of
meltdown.

Session #16

After she settled in, I said, "Tripsy, we really need to address some issues here. And I'm not going to listen to one more word of yours until—"

Like a cat on a hot griddle, she jumped up and headed for the door, turned half-way around toward me: "I've gone off my meds!"

I jumped up and cut her off, my arm across the doorway. "Were these prescribed medications; by a licensed medical doctor, I mean?" She wasn't supposed to be on any medications, at least none I've prescribed. *Not yet*, I thought, looking at my Special Edition BigPharma Collection.

Looking away, she said, "Dayum right, dorkus. Meds for this, meds for that. If you're up, there's stuff to bring you down. If you're down, there's magic to send you to Venus. Bleeding too much? Take this little pill, darlin'. Head not screwed on straight? Try this one! Hot flashes? Pop this one! Jeeeez! And then I come in here and see all this." Her hand swept across the room, referring to the BigPharma literature that occupied more than a few of my shelves. It was all more colorful than any of the dull and lifeless academic books and journals that shared the space. Those pharm'ers had such clever marketing experts, showering us shrinks with all that high art. Now, too, they add provocative scents that hijack our neuronal control and communications centers, if you can believe that. What's next, oxytocin in our air, and LSD in our drinking water?

"I was told that even though some doctors prescribed them, you weren't actually on any medications. What were you taking yours for? How long were you on them? And why'd you go off your medication?" I gently motioned for her to sit down.

Her warm breath fell over me in short rhythmic waves and I suddenly felt a slight calming sensation. *Indigo Children* were reported to have this effect on people and animals. Did I have the same effect on her, encouraging her to open up and share more? Thing is, I was far from being an *Indigo*.

She looked at me ever so briefly and moved back to the couch, touched the pillows, looked out the window. The sun threw bright, delicate lines across the floor, shimmering a lively melody as the drapes moved. She seemed to find some small comfort in those slow-moving waves of light, her fingers dancing to the tune.

"Took 'em for depression, borderline schiz, the usual deal for normal chicks like me. How long? Foreverrrrr. My mom practically nursed me on 'em. Why the heck did I go off 'em!? They made me stupid, dorkus! I'd be sittin' in calculus class, workin' on some simple first-order differential equation, one I knew the answer to, and I'd completely flake out. I couldn't get the answer from my brain to the pencil to the paper. It was sooo frustrating! So I just stopped, like, cold turkey. Meds. They make you a Stepford wife. You'd pro'ly love that, huh, dorkus?"

"That can be very dangerous, Tripsy."

"What, criticizing you? Gonna arrest me, Dr. Dorkus?"

My first reaction was to react to her words. I stopped immediately, because I knew any negative reaction would propel her deeper into whatever hole she'd dug for herself that day. I just hoped it was nothing close to six feet down.

"I meant, it's dangerous to go off that kind of medication cold turkey. It can lead to all kinds of rebound effects that can make you—"

"What, dorkus? Suicidal?" She threw back her head and laughed deeply.

Her laughter was filled with a thousand beautiful harmonics that sang to every atom in my body, and I secretly hoped her dynamic nature would materialize in the form of a special forty-year-old woman who would understand me and take me as is: a dorkus. I thought quickly of another stupid thing to say, but nothing came to mind. I guess my stupidity surfaced only when I wasn't looking.

She said, "Like I don't know this stuff. Sometimes I wonder who the doc is here. Doesn't it make you wonder, shrink boy?"

I could only manage a weak smile, thinking how my father would say sarcastic things like that to me: "Son, I just hope when you grow up you're not as brilliant as you are this morning."

"I wanna kill myself right now! I know intellectually that time and a guarded regimen of low doses of that crap I was taking before will slowly make me better, but like I said before when you're young and messed up, time is utterly meaningless. Nothing matters, least of all yourself. Despair and chemical depression and schiz are all tied in so closely to the same outcome: you feel like crap, that you can't go on, and that nothing matters at all."

"Can you access that intellectual part of you? You do it sometimes when you talk with me."

"Yeah, I guess. If I concentrate on it, or maybe if I . . . I dunno."

"You get very passionate when you talk about all this, you know?"

The bright sun-lines through the window marched slowly toward my bookshelves. She followed the lines until they touched the wood. Must have been a long five minutes before she spoke again.

"Don't try to make me feel good, dorkus. It'll piss me off more than the meds."

We both laughed, looked at each other briefly, then looked away, clearly embarrassed, but at the same time—hopeful. And in that moment, I felt my thought was a deeply shared one by a young woman desperately in need of . . . something I wasn't sure I could provide.

"I wish you'd tell me about your diary."

A mischievous look crossed her face: "Show me yours and I'll show you mine."

Taken aback by her suggestive statement, I paused, thought about saying something maybe remotely clever, then fell silent again.

"I know I act slutty sometimes. Bothers you, doesn't it?"

"Look, Tripsy, I'm a middle-aged psychiatrist who struggles with many issues each and every day." In all my years of talking with people, I'd never said anything like that. And there was nothing I could do to stop it from coming out of my mouth. I bit my tongue, but it kept on working: "Some days are better than others, but they all seem to suck lately."

For the first time, she looked at me for longer than a few seconds. "Maybe you're more messed up than me." Her eyes still on me.

To show who was still in charge here, I met her gaze: "I don't know. Maybe some people are more chemically challenged than others." I then noticed a slight smile form over her delicate skin.

"You're avoiding the subject, dorkus."

"Since when does a pot call a kettle black?"

A look of amusement on her: "When it's black, you moron."

We both laughed. Not so uncomfortably this time.

"Why don't you tell me about your diary?"

As if hitting an overhead slam, she countered, "Tell me about yours."

I paused, careful not to appear defensive. "This is about you, Tripsy. I'm not the patient here." As soon as I said that, I knew it to be patently false. She knew it, too.

Some noise outside the window behind my desk distracted me momentarily. I turned to investigate. When I turned back, she was gone. How the hell does she do that!? Feeling dejected and maybe a bit confused, I rose and walked around the desk, looked up at the diaries, wondering what she saw up there. Or was she looking at Jimi? Brian? What did she see that I did not, could not?

Several pillows were scattered on the floor. I picked them up and replaced them in their perfect positions as before, when I observed that one of her long scarves was elegantly draped over an arm of the couch. A beautiful, multicolored waterfall. It was so spectacular and arresting that I just stood there, staring as if it were some newly discovered Old Master's painting from the High Renaissance, one worth millions and millions. A single tear fell from my eye, a small reverent salute.

My father would have immediately ordered me to snap a picture of it so he could auction it off to the highest Palm Beach robber baron, but I just stood there, in awe, as the sun's golden light moved across the delicate folds of color, shape and texture, changing important aspects of the scene in the most subtle yet perceptible of ways.

There were a hundred individual masterpieces in that one scene, each one marked by incremental movements of a light coming from miles and miles away. Armed with that kind of math, I might be able to determine what the hell my reality truly was, but I wasn't going to count on it just yet.

Instead, I opted for something I could understand: Tripsy's file. No, it wasn't a tome. It was about sixty pages, and most observations just didn't fit right. The only thing I believed was that she suffered from anxiety and maybe depression. Still, she had that extraplanetary energy and a presence of mind no other kid had. That kind of lucidity impressed me. And scared the crap out of me.

When I leafed through her file again, randomly selecting a page the way one might choose a puppy in a bin full of cloned puppies, I was hopeful to gain some new understanding. Instead, I suddenly felt lost in a dark and seemingly empty space. The notion that all "empty space" is filled with dark matter and dark energy made me feel worse, because there was so much more to "reality" than tv, politics, mountains, salt water, neutrons and even life itself.

More than anything, I was confused about how to characterize Tripsy's unusual behaviors.

Filled with those confusing thoughts, I looked at Dr. Kelley's notes again, trying to ground myself in some reality. Yes, again. Even if that reality was not my own.

The more I pondered what reality was, the further from it I felt. If I couldn't comprehend my own sense of it, how could I understand Tripsy and her behaviors, all 9,936 of them?

My own case notes showed a growing pattern of behavior that intrigued me. I sensed that Tripsy was guiding me along, and I was going to follow wherever it led.

Also, those crazy doodles of mine were revealing something new each time I studied her case file and my session notes with her. I could discern what could only be palm trees and. . . ."

2

Some Alternatives to Killing Yourself

Normally for most patients I spend only minimal time discussing how and why they wish to kill themselves. I've hypothesized that dwelling on that subject for too long can reinforce their own beliefs about it, thus possibly leading to an early demise. Tripsy's method, however, was quite different from mine, as you doubtless saw in the last chapter.

While I'm still reconciling these findings with my own professional and personal beliefs, I do acknowledge that her "method," if you'll allow me to call it that, bears further study. My question to her was, "If it works well for you, will it work equally so for others not of your intelligence?" Her response was, "Listen, dorkus, I'm dumbing this down for you and your crew."

At the beginning of session 17, Tripsy immediately changed subjects and launched into a monologue about alternatives to killing one's self. Seemingly, I was only permitted to sit in my own office, tend to her needs, listen to her expertise, record her words, and take the occasional personal note. Life as usual around Tripsy.

With other patients, I sometimes caught myself doodling in my notebook, a habit you may find off-putting. However, it does serve a great purpose: it has, in the past, brought out aspects of my subconscious that have provided valuable insight to a case at hand. In looking back at my notes here with Tripsy, I have yet to find the high volume of doodles as I have done with all other patients. Something was definitely off here. Was it my lazy behavior? There was more to it than that. I knew there was.

As Tripsy may have eloquently put my dilemma: "The heck does that mean, dorkus?"

Who knows? Maybe only the future doodles will tell. . . .

I should probably pause here and confess something to you: I almost chose another specialty when I was nearing the end of my medical-school studies. Treating adolescent cancer patients appealed to me because they were the strongest and most resilient humans on earth. I was continually amazed at how well they dealt with the prospect of dying so young, missing puberty, high school, the prom, losing their virginity, college, partying, finding that first job, getting married, etc. They accepted death better than adults. I saw these young cancer patients as unsung heroes.

Now that I look back on my choice, I can safely say that I chose to treat teen suicides because they posed a greater challenge to me, that is, encouraging me to bring a human back from the brink of death, using good listening techniques, behavioral modification and accurate drugs. I also knew there was still a chance I could help these kids. I needed to know there was always a chance.

Cancer usually wins, mostly because all the real cures are withheld from us. I couldn't accept that fact, so I chose another specialty.

Suicide usually does not win, although the rate of suicide has increased more than 30% in the last twenty years. Honestly, I don't trust most statistics out there, because those behind them have an agenda they're pushing. I'm willing to bet that the rate has probably increased more than 50% in twenty years, and this statistic includes our beloved military personnel, more than twenty of whom take their own lives each day.

Still, there was always hope among the living.

Therefore, I felt I had a fighting chance to help kids find their own strength and will to live again. The fascinating aspect of neurochemistry is that it can be regulated by changing one's behavior over a long period of time. It's often an uphill struggle, one most people give up on, but for those who persevere it can be life changing. I admire those children who choose to stick with therapy until it makes them whole.

They truly are unique creatures, those young kids, and I wish that kind of success for all others, even though it usually does not happen with most children. Abnormal neurochemistry and neuroanatomy can be powerful demons that overwhelm most kids.

That very thought saddened me to the core yet fueled my inexorable willingness to find ways to defeat the demonic intrusion.

Session #17

"I need HELLLLLLLLLLP!" Eyes screwed up tightly, she screamed it from my door.

"Forgive me, Tripsy, if I appear taken aback. Are we now on a new subject here?" I sat on the couch as she walked in and stopped just inside the door. "Please close the door and come in."

"Gawd, dorkus, do you have to make this harder than it already is? You're in my seat."

Don't ask me how the blazes I decided on this approach today. Maybe I was at a loss for what to do and was experimenting randomly. Maybe I was being my usual lazy self. Or just being stupid. Maybe all the above. Like one of my old professors told me: "When in doubt where to start, start anywhere."

"Just trying to clarify things a bit. Okay, so . . . from whom might you ask for help?" Hesitatingly, I moved to my desk and turned to watch her plop down, not even touching the pillows or blanket.

"From a friend . . . my family, I guess; the weenies they are. . . . My priest, although he'd pro'ly wanna sex me, too."

"Let's not go there right now. The Roman Catholic Church doesn't need another accuser."

"Baloney, doofus! I've seen that guy's eyes peel my clothes off!"

"I thought priests preferred . . . never mind."

She ignored me. "Don't tell me I don't know when some guy wants to bone me. You have no clue what it's like to be a girl, let alone one who's desired by all you buttheads."

Right she was: I had no clue what it was like to be Tripsy, to be thought of as a desirable object. I had absolutely no idea, and I felt horrible for it, especially since my dream as a young man was to be worshiped by young girls who loved The Godda Baddass Rock. Shame on me. Right now, the least I could do was make some lame attempt at sympathy and understanding.

After a vain attempt, I realized I felt sad for her and how the world seems to view her. Mostly because I felt she may never find a man who truly loves her as she is. This is a stereotypical conundrum for beautiful women whose high intellect usurps their own exceptional looks. Compounding these dilemmas was the fact she was emotionally challenged, as well, and I wondered if I could do any good at all. Again, maybe I should abandon my training and do as I usually do: listen and analyze.

When the room fell silent, even the air seemed to stop moving, leaving all the tiny dust particles suspended, nowhere to go except straight down. After a deep breath, she exhaled, followed the dust to the floor, spread her legs wide and dropped her arms and head in a deep stretch.

"Okay, I understand. I have no clue. How about we get back to those alternatives? And next time, Tripsy, would you please stay on the couch?"

Still in her stretch, she mumbled, "I like to stretch out. Sorry if it bothers you." She looked genuinely hurt and pressed her face against the cool tiles. "Maybe a suicide center or something. I've read about 'em, even called one a coupla times."

Wanting to apologize to her for my remark, I stopped and decided to let it pass. Leaning forward to hear her, I said, "What did they say?"

"They were zeros." She pulled up from the stretch, rose, and reached both arms high to the ceiling. "Too nice and all but couldn't relate." She then mumbled, "Sending out lambs to greet the she-wolf."

"Couldn't relate to the wolf in you?" I looked down at the highlighted line in her case file: 181 IQ. "Most people aren't like you, Tripsy. They don't get you. You intimidate people. In ways even they don't know. It's on a deeply primitive level not accessed by modern humans. All they know is, you scare the poop out of them." Except Tyra Bailey.

The air in the room still refused to move. It became almost suffocating. The dust kept falling in a silent snowstorm, though.

"Do I scare you?" She looked up at me, clearly concerned.

"Scared isn't the right word, Tripsy. Sometimes, though, I'm not sure what to expect from you. And I certainly can't relate to a young person with a 181 IQ who intends to kill herself when she has so much to offer."

Slowly dropping her arms, she went into another impossible yoga pose, her arms and legs tied up like a pretzel. She looked up at me: "How's that supposed to make me feel?"

"You're just going to have to reconcile the fact that most of us normals aren't like you. The only thing I can do most of the time is listen and assess."

"Yeah, maybe you do listen. You're still a dork, though. Anyhoo, like I said, why bare my soul to someone who won't get me at all, in the hope they might know what to do with me or how to help me? Kinda like seein' a podiatrist for a brain tumor."

How does one respond to that? She was right, though. "Listen, Tripsy, I know it seems that way, and my job is to help you help yourself. A person

of your unusual caliber is obligated to live and prosper and help others, too."

"A legal obligation?"

"Maybe a *galactic* obligation, who knows?" I was reaching here, but something told me it was the right thing.

Wasn't there some kind of treatment out there on the fringes of this still-nascent field of psychiatry that I could try with her? If I were at a loss for what to do before, I was totally lost now, not even certain what was the right thing to say. I know that other psychiatrists who read this will think me an imbecile. Maybe they're right. I've spent too many years trying to punish my long-dead father, and have wound up hurting myself and maybe even my young patients. How could I make this right . . . for Tripsy or me? Others would medicate her into submission and call that a victory for them, for the profession. It was the lazy man's way to practice medicine and heal patients, but it's what the AMA and APA mandate, given their intimate ties to BigPharma. What am I saying? The pharm'ers control the AMA and APA.

What crap, all of it.

"Duh. Tell me about your diaries, dorkus."

"About my diaries? I don't know. I guess I write about everything, whatever bothers me and starts to itch in the back of my mind. My diaries were a way for me to vent my frustrations. I didn't have any real friends growing up, and I needed people or someone to talk with. Someone who would listen and hopefully understand me, maybe even guide me along."

Tripsy suddenly turned and faced me and pulled her legs up to her chest, cocked her head sideways, a cartoonish puppy, curious and quizzical. "Poetry. Betcha that's what you need to focus on, dorkus. Poetry. It's the math of love."

Not knowing how to respond to that comment, I nodded like I understood, then continued: "My family's very wealthy. Father was—how to put it?—a bastard who loved to control everything. And I mean everything." I paused briefly to look at the clock on the wall near the door. "Look, Tripsy, we have only about fifteen minutes left."

She pulled herself upright and sat on the couch again, crossed one leg over the other, almost professorially, looking well beyond her seventeen years. In that moment, she resembled my beloved Zxta.

I continued: "By the time I was fifteen, I had read every book about the great physicists: Rutherford, Heisenberg, Bohr, Planck. And I knew I wanted to be like them. In spirit, as least."

Nodded her head: "You know intellectual stuff, dorkus. You've contributed something to the world." Then she looked down at the tiles. "No one sees me as I see myself, not even my teachers. They all go, 'Uh-oh, here comes mass trouble and sexification.' "

With that, she left. On her way out, she sat down with Tyra and put her arm around her, whispered something in Tyra's ear, then departed.

I walked to my door and looked at Tyra, who looked over at me and smiled, said, "Hi."

How does one interpret Tyra's coming out? The emergence of her personality defied logic, at least the stuff I'd learned in medicine thus far. Now thrown completely off guard, with no meaningful insight here (or anywhere, for that matter), I moved back to my desk, opened my note pad and began to write and doodle, mostly random items.

While my notes revealed the structured and sometimes scientific approach to my work, doodles opened up a path into a deep emotional abyss of thoughts, ideas, wishes and beliefs that rarely seem to rise into my consciousness. Only recently did I start doodling during sessions with Tripsy, and only infrequently.

After a few hours, I got up and placed all the drawings next to each other, each in temporal sequence. And I saw a definite pattern, a method to Tripsy's wandering dialogue. I was finally getting past her explosive entrances and theatrics, and appreciating her thoughts. Suddenly I felt like I was the only man in the world who knew this important fact. Now what was I going to do with my newfound information?

Rather than structure our sessions in the classical sense of treatment, I decided to consult my subconscious, my inner "mentor," or my CHILD. I know it sounds silly, but it really works. For a dorkus like me, mind you.

C is for the child or little kid in me; H is for heart or my subjective and emotional side; I is for intuition or the gathering of raw data via all possible sensory inputs, well more than the five we know now; L is for cold stainless-steel logic or pure objectivity; and D is for the little demon in me, the mischievous and wild devil. Together, these very real beings in the subconscious design and build and shape our lives, from birth to the grave.

The human subconscious is the engine that drives everything we do in life. It is also the entity that is in direct, continuous communication with The Universe. We get valuable information through dreams and dreaming. Maybe I should write a paper on it sometime.

Lately, I had been ignoring my CHILD. Shame on me.

Not this time, I vowed. Luckily, it had forgiven me and was now communicating with me via doodles and poems, or just little passages that came to mind.

My CHILD pointed me toward encouraging Tripsy to control where this treatment went. I was no longer sure it could be called "treatment" in the conventional sense but, then again, convention didn't matter here.

I was no longer sure of a lot of things at this point, so much so that I could hear my father now: "Son, you're nothing short of a moron even to think about allowing a patient to control their own progress. Patients are too weak-minded to be left to such important decisions. Pull your head outta that skinny ass of yours and practice some real medicine for a change. And fetch me another coffee, black, no sugar, while you're at it." He never said thank you, by the way. To anyone.

Dear old father, my consummate cheerleader. No wonder I moved to California. Don't laugh. I actually considered a post in Antarctica, until I learned the supply planes didn't always come on time. Always had to have my special tea each day. Sometimes there's just no compromising.

Session #18

Tripsy seemed to glide over the lawn outside my office, on an air of calm and peace, occasionally looking up into the trees to admire their beauty. Soon as she entered my building, she threw her head back and blew it all out: "I wanna go on walkabout for a month and flippin' CHILLLLLLLLLL!"

"We're definitely not discussing why you would like to kill yourself anymore, are we?" I held the door for her.

"You don't have to hold the door open for me every time, you know?"

"I prefer to formally welcome you to our sessions, Tripsy."

She threw one of her scarves at me. It landed across my chest. I wasn't sure whether she was being playful or genuinely trying to get my attention.

"Try to keep up, dorkus. I'm going slowly here. Your only job in life is to listen, record all this suicide talk with my shrink, and take some notes. Make it all meaningful, will you?"

"You do that to everyone?"

"Actually, no."

Today she was wearing a long-sleeved blouse in a bright summer tangerine, full-length skirt of various blues, with . . . those jungle boots.

"What was I just saying?"

"Something . . . aboriginal. By the way, you look nice today, Tripsy." She was more womanly than ever, truth be told; more beautiful than the first time I saw her. It was definitely the look of a more mature woman. I almost wanted to say sophisticated, too, even with the jungle boots. An urban-edge chic only she could pull off.

"Dorkus has a sense of humor . . . yes, walkabout. It does wonders for the soul, bonehead, did you know that? Taking a long-assed walk into nowhereland, maybe up in the woods by Big Sur."

"What about bears and mountain lions?" I retreated to the safety of my 300-pound desk.

"Repeat after me, doofus: stick to the trails, hike during the day, don't carry any food outside your backpack, and make plenty of noise while walking; nothing stealthy, hear me?"

I just smiled at her, maybe even nodded my head a few times. The latest tactic of a mature, sophisticated shrink, then: "It's good you're out getting fresh air, Tripsy."

"I hear that trees account for more than twenty percent of the methane output worldwide. Fresh air can be defined in many ways."

I smiled again. "Did you know that humans are a huge source of CO_2? We exhale it each time we breathe, plus it diffuses from our skin every waking moment. Just go hang out in a pool or bath for ten minutes and you'll see those little bubbles of it all over your skin. Cool, huh?"

She gave a little smirk, appeared to ignore me: "Then why didn't you suggest goin' for a hike or something?"

"Just a thought. . . ."

"You should listen more, speak less . . . Being out in nature is like getting grounded again. Pun intended. You're one with the earth. I mean, dude, this is where we came from! The soil! Air! Water! Outside of human-made stuff, we feel like animals again, free and wild and unencumbered by society's ills and chills. I'll betcha in about fifty years, you scientist types'll have figured out how all this chemistry works and how to manipulate it, huh?"

"I think it's possible. We're making strides each day, you know."

"Uh-huh. Scientists everywhere making up stuff as they go along just to get published. You're definitely making headway."

"Why don't we make some headway here, Tripsy?"

"I thought we were, doofus, getting beyond suicide. And don't ask me about my diary, okay?" She pulled on her top, grabbed her stuff.

"Okay, how about your father?"

"Piss on my 'rents. And dirty-wee on you, too, dorkus!" With that, she ran out. Again.

And here I thought I was doing so well with this special child. In my line of work, if a patient doesn't backslide once in awhile, then it's possible she may be faking her recovery, so I didn't place blame. It was only normal, just part of the process.

At least that's what I hoped. . . .

Session #20

Tripsy suddenly appeared right outside my window: "Give the anger, hurt or whatever time to pass!"

"This is like the last one," I yelled back, waving at her, but she'd already zoomed past the window, ran down the hall and into my office, settled in on the couch, and lit up a hooter.

"No, it's different, so don't argue. This is letting time really heal you, without your being chained to some bedpost in agony." She turned her head to the window, looked out longingly. "Can we go outside again?"

I was surprised she didn't simply do as Tripsy did and dragged us both out there without permission or word of any sort. "Yes, of course. In fact, if you prefer it out there, we can meet there instead for the next few sessions, provided it's not raining."

"I love the rain!" With that she grabbed her gear and was gone before I could get up. What else was new?

We took our seats under the same tree. A mixed scent of lavender, sage and orange followed a mild breeze across our path, setting the tone for this session: calm, peace, beauty, strength. At least that's what the aromatherapy book promised.

She perked up, looking for the sources, spied them, then jumped up and ran to them. Waving her hand through the lavender bushes, she looked up at the orange tree, picked several ripe ones, and returned to the chair, handed me an orange.

"Ah, thanks," I said, peeling it clumsily with my two left thumbs. It squirted in my face. I looked over to see if she'd seen the dork in action. Affirmative.

Eyes closed, a huge smile across her face, she seemed to relish every molecule of her bounty. "What a great scent!" She peeled it with her long, slender fingers, and slid each piece slowly into her mouth and savored every molecule. "The only stuff you could smell in Germany was cow poo. Everyone had a big pile of it, mixed with hay, in front of their house. You walk up to a neighbor's place to drop in for dinner, and the first thing you see is a mountain of poo. You walk inside and the first thing you smell is more poo." Her orange gone, she pulled off the small delicate leaves and flowers from the lavender, massaged the essence around her face.

"That's what you recall about Germany—poo?"

"Yeah. No, not all of it."

"What else?"

She was thousands of miles away. "Sometimes, it's enough just to chill out and let everything go, let it all wash away somehow. Take off from work, if you have a job, and go on medical leave or something. Sit around the house, take a walk every day, exercise, go to the bookstore, watch a bunch of movies, whatever it takes to distract you."

"To allow time to heal you?"

"Yeah. There's that time thing again."

I could smell the lavender coming off her face, mixed with pheromones and unknown girl-chemicals that would likely drive anyone to distraction. I was starting to feel alive for the first time since I dreamed of being The Godda Baddass Rock so long ago. Maybe it was Jimi and Brian looking down at me all these years, imparting something that would somehow transform me.

"What are your thoughts while you're letting time do its thing?" I absently ate another orange and allowed a few drops to run down my chin and onto my shirt. The scent, mixed with lavender, was intoxicating.

"I dunno. Anything. Just don't allow yourself to pull that trigger or jump in front of a bus, that's all. Do anything to stall. I mean, you don't really wanna off yourself anyway."

Confusion was again setting in. Just a week ago, she was adamant about destroying herself in countless ways, now this? Was she self-medicating? Was someone else intervening without my knowledge?

"Then why threaten it?"

"You ask too many questions, dorkus! Where was I!? Oh! That's the point of bein' distracted, dude: you're not thinking about the most devastating thought of all—killing yourself. Now do you get it?"

"No." At least I didn't think so.

Several small birds, screeching at each other, swooped down from their perches, dropped several white blotches of poop on my shirt. Tripsy tossed her head back and loosed a melodic laugh. Her hand delicately balanced her drink as it rose with the laughter. "How's it feel to get shit on, dorkus?"

"The story of my life." I wiped off the mess with a handkerchief. "And I think the proper phrase here would be 'shat upon.' "

"Forget grammar. The result's the same: three little birdies crapped all over your hundred-dollar shirt."

Wiped off the impressionistic mess. Actually, true to my nature, just rubbed it in more and more.

"These oranges are great. Mind if I—"

Before I could answer, she was already there, gathering up her shirt and dropping the fruit into the makeshift bag. When her shirt was full, she walked past me, turning only briefly: "Later, dorkus!"

I couldn't recall the last time I asked myself, *What the hell just happened here?* With Tripsy, it happened several times a week, even in her absence.

On one hand, I thought I was treating a young suicide. On the other, I sometimes felt it was I on the couch, with Tripsy leading me down a long, tortuous and painful road, drawing out my deepest thoughts, feelings, fears. . . .

The scent of lavender and oranges swirled in the air around me, so I closed my eyes briefly and just sat there, taking it all in and hoping it would replace the noise inside my polluted skull.

I could hear some pleasant music coming from an upstairs room deep in my so-called mind, and I did something I'd not done in many years—I strummed and picked on an air guitar—a 1968 Fender Stratocaster. An original. Maybe something touched by Jimi himself.

My voice then took on that sandy and smoky tenor-baritone of Brian Johnson's, and I belted out a small poem, something I'd written long ago. Wasn't meant to be a song, really. A ballad, at best:

```
Hey  hey,  Old  Man,  why  such
tears of sorrow?

Sorrow?  What  do  you  know  of
sorrow?

I  have  drunk  from  the  inner
ovens of your sun and played
on  the  feathery  tendrils  of
midnight lightning.

My  song  echoes  distant  among
ghostly  hypergiants  of  the
celestia.
```

Tripsy South

I twirl The Great Flat Earth on
a single digit, while my warm
breath spins Hurricane Sally
over the high seas.

So I say again: What do you
know of sorrow?

The tears I weep created the
great Pacific pool in which I
swim and dive and feast.

Silver rivulets fall from
my countenance and seed the
heavenly rivers and streams of
the north and south.

These tears of what you call
sorrow run blood red among
the craggy masses of land so
enriched with my intoxicating
ferrics.

No, my young earthling, mine
tears know no sorrow. Only
the dreams and fantasies and
promises of your tomorrow.

Session #21

Today I walked out early and sat under the trees again, awaiting her arrival. My nose was running from a slight cold I'd contracted from one of the younger kids who blew both of his lungs and a mouthful of light-green mush all over my face two days ago. I just love children.

The bus stop was just across and down the street, and I could see it clearly. I knew she took the Waterfront Shuttle from Chase Palm Park down to my office, which had a lovely view from the second-floor offices. I actually had another office upstairs, a reading room, and never let patients or staff up there. Funny thing, I almost wanted to go up there today, to see the cobalt-blue Pacific.

Cobalt blue . . . her eyes had the same color, depth, tone and texture, with a ring of light-brown around the iris. If one took the time to look into her eyes, really study them, they'd see a beautiful coral atoll atop an infinitely black volcano, surrounded by the magnificent Pacific.

"Where the blazes is your head, son?" my father would doubtless ask if he were witnessing this. The question would then be followed by a full-handed slap across the top of my head. Thank goodness he was long gone.

Distracted by nightmarish thoughts about my father, I missed Tripsy's exit from the tram. I caught her running over to our perch under the trees. She tossed her head back and yelled, "Talk to my significant other about problems between us, or find someone new to connect with!"

Oookay. Looking up into the tree, I wondered when the squadron of birds would dive-bomb me again. "What if you're incapable of talking to him?" I shot back, unsure where this was going.

Seeing my worried look, she smiled and said, "Or her. Think optimistically, will you!?" she said, reaching out to slap my arm and sending 500 electric spears right through my heart.

I stuttered, then: "Uhhh, okay. . . ."

"See? This is where it all begins! With so-called adults like you. You're supposed to be this paragon of smartness, and you turn out to be an evil clown. Gawd. If you actually have someone you could connect with, then it's possible to talk with them about anything."

"Hypothetically," I said, putting on my sweater and wiping my nose. "It's starting to get cold here." That was a lie; I just didn't want to get bird crap on another expensive shirt. That was another lie. If she touched me again, I would surely have an explosive myocardial infarc. Or just fart. I really should have retreated to the local Army-Navy store for some body armor or, better yet, built a Faraday cage.

Not sure what that is? Imagine a metal cage, with a direct contact to the earth, called "ground," that receives electricity from outside sources and immediately shunts them harmlessly to ground, thus protecting the object inside the cage from unwanted electromagnetic radiation. Mesh size depended on the wavelength of the incoming or offending radiation.

"Yeah, okay, hypothetically. Point is, ya gotta initiate some kinda dialog to sorta . . . distract you," she said, tossing a small branch at me.

"As you've suggested the last few sessions, right?"

She looked around at all the trees, the gardens, the hedges that lined an entire section of the yard, screening them off almost completely from the street, except a small gap through which I could always view her bus stop. "It's all about distractions and letting the passage of time do its work on you. With this, I mean talking with someone special or close to you, it's not just about distraction. It's about a connection with another warm body."

"How about your cat?"

"Doesn't work the same. You're lookin' for some human feedback that's reasonably intel."

"Smart?"

"That's what intel means."

"I thought that was CIA-speak for the stuff that's gathered during illegal break-ins and the like?"

"Forget spy crap. Intel means intelligent, doofus. Anyway, it's important to have that connection first, then to have the other side be able to say something meaningful. And I don't mean, 'Oh, baby, I love you!' Forget that sweet-ass, romance-on-a-stick crap. I mean, they should consider what you say, and have something relevant to say back to you."

"What if they're not wired for that? Or what if they really don't know how? A lot of people don't know how to listen and respond accordingly."

"Okay. Then find someone else to connect with, and ultimately talk with. Someone who will listen and reciprocate. Someone who may have already gone through it. Someone like that, with experience, is like a light at the end of some long, dark tunnel. Those who've gone through and survived it give us hope."

"Something you can't give yourself?"

"Yeah, I guess. It's tough to see things objectively when everything just hurts, in general. And I mean everything."

"So you acknowledge that it can be difficult to talk to yourself about suicide, right? After all, this was one of the topics a few sessions ago."

Silent for a moment, then: "I know, I know. Try not to turn this into some kinda contract thing, okay? What I meant was, you have to at least try to do it on your own. If you don't have the minerals to—"

"Minerals?"

She laughed, then: "Balls, gumption, wherewithal. Jesus flippin' Christ, what time zone d'you grow up in? You're supposed to be the expert in suicide, especially with kids, and here it's like you're practicing alchemy without a license. Berlitz needs a course in Current American Kid-Speak for timeshares like you."

"Timeshares."

She got up, turned to me: "Is English a second language for you? Wrinkled skin, blue hair, Viagra . . . ollllllld people!"

"I'll look into it."

"My point's this: first try to talk to yourself." Something caught her eye, and she turned around and looked up slightly. "If self ain't listening, then talk to a significant other. If they can't understand, then find a new friend. If that doesn't work, then try the cat. Talk to the cat before you feed her, though. Otherwise, she'll scarf down your can of chunky albacore, find the nearest warm and cozy spot and go into a tuna coma for days."

A blue jay landed on a branch just over her head, cocked its head down to inspect the otherworldly human. Her, not me.

"You seem to know cats well."

She pulled out a slice of orange, gently handed it up to the blue jay. The bird hopped onto her arm, took the gigantic slice, flew off. "I know the nature of animals, dorkus. . . ."

Not wanting to comment just yet, I just took it all in, now more confused and fascinated than ever before. Amazing, I thought, watching her feed the bird, and seeing the bird react as though she were a member of the flock. It didn't hesitate in the least when it approached Tripsy.

"So you think a suicidal person can actually reach out and change someone's life?"

"Not only that. They can alter their own life by doing it. When people read or hear about how someone who's as afraid of life as they are, and yet still kicked suicide in the balls, they're drawn to it. Very, very few people are so chemically inert that they can't find help in one form or another."

"So, does someone like me change your life . . . somehow?"

"Forget that. I just wanna entertain you, dorkus. If you pass on what I say to someone and it saves a life, cool. If not, cie la flippin' vie."

"You clearly are very serious, but there has to be more to your purpose than that. What does all this mean to you, to anyone?"

"It means that you should have some agenda in life, worship it, feed it, grow it, and then pass it on somehow."

Hadn't my Zxta said something similar? "So, again, you'd like to reach out to other suicidal people with your message—"

"Hey, we're just chattin' here . . . gimme some fuego, will ya? My hooter needs a strike."

Fumbling around for my lighter I'd bought for times like this, she reached over, leaned on my lap and grabbed the lighter from me, lit her hooter, blew out a long, steady stream in my face, pulled back and relaxed again.

"Oh . . . I was under the distinct impression that you had a grand plan for all this."

"Maybe I'm just entertaining you." The blue jay came back with a SCREECH! and landed on her shoulder. She casually handed it another slice, shooed it away, turned to me.

"I refuse to believe that."

"Good, 'cos I'm just pullin' your chain, dorkus." She sensed my discomfort, said, "Relax. It'll all be revealed someday soon. Keep on doodlin' and scribblin' out that poetry."

That's what I was afraid of, especially since I was talking with a seventeen-year-old suicide.

"How long you been sick, dorkus?"

"I've been fighting this thing for days now." Actually, it was about two hours.

"You practice pain by the mile, dorkus. Don't fight the cold, entertain it. See ya!"

Was she poking fun at me again, or was there some truth to that statement? How does one entertain a cold? Welcome it? Relish in its pain and misery? Is that what I did?

After that session, I consulted my notes, which I'd scribbled down in haste. There was one long list of Tripsy's traits: selfish, jealous, insecure, frustrated, distrustful, disloyal, self-centered, self-destructive, angry, passionate, mean-spirited, egomaniacal, bossy. I then recalled all the good things I could about her, weighed them against those traits, and came up with a big nothing. I then looked over a shorter list of traits that appeared to be missing from her personality: love, friendship, sincerity, loyalty, laughter, modesty, and the ability to laugh at herself. Little made sense.

To call her anxious and depressed, maybe borderline schizophrenic, was also probably careless, although I had no ready explanation for my assessment just yet. Call me an idiot, but somehow I knew something was askew. How I sensed her and how she actually came across just didn't add up. Was it because I saw her inaccurately? In the past, I've had no problem admitting when I was wrong. This time, I felt I wasn't wrong. Though I had nothing to support it, except the nagging voice of my subconscious. That lack of supporting evidence concerned me.

With all of Tripsy's characteristics I'd listed over our many sessions, I obsessed over coming up with another brilliant acronym like CHILD, a grand unifying theory that would explain everything about her in one simple equation.

I knew it existed, but it just wouldn't surface.

Two new doodles: a coconut palm arching over a tiny beach bar under an impossibly bright sun.

After listening to Tripsy, I secretly prayed I would find that special forty-something woman. But who would ever have me?

Closed my eyes and my hand began autowriting, kind of like a planchette over a Ouija board. When I opened my eyes, this appeared, a continuation of the last poem or tiny story, whatever you want to call it:

```
When we bumped into each other,
our collision created a sizable
bow wave that sacked the German
steamer Ursula Rickmers.

We    rolled    and    tossed    about
for     hours,     expanding     and
contracting, adding a few other
molecules here and there, some
tearing off during the pitching
```

of the giant waves.

Ours was an endless tango in
the morning, disco and smooth
jazz by midnight, building
needed strength for the long
voyage up into the jet stream.

Session #22

Okay, it was good to break things up a bit and sit outside, but did we really accomplish anything? The past twenty-one sessions with Tripsy, conducted over five-plus months, seemed a blur to me, and I wasn't in great shape to analyze any of the data I'd collected from our meetings. Not just yet.

No, today would be an indoor event, so I had the cleaning service come in again this week to spruce up my space. Why bother, given it's already spotless? Why don't you ask me that sometime next year?

Meantime, I admired Tripsy as she danced across the lawn, touched the big oak trees where we sat, then came inside and launched into her usual introduction: "Check myself into a mental-health clinic or hospital for thirty days!"

Now we seemed to be hitting on familiar topics again. I was sitting on the chair next to the couch, holding up the blanket for her. More than ever, I wanted to make her feel at home, despite my best internal urges to medicate this girl. "Why?" I asked, draping the blanket over her. "You were there only six months ago."

Ignoring me, she said, "Dude, you can get all kindsa free stuff at The Nut'tel!" Pulled out her humidor stuffed with fresh hooters.

The last time I saw a humidor of that quality was at a snob party in Palm Beach. Tripsy's sterling-silver container had an image of two lovers sitting together at a tiki bar, the setting sun a huge ball of fire that ignited the atmosphere.

I asked to see it and she handed it over. The elegant inscription read: "Good luck, Indigo Girl. CMK." And then: "Many uncertain tomorrows."

Handed it back to her, continued: "That's taking unfair advantage of a state-sponsored system, don't you think?"

I looked on in amazement as she lit a perfectly rolled joint, sucked in a lungful of very potent British Columbian weed, held it for the longest time, then steadily exhaled a stream of the sweetest ganja I'd ever smelled. Yeah, yeah, you can knock me for letting a seventeen year old smoke marijuana in my office. Knock me all you wish. Thing is, sometimes it took some pretty unorthodox methods to treat special patients, and I didn't care whose laws I broke, as long as it worked. Would you rather I just say forget it all and medicate her with little yellow pills at $300 a pop? I should mention this: she now had a medical marijuana card from the State of California, so there.

"Forget you! I'm suicidal, or have you been severely comatose this whole time!?"

"I was just saying—"

"Leave it! I'm serious. It could be the most important step a suicide can take, walking into a hospital and declaring herself suicidal and messed up. Better yet, I could just come here and stay with you for thirty days. I mean, look at this place!"

Looking around in wonder, she got up, danced around. "You really outta try this, dorkus." A perfect pirouette. "It's great exercise!"

"There is a downside to this scenario, you know?"

"So what's the downside?" She fell back onto the couch.

"You know what the downside is," I said, wanting to give up. "The downside is that you wind up staying for a lot longer than you imagined, if you're not careful, and possibly with less-understanding people who will control your spirit."

"Why?" A huge smile on her face.

"Because if the state believes you're suicidal, it will keep you a lot longer than your requested thirty days. I promise you. There's our little 5150 law that provides for it. And what if someone in there provokes you into a fight, and you hurt them? It'll only get worse."

"5150's good for only three days. Look, dorkus, I still think it's a cool idea, so roll with it, will ya? Anyway, you can voluntarily check yourself into the nuthouse for at least seventy-two hours and up to thirty days, and allow them to evaluate you for that time. It gives you some breathing room, remember?"

"I'm a psychiatrist, so I know this, Tripsy. You sure you're not cold?" I got up, reached my arms high to stretch.

"I like it cool. Shut up and sit down."

"I'm an old man. My bones need stretching."

"What . . . ever. Anyway, it buys some needed time for you to sort yourself out, find your inner self again. Know what I mean?"

"Of course, but—" I tried to do a squat, heard my knees go CREAK!

"Damn, doofus, was that you!?" She laughed liked I'd just farted. "If they think it's cool to keep you longer, then I guess that's what happens. I mean, you don't hafta pay rent or buy food or anything, right?"

"Someone has to pay for your stay, like parents, taxpayers. Someone. It's not free, Tripsy, plus you do pay for your own smokes. And no marijuana, even with a pot card."

"I know how to bogart from other people. I could live in that place for at least a month and not pay for a damn thing. Got a strike? And don't worry about the hooters. I know people who bring in all kindsa meds."

Pulled out a lighter, fired up her second hooter. "I've heard of women who sell their bodies in those places, so, yes, I do know how some people do it."

"I wouldn't do that, dorkus. My bod's off limits to men . . . and women."

"Please continue, Tripsy."

"Anyway, you also get free meds, especially if you show the right symptoms."

"Now you're taking unfair advantage of the system."

"No, listen. I'm just tryin' to educate you, dorkus. You're waaaay outta touch with how to milk The Man."

"I don't like milking 'The Man,' Tripsy. I like paying my taxes and receiving only my fair share."

"Let's move on, dorkus. I can check myself into a cool place without having to pay a dime, and they'll check me out for at least thirty days free of charge. The whole time they're feeding me decent food three times a day, plus giving me good meds that'll keep me from offin' myself."

"All true."

"It's a good place for some people to unwind."

"True. For some."

"It took us a whole hour to get to a space where we're both on even ground, Dr. Dorkus. You should consider another day job. Ever try flippin' burgers?"

"I did, actually. I wasn't good at it. I enjoyed watching them burn. My manager told me I was the only griller he knew who could take a perfectly good piece of beef and turn it into a block of iron. Called me an alchemist, he did." Hmmm, wonder what that was a sign of, watching dead cows go the way of dead metal?

Small laugh, then: "Alchemist, huh? Well, you're not too good at this one, either, so we need to find you something that works for you. Let's see . . . what's your passion in life?"

"Physics. Reversing bad chemistry." That was a lie, I thought, looking up at Jimi and Brian.

"Hmmm, where would someone like you fit in? Ahhh, I got it: oil-spill research in the Arctic. When Exxon dumps its load on the shore, you can come along and reverse the bad chemistry."

She blew out a huge smoke ring that traveled the length of the room and glanced off my bookshelves and enveloped me.

"Speaking of chemistry, what happened to you such that you stopped writing in your diary?" I ventured, knowing where this would lead.

"And we were doing so well together. Time to run."

One item was true: she had dropped her guard recently. How would I now get her to open up about her diary? What was in her past that she didn't wish to revisit or reveal? While she dealt with her demons, I tried unsuccessfully to figure her out. Colleagues would call what ails me an obsession with this girl. The case, not the girl.

Dad would say, "Yeah, right, uh-huh."

Tripsy showed a level of intelligence and wisdom that was beyond her peers' most intricate thoughts. Some people are just born old souls. They know about the world, how it works, how to get around. And they had already been around the block long before they were out of diapers. Face it: some people are softwired to understand The Universe. *Indigo Children.*

I felt Tripsy was probably one of those very few. She knew it, too.

There was a psychiatric term for it, *unio mystica*—in touch with God or some higher form—but I felt it didn't adequately describe Tripsy's overall behavior.

The plain fact was, she probably was intimately tied to some higher source of energy, because Tripsy was like nothing I had ever seen before, let alone attempted to treat. I only wish I could've dug up more information about *Indigo Children*. Fact is, almost nothing existed, except in the TOP SECRET annals of CIA and Russian FSB filing cabinets.

When I thought about her in this light, I began to wonder if she were guiding me somewhere. Normally I don't spend a lot of time doing research on my patients, a sorry trait that puts me in that "middle of the road" category. But I found myself looking back on my sessions with her and seeing a slowly emerging pattern. Now, if I were only reasonably intelligent enough to discern it.

The only thing I could come up with so far was that she never repeated her problems in our sessions. They were all independent and distinct. She didn't fit the model of someone who suffered from dissociative identity disorder—what some still term multiple personality disorder. She seemed to retain her same personality, yet act out many different fictitious disorders.

I thought of Munchhausen syndrome, but something in the back of my mind dismissed it. She needed my attention for something, but it didn't appear to be a pathological state. She simply came in for each session, sat down, screamed out some malady or problem, abused me verbally, then carried on about her problem. Thing is, she was focused on only one problem for each session. Where was she going with all this?

Where was I going?

Far as I could tell, I was still along for the ride.

If I dear old father were here, he'd say, "Son, do not pass GO and do not collect $200. Go straight to hell. It's where you belong."

Session #23

It rained every cat and dog in California, plus the odd illegal from Mexico, so I decided to go upstairs and have our session in my private reading room. My charge nurse lifted an eyebrow as I trudged up the steps, but I knew it best to ignore the unspoken comment. She had never had to intervene in any of my cases in the past, so she probably knew darned well that I wouldn't do anything unethical or immoral with Tripsy. At least I hoped she thought that well of me.

What she did know was that Tripsy was becoming more of a handful each session, and I was seemingly getting nowhere with her, so maybe the reading room was a good idea after all. I probably should've briefed my staff about Tripsy, like I had always done with unusual patients, but I decided not to in her case. There were too many unknown variables that may have put me and my lousy career under a microscope, and I wasn't in the mood to be questioned harshly by any staff member, or anyone at all. After all, they reported to me. I was the boss. The guy in charge.

When Tripsy came tearing into the building, she yelled something at the receptionist, then stormed into my office.

Several of my staff looked up at her and smiled. One even said hello and welcomed her.

"Stop drinkin', smokin', shootin', snortin', vapin' or inhalin'!" she yelled at the empty room, then lit up one of those you-know-whats, the fan already sucking out her hooter-smoke and delivering it to an awaiting flock of birds outside the window behind my desk.

"As she lights up a hooter," I said, standing behind her at the door. "I was just setting things up in my reading room upstairs, so let's walk up, shall we?" I waved my arm to the stairwell, beckoning her.

Her left arm slowly extended in an elegant balletic pose, those long, slender fingers slowly doing the hula and forming a . . . and she flipped me off oh so elegantly. "Bite me, dorkus. This is one of the best things you can do to help yourself! Abusing some other chemical only compounds the suicidal impulses. I used to shoot all kindsa stuff into me, and it made healing impossible! I was too busy dealing with the last high or crash to think about taking my own life. It was a wreck of a life."

Through a tight-lipped smile, I said, "Follow me, Tripsy . . . For some, though, doesn't this form of abuse distract them from suicide?" I turned briefly to see her following me up the stairs, then thought about whether she really did abuse drugs to that extent. To me, she seemed so unbelievably lucid all the time. So, how could I know the truth unless she revealed it to me? Nothing in her past records or interviews with physicians or parents revealed anything terribly useful. They were all too lazy to take any interest in her. The MRIs, x-rays and lab tests revealed nothing remarkable. Except those keen observations by Dr. Kelley. So few yet so accurate. She said Tripsy was gifted and wanted to share it with the world. Share what, exactly?

How did she conclude Tripsy was an *Indigo Child*? Did she conduct some kind of test? My efforts to reach her were unsuccessful, so I was on my own here. And how did I come to the same conclusion, independent of Dr. Kelley? Was there some message from my subconscious that suggested this possibility?

Bottom line: Tripsy simply was not a user. Was she a poser? If so, why? Added these to the growing list of unanswered questions.

The room was largely empty, except for two very comfortable overstuffed chairs that sat at forty-five degrees to each other and only a foot apart, closer than the two chairs outside. A lovely stone fireplace, behind both chairs, slowly burned down a sizable chunk of old oak. I had made a point to light it before our session.

She took up residence on one of the chairs, my favorite one, more so because it was the first really nice chair I had bought when I started my practice fifteen years ago. The second chair came a year later.

She walked over to the fire, stoked it: "I forgot what you were sayin', dorkus."

As I sat down and gathered two comfy pillows on either side of me, I propped my feet up on one of the two large ottomans and repeated myself: "Doesn't this form of abuse you mentioned distract them from suicide?"

She lit up that joint again, said, "I guess for some, yeah. Not me, though. I think about it all the time! Thing is, you can't have a clean head for thinking while you're hopped up on all this other crap! How can you make any rational decisions about doin' yourself if you're drunk or high?"

As she pontificated this, I stared intently at her hooter, a long trail of smoke rising up to the ceiling and curling around itself like that otherworldly python. Ah, the recursive dynamics of illicit hooter-smoke.

"Okay, so maybe your argument is valid for a minority of people, but I'd say the majority of suicides who also dip into booze, say, are only

falling faster into that dark hole. On purpose."

"So your advice is to stop drinking or smoking or shooting, then deal with the suicidal thoughts, that it? Most people don't have it in them to function that linearly. For men, especially, they just pull out a gun and do the point-and-shoot thing."

I was pleased that she had such good eye contact with me now. I could get used to this overnight maturity. Maybe this change of venue wasn't such a bad idea. Maybe I wasn't so "middle of the road" after all. Or maybe this was just another day of surprises that weren't likely to repeat themselves anytime soon. In my world, anything was possible, even good things.

I could hear my father now: "Don't be too impressed with yourself, son. Sometimes even the mediocre get lucky."

Thanks, father.

"Find some cool way to stop abusing drugs—whatever drug it may be—so you can deal with the suicide thing. There are ways to kick those nasty habits, or haven't you been paying attention to your own advice all these years."

"I don't miss much."

"Okay, if that's true, then you should be the first one to tell people to wean themselves from anything other than toast and Perrier."

"Patients don't usually change that quickly, Tripsy. And it's almost never linear, like you suggested."

"It doesn't have to be linear, dorkus! One day, work on dropping the booze, another day work on dealing with the thoughts of offin' yourself. You take me so literally! Jeeeeez!"

"I listen to what you say and try to make some intelligent sense of it. It's the only way I can interpret your comments at the moment."

"I'll give you this much: you do listen well. After that is where you mess up. You're so rational and . . . literal. There're no gray areas in your life. It's either this or that. But what about things that fall in between? You just discard those?" She drank her glass of water, set it on the small side table, then went into a full splits position in front of our ottomans.

I looked down at her, amazed at her fluidity, her dexterity. "No, I—"

Her head now up: "Oh, I know: you take what doesn't fit neatly into either a black box or a white box, and then shove it into one of them and call it black or white. That's changing the essence of what constitutes a gray area. You make convenient color changes, dorkus."

"Where did you study this system of logic?"

"I'm an observer. I study people."

I bent down and gently touched her arm. "Then please tell me why your mom is so worried about what you write in your diary. She called me about it again."

The wrong thing to say, obviously: she shook off my hand, jerked upright, gathered her bag. At the door, she turned around, said, "Things aren't just black or white, dorkus. There're a lotta pastels in my life. And I happen to like the grays." With that, she was off.

What did that mean, she liked the grays? I took it literally again, as usual, analyzing her dress: very colorful yet elegant pastels. Wasn't that the definition of a pastel: brilliant color, dulled with gray? The further I got with Tripsy, the more I felt myself backsliding. More confused than ever, I went back downstairs to my office and composed an email to her mother, asking if she'd ever read Tripsy's diary, knowing full well this could blow up in my face.

Within minutes, Tripsy's mother replied: "Dr. Moore, Yes, I have taken it upon myself as her mother to read it. I am concerned because of her long list of suicidal statements. In fact, they go on and on for dozens of pages. And her language is rather odd, too, as if it belonged to someone else. What does this mean?" –Sheila

When I requested that she email me some of the passages, I knew I was walking on black ice, the scariest ice to find yourself on.

Session #24

Several of my staff had gone home early, so no one noticed Tripsy's stealthy entrance. She walked barefoot over the tiled floor in my office, sneaked up behind me as I was replacing a book on my bookshelf and delivered it: "I'm checkin' myself into a drug-rehab clinic!"

If I didn't shoot six feet straight up and hit the high ceiling, it was because I could only shoot up three vertical feet under those unusual circumstances. I thought I screamed "Holy crap!" in the key of ten little kittens, but who knows? I hadn't yet turned on my digital recorder. Maybe it's best I didn't know how I reacted.

"Don't gimme crap for making this a separate issue. This isn't merely an extension of our last session, dorkus."

"Would you please stop calling me these silly names? I do you the courtesy of calling you by your name, something you told me the first time we met, remember?" Feeling somewhat agitated, yes I was. I took several deep breaths, then thought about it: actually, I kinda liked her pet names for me, but if I didn't say something she'd probably truly think me a hack. Didn't she just say that anyway?

"Would you settle for Dr. Dorkus?"

"I'll make a note of this being an entirely new session." A cool breeze whipped through the yard and managed a way through the impossibly tiny cracks around the windows. I felt a momentary shiver as I made my way to my desk, lowered myself to the chair, and scribbled something down on my notepad.

After a moment of scribbles and doodles, I looked up: Tripsy was standing next to my desk, mere inches away from me. That heat again! Or was it her electric field or *Indigo* aura? Did it matter? I looked up and into her eyes, suddenly feeling very very small and insignificant. When one is lowered to this state of vulnerability, there're three choices: fight, flight or freeze.

"And while you're at it, moonface, note that this step happens only when you realize there's a problem, and—big 'and' here—you take a step to right it." She nudged my knee with her hand. "Got it?"

"Yes. You're going to have to tell me something here, just for my edification: why do you run away every time I start talking about your diary? It's clearly something that makes you feel uncomfortable."

For a moment, she seemed to pull back. At least she considered my query. That much was evident. Her eyes didn't leave me. A million different thoughts all competed for the same small neural funnel at the base of my brain, straining to warn me about something. What was it? Was she embarrassed? Frightened? One couldn't always tell simply by observing this girl.

She maintained her composure, though: "Most people actually know when it's time to check into a clinic like that. You know that?" She turned and went back to the couch, sat down and faced me, legs spread wide apart in a perfect stretch, one toe touching one end of the couch, the other touching the other end, with her sitting right at the edge.

Somewhat frustrated, I turned away, to the same place where she went when she was uneasy—my diaries. But now I became focused on my warrior-poet, Zxta, forever entombed in bronze. I wondered if there were anyone like her out there in the universe. Zxta, not Tripsy.

I said, "My feeling is, that's not true. The patients I see are sometimes so far gone they can't think for themselves; rationally, at least."

"Well, it is true."

I turned back to her again, adjusted the two pillows on either side of me, looking for a source of comfort. "According to whom? You?"

A smirk. "The average doper pulls herself outta her own hole without outside intervention. She's not a total flake!"

"Never said she was."

"And most people know when and why they've hit rock bottom," she said.

"If there is, in fact, rock that far down. It's usually mud and detritus."

"Whatever, smartass. When you can't go down any further, you know it."

"I thought that was the moment just before you pulled the trigger."

"You've been misinformed, dorkus. Where do you get your information? I mean, it sounds like you've been watching too much tv lately. Ya really should get out and experience the real world more, instead of locking yourself up in this . . . cave." She waved her arm around my precious office.

"This cave, as you put it, is my existence, Tripsy. I work here. I have obligations here: staff, patients, overhead, the like. I also watch BBC News and read a lot." The sad fact was that—lately, at least—I was not honoring all of my obligations, nor was I watching any news or reading much of anything. I had indeed slipped a bit. . . .

"Well, birdbrain, the real world doesn't exist in here. 'Sides, from what I see, you're not totally into your work."

I wondered whether she'd seen through me and how lazy I really was? For some unknown reason, I wasn't embarrassed. That thought, alone, made me uncomfortable.

Now looking at me again, she leaned forward as if to share some dark secret. "If you want real info, ya gotta go out and find it in real places. Hint: this ain't real, what ya got goin' on here." That sweeping hand motion again.

A small bird landed outside the front window, pecked on it, an excuse to break eye contact with her. "Then why are you here?"

"To help you, dorkus. You need it as much as I do."

The noisy little bird cocked its head at me, pecked on the window again, then seemingly shook its head in disgust, flew off. "I'm beginning to wonder who's helping whom here. And what makes you think I need any help?"

She heard the bird, looked up. "You talkin' to the tweet or me, dorkus? Anyway, I like the way you talk. Now, you think you can get the hell outside this pretty office sometime and get a real-world education?"

"Okay, I'll get out more. Can we get back to the drug-rehab topic?"

"Sure. What else ya need to know? I've already told you all ya need to survive, but since you weren't listening, I'll repeat myself. Listen up here: drugged-out kids aren't as stupid as you adults think we are. When we're right outta sixth grade, we can survive on the streets. Maybe what you see ain't the best example of the all-American teen, but hey, who gives a crap? Animals in the wild survive just like we do. That's what life is all about: survival, right? Well, we survive just fine. And when we turn to drugs and alcohol, it's for a reason."

"Which is?" I felt I'd heard the answer a thousand times before.

"That's for another book. For now, I'll just leave it at this: drugs change our chemistry in ways that parents and sib's and candy and nice clothes and a cool car change our chemistry. We feel safe and loved when we have all this crap. When some of us don't get these things, we turn to alternate means. And sometimes those alternates push us down a long slope that ends at some bottom of hell. Like I was sayin' before, we know when we've hit that bottom. It's dark and cold and devoid of life. It's the last place we wanna be. So some of us—most of us—say fuck it and pull ourselves out. One way out is checkin' into a clinic where dopes like you try to help."

"You're welcome."

"When I'm done with all this, I might thank you, dorkus, but not now. You ain't earned it yet. What's wrong with you, anyway? You're not your usual cheery self."

"I'm not here for the thank-yous, Tripsy." That bit of spring-loaded defensiveness got out without my permission.

"Okay, so you'd rather ignore my question . . . Remind me again why you're here, dorkus."

"Maybe you should remind me why you're here. What do you want from me? Or for yourself?"

No reaction. "What about all those doodles you've been doin' all this time?"

Oh, boy. "They help me understand things better . . . on a subconscious level."

"If they don't work, you could always read some of those tea leaves. The ones that smell like Lipton."

A typical smart-ass answer. I'd heard things like it from other teens who were angry at the world. In her case, The Universe. When I looked up again, she was gone. I pulled myself up and walked to the window, saw her running to the bus stop, then looking down the street. The bus drove up and I felt a sudden tinge of sadness. Why?

When all passengers had loaded, it pulled away. Tripsy was still standing there, looking down the street. A moment later, Henry rolled up and stopped a few yards from the stop where Tripsy was standing. She walked over to him, waved. He nodded his mop of unruly salt and pepper hair, then extended his hand.

If I could've given an arm right then to learn what they were talking about, I think I may have. . . .

Session #25

This was unusual for me: at six months of working with Tripsy, I had yet to prescribe any sort of medication whatsoever. Why? My subconscious CHILD ganged up and threaten to cut off my privates if I interfered with Tripsy's plan.

Plan!?

Only one other mental-health professional who saw Tripsy did not prescribe her any medication: Dr. Kelley. Though she was a psychologist, Dr. Kelley did not even recommend that she be medicated. In fact, I recall seeing some scribble of hers that said, "DO NOT MEDICATE." But she did not elaborate further. Shame on me for not following up on my calls to this Dr. Kelley.

At this point in my working with her, I was still at a loss to explain her behavior. And I wondered what the high-end psychiatrists would say to all this? How would they diagnose Tripsy's behaviors? I should find out, sooner than later. If there were something that would help her, then I owed it to her and her parents, distant and uncaring as they seemed, especially the asshole father. Please don't get me wrong here: I don't hate fathers—except mine. I just hate *bullies*.

Even though we didn't progress as far as I had hoped during one of the previous sessions, I felt holding the session in my private reading room was still a good idea, so I walked up to the room and sat down, awaiting her arrival. While I was feeling sorry for myself, she barged in: "Crash Alcoholics Anonymous or some other twelve-step program!"

"AHHHHHH!" I jumped out of my chair and stood ramrod straight, sucked in all the available air in the room, held my breath to calm down a notch.

Yes, you heard me correctly: I screamed bloody murder in my own private reading room, my sanctuary. And, yes, I heard it this time. Didn't have any need for a recording device: I'd remember this one for quite some time. Never before had I felt so insecure and intimidated by a patient! Why now and why me?

She stood in front of me, a small challenge: "What the eff, dorkus? Need me to call a doctor. Or maybe your shrink?" She seemed genuinely concerned and touched my forehead. It was as if her own outbursts were the norm and my 130-dB scream was clearly out of order, if not indicative of an impending heart attack. At least she was concerned about me. Or maybe worried she'd have to give an old fart CPR.

"You think anyone can hear me when I scream this out, dorkus?"

A wave of embarrassment pulled me deep into my chair again, so I grabbed a glass of water from one of the small end tables, and emptied it in two gulps. I was not usually a gulper. "This room is isolated, Tripsy. No one can hear us. That's why I like coming here. It's more peaceful and private. Never had any cause to expect a loud outburst before."

"Whatever. The next best thing is to crash a twelve-step and tell everyone your name. That's the first step."

"Have you hit rock bottom at this point?" I asked, trying to calm myself further, especially my breathing and heart rate.

"Probably not. At least for most. At this stage, you're not as desperate as you were, checking yourself into a clinic. A clinic is where you know there's some chance you may not come out the other door."

"Why do you say that?"

"The same reason you gave me for voluntarily checkin' into a psych ward: because they may find you so creeped up they'll wanna 5150 you 'for observation' for a looooong-ass time. Still, some of us do it, knowing it could lead to some kinda salvation. If there's some kinda chance, even a small one, we can survive and get whole again, most of us will jump all over it. That's what we are, dorkus: *survivors*. But we're also more than that; we wanna thrive in some way. Yeah, some of us are happy just to maintain, but others want more, a lot more. We're not blind! We can see people around us with a life. They've got the house with kids and the Mercedes and the 36-foot motor yacht parked in the harbor. We see that stuff and we want it, too. We know it exists, 'cos it's all over. It's not hard to put two and two together and see that there are ways to get it without gettin' felonious."

"So that's the dream? To thrive on material wealth?" I took my pulse: down to 180 beats per minute, and steadily declining. I'd broken out in a sweat, though. My new shirt was dotted with it.

"No, not really. But getting to that point means some accomplishment to us. By taking that first step, and at least admitting we need help, may save us. What's totally cool about it is that someone didn't step up and offer help; we took the step on our own."

"And that step allows you to cope with being suicidal?"

"It gives you a chance to sit down and breathe, yeah. And when you breathe a little, you can look at all the other crap in your life, and that includes killin' yourself."

"You're telling me that suicide isn't necessarily the most important topic on a suicide's mind." She handed me a handkerchief from her large bag. I took it absently, wiped my face.

"You catch on fast, homeboy. It doesn't include those suicides who're so far down the rabbit hole nothin's bringin' 'em out."

"I'll try to catch up to you, Tripsy. Meantime, I have to tell you something: I spoke with your parents yesterday about our progress. I told them I felt I wasn't the right person to help you."

In a flash, she was on her feet: "What the fu-fu-fu-fuuuuuu, dorkus! We talk all the time here! You ask me stuff and I tell you—"

"Crap. You tell me crap, Tripsy." I was more uncomfortable than ever, although relieved at having told her the truth. Was it the truth? Was she really feeding me garbage, or had I so far failed to see the real pattern, the meaning behind all this? Gathering data is one thing. After that, a good researcher has to analyze it and come up with an accurate diagnosis, a result one can use to make things better.

Looking away, she said, "That's not true. You just haven't figured it out yet."

"You're right: I have no idea what you mean, what you're up to, and what your motives are." I felt like a complete idiot: wrapped up, sewn up and polished off.

"Exactly." A long pause, then: "Sometimes you complicate things to stay in business, dorkus."

Had to stop and think about that one. "I told your parents that I felt they should find you someone—"

Not quite the same level of urgency as before, mind you, but she grabbed her stuff and moved out pretty smartly, leaving me standing there, alone. Very alone. With my dangerous thoughts about how poorly I had dealt with this situation.

Did I just subconsciously kick her out? Had I had enough of this young girl and her antics? And here I thought I was just beginning to figure her out. Why was I quitting at this point? It was a sad fact: most people quit before finishing something, and they had no idea how close they were to actually completing their goal. I knew this intellectually, but my basket-case head was in denial.

Session #26

After our last session, I called what some might say is a colleague of mine, Dr. C. Jay Cullins. Hell, even his name sounded cool. He was one of those high-end psychiatrists who billed at about $400 or $500 an hour. And the hour is about thirty minutes. For some reason, probably important to me, I wasn't the least bit embarrassed about referring Tripsy to him. He was actually quite gracious, too, and invited me to lunch sometime. I was so taken aback that I most assuredly said something stupid. Some guys just lack the *cool*. I was one of those unfortunates.

No one ever accused me of being cool.

Nearly a week later, five minutes before my next session with Tripsy, Dr. C. Jay Cullins called. He had three words to describe her: "No. Damned. Clue." The guy hung up on me before I could ask him what outfit I should wear to our lunch in Montecito.

My euphoria over his having failed eclipsed my feeling uncool.

Just as I replaced the phone, Tripsy walked to my desk, stood over me like a netherworld demon and did her thing: "Experiment with suicide, but don't kill myself!"

This one was beyond me and I didn't give a hoot. At least she hadn't run off like I felt she would, and was still in my care. And I don't give another hoot if what I was doing isn't "care" to my peers and other professionals. The high-end Dr. C. Jay Cullins couldn't crack the case. That was all that mattered at the moment. Maybe this mattered, too: that I was still in the running to figure out this extraordinary girl. Woo-hoo!

She waved her hands in front of my face, snapping me back to reality. Her reality: "It's simple, stupid: you find some thrilling way to kill yourself, do it only, like, half-way, then come back to life. Like a shock to the system."

"You're kidding, right?"

"No, listen! The point is not to kill yourself, but to get to the edge to see what's up."

"To shock you into loving life?"

"Yeah, sorta. Most don't really wanna die. They need a little convincing, though, so this might do it. Scare the hell out of 'em and they'll jet back home to mommy's milk and cookies."

"And this will put the fear of God in them?"

"Well, maybe not directly. But it'll at least cross out one choice they have in life: offin' themselves. That's gotta be good, right?"

"Yes, yes, it is good. I'm just wondering if being scared straight is necessarily the answer."

"There's no one answer, dorkus. Ya gotta roll with it. Sometimes it may take a few different strategies."

"Strategies. Hmmm. Doesn't that suggest long-term thinking."

"Okay, then. What's the right term, smartass?"

"Tactics."

"Sounds so . . . military shoot-'em-up."

"It is what it is, Tripsy."

"Okay, so this tactic makes you think about other stuff."

"Still about killing yourself, you mean?"

"No, I think at this point, they're probably ready to join some church like an obedient little twerp."

"That sounds like some resignation."

"In a way it is, 'cos it's a sign of failure, and they just have to get over that. Time is the only thing that really works. Unless they're stuck in the same cycle."

"And if they are?"

"Maybe they should try another suicide . . . and not miss."

"I'm surprised to hear that from you, of all people."

"I wasn't serious."

"If you get serious for a moment, then what's the answer?"

"Sometimes it takes more than one shock to show people that life's worth living."

"And living *well*."

"That goes without saying, dorkus . . . oh, look at the time!" She looked down at her oversized Swatch, whose little hand was on the 5 and big hand was on the 1.

I was in shock: "It appears you've overstayed your session, Tripsy."

Spreading smile over her face.

Yes, it was contagious.

3

How Do You Want to Kill Yourself?

This is where things got really creative. Morbid as it sounds, Tripsy unleashed a white-knuckle ride of colorful ways to end her life. After a couple of weeks of this, I stopped taking notes and just listened and observed her. I did doodle, though. She was quite animated—no, *passionate*—during her discussions about how to commit the highest of mortal sins against a human mind, body and soul.

While I don't believe in God or support any religion, mostly because I hadn't found any so-called God/gods worth worshiping, I found myself searching for more meaning about why a young person would even think of doing these things to herself. It amounts to nothing less than torture of the soul, if one actually existed. After hearing all this, I was wondering if a soul in this much trouble could possibly redeem itself.

But, then again, Tripsy was no ordinary soul. Somehow, I didn't feel that any organized religion could help me explain the inner workings of this young woman. I probably needed to consult a particle physicist. Or an exorcist, now that I considered this more. I was relieved when I recalled that there were several excellent exorcists still on the payroll in parts of West Africa, Haiti and Palm Beach.

Honestly, I don't recall hearing about so many different ways to commit suicide, at least not from my previous patients. The traditional attempts or thoughts about suicide were usually overdoses, especially by females, although a bullet through the mouth occasionally reared itself, limited mostly to males.

Most people who want to end their pain didn't enjoy the thought of throwing themselves in front of a moving bus at rush hour. That simply brings more pain, and they ended up feeling extremely anxious and agitated for it. No, their m.o. was typically to do it quietly and painlessly, which usually meant popping something that would make them go comatose indefinitely. Clearly, the typical suicide is not as creative in options as Tripsy had been.

Tripsy's approach to suicide, while novel and at times horrific, echoed her high thinking and creative intelligence. It was worth exploring, because it revealed how she thought through things and came to conclusions and solutions. If I have said before Tripsy was wise beyond her years, I say that again. With emphasis added. I had an independent research librarian friend of mine look for information about *Indigo Children*. She found very little, only hints that American and Russian intelligence were still experimenting with these kids. There had to be someone who could shed light on this unique phenomenon. I hated not being able to figure out something. This was beyond frustrating, it was maddening.

Tripsy's thoughts on creative suicide were not unlike those found in a wildly popular cartoon book that depicted animals in various stages of suicide attempts. I wonder if Tripsy secretly consulted with the author on those various ways to kill herself. And I don't mean that the author gave her advice. Far from it. Tripsy probably educated him far beyond what he depicted in his cartoons. No disrespect intended to the author, of course. Tripsy was a force of nature and no man or woman could match it, present company included. Sometimes, I was given to exaggeration.

While funny and downright comical at times, Tripsy's approach showed an underlying creativity I wanted to explore. She brought this out more and more, drawing me closer. Or was it further and further down that proverbial hole full of gooey dark matter?

Please don't get the impression I've never studied these various methods as a means to commit this act of violence. We, of course, had long discussions in med school about it, and I spent many long hours with fellow residents and my mentor, familiarizing myself with every possible avenue of self-death.

When attending at various hospitals, emergency rooms and private clinics, I did see a somewhat larger variety of techniques to commit suicide. Still, they mostly centered around "non-violent" means of taking their own lives. Only a handful in a hundred or so would attempt the truly violent means, say, using a shotgun or spreading themselves across active railroad tracks. And they were almost always young males, raising many questions, not the least of which was: "Was testosterone a major culprit in how someone took their own life or was it somehow cultural and learned?"

I'm not so naive to believe that testosterone is the only chemical at work here. Far from it. It did, however, appear to play more than a minor role in how young men took their own lives.

Never would I be so careless to release that kind of opinion without further careful thought and study. Suffice it to say here, in the privacy of my own thoughts, that I feel the chemical that confers such maleness on so many is probably what causes many of the ills of this world, and not simply influencing how a young person ends her life.

One last note on that topic: what I also found sobering is that females are twice as likely to attempt suicide, but males are four times more likely to succeed in killing themselves.

In fifty years, my hypothesis will be either proven true or rendered false. I truly feel that there's much truth to it. Then again, that's why we call these our "pet hypotheses," yes? I know many of you refuse to believe that our behaviors are all defined by chemistry, but they are. Really. I've had this belief for decades. Interestingly, only in the past ten or so years have the media picked up on results from scientific studies that have demonstrated chemistry, in one form or another, is responsible for our behaviors. Of course, when I say chemistry, it encompasses all the various reactions that occur when a behavior or an action actually happens. So much is involved.

Alas, this important subject is not the primary focus of this book. For now, I will restate my hypothesis: all behaviors are conducted by chemistry, especially in the brain. What's more, we humans have less control over our behaviors and lives than we would like to believe. Yes, I do subscribe to the concept of fate . . . it is indeed written somewhere, perhaps in our DNA, we are continuous communication with some higher power that I believe to be The Universe.

Some of you would like to string me up for saying this, yes? Good for you. In the very least, your resistance will provide science a system to check its progress, and to ensure that those practitioners of science continue to do the right thing.

One would hope. . . .

Session #27

Outside my window, the wind-driven rain splashed against the trees, buildings and ground, paused to catch a breath, then commenced once again, creating a gentle symphonic cycle. I caught myself humming to it and wishing I could record all those beautiful harmonics. Oh, how Mother Nature sings to us!

Teapot whistled, interrupting my song: the Lipton gourmet tea was nearly ready for consumption. Without really thinking about it, I took the pot from the burner, turned it off, stared at the little hot plate. Looked outside because the rain had turned on again, a mesmerizing adagio befitting Mozart himself. Saw her standing there, wet as water, swaying gently back and forth.

"A bullet through the brain pan!" Hers was the look of a soggy homeless dog.

Oh, fudge. Set the tea aside, made a little sigh of exasperation, walked outside. "That's quite a colorful way to start off this topic."

Soaked to the skin, she stretched her arms skyward, her muscular curves accentuated under the wet clothes. "Noir on noir, genius. Get used to it. It's the color of the ultimate piss off, you."

"And here I thought it was red." After a few minutes, I was soaked, too, and taking on more water. Would I soon keel over and sink?

"Get real! And kill the lame-ass jokes, will you? They're diluting mine."

"C'mon, Tripsy, I was just adding to the color palette. Yours was a bit dark on dark. I thought you didn't like just black and white—oh, never mind."

"Follow me, dorkus," she instructed, and walked past me and into the back area of the office complex. The sounds of the little winter shower ceased. Nothing but peace back here. She wiped off the water, plopped down on her chair. "I love violence. My dad was a bandit, a lifetime terrorist. Who could've grown up in such sweetness and not been influenced so positively?"

I pulled out a large plastic bag I'd brought out with me, draped it over my chair, sat down. "Okay, I get your sarcasm."

"Shut up so I can get on with this thing . . . a bullet through the brain pan will normally do the trick. Thing is, ya gotta make sure you start in the right place."

"I'm sure you know all the right locales."

"Stand by, dorkus, I'm getting there! Ever heard of progressive disclosure?"

I nodded eagerly, still wringing the water from my clothes.

"Good. Here goes: first, ya gotta use somethin' bigger'n a .22. Those little things are like BBs and don't do much other'n rattle around your head and scramble thing up like eggs on high burner. I recommend using at least a nine-mm bullet, which will go through most points on the average skull; neanderthals and thick-headed knuckle-draggers excluded. Now, if you're a girl like me, you can get away with pointing the pistol—"

"I hate to interrupt your excellent instruction, but what types of weapons are we talking about?"

"You can get a small pistol like a Ruger, which fits well in the hands of most girls. It doesn't have a kick, so you can fire it without the thing getting blasted outta your hand."

"Not that it'll make much of a difference when you've got a two-inch-diameter hole your head, but why care about whether the pistol will fall out of your hand afterward?"

"In case you miss and the pistol slams off the wall and shoots you in the kneecap or something."

"Then you'll really be in trouble: you have to call an ambulance and go to the emergency room and get that kneecap glued back on and the bullet hole sewn up so you can get back home and do it right the second time."

"At least I'm teachin' you well, dorkus. Yeah, something like that. Anyway, dig this: since there're so many different places you could actually put the pistol when shooting, I'll just tell you where not to point it."

"I'm all ears."

"That's exactly where you wouldn't wanna put it. But, then again, I have to remember who I'm talking at."

"Why? It goes through the head."

"Yeah, but it may not blast off the right stuff."

"It would probably go through the medulla."

"Is that a neighborhood where you live?"

Big sigh. "Please continue, Tripsy. . . ."

"I was just joking, dorkus. I know what the medulla is. Sooo, don't stick the thing in your ear. Don't put it on the side of your face or you'll just blow your pearly whites all over the floor like a buncha Vegas dice. Nope, don't do that. Don't put it directly under your chin or you might only rip off your nose. In your case, dorkus, it would be an improvement. For us suicidal chicks, it's a waste o' lead."

"You talk like a cowboy. Who've you been hanging around lately?"

"Listen, dorkus! If you shoot yourself in the jaw, you break your jaw, some teeth, and maybe pop out an eye. That'll only get you a one-way ticket to the emergency room and about six months of plastic surgery. The 'rents'll hate you, for sure."

I mumbled something I hoped she wouldn't hear: "Not to mention years of therapy with some guy like me."

"All the more reason for us girls not to go there."

"What about the guys?"

"Those dickheads? They're pro'ly using an antiaircraft gun or some big ten-inch thing from a battleship, which we'll talk about later, so shut up and lemme finish. Just don't shoot anything lower than the nose and nothing forward of the ears. Get it?"

"Does this superb instruction come with a manual, Tripsy?"

"Did I mention that you should put two bullets in the gun, one for your therapist and one for yourself?"

"I'm getting it. Keep going. And while you're at it, let's talk about your diary."

For the briefest of moments, she paused, then: "What the flippin' flip, dorkus . . . always aim for the center of the brain, just above the ear. And try to go the length of the head. It takes out more of what matters—gray matter, that is—instead of from the side. Listen up: it's better to go through the front of the face first, 'cos the skull's thinner there. If you start at the back of the head, where it's still kinda neanderthalic, the bullet has to penetrate too much skull initially. Yeah, yeah, I know those ballistics perverts'll tell ya a nine-mil will go through the thickest of skulls, but it's not true unless you aim dead center of the bone from less than a foot away."

"Or else you risk a glancing shot?"

With renewed energy, she hopped up, threw her arms outward. "Yes, grasshoppa! It's also hard to hold a pistol to the back of your head, so just be a smart little suicide and aim from the front. Besides, you get to see it coming right before you blast away your last thought."

"And your favorite spots are?"

Pointing her hand like a gun, she says, "My money shot? I like the left eye, nose or mouth, remembering to aim dead center of the brain so you take out your inner reptile and all that ancient software that keeps your clock goin'."

"Right, you don't want to miss those vital parts. Tripsy, please allow me to break this to you: even if you use a nine-mm pistol to effect this killing, and you shoot yourself somewhere in the head, chances are you're going to be brain dead anyway."

"Prick up those ears, dude: the point is not to chance it. I'd hate to wind up in ICU for a year, hooked up to all that hardware keeping me breathin' and eatin' baby food through an i.v."

"Just adding my two cents." The cold was now getting to me: I put on my jacket over my nice shirt, zipped it up.

"Keep your pennies. I'm dealin' in Benjamins here, get it?" She was still wearing that flimsy outfit, seemingly unaffected by the cold. Otherworldly, this woman.

"Okay, Tripsy. Whatever you say."

"I'm glad we finally agree on that . . . so, my fave is through the mouth, aimed slightly upward." She made a finger-gun and stuck it in her mouth.

"Hey, for the record, Tripsy. I wouldn't even bother with a nine-mil."

"Oh, yeah? What would you use, Generalissimo?"

"I like the antiaircraft gun idea you had earlier."

"You just wanna send what's left of your little mind into outer space, don'tcha? Oh, yeah, you also only wanna have one bullet in the gun."

"I thought you said two before?"

"One will already have gone through your therapist's head. The other one is reserved for yourself. Like I said, you only wanna have one bullet in the gun, in case some little shit like a brother or sister comes along and finds you with a loaded gun."

"After you're dead, you mean?"

"Of course. And then the little poopers take the gun and blast some fool like mom or dad."

"Everything's great 'til something goes wrong, Tripsy."

"What the hell, dorkus. And stop trying to be profound. Doesn't become you."

"Okay, forget that statement. About your parents, you hate them anyway. And that brings me to an important question, Tripsy: shall we talk about your parents? Maybe your diary?"

Usually, she flinched at my probing her, or just blithely walked away. Now, though, she paused. "The name of the game is suicide, smart guy. You only wanna take one life."

"So I guess the therapist gets spared."

"You'd be my exception. . . ."

"That brings me to a general question."

"Send it."

"What brought you here in the first place, if you weren't willing to share your deep thoughts?" A quick glance at my watch: we had gone over our one-hour limit. I decided to press on, sensing . . . something.

Suddenly, she slumped in her chair like a Raggedy Ann doll tossed in a corner. She flopped her head away from me, then back again. "I guess I'd hit rock bottom."

"How did you know?"

Sitting up straighter now, she said, "I defined it as the worst I'd ever felt in my entire life, a place I'd not wanna stay too long, like a dingy Italian hotel room filled with a thousand mosquitoes I had to swat all night just so I could lie down and zzzz."

I pulled my chair closer to hers. "How do you know it couldn't get worse than what you defined as rock bottom anyway? When we really look at things, they could always be much worse."

"It could. I know that for sure. Thing is, dude, I also knew that there was a point of no return and if I hit that point, which was only a few feet beyond rock bottom, I'd never recover. Simple as that."

"How'd you get to rock bottom?"

"Good question. You ask good questions." Her gaze was now off, somewhere beyond the trees, the hedges, the street. "If I could only train you to come up with some clever solutions to all my teeny dilemmas, you'd soon be in Stockholm collecting your prize."

Now looking at me again: "It's like this: I knew I could only start to heal after hitting rock bottom. That's sort of a mental point where people either say forget it and keep going down, or they see it as a wake-up call and they start to climb out. It's a well that's infinitely deep and has no light above. That's what it seems like in the beginning."

"So you find yourself at rock—"

"Wooo, dude, not to so fast. You skipped a few steps. Back up here. First of all, we haven't hit rock bottom yet."

"I thought we had."

"No, dummy, we were approaching it on a slow and steady collision course, but we were still miles from it. Pay attention."

"I'm all ears."

"That's what concerns me: you need to be all everything except the mouth. Open your brain, listen and assimilate."

"Okay. I'm trying," I assured her.

"I knew I was a few miles from rock bottom. My goal was to get healed. But the one thing standing in my way was hitting that proverbial end of the abyss. Since I wasn't there yet, I was impatient to get there. You following me?"

"Keep going. I'll catch up sooner or later." I felt confused, but not because she exhibited that avoidance behavior again. She was fascinating, or was I just lost?

"Good. Check this out: since I had a pretty good idea of where rock bottom was—I had a map—I just decided I'd rappel down there on my own."

"You mean you facilitated getting into the worst shape you possibly could, without losing the mental faculties to realize where you were and how you might recover?"

He arms were now waving wildly. "DAAAAAAM! So, yeah, I did what I had to do to mess myself up so much I couldn't go further without killing myself."

"And that's when you came to see me." Stuck out my chest. A little.

"You like to skip steps and just go right to the bank, don'tcha? No, I didn't just come see you after I'd smashed into rock bottom. I spent thirty days in a mental unit, then my mother sent me here."

My chest sunk inward slightly.

"If you wanna heal, I mean, truly recover on your own, ya gotta find the edge of reality, 'cos the margins define the rest of your life, dorkus. They give it weight and balance." She moved her chair closer to mine, now almost touching. "*Your* reality. Most people live in a teeny tiny envelope of safety. Forget that. I've gone out there and defined my margins, and when I felt they were constricting, I widened 'em on my own."

"How?"

"It's called 'stretching' in some professional circles. Obviously not yours."

"Good point. I know about stretching, but it's more a colloquial term than a formal one."

"Anyhoo, dorkus, I keep on pushing those boundaries out there, expanding my balloon."

"Maybe that's how you can get to your rock bottom on your own. Sounds like you rappelled, as you put it, to a space where you wanted to go and knew where you were going. Some will find that approach sadistic, at best."

"Forget 'em. They're the ones who are scared of their own internal shadows. They can't live in the dark, that can't live alone, especially with themselves, and they sure as hell can't live with anyone else peacefully. They're always just criticizin' or judging, even if they don't know they're doing it. That's the worst kind, dorkus: those without any self-awareness. They all think they crashed right through rock bottom and defined a whole new kinda hell, but they fail to realize they're still flailing at the surface. Leave 'em."

"I thought you'd like to help everyone."

"Piss on that, dorkus. I told you more than once that I'm here to enlighten and entertain you. What you do with this is up to you."

At best, I still had only a vague idea about what was going on here, so what I would do with it remained to be seen. By me, at least. "I don't follow."

"It's entertaining . . . it's stimulating . . . and it scares the crap outta you because it's so unfamiliar and unconventional. Even if you could define it, you wouldn't know what to do with it."

"I'll reserve comment on that one. Tripsy, we're way past the usual time, so—"

"How is it that I'm the only one here who never reserves comment on any subject on any level at any time?"

I put my hand on hers. "Except when I mention the diary or your past, Tripsy?"

It was about sixty degrees now, perfect for a brisk walk or jog, maybe even a nice bike ride along the beach. The sky had cleared here and there, allowing the sun to drift through, but not enough to warm me up.

She pulled her hand away, looked up into the tree. "I'm a 'bring it on, baby!' kinda chick and you're all, 'excuse me, please, I need to check my calendar.'"

"You're enlightened, Tripsy, what can I say? Wise well beyond your seventeen years. I wonder where it comes from." I almost didn't want to think of the term *Indigo Child*, because I knew little about it, only its very general concepts. It was like great art: you can't describe it, but you know it when you see it because it pierces your very soul. I knew this about Tripsy: she was no ordinary teenager. Tomboy meets Dr. Richard Feynman.

"First you listen . . . then you feel . . . then you experience . . . then you assimilate . . . then you practice . . . then you excel . . . then you preach. You like to speed-walk from listen to preach. It's a bad habit I'd work on if I were you, dorkus, cuz you miss all those little details."

All those singing details, indeed. "Noted. So you think I'm a charlatan?"

"You know the basic package okay, but you need to fill in all the gaps before you can call yourself an evangelist."

Touché. "And you are?"

"I'm an evangelista, dorkus. Been there, done that, writing the book."

"I didn't know you wanted to write a book. You stopped writing in your diary some time ago, your mother said."

She stuck her tongue out at me at the mention of her mother. "Remember: first you listen, then you feel, then you—"

"I understand, Tripsy. Like I said, wise beyond your years. Where'd you say you were from?"

"Santa Barbara."

"USA, Flat Planet Earth, Milky Way Galaxy?"

"Let's not get lost in little details, dorkus. 'Sides, you don't give a hoot about details anymore, 'member?"

"What's that mean?" Sitting up a little straighter now, I was.

"Do you really care about the kids you treat? I mean, c'mon, dorkus. Look at you. You're a wet, mushy lump o' flippin' disinterest, if I ever saw one."

"And you glean this information how, Tripsy?"

"By the questions you ask, how sorta casual you are, how you try to squeeze in the 'diary' or 'my past' thing at the end of sessions. You're just punchin' a ticket, doc. Simple as that." A chime from her cell phone. "Oh, crap! I'm late."

"For what?"

"My parkour class. Sorta this fluidic street gymnastics. Jackie Chan on rocket fuel."

"What?"

She pulled out a pair of stretch pants from her bag, slipped them on under her skirt. Tossed the skirt in the bag, looked up at me. "C'mon, sport, haven't you ever drunk some chick's bathwater before? You guys should bottle that magic. Trust me, it's more than just an aphrodisiac. Gotta run!"

What did she just say? Bathwater? Bottle it? What!? I had to admit something, though: she was more voluble in positive ways than ever before. Something was happening here, and it wasn't my technique or presence. I was just a bystander and she knew it. As usual.

My dad would have said, "You make a great doormat, son."

Session #28

"Illegal drug overdose!" Tripsy looked around my office and smirked, not because she was pissed off; she wanted something different. "I liked it better outside. Why do we have to be in here again?"

"I told you on the phone it's getting cold outside." Rather than sit behind my desk, I pulled out an old wooden Catholic teacher's chair, something specifically designed for discomfort, sat down a foot from the couch. "A lot of people use that method, Tripsy, overdosing on something right out of the bathroom cabinet. In fact, it's an epidemic now, especially among teenage girls."

Sort of ignored me: "The hard core ones? They just grab a gun. That was my first thought, too. But most dudes who use illegal drugs are already using and have nothing else, or they know someone who's a user and can get it easily."

"So, to you, it's really a matter of convenience?"

Off came the scarves and sweater, then the jungle boots. Those yoga stretches again, both hands on the floor in front of her. "Dude, you're amazin'. Suicides are the laziest people on this planet. Not much prep goes into the deed, ya look at all the statistics. It's like some run-of-the-mill assembly-line job: pick up this part . . . put it into that part . . . push parts off the line . . . pick up this part. Didn't you ever watch that rerun of *I Love Lucy* where she's max'd out on brain bytes and, just to keep up and not get fired, starts shovin' bonbons in her mouth?"

Stretched to the side, then the other, looked up at my diaries, then over to Zxta.

I was trying to imagine Lucy at that assembly-line table, stuffing bonbons into her beautiful face. "I never watch tv. Only the occasional film on my computer . . . you're looking at my diaries again. What's the interest?"

Blowing me off, she continued: "How to off yourself with illegal drugs. The most obvious is weed, but you can't do much with it unless you, like, go out into a bone-dry forest and use it to start a forest fire with you in the middle of it. Other'n that, forget it. You can't OD on weed."

"You could choke on it."

"You should write a book on suicide."

Honestly, I thought I had. In fact, it's that little ten-pound, dust-covered paperweight sitting impassively on my desk, remember?

I lowered my head, ashamed. "It's on a back burner."

She hopped up like a cat, padded over to my desk, ran a long, slender finger over the top of my beloved manuscript . . . inspected it . . . looked at me again. "Back burner, huh? Way things look to me, dorkus, it hasn't even made it to the kitchen yet."

"Thank you for that, Tripsy."

She sat down again. "Fire the chef, dorkus. All this talk of back burners is making me hungry."

"Can I have one of my staff order you something, Tripsy? There're some great food trucks outside today."

"Dude, not in the mood for medical-grade tacos, EPA-blessed burritos, or an FDA-approved chimichanga. Gimme a cabbage patch and some vinaigrette."

Something shot out of my nose and I belly-laughed.

She ignored me and pressed on: "Listen up: the top two drugs that do it for you are coke and heroin, or the latest derivations of each. You either inhale it or shoot it. Either way, the stuff is potent enough in small doses to freeze your clock like fentanyl: all you do is look at the stuff and your're dead."

"Clock?" I laughed, knowing it was something arcane, known only to cool people like her, and probably Dr. C. Jay Cullins. I was still reeling from her "fire the chef" comment. What exactly did that mean?

"Heart. Your ticker. Remember that book I was tellin' you about?"

"Yes, the one about youth slang."

"Youth. Slang. You're a curious sort, know that, dorkus?"

"I'm learning more about my predicament every day." My father used to tell me that, too.

"Soooo, if you hoover about ten grams of coke at one sitting, you're probably gonna stop ticking within half a minute. Questions?"

I snickered. "Reminds me of a scene from a Cheech and Chong film from—"

"The Ajax whore!"

"Yes, ma'am," I said, getting up and pulling down an old diary, something from my childhood.

"While you're at it, you may as well turn it into some fun: draw a line of the stuff in the shape of your face or something."

Without looking at her, I said, "That may take some time. And time isn't what suicides have much of, is it?"

"True. I was just tryin' to make it more fun. What're you readin'?"

I turned around, looked at her, held up the diary. "Suicide is anything but."

She stared at the diary, piqued. "You win that one."

"What about heroin?" Sitting down again, I leafed through the pages, smiling here and there, then frowning.

She studied me, my expressions, wondering what I was reading with such interest. "That's even easier. Ya gotta shoot it into a vein, though, and that can be a bitch for first-timers. Not many suicides are gonna—"

"Why do you refer to all of these kids as *suicides*? That's not at all encouraging." I must admit that I've also used this term, disparaging as it sounds.

"Because they all think that suicide is the goal. It doesn't mean that all of them want or will succeed. It's the goal in that moment, according to some part of their mind. Plus, it sounds cool, like you're a member of some elite hit squad. Don't read into it too much."

"Just clarifying things a bit. And I don't necessarily feel that suicide is the goal."

"What do you feel, professor?"

"Ending or avoiding pain."

"Cool, I'll buy that. Now dig what I'm selling: the goal beyond that is suicide. That's not open for debate, dorkus."

"Let's agree to disagree, shall we?" I looked up from my diary.

"Shut up and keep listening. If we take away all the conveniences of modern humans, we're left with only the basics to get by. Like food, water, shelter, and a comfy place for your type to read the paper. Without the immediate means to off yourself, you'll have to resort to something you don't wanna do."

"Think." I leafed through more pages. A worried look suddenly appeared on my face.

"I'm impressed. And when you sit around and ponder stuff, you start to . . . dorkus?"

"Huh? Oh. Uh. Ask questions."

"Pay attention to me!" she snapped, grabbing the diary. "Like I was sayin', one of the first questions usually is, 'What the heck am I doing?' When you ask yourself questions, you then do something that no one likes to do: you answer yourself." The diary, heavy in her hands, stopped her momentarily.

I reached out, took the diary from her. "People don't trust their own answers."

She started stretching. "They're insecure, dude! I see it all the time: people have pretty much all the answers inside 'em. And I don't mean they know brain surgery or stuff like that. They do know what's generally right and wrong, and they can find a reasonably clear path to where they wanna go. It ain't rocket science."

"Actually, Tripsy, it's rocket science on every level."

"I know, I know: quantum mechanics rules all. I'm not challenging people to go that deep here. I'm not even askin' 'em to jump in the pool with me. Even though it's less than six inches, most would still find a way to drown. I'm just tellin' you that all you need to do is stop . . . listen to yourself for a few minutes . . . listen again . . . then ask a question . . . and find a bunch of possible answers. Just throw 'em all out there like darts. Doesn't matter what you hit, long as you hit something, even just the air. When you see that some of your answers are wrong, you scratch off the veneer and look underneath yourself a little. And you question your own answers for the first time in your life."

"You become self-aware." I replaced the diary on the highest shelf, still well within her reach.

"Yeah, you develop consciousness instead of just walking through your world like a stick figure."

"I'd like to hear more about how to kill yourself with illegal drugs."

"Tangent. Sorry. I won't go into all the different kinds you can use, unless you wanna be here all weekend." She stopped stretching, returned to the couch, curled up at one end, only her painted toes showed: like colorful M&Ms.

For once, I did not respond.

More surprised than I, she continued: "Uh-huh. Let's get back to using illegal stuff to do the deed. If you're shooting up, hit a good working vein with enough of the stuff to kill you. You don't wanna wake up hours later, paralyzed from the neck down with your dog looking at you like you're the only steak in the building. That would suck. Especially since you'd be awake to watch yourself get taken apart a bite at a time."

"I get the picture, Tripsy."

"Cool, cuz that freaks me out, being consumed by an animal, especially a stupid dog. My cat would never even think of eating me. Dogs eat people, so let's leave it at that."

"I think it's safe to say it's an atavistic fear in all of us."

"So anyway, make sure you've added a true overdose of your drug of choice to your syringe. At least look it up on the web for the LD-50, which is the dosage that killed fifty percent of rats or guinea pigs in that messed-up experiment. See? This means ya gotta think, dorkus! Most people will just find the nearest bottle of vicodin and chase twenty pills with a finger of Stoli. Some die, some don't. If you're popping pills, make sure you take the right dose, you moron, or you're not gonna do it right. And ya gotta use the right drug, too. I saw where this one chick popped a bottle of chewable baby aspirin. It wasn't even enough to kill the headache she got after her mom slapped the crap out of her for trying to off herself."

The clock on the wall signaled the end of the session. Neither of us moved. We just sat there, looking at the other and wondering what was going on in her beautiful mind. Other than killing herself, I mean.

"Tripsy, the reason why I usually leave those touchy questions to the end, rather than throw them out in the beginning, is because you seem more relaxed toward the end of sessions. I'm not trying to be lazy working with you. I'm hoping you'll take these deep thoughts and do some serious thinking."

Unfolding herself, she stretched out a moment, picked up her things, walked to the door. "I'm not ready to talk about that stuff." With that, she left. Calmly. Quietly.

While I should have felt relief at her mature exit, I was saddened by her departure. I opened a bottle of Sumarroca cava, a lovely Spanish sparkling wine. What the hell was I saying? A goddamn champagne. And screw the French when they raise an objection. After all, champagne had become so commonplace nowadays, like Coke, Xerox, Kleenex, Q-tips. Each of them now refers even to the generic varieties. What do they call that? Anepronym? Or is it metonym?

If my father were here, he'd say, "Growing a pair of balls, are you, son?"

After a few gulps, my planchette began autowriting again:

this noon I swim through a
midnight sky, over and under a
hurricane's eye

stirring every electron from
wild slumber, lucifer's
entourage of untold number

following in my wake, so
dutiful they are, carving
lightning to splinters so wide
and far

ghastly photonics surge across
the earthly plane, raising
dust and sea so insane

and so another submystery
begins anew, this hot frothy
mix of celestiobrew

Session #29

For the first time in seven months, I felt she was opening up. Knowing how volatile she could be, I didn't always press delicate points, except her diary and some of her past. Thing is, if I don't continually challenge her, we will get nowhere and all she will do is vent. Or is there more to her rants than that?

Remember those doodles I'd been making recently? Well, they revealed some interesting aspects to these rants: for one, her subject matter has a pattern. It appeared silly at first, but then I began to see how she'd bring up seemingly random bits of information that now appear to form an interesting outline to the whole notion of suicide.

What else? Her face was a bit softer than in previous meetings. I felt more encouraged, so I scooted my chair closer to "her" couch, propped my feet up on an arm of the couch, and awaited her imminent arrival. . . .

My beloved diaries and Zxta were about the only things she noticed when she walked into my office. Except me, of course.

"Woo-hoo! Alcohol poisoning!"

"Great, let's blend a pitcher of margaritas."

" 'Bout time you got comfy in your own office, dorkus."

"If it's good enough for you, it should be for me."

"You should take more cues from me, doofus."

"Tripsy, you don't give me enough to go on. We've been doing this for seven months, and you still have yet to talk about some deep issues I know are disturbing you. I wonder why you bother even to come back." Smooth move, dorkus.

That pouty look, the one with a dash of anger, flashed across her face.

I looked away, raised my head up, closed my eyes. Exasperated. Again. "Okay, what about alcohol poisoning?"

"Alcohol poisoning is great, but you almost always end up puking like a bulemic. The last thing ya wanna feel is nauseated before you die. It's the worst feeling ever, next to two-day diarrhea. Buuuut, if ya gotta go that way, then ya gotta go that way. And don't drink beer or cider. You'd hafta down more than a case to do it, and by that time you'd be passed out over the toilet with vomit all over your pretty dress."

"I guess anything under fifty proof is off limits, too?" My eyes focused back on her, trying desperately to look positive and upbeat.

"Unless you wanna go wine tasting before the evil deed, forget that stuff. Suicide-wine's only used by middle-aged women with fake boobs, bad tummy tucks and cheating husbands. They call those bitches sidewinders, with a 'c.' "

Suicide-wine. Sidewinder. I held back a laugh, paused a moment. "And you know this how?"

"I read a magazine once, dorkus. Anyway, they suck at killing themselves, but they're great at getting lots of new attention. It only lasts a few weeks, though."

"Wine's good for you, you know?"

"If there's ever a kick-ass two hundred-proof vino, I'm all in. Hey, maybe splash a little no-name box wine over moonshine."

"A little wine, or maybe just plain old alcohol, is good for you, Tripsy. This is just my pet hypothesis, but I think the reason why people who drink a moderate amount of alcohol don't get certain diseases is that the alcohol binds to toxins that are easily soluble in alcohol, which means the liver can then sequester them and prevent them from forming more volatile and damaging compounds in the body. Without that alcohol to dissolve those harmful chemicals, the human body falls victim to their deleterious effects. We already know the great benefits of a glass or two of red wine each night, and it's not just the resveratrol."

She gave me one of her signature looks: slight tilt of that pretty head, tiny smirk, one eyebrow raised. "Where's my *Handbook of Chemistry and Physics* when I need it, dorkus?"

I may have rolled my eyes. "Okay, what else?"

"Slice an artery."

"Ouch." I meant it. Many suicides had tried this approach. The result was always a mess. Even well after the evil deed.

"Be sure you choose a prominent one, 'cos arteries are buried deep in muscle. Don't ask. I took a few anatomy and physiology classes. Ya gotta slice along the length of artery, not across, 'cos it'll clot too soon if you cut only across. The clot'll plug up the hole within a couple of minutes, depending on your clotting time."

"You sure you're not a med student?" I was now wondering where the heck she got this information. Intel, excuse me.

"I could probably teach med school, dorkus. Personally, I love the brachial artery. It's pretty accessible and bleeds like a river when you rip it open. Buuuut, if you're not into slicing, then jump off a building or some other high place. Just make sure it's high enough to kill you, or you'll just break yourself like an egg and be in a straitjacket, in a psych ward for a year."

"What should you land on?"

"Some place hard, rockodon. Concrete or asphalt is always good. Just make damn sure your landing ain't a soft one. Or in cold, deep water with a ragin' current. I still like jumpin' off the Golden Gate Bridge. That's my fave suicide spot. Or, if I'm in the Tampa Bay area, the super-sexy Sunshine Skyway Bridge! Dude, they even have a suicide box to put your keys, valuables and a goodbye letter. Cool."

Golden Gate Bridge. I ignored the rest. "Skydiving okay?"

"Yeah, but there ya gotta think again! See? If ya really really wanna off yourself, and you actually go through the pain of dreaming up a cool way to do it, then you're effed up in ways that suicide won't cure."

"I don't follow."

"Even if you decided not to kill yourself, you'd still be in therapy or the funny farm for years. Let's move on. I hate talking about this thinkin' part. Most people never do it anyway. Sooo, you could run into heavy traffic at night so they don't see you until the last second. I don't like this one cuz too much can go wrong."

"That's a rather ambiguous statement, Tripsy."

Tripsy pulled herself closer to me, then got really animated. "First of all, the traffic's gotta be movin' like at least sixty miles an hour and you need a direct hit and not a glancing blow off a fender. Any less and you're just gonna get tossed in the air like a bean bag, and, if you suffer the luck of the living, probably land on some soft grass or Tempur-pedic mud."

"Then you could drown in mud."

"That was a funny. Write that down and use it again sometime when I'm not here. So remember: faster than sixty, head-on shot. Freeways are best, especially at night. And you might wanna close your eyes, too. Just remember to choose a good collision course before you do, or you might fall through to the pavement and turn the zone into a demolition derby, all those cars trying to avoid hitting you."

"The thought of throwing myself in traffic gives me the shivers."

"How would you off yourself, doc?"

"I wouldn't, Tripsy, so let's not go there, okay." It wasn't a question.

She reached out, touched my arm. "No, sweetness, let's go there. Besides it's good for my therapy. Answer the question or I'm outta here."

A long pause, then: "I would lock myself in a quiet room, no one around, raid BigPharma, and take some lethal pills. Definitely pills."

"I figured you'd go for the bullet through the brain pan."

"Too messy. I'd hate for anyone to see me that way. Plus I have too much respect for first-responders. Wouldn't want to traumatize them." Even though part of me didn't give a hoot about how I might look dead, I still harbored nightmarish feelings about being found in such a sorry state by good people. They could never un-see that horror.

"Dorkus, you're a gentlemen, even in death. With that, I'm off to get a haircut." She saw me frown. "Don't worry, only an inch."

I was pleased she took the time to care for her looks. Maybe I shouldn't be so concerned about her? Still, she was an enigma. . . .

"Wait, Tripsy—" Before I could respond, she was outside, sprinting to the bus stop.

Session #30

Just as I was preparing for her arrival, the latest notice from iTunes popped into my email box: Animal Planet had a cool new video for me to check out. Since Tripsy wasn't due for another six minutes, I logged onto my account and watched the first few frames. Two lionesses were dismantling a baby elephant, ten pounds at a time. I should watch such motivating content before every session.

I sensed her warm breath more than actually heard her, as she inched slowly forward and stood directly behind me: "Ripped up by a wild animal!"

It would be silly to tell you I jumped out of my pants again. How high? I did not hit the ceiling this time, but I definitely launched . . . and came crashing down in a heap. Following a few seconds of composure, I said, "What a horrible thought. My goodness!" My laugh was clearly masking my discomfort at the thought of being torn to small pieces by a pack of raging animals. How primal!

As she straightened out the pillows and blanket, I watched her move. So graceful. No, so stealthy! Or is it stealthily? Reminder to self: look it up, idiot.

"For once I agree with you, dorkus: I hate the thought of it, too. I did read a few times where some guys have jumped into a polar bear pit or lions' den at local zoos. Anyway, if you're goin' domestic, choose a good killing breed like pit bull or Rottweiler. I hear Rott's are becoming real pussies through too much breeding with dogs that ain't seen combat. Ya gotta have a dog that's been in the shit, homeboy."

Hopped up, pulled down one of my diaries.

"If wild's your game, choose something really big like a bear, lion or tiger, or maybe a big shark. You can find most of 'em at the zoo or aquarium. Personally, I'd forgo the anaconda."

"Is there ever a time you're not so vulgar and candid?"

From the corner of my eye, I noticed she followed my every move. Not admitting her keen interest in my writings, she continued on her one-track course: "Anaconda? Ya die too slowly. 'Sides, they take forflippinever to squeeze the life outta you, then they spend hours dislocatin' their jaw just to get it over your head and shoulders. Forget that. I'd be like, would you hurry the hell up and kill me, you slimy, phallic weenie?"

"Okay, so no reptiles, except maybe a poisonous snake." I laid the book on the arm of the couch, next to her feet.

She just stared at it. "No, crocs and gators are good, but they hafta be real real hungry or they'll just grab you and shake you like Raggedy Ann, roll you into a burrito and then stuff you under a rock to tenderize you, like a dog with a steak bone buried in the back yard."

"What's wrong with that? It seems to fulfill the criterion, that is, it'll definitely kill you."

"You wouldn't die from your wounds, you'd die from a monster-megadose of boredom, all scrunched up like some disarticulated Barbie doll. Like I said, forget that. Ya gotta find some starving croc who ain't had a dead chicken in, like, months. When he sees you, he drools like a faucet. That's the way to go, if you dig that sorta exit."

"Not my cup of tea," I said, recalling that film clip about the lionesses taking apart the baby elephant.

"Me, neither. Course, unless you dig pain, you should take some painkillers before you throw yourself to the wolves, 'cos it might hurt a bit to be torn to pieces before your lights go out. That would majorly suck."

"The human body has a shock system that engages when you're in that kind of trouble. An endogenous painkiller. There's also a special mechanism that shocks you into a heart attack. Vagal inhibition."

"Vegas. You get both horns not to mention the whole flippin' bull for the first few seconds until that so-called 'shock system' of yours kicks in. And what if it doesn't? You're stuck with sharp teeth up your ass. Nope, I'd go for the pills or alcohol before jumpin' in bed with Jaws. Come to think of it, you could get high-high or buzz-drunk first, then walk down to the zoo and hop the fence."

"Wouldn't you be too intoxicated to find your way there, much less be able to scale a tall fence?"

"Uber on over. When you get there, have the driver walk you to your final destination."

"I doubt you'd have much cooperation there."

"Give 'em a Benjamin and tell 'em it's for a science project. A guy pullin' in two hundred on a ten-hour shift'll carry you by hand and drop you over the fence himself, guaranteed. Where there's a Benjamin, there's a way. Trust me."

I looked at my diary, wondering how she'd respond. "I do, Tripsy. More than you know." Knowing she was about to leave, I turned away, walked to the window behind my desk, looked out. "I guess time's about up."

"Eager to get rid of me, dorkus?"

"No, it's just that you're usually out of here like a light, so I thought I'd save you a few minutes."

My father would say, "Death before dishonor? Good choice, son."

When was the last time she looked up at my diaries? Her own was safely tucked away in a box up in the attic of her parents' home. From what her mother has said to me about Tripsy's, mine looked like hers in some ways: small size, ratty covers, the kind with years of character spots and tears. She reached out and touched my diary, which I'd placed on the couch, then pulled her hand back suddenly as if it had burned her. Was that for effect or was she genuinely moved by my gesture, my willingness to open up to her?

Not turning around, I heard her leave. When the door closed, only then did I turn and see my diary still perched in the same position on the couch. Did she open it? Hell, I knew she was curious to see what I'd written. Didn't matter what the subject matter was.

No, it looked like she hadn't touched it.

Well, there was always next week. Sat back and doodled, wrote some session notes. Zxta grew little bronze-bust legs and toodled on over, winked at me. Again.

Session #32

I'd been on the couch for hours today, reading journals, since I had no patients to see. So much for getting out in the real world.

Sometimes, like every six months, I scheduled a whole day to read medical and scientific journals. Today, I did have one patient, though. I was in the middle of an article about the moral implications of using potassium chloride (KCl) to stop the heart of a death-row inmate. One night when I was still in medical school, I actually injected a small amount of it into my forearm: it felt like a hundred killer bees had jammed their stingers into me at the same time, and injected me with, well, KCl. I screamed loud enough to wake up the entire psych ward where I was doing rounds that night.

When Tripsy saw me sprawled out on "her" couch, she made a sweeping motion with her right hand. "Dig it: KCl, the drug of lethal injections."

Coincidence? "They use that to stop hearts during lethal injections of death-row inmates. It stings like—"

"Duhhhh, dorkus! It depolarizes cells down to zero, or something lame-ass I heard in physiology once. Drains your heart cells of all their battery power."

"It depolarizes cells by potassium ions diffusing into cardiocytes, not to mention many other living cells, thus—"

"Spare us, dorkus. Tell me somethin': ya think some suicide's gonna give a crap about whether her cardiocytes're sufficiently depolarized? When ya get it in your veins, this stings like a motherfu-fu-fu-fuuuuu, so take some painkiller beforehand. And ya gotta make sure the concentration is 10 millimolar or greater, or you'll just have teeny heart attacks for hours. What a tease that would be, wonderin' if the next shock's gonna be enough to kill ya. So inject about 10 mil's of this stuff into a good vein. Like I said, it's cool if you take painkiller before. See? There's that double-hit again: use pills or alcohol to dull the pain, then shoot up the heart-stopper."

"Nothing like trying to end the pain." Which pain in her, though, remained to be discovered. Normally, suicides are in terrible emotional pain, which has a physical basis, and they use physical pain to punish themselves until they finally expire or, in some cases, find a way to heal.

"Now you're gettin' it, dorkus!" With that, she turned over on the couch and fell fast asleep . . . woke up exactly one hour later . . . grabbed her things and walked out. At the door, turned to me: "Maybe a bullet is better after all, dorkus. . . ."

My folder of doodles called out to me so I leafed through it again. Maybe this was just a bad month, but nothing really sprang out at me. Except . . . the lack of wavy lines that I interpreted as giant ocean waves. Metaphorically, I believed them to symbolize extreme danger, or perhaps large-magnitude chaos.

The paucity of that chaos made me wonder what was occurring with Tripsy. Was this a calming period, a time of transition? Was she making real progress? Consistently, I mean. Time will reveal all, I hope.

After she left, I read some of the things I'd written nearly thirty years ago. Each snippet brought tears to my eyes. With each passing page, I saw some of Tripsy in there, wondered if I had gone through what she's into now. Still going through. Only difference is, I found ways to mitigate my own pain and learned how to work through it. Looking around my office, I thought how much I isolate myself from the world. Tripsy was right about that.

My office here and the reading room upstairs were the only spaces I felt reasonably comfortable. But Tripsy was spot on when she said I needed to get out in the real world.

Maybe someday. . . .

Session #33

Even the threat of rain didn't deter Tripsy this afternoon: she wore a neon-aqua mini dress with her usual jungle boots and a stylish t-shirt. I must mention that she also wore the most beautiful lavender and sage scarf I'd ever seen. Looked like a series of waterfalls coming together in a spectacular flow that seemed to explode at both ends in a riot of blue and green hues. I've always loved those colors, a wild yet consonant palette of pastels that evoked certain emotions I won't go into here.

She took her place on the couch, fluffed up the pillows, draped the blanket over herself. "Drown myself at sea." It popped out of her mouth like an ejected chicken bone.

"Sounds vaguely romantic . . . in a creepy, maritime kind of way," I offered.

"This one really sucks, dorkus! Wouldn't ya hate to be all alone at sea, miles from shore and double-cheeseburgers, and then just drop over the side into some forever abyss? Not my way to expire. Huh-uh."

I sat back down, hunched over my desk. "How would you drown yourself?"

"This is just a hypothetical, 'cos it gives me the creeps, too. Ya gotta get a boat, skiff or dinghy first, and motor out about two miles where there's no traffic. A strong current helps, too."

"Getting hit by a billion-ton, ocean-going cargo vessel would ruin a perfectly romantic evening, I imagine."

"You tie a 150-pound dumbbell to your ankles—both of 'em— toss it over the side, and then follow it down down down. Thing is, the pressure's gonna squeeze the air outta your lungs as you go, so pray you pass out before suckin' in a lungful of water. Your last thoughts'll be of runnin' to the store for some cough medicine."

"What would you rather be thinking about as you're life slowly fades to black?"

"I wanna go out not thinkin' at all. My life is over! It's gone. Screw all thought and emotion and whatever. I just wanna go go go and not be burdened by anything any longer."

"So your pain would then cease?"

"At twenty thousand leagues under the sea, one would think, dorkus."

That one made me smile, something I couldn't hold back. "What about all those would-be rescuers who spent all that time, money, effort and emotion looking for you? What about their pain and frustration?"

Tripsy went on and on for nearly an hour, my head nodding here and there, my hand absently doodling and filling sheets of paper, one after another, taking some otherworldly form of dictation.

After she concluded her monologue and gathered her things, I pulled myself from my chair and moved to the open window. I hoped the afternoon breeze would send a nice cold chill up and down my spine and into my brain, enough to freeze any further thoughts about this special child taking her own life.

When I turned around, she had already slipped quietly out the door.

Looked back at the sheaf of doodles, all twenty-five pages: palms, beach bar, setting sun, and . . . Zxta. What!?

My CHILD was trying to tell me something, but in a language I had yet to learn. Some static popped through and it sounded like, "NERONIX. NEURONIX. NEURONIX.

I recall the paper I'd written about NeuronIX: *The Laws of Neurophysicochemistry and Correlative Behavior*. It's in Appendix C, should you be so inclined to read it.

Here's a snippet: "A future goal will be to remake an entire human being on all levels, so deceased organisms can be resurrected with 100% accuracy."

What the blazes did this staticky message, NEURONIX, have to do with Tripsy?

Seems my poor mind was growing more and more static these days, kind of like cultivating herbs in a little garden. Why would I knowingly grow this highly charged "static"?

Was there really an underlying message?

Help me out here, will you!?"

4

Collateral Damage

How many a child actually considers collateral damage when killing herself? I feel they don't have sufficient energy for themselves to think about whether their act will hurt or kill someone else. Suicide is the ultimate in selfishness and not the least bit courteous, although some do see it as a selfless act, given they're removing what they see as bad DNA from the gene pool.

My concern if Tripsy actually did attempt suicide was that she would take others with her. While killing herself is tragic enough, the mere thought of her killing innocent people, or even subjecting them to her death is unconscionable. And I would be held responsible. That selfish thought bounced around my empty skull.

Tripsy tended to vent in long diatribes that alternated between loving and hating life and all in it. One day I'd wonder how this highly intelligent, thinking girl could possibly go wrong in this chaotic world. The next, I'd be wondering how this world and all in it could possibly survive Tripsy. Even more worrisome: were there others like her out there? I wondered how I would react if I met another *Indigo Child*.

When a person commits suicide, it begins with an external stimulus or an internal chemical event that goes horribly wrong. Something somewhere in that magnificent brain is amiss. I truly doubt anyone would take her own life if she were in great neurochemical shape, that is, her brain functions were normal (whatever normal truly is).

We do know that certain brain regions are responsible for personality, emotion, muscle action, conscious and subconscious thought, controlling the release of neurotransmitters and hormones, and so on. It's no wonder that if one or more of these systems, or subsets of them, are compromised or damaged in some way, that the correlating behaviors also will be affected, sometimes adversely. While the brain is largely modular, its moving parts are intimately linked in ways we don't yet understand.

As Tripsy would say: "Duhhh!"

Interestingly, more than 90% of all suicides have been described as having suffered from a mental illness, some of which are treatable to some extent. The most prevalent is depression, and I have a great cure for that one: intense, daily exercise, followed by a long cold shower. It works like shock treatment, although no one other than myself acknowledges this fact, except Navy SEALs.

Many in the field of psychiatry still hold fast to the belief that behaviors are largely unto themselves, and still have not grasped the notion that chemistry drives all behaviors. Not a single human or animal or plant behavior occurs without some form of chemical action, as I've stated previously. Just so you know: I cannot belabor that point. We're a bag of mixed chemicals under a scaffolding of delicate anatomy, and we largely do not consciously control very much. Our so-called self wishes this were not the case, and often goes to great lengths to fool us into feeling otherwise.

With these ideas in mind, I try to understand the underlying chemistry that drives a young person, or any person, even to contemplate suicide, which is the ultimate easy way to free oneself from intense, chronic pain, imaginary or not. Since young people don't understand the concept of "time" as well as adults do, young folks tend to see horrible pain as unending. The human brain at, say, ten years old, is wired to absorb lots of information when life is going well. When things are great, the brain fools the child into thinking that these good times will last forever. That's why I tell kids to get out there and absorb more more more!

Of course, there is a flip side.

Try to tell them that they'll survive puberty; just wait a couple of years. They'll tell you to go sex yourself, that they'd rather be dead. And so they not only consider suicide, but actually follow through in some cases. Those who succeed leave behind a trail of unanswered questions that I feel could have been answered to everyone's satisfaction should they have been addressed properly.

While I state I do not heal people—that I simply listen—my innermost heart strives to discover what ails these children. I struggle to find these answers on a daily basis, and then make every attempt to correct the problems, mostly with behavioral therapy. Until we can heal the brain directly, we are saddled with the grossly inaccurate approach of chasing down only the behavioral correlates of compromised neural circuits. As I suggested above, since behavior and chemistry are intimately associated, it's possible to reverse "bad" chemistry by changing certain behaviors. I hate to use the term "bad chemistry," but it's pretty accurate as it describes abnormal or malfunctioning chemistry.

Again, if you're interested in these subjects, please read *The Laws of Neurophysicochemistry and Correlative Behavior* in Appendix C. It's not for the faint of heart, so be forewarned. It does delve into some fascinating hypotheses about the interrelationship of chemistry and subsequent behaviors, and how those can be 100% transferred to a whole new human being or other organic being.

Interestingly, reversing bad chemistry usually cannot be done by the affected person alone. Why? We're just too strangled by our own thoughts, emotions and bad habits, while in the throes of those painful behaviors, that we often fail to see the light at the end of a potentially long and dark tunnel, and if we do, it's perceived as an oncoming train. Yes, some people do get themselves into rehab and beat their addictions, but those are rare cases. Most people must be forced into rehab or therapy. Humans are just too weak and ignorant to seek help on their own, let alone cure themselves.

Unfortunately, when bad chemistry sets in at a young age, it shapes a child's personality into one completely unlike what one would expect had the child been "normal." And there's usually not much that can be done to reverse it, unless it's something like an underactive or overactive thyroid gland or maybe a malfunctioning pituitary gland. In those cases, we can use hormone-replacement therapies to treat the child. In most cases, though, we can treat bad chemistry only so much.

And don't even get me started on so-called shock therapy. Not one single psychiatrist in the world knows how this "therapy" works or whether it actually helps patients, but they continue to use it anyway. American medicine.

So, where does all this lead us with respect to Tripsy's inflicting collateral damage when she kills herself? I'm not sure yet. I do believe that Tripsy may have suffered some chemical or anatomical damage to her brain that resulted from extreme bouts of emotional and/or physical abuse. Her parents? Boyfriend? Others? I don't know. She internalized this anger and converted it to a destructive force that now manifested itself as a willingness to harm others, not just herself. Or so it would seem. Worse, she may encourage others to do the same, instead of changing their harmful behaviors and breaking the painful cycle of suicidal thoughts and behaviors.

Of course, this is all just speculation. I could be completely incorrect in my assessment of Tripsy and her unusual behaviors. Let's just have Tripsy tell it like it is, shall we?

Session #35

So, tell me: what does this lovely day have in store for me? I thought.

"Make a suicide pact with a friend!"

Before I could answer my own question, her words echoed off my walls, my bookshelves, my ceiling . . . and hit me squarely in the face, as usual. I never seemed to be prepared for her entrances, even at session #35.

The walls shimmered with secondary, tertiary and quaternary harmonics, just like the peach-stained walls did in my parents' mansion the night I told them I wanted to be a rock musician. All those singing details. This time, though, I understood them better.

"Yeah, dorkus, that'll get people rollin'. Look, it's raining! Let's go outside!"

You'll be proud to hear that I also gave up trying to compose myself after her opening salvo. "No. As you said, it's raining, Tripsy. Nice to see you today. Take a seat, please."

She towered over my desk: "You wanna talk? Then we talk out there." She pointed out the window, shot out the door, a rainbow-colored flash beckoning me to follow. Or else.

Not joining her right away, I watched her dance on the lawn, her clothes now a flimsy wet paper towel. Ah, what the heck: I grabbed my rain jacket and hat, and joined her. I had lost control of this situation the second she walked into my office nine months ago. What was I doing now, humoring her? No, there was more to it than that. I knew somewhere inside me that this was going somewhere. Where, I didn't know, but I did trust my subconscious CHILD enough to keep going.

She was sitting on one of the chairs, looking up into the tree, millions of silver beads bathing the great oak leaves.

I handed her a towel and blanket, diligently fixed my seat. As I prepared to sit down, she pulled the towel out from under me, shook it out into what I would describe as a disorganized mess, then spread it haphazardly on my chair. My chair. Haphazardly.

"A pact? It'll make people wonder how two or more smart young people would want to kill themselves. Some would even call you not-so-smart for doing so."

"Forget that. They'd be grievin' over us for years."

"People do get on with their lives, Tripsy, even after horrible events.

It's a necessary adaptation of evolution and continuity."

Rolled her eyes at me: "At least I'd get their attention for a little while. Make 'em feel the pain a little. What I had to feel all this time."

Perhaps not pain, but pity? I thought.

Despite my weak, nonverbal protest, she lit up a hooter, blew huge smoke rings into the tree. On her second launch, a squadron of little birds made uncharacteristic chirpy sounds, slightly off-key, even to a non-bird brain like me. She looked up at them: "See? They like this stuff, dorkus. Reminds me of the time some science geeks gave Molly to an octopus in a holding tank. It got all gooey and started lovin' on the water filter. Animals have feelings, too, dorkus, even if they're sometimes misdirected."

"Tripsy, it might be okay to do this in my office, but—"

Again, she blew me off: "Sooooo, I'd invite one of my girlfriends to join in. We'd make a pact together about doin' something mind-blowin'."

This girl never listens. I settled into the chair more, approaching exhaustion, and it wasn't even noon yet. "Thelma and Louise?"

"Drivin' off a cliff in the middle o' nowhere ain't my idea of cleverness, bonehead. Those two hicks didn't think it through very well at all. They got cornered and had only one way out. Not much of a choice."

"And you have? Thought about it, I mean." I looked up and thought I saw one of the little birds intentionally perched in the middle of her hooter-cloud, snapping at invisible miniature worms.

"Yuuuuup."

Pulling my eyes from the rather odd sight, I offered: "So, who would write the pact?"

"Me, of course."

"Why you?"

"None of my friends can spell for crap. I'd hate to get to the defining moment and not be able to read what they wrote."

I snorted out what could be mistaken for a laugh, sat up and looked over at her. "Okay, who decides what method you'll use to kill both of you?"

"Again, that would be me."

"Because you can read the manual on how to kill yourself and a good friend?"

"I'd do it all, okay!?"

"One more question, please."

"Jeeeeez!"

"Who goes first?"

"I'd make it so we both go together."

Our conversation now silent, the sky thundered overhead. Both of us looked up into the tree and out over the yard. The rain shot down in thick gray sheets that could only have been Hecho en Hell, all that dullness and depression, not to mention all the dust they exported. I looked at her again: wet hair cascaded down in drippy strawberry-blonde tangles, framing her bright face, a sudden look of consternation erasing the light, one stroke at a time.

"What if the method works on your friend and spares your life, Tripsy?"

"I'd try and try again 'til I got it right." Her voice was half an octave higher, pitching above the thunder and adding to the music.

"What if you suddenly fall unconscious? Your friend is now dead. They'll patch you up, try you for murder, probably find you guilty, and ship you up to Pelican Bay Prison for the rest of your life." I'd been watching a small puddle at my feet turn into a big puddle at my feet. I then turned to her: "Oops. Look at it this way, Tripsy: you'd be the life of the party up there." Or maybe a ringleader of some Aryan gang.

She threw her towel at me. "Jeezo-flip, do you have to be so morbid? Are there girls in Pelican Bay?"

"Me morbid? Just a thought. Yes, there are so-called girls up there, but they're really guys. Just kidding about Pelican Bay." Pulling the towel from my head, I wiped my face and instantly smelled her body lotion, bath soap and maybe a hint of perfume. What was it? Nothing a child would wear. Her mother's? And what was that other scent? Must be her essence. It hit me strangely. I now felt slightly drunk. Was that just a spritz of oxytocin or something otherworldly we mere mortals weren't familiar with—yet?

She took her towel back, said, "I'd say what the heck and just try it again. If I go to prison for bein' stupid, then I deserve it. I could always hang myself from a wall, I suppose."

"You'd lose the larger effect of getting people's attention, remember?"

"Then I'd find the nearest wormhole and jet back to the moment just before I messed up last time, and then get it right. *Groundhog Day* for suicides. Now that I think on it, I could do it a thousand times, just for fun. Maybe even take some snaps for everyone. Satisfied, dorkus?"

"You don't give up, Tripsy. I'll give you that." Yes, there was definitely a moderately concentrated scent there, gently mixed with her own oils. Her chemistry was intoxicating. Literally. I know people don't understand this just yet, but we humans are intensely sensitive to chemicals given off by other animals, especially our own kind. I knew I was being manipulated by her essence, and it drove me nuts. More so because I had no control over it. When I realized that thought of having no control over it, I then had some control over it. I simply modified my behavior to counter the effects.

Didn't work as planned.

"If chicks like me gave up, you'd be out of a job."

The rain now stopped and the sun melted a large hole in the clouds and threatened to push back the darkness.

"Good thing I'm still your patient. See you later, 'gator!" She dropped everything, grabbed her bag and was off at a dead sprint.

The thirty or so pages of doodles in my lap had gotten wet. Some of the scribbles were now mush and smudges, revealing wholly new patterns. I lamented over having lost the meaning of the previous iteration, i.e. before the rain had morphed them into a new verse.

As I turned the pages, a story unfolded under that oak tree, and I read it over and over well into the evening. And when I retired to my office, I studied it again. The effects of the rain continued to act on the doodles, changing them over time, a slow-acting doodle-mutating virus.

By the time I'd looked at the pages for the fortieth time, the story had evolved even further, an intriguing film that gave up new information. At that point, I wrote down some thoughts in a notebook, then carefully transcribed those into my computer so I didn't lose the newly acquired information.

As midnight rolled into one a.m., I had transcribed more than twenty pages of my new interpretations of the doodles. It was now time to allow my subconscious to distill the contents, so I read through the transcription again.

And again. . . .

Slowly, too, this unfolded:

```
In the still moments before dawn,
when the deep lavender sky
paints with a broad dark-pastel brush,
```

Tripsy South

I invest morning thots on a good wind,
and several noble gases of my breath
displace the coolness of yesterday's
unfulfilled wishes,
made by false hearts on slow journeys
back through days that promised so much and
delivered frosty sorrow.

My high hopes diffuse into pink clouds
that soon warm and bubble,
pushing morning into afternoon,
flowing solemnly with faith anew
that descends in a cleansing evening rain,

silver drops into rivulets

rivulets into streams

streams into rivers

rivers into the beautiful promise of tomorrow

5

Things to Do Before You Off Yourself

Surprisingly, suicide depletes an extraordinary amount of energy from a person, especially if they should get lucky and fail. Do you have any idea how long a person thinks about killing themselves before the actually deed? Years, in some cases.

What does that tell you?

It should suggest that those folks have no interest whatsoever in killing themselves. The underlying motive is to remain alive as long as possible. I've listened to all of it. This normally isn't an act embarked upon on a mere whim by drunken frat boys with a death wish. Most suicides are committed by males, with only about 15-20% by females.

And, like I said earlier, although females make twice the number of suicide attempts, males succeed four times more, although in the past few years, teen girls have been succeeding a lot more. Society's pressures and stressors, especially from very unfriendly social media? Lack of parenting? Poor schooling? No support from friends? No hope for the future?

These statistics lead me to believe there's an inherent chemical factor that is lacking in males or perhaps that is present in abundance in females that protects them from self-harm, although not lately, it seemed. I seriously doubt there's some chemical that's in greater concentration in males that makes them kill themselves more often. Testosterone is overrated as a demon molecule.

No, it's more likely that males lack protective chemical pathways and associated neuroanatomy that are fully developed in females. Females have been blessed with a far better overall chemistry, especially with evolutionary survival pathways that enable them to function more efficiently in life. After all, females are burdened with childbirth and rearing, not to mention propagation of the species.

Still, something in society was slowly eroding that protective measure in teen girls, and it disturbed me greatly, because suicide among teen girls had increased to a staggering rate and no one seemed to be doing anything to mitigate the issues. It was now an American epidemic, although the card-carrying members of the AMA and APA were still patting themselves on the back for a job well done, such vulgar self-congratulations in the middle of a worldwide crisis.

It's still saddening that males are left out there hanging on a limb without much help at all. We're burdened with societal views of us as strong and silent, and must cope with stress and depression and loss and other emotional insults without the same physiological mechanisms that are conferred upon females.

Again, all my own opinion, based on personal observations of hundreds of children. I've been panned at parties and symposia and casual get-togethers for these views, although I do feel that most people probably do creep home and consider them seriously, especially when not among colleagues they fear might be looking over their shoulder, snickering and deriding them for even considering those heretic thoughts.

So, back to the subject of what to do before you venture off into the deep, dark goodnight. My patients have told me that they hope their friends and parents, etc. will suffer greatly from the trauma of the loss. In older patients, this has extended to spouses and significant others. Simply put, suicides are trying to send a message in the most desperate way possible, and when people don't listen, the evil deed is carried forth into a final and complete tragedy.

Tripsy told me of her plans to leave something useful behind, something that would influence others not to go her route. While she spoke of revenge in great fits of anger, I feel she really wanted to spare her loved ones the trauma of it all, should it ever arise, and simply leave behind something useful for young people contemplating suicide.

I think she also realized the need to somehow educate her loved ones about how and why she chose this course of action. I'm sure that, while they may not understand the underlying cause, sending their child to a mental-health professional shows they do care and are at a loss for how to care for their own child.

I think Dr. Kelley's observations were probably accurate, even though Tripsy's parents disagreed. At least they sent her to another mental-health professional, even if he was a middle-of-the-road shrink.

Session #37

After this morning's tearful session with the family of a young male suicide, I needed a break. No, a long vacation to a place with a tiki bar and warm sunshine. The mother, who had once screamed at me and slapped me across my face in front of my entire staff for not treating her son "properly," as she put it, had praised me for an hour, recalling how much her son had improved.

One thing, though: she never apologized for that slapping, acting as if it never happened. A hazard of the trade, I've discovered over the years.

My eyes now closed, I wondered what Bermuda would be like this time of year. How about New Zealand? Did New Zealand have tiki bars?

"Leave behind a nice letter!"

The outburst came from just inside my door, which I thought I had closed. Evidently, I had slipped up on several things this fine morning, as I reveled in the high compliments from the boy's bipolar mother who had a wicked right cross.

It would probably be a bit of an exaggeration if I described myself as being fed up with this girl's crap. How shall I put it? Exasperated? Exhausted? Extinguished? Ex-[fill in the blank].

I smiled that little fake smile I give when I'd rather kill whatever was in front of me, destroying my peace. "A letter," I said, a little too flatly.

Walking in, she passed me and raised an eyebrow at my sarcasm, subtle as it was. "Ya can't just whack yourself without leaving something behind, dorkus."

A part of me wanted to commit Tripsy under 5150, mostly because she'd rebuffed my every attempt to help her open up and release that negative energy, but . . . I could not. There was some message there. Something she was trying to tell me in her own controlling way, yet this was the only way to tell it. Like our brain during a dream state: it's sending our conscious self a message, although it's in the code of a metaphor, something to figure out and act on, and it's saying, "Good flippin' luck."

Maybe it's the only way she knows? The only way she can communicate? Maybe I should deal with this dream, this metaphor the same way I do with my actual dreams, since human dreams are expressed in a child's language, about the age of six: look at and regard the dream as a six year old would, through a child's senses, using a child's language and skill sets. Another challenge is to have that same six year old translate a dream that scares her to death. What six year old would even think of doing that?

In my last dream, I was on a school bus filled with people I didn't know. We drove down into the ocean like we would drive down a steep hill in the countryside. No one moved. As the water filled up around us, I tried to open the window on my side. It released slightly and swayed out, but wouldn't open all the way. No one moved to help me. They just sat there impassively.

The six year old in me said, "They wouldn't let me out. They wouldn't help me."

In another recent dream, I sat in an old bus station with church pews. We had to set up shooting targets on the pews in front of us, then do target practice with pistols. Everyone was able to set up their makeshift targets, but the supervisor was very slow to get my targets and something to hold them up. No one else offered help. They were oblivious to me.

Again, the six year old in me said, "She wouldn't help me. No one would help me."

The theme in most of my dreams I can remember is this: *no one will help me.* Clearly, my hypothesis about using a six year old to interpret dreams begged further testing, but it had been highly accurate with my own dreams for many years, and it saved me much heartache and drama on many occasions and, since no one would ever help me, forced me to help myself on all levels. That, in itself, was exhausting, becoming my own mentor.

I pulled off my tie, placed it on my desk, now resigned to the dilemma:

no one will help me. Even though I was completely on my own, there was some measure of hope. After all, I was a middle-of-the-road psychiatrist. "Who would even think to do something like this at a time like suicide?"

"Obviously, you'd be surprised who thinks about this stuff. Haven't you been listening? Sometimes suicide's all about getting even, man! Inflicting major pain on someone you love."

"If that's love, Tripsy. . . ."

Now on the floor, legs crossed.

"Don't go there. You have no idea about teen love. I know you'd tell me it's all chemistry and quantum flippin' physics, but to us it's all irrational, illogical, syrupy romance. There's nothing in our bodies that tells us about your half-ass science, so drop it in a gutter. Just like a year to a kid is a lifetime, love to us is the ultimate emotion and we seek it out like honey. Romance means flowers, looong handwritten letters that go nowhere and loop back on themselves like morning glory vines, special songs between two lovers, deep wet kissing for days, spending time together talkin' about . . . nothin' at all."

"Obviously it's not 'nothin' at all.' "

"No, to us it's everything. Have you ever listened to a conversation between two teen lovers?"

"All the time."

"When!?"

"I'm a student of human behavior, Tripsy. I do know how to listen and observe. Besides, I was a teenager, too."

"Then why're you such an idiot at this?"

The statement stopped me cold, wondering if she really meant it. All I could do was look up at my diaries and wonder where I had gone wrong: didn't stand up to my abusive father at key turning points in my life? Chose to treat kids instead of "safer" adults with lots of disposable cash? Allowed this young woman to bully me into listening to her nine-month-long diatribe? I was getting paid, wasn't I? Heck, I didn't care about the money: I'd never been on a vacation in my adult life, never bought an expensive house or car. Never spent the money I'd earned over the last fifteen years. Never got out and enjoyed life. All my frugality earned me was a savings account with more than two million dollars in it. Big whoop.

I couldn't look her in the eye now. "I don't feel I am. I just know things that are different from you and your experiences, some things you don't agree with." I may have looked at her on that last word, but don't count on it.

"Not that I don't agree with what you know, dorkus. Some things you say are just stupid, that's all. Like you don't really know much. Makes me wonder why I'm here."

Had I failed her this badly? Really? Why was I truly here? Why was she here? After all, she had come to me. "As you pointed out before, to teach me a thing or two about teen suicide, Tripsy."

"At least you remember stuff I say, dorkus. . . ." Lying down now. "Like I said, it's cool to leave something behind. A long letter to the 'rents is cool. If your boyfriend's the cause of it all, send him a little hot-poker-up-your-ass letter, too. Tell 'im how you had herpes and HIV and some pussy virus that'll rot his weenie off after you die."

"That's completely irresponsible." Looking at her now, I added, "And cruel." Was that responding to her statement about STDs . . . or how she was treating me?

"Duhhh. What the hell ya think suicide is!? You need to wake up and pay some attention here, Dr. Moore. 'The Big Whack' isn't some paddling ya get at detention for passing notes in class. Fuuu-uuu-uuuck. The point is to inflict as much damage as possible. And who cares who gets hurt? I'm already killing myself! Ya think I care if I hurt someone's feelin's? Honestly?"

"Tell me more about the letter."

"Depends on who ya wanna mess with the most."

"Why not just leave a trail of letters for everyone?"

"Who has the energy? One's fine. Personally, I'd leave one for the 'rents. Thank 'em for all those wonderful years of support and love and kindness and understanding."

"What would you really say?"

"Thanks for the memories, all three of 'em."

Got myself a cup of tea on that note, stood by the bookcase. "You could just put that on a Post-It note."

"So imaginative, dorkus." She threw a pillow at my head. Good shot.

"What else would you leave behind? A will, even though you're a minor?" Picked up the pillow, placed it on the couch near her feet.

"Yeah, a will would be interesting, huh? I hereby bequeath to my asshole 'rents my rusty tricycle, my collection of love letters since third grade, my turtles and snakes, ParksTheCat, and Smooch the velociraptor—and if you dare use 'em for sushi, I'll come back and harm you with cruelty."

Tripsy was channeling Archilochus. "So the material things mean nothing? And what about your diary?"

"When I die, dorkus, I'll leave my diary to you."

"Some parents, not necessarily yours, tend to destroy the belongings of children who have died, so that might be good, Tripsy. In the least, we might get some closure to these issues of anger and hatred you have." Was it really anger that plagued this woman? My prospective answers ran the continuum from everything to nothing at all.

She studied a pillow, picked at the fabric, pulled loose threads, tossed it to the floor. "The 'rents, they wanna forget it all."

"The pain can be too great for some. Most, actually. And, you know? I don't think most parents ever do forget something like the death of a child. The child is supposed to outlive the parents, unless the parents intentionally kill her. Even then, I'll bet remorse sets in at some point."

"They deserve it. It's their fault I'm here anyway."

"Really?"

"Uh-huh. They gave me these mangled genes, made me go to ballet when I wanted to play baseball, dragged me to piano when I begged to jam on my guitar. It's their fault. Let 'em stew in it. You should tell 'rents to keep everything and go up in my room everyday and touch everything and look at it and smell it and feel it. I sooo hope they cry their hearts dry."

"There's more anger than objective thought here, Tripsy. Where are you going with this?"

"Maybe nowhere. Maybe I just wanna let certain people know, 'Hey, I'm checkin' out now! I'm gone! And I won't be back anytime soon, so don't put out a plate for me at dinner!' "

"What prized items would you want to leave people you care about?"

"The hell do I care?"

"It doesn't have to be expensive things, Tripsy. You can will something precious like your collection of stamps or postcards from friends in Europe you told me about. And don't forget the diary."

She stopped fidgeting, looked up at my diaries. "You said they'd throw 'em away."

"I said some parents do. I don't think yours would, though. They find you too precious."

"Oh, like you know."

"Yes, I do. Your mother's told me on many occasions. From what I hear, Tripsy, several people in your life feel you're most special. Maybe even your father."

"Can we please not go there, doc? Huh?"

"As you wish."

"Okay, okay, so maybe I could leave something for them, something not so hurtful. Ah, forget that! See? You got me all tangled up in this broken hearts club!"

"Delightful. . . ."

"I'd wear my best clothes, though."

"Why?"

"Well, if I'm gonna go to hell and meet Jimi Hendrix, I wanna look ooooo soooo hot-hot!"

"I thought it didn't matter." At that point, I wanted to go to hell and meet Jimi.

"Like hell! Jimi's gonna be in his cool sixties rag pants and tie-dye t-shirt, I wanna be in a miniskirt, and maybe even get my hair done!"

"Oookay." This was too much. But I listened. As usual.

"You're dreamin' about seein' me in a miniskirt, aren'tcha?"

"Knock it off, Emma!"

That stopped her. She lowered her head to gather her thoughts, whispered, "Emma" as if hearing it for the first time, repeated it several times so she wouldn't forget the sound of it. She turned it into a distinct humming tune. One chord, yes, but a sweet melody.

"Sooo, Tripsy, anything else we could leave behind or maybe do?"

"I'd wanna have some cool music goin'. Something that chills me as life fades to black."

"Hendrix?"

"You on crack? Hendrix'd rock me out. I'd pro'ly be up ragin' all night, I put his jams on. Nope. I need somethin' to mellow meself out, dude. Like Zero 7 or Maserati or Tristeza. Maybe even some ocean waves. Forget that, I could just go down to the beach, and chill and kill."

"Very funny. I'm shocked you're not into rap or hip hop."

"They don't move me, dorkus. Too lame, all that contrived dissonance."

Dissonance. I gave a weak smile.

"Know what'd be a huuuuge nuclear rage?"

"No idea."

"Leave a big mess. Like The Who used to do at all their hotel rooms. I mean, trash my room, maybe even the whole house."

"That would surely get someone's attention. They'd already have a heck of a mess to clean up, so why do that?"

"It's all about the rage, dorkus. The rage. If you have to feel it, someone else does, too. It's all meaningless if you have to go through it all alone, without anyone understanding how you felt, what you were going through, what your thoughts were, how lonely you were every single day, and there's nothing you could do to help yourself. And no one'd listen or help, 'cos they're too busy pickin' up the kids from soccer practice, buying groceries, taking dad to work, goin' to the library. All that 'rent crap."

"Sometimes children have to understand they're a part of a household, a part of something larger than they are. Those who don't get this end up feeling the world owes them something, and they become entitled."

"Oh, so I'm supposed to accept the 'fact' that I'm just being selfish, because I'm really just a little satellite—one of many, according to you— orbiting around a larger, more substantial 'higher being,' is that it? Did I accurately capture the essence of all that fresh monkey poo, doc?"

"With a dash of insecurity thrown in, I'd say you did pretty well."

"Let's move on, dorkus. I'd love to leave a big mess for those a-holes to pick up. A teeny little memento from their little nanosatellite."

"What would you do?"

"Rip down the walls with a pair of claws . . . smear some ice cream and ketchup in patterns that could only be mistaken for late impressionism."

"Or a mistake of the brush," I muttered. "Ah, so you're going to get artistic, I see." I stared up at the ceiling. For now, I was tuning her out. The notes of her voice were starting to fall off the page and onto the floor, creating a whole new tune. Or was I intentionally wiping them off and making my own music?

"The object of this exercise is to get creative and stay creative. If you just lie down on your bean-bag sofa and pop yourself with a nine-mil that blasts your last thoughts onto a six-thousand-dollar handmade rug from Turkey, you've done everyone a few favors."

"I'm not sure I understand."

"Only a moron would kill himself and not leave a cool signature. Second, all the 'dults have to do is grab the bean bag and throw pillow, with him in the tangled mess, and archive it at the morgue."

"Tripsy, I think you're failing to see that some people just want to kill themselves and aren't into the pomp and circumstance that you're prescribing now. Suicide isn't a pageant or an affair like the Academy Awards."

"No, you're missing the point here! Listen to me! I'm trying to clue you in on how a lotta teen suicides think—"

"As a psychiatrist with a long-standing history of treating suicidal teens, I feel I know how suicides think, Tripsy. I deal with it every day, and they share their thoughts and feelings."

She paused long enough for me to finish, then: "Those that off themselves as you said probably don't wanna send out a message to anyone. They just wanna be dead and gone. Most people do not want to kill themselves, Dr. Moore. Most people want to send out messages to people who obviously aren't listening. I'm trying to suggest some ways that these people send these messages to their 'rents and so-called loved ones. That's all. And don't look at me like I'm some stupid little kid. I'm not. I know what's goin' on here."

"What is going on here?"

"You're taking my small statements and generalizing waaaay outta proportion to my original argument. Let's agree that some people out there will kill themselves no matter what anyone does or says, and that they will do it as fast as possible with whatever weapon might be lying around?"

"I agree."

"Okay, then. I know there may be nothing at all we can do for those types. I don't know chemistry like you do, but I know that some people have this certain vibe that resonates evil. It's like some off-planet demon seed. They smell funny, they look totally goth or wickedly depressed, and they give off this black aura I can sense from yards away."

"You have a gift." Was this the *Indigo Child* emerging, the empath who reads people?

"So, doc, back to the messy exit?"

"Sure." Why not? *Indigo* on one hand, brat on the other.

"Like I said, rip down the walls and paint 'em with kitchen condiments. Rearrange the place in ultra-modern tornado fashion."

"Hurricanes not good enough? They're in vogue this year, you know."

"Ever seen the after-effects of a tornado inside a 200-square-foot closed box?"

"Enough said."

"Trust me, I know how to reduce a two-story, four-bedroom suburban dwelling to wood chips and saw dust."

"We're now talking total destruction here, not just a little ransacking of one's bedroom, Tripsy."

"Okay, we can go there."

"What else on this topic?" Tried not to sound impatient.

"To do before you turn off your lights? Call all your family, friends and asshole colleagues and tell 'em the good news. Send out invitations!"

"That takes some planning, Tripsy."

"So? Some people really wanna make a statement here. Some would actually do it. I'm just relaying it. You could invite your family and friends to witness it."

"How would you get them there?"

"Captive audience: tie 'em all up. Tell 'em it's a little game and they have to go along or you'll shoot yourself in front of 'em."

"And then just do it?"

"Yup. You might even find a cool public space then trash that to hell!"

"If you want to run up your parents' and the taxpayers' bills, then this sounds like a good avenue." I still had my eyes glued to the ceiling, staring at who-knows-what Rorschach pattern up there; thought I saw a few pistols floating around. Nothing short of reading tea leaves.

"Tell me, dorkus, who cares about earthly bills when you're on your way to the greater cosmos?"

"I get it."

"Also, you can rent some space somewhere or the use of the local carousel or theme park or entertainment attraction."

"You're turning this into a show?" I looked over at her now, my eyebrows raised up high, thinking how silly all this sounded.

"Just a suggestion."

"It detracts from the act itself, doesn't it?"

"Not really. Especially once the shock's worn off and the 'rents or your so-called loved ones have had a chance to figure out that their sweet, darling daughter just blew her super-high SAT scores all over some thousand-dollar-a-night hotel room. Stop interrupting me with silly comments."

"All right." Finding a pattern of pistols on the ceiling, I looked at it harder, then stood up.

"Let's see . . . I like this one: invite a Hollywood screenwriter, one of the unknowns, to interview you beforehand, then witness it. She can write a cool script and launch her career."

I looked down again, momentarily distracted by her. "That is absolutely morbid, Tripsy."

"Forget morbid, button-down! It's creative! I'm trying to milk it for everything and leave something useful behind. You do understand this, yes?"

"I think I do. Sometimes. No, I definitely do not." *Please get to the useful part, will you, Tripsy?*

"Along those 'morbid' lines, do the same with a local rock or alternative band that's looking for some new inspiration, something gothicky, total dope. Better yet, hire the band to play before. Don't tell them what's gonna go down, though, or they'll get arrested and charged with accessory to murder."

"That would be unfortunate, especially for talented young souls starting their music career."

"Throw a big-ass party for all your friends, family, colleagues, or the whole bloomin' town. Don't tell anyone what you're gonna do. At the height of the evening, walk up to microphone, say piss off to everybody, and do your ugly deed. Make sure they get this stuff on video, please. Hell, live-stream it across the universe. Maybe CNN'll pick it up."

"Just so you know, Tripsy: a kid in Florida tried that five or six years back. He even advertised tickets to his 'concert.' "

"What happened?"

"They arrested him and took him to the nearest psych ward."

"So my plan wasn't original. Big deal. Okay, here's something safe and sane for you: rob a bank and make sure you get away with it."

"How?"

"Ahhhh! Betcha you'll try this tomorrow!"

"Not my idea of a good time, Tripsy, but please continue."

"I mean rob a bank! Go up to the teller the moment they open, jump over the partition and grab all the cash before anyone has a chance to notice you. Make sure you wear something colorful and mismatched so the witnesses can't ID you clearly."

"Confuse their minds in the middle of the turmoil?"

"Hell, yeah!"

"What if you get the dye pack?"

"What!?"

"Ohhh, boy. Tripsy, let's leave the bank-robbing to the pros."

"Forget that! The 'pros' usually get caught!"

"And you wouldn't, especially carrying a dye pack that will probably burst into a rainbow of infrared and ultraviolet paints that stain you indefinitely. And all the police have to do is shine a little IR or UV light over you and your skin, and you light up like a Christmas tree. Even in the darkest of your hours, Tripsy."

"Oh, now I see. Okay, forget it. Obviously then you don't wanna do anything too felonious or you might get caught and then won't be able to turn your lights off."

"Exactly. Maybe you should just stick to applying the tornado."

"Eff that—"

The pattern now came in clearly. It was better than one of my doodles. "You don't write anything in your diary, do you?" I fully expected to hear the rustling of pillows and blanket.

"Maybe you should read my diary, dorkus." She got up, smoothed out her skirt and shirt, put on her sweater.

"If it's germane to this lengthy discussion we've been having, then fine, I will."

As she walked out, turned and said, "Guess you'll hafta wait 'til I'm gone, doofus," and walked away.

6

Broadcasting the Big Event

I couldn't help but feel mortified when Tripsy began talking about broadcasting her suicide, although certain elements of the last chapter should have been a harbinger. Being a middle-of-the-road shrink, some things may be lost on me. . . .

The mere thought of recording such an event made the act of suicide itself all the more horrible. Why anyone would even have thoughts about putting this down for posterity was beyond comprehension—mine, at least—but, then again, I realized it was just another medium, like a book. We're such visual creatures, we humans, that we often go to great lengths not to see what we deem horrific.

Our eyes seem to sense the worst of things, while our ears and other senses only add supporting information. I guess it's because by recording one's death, especially a child's, we are somehow sanctioning it without doing something to prevent it. And that's not simply morally wrong. It's just plain despicable on all levels.

So, shall we entertain this horrible thought? Tripsy seemed to feel it was important, even in the face of her knowing that it may be fleeting. I tried to explain that most people have such short attention spans and can only attend to so many inputs at once.

We humans tend to process so little, while so much still goes on all around us. All the time. And it never stops. Until death visits us.

This girl wasn't as naive as I first thought. Quite the contrary. She had her grand plan and would stick to it, regardless of what wisdom I could impart on her. Did the word wisdom escape my pen? If so, then it appears to have escaped my editor's eraser, as well.

While I still find it reprehensible to record such an event, I do see her point in some deep, dark way: if something so horrific can be captured and displayed for all visual creatures to behold, then maybe it will frighten them enough to at least want to comprehend it. Either that or it'll scare them away and cause them to suppress any thoughts of committing it.

I didn't know the right answers.

Perhaps Tripsy did. My doodles seemed to suggest so. . . .

Session #38

I knew she was standing right there in front of my desk, as my head and its few working parts appeared to be thoroughly engrossed in one of my diaries. Truth? I was somehow dreading this session, not so much because of Tripsy. I'll tell you some other time, okay?

She practically whispered it: "Do a death blog."

Ever felt like walking away from it all? Just literally dropping whatever you're doing and walking out the door to something new and different? Maybe if you're lucky, stress free? That was my feeling now, more than ever before. As I looked up, there she was: a vacant look in her eyes. Was she losing the little ground she'd made here over the last nine months? My heart seemed to drop momentarily, just thinking it. It would have been so easy to wish myself a myocardial infarc—a heart attack. The easy way out. My goodness, was I considering suicide!? The mere thought curled my toes involuntarily inside my loafers. I think I lost a toenail in the process.

Suicide.

Me?

"I can't believe I'm hearing this, Tripsy." Off came the tie, given to me by one of my suicides, the day before she took her lovely life. It held a hundred pink pigs in a field of puke-green, and I tried not to look at it, but my young patient loved pink pigs and the color of puke—I mean, green lima beans. The gift-tie had been slowly contracting around my neck, fiber by fiber . . . like boiling a frog so slowly, it consented without protest. No, like that storied python that took my breath away nine months ago. Remember? Back then, it was disguised as hooter-smoke. Damn, I was losing it.

Please do not think she was oblivious to how she affected my own behaviors. She didn't miss a beat, witnessing my actions.

"Why the hell not? By now, dorkus, you shouldn't be surprised about anything I say." Although it was probably just my imagination, her speech seemed slurred, like she had just inhaled a bottle of champagne, and the spirits became entangled with her tongue, making it flop about in a mild hissy fit.

"It's not so much that."

"Then what?"

I tossed my two-dollar puke-green tie and all those pink pigs in the trash can, looked down at it. If you look at a stationary object long enough, it appears to move. My tie writhed as if bathed in acid. I quickly withdrew it from the trash, placed it inside one of my desk drawers.

The pigs safely tucked away, I said, "Uhhh, nothing. Please continue."

"You'll love this: I can think of a hundred different ways of broadcasting this thing, but I'll stick to a few. You can post your impending offing on a blog or website or have some kid write an app that blasts it to everyone's phone."

"That's called spamming and there are laws against it."

"Who gives a crap what it's called? You authority figures always try to put a doomy label on everything to scare the rest of us. Thing is, the collective is smarter'n you. You just don't know it. Now pay attention. You could use a real site or something like that, and put up some notices."

"The authorities would find you somehow."

On the couch again, big smile on her face: "Now where was I? Oh, you could do it anonymously. Make up some new identity, post pictures that don't show who you really are, videotape only your body, not your face, stuff like that."

"Okay, I'll bite. What would you say on this death blog?"

"Now that was a decent question."

"Thank you."

"No problemo. And now I'll answer it: start with a little history of me, about how I got here, and maybe what drove me to wantin' to off myself and maybe a few others, too."

I now followed her. Looked up at the ceiling, thought about the possibilities. "Could be informative."

"A little history, then some specifics about current affairs, like what I'm thinkin' each day as I count down to my day of death. That would freak some people out, dorkus! I mean, think about it! Millions of people tune into a colorful death blog with a live-streaming video that counts down, maybe hour by hour, the last hours of a desperate young woman's miserable life."

"Interesting as it is, it's grotesque. I think you know that. A young woman went to prison for fifteen months for encouraging her boyfriend to kill himself. Pretty sickening."

"People love this kinda entertainment. It's modern-day caligulation. Look at all those torqued and caligulated reality tv shows. People'll freak when they see this!"

I looked up, rolled my eyes. "Ooookay . . . so why do you think people would love that kind of entertainment?"

"You mean, why is it a fact!? And where's that rad tie you had on?"

"Yes to the first question. In here . . ." I pointed. ". . . is the answer to the second question." I pulled out the ugly tie that Tripsy thought was "rad," put it back on, buttoned my shirt at the top, cinched up the beautiful tie with the pink pigs swimming in lima bean-green puke something or another.

"So, like I said, why do you feel it's such a fascination?" I touched my lovely tie, stroking it up and down, trying to calm down the little piglets I'd just traumatized.

"Cuz people are stunningly morbid. Society has taught us kids to love and accept violence and mayhem. You're a moron if you don't see it all around us. It's programmed into us to be attracted to this stuff. We all live these silent, desperate lives of just conforming to the government and media propaganda, what society tells us, what our religion tells us, what our 'rents tell us. And we do it all for someone else, not for ourselves. It's maddening! Like people on this planet don't have their own lives! They're told what to do, how to do it, when to do it, and are threatened with myriad monkey poo if they don't. Ya gotta be kiddin' me! What kinda life is that!? I mean, if someone told me what to do all the time, I'd kill that noise."

People have told Tripsy what to do all the time: feed the dog, do your homework, go to the shrink. What the blazes was she talking about?

"There has to be some semblance of organization in society, Tripsy, or it doesn't work. There has to be some rule of law that gives people guides for conducting themselves, both in public and private."

"Oh, yeah, right! That little book . . . what the hell's it called? Oh, the *Koran*. That bitch is just another damn rule, too. And the *Ten Commandments* and the *Code of Hammurabi*! Tell people how to live."

"It's a start. It's not perfect, I'll admit. Then again, neither is life, in general."

She was on her feet now, gesturing wildly. "People like you make all the rules! Not my scene, dorkus!" She's stopped now, facing me.

"As you grow, Tripsy, you also will set rules for yourself, for others. Now, please tell me more about the death blog. There's some useful information there."

Put her hands on the front of my desk, leaned over: "Oooookay, it's drama at its highest. I mean, you're allowing people into your life as it's ending. It shows them how they should appreciate their lives . . . maybe."

"So that's what this is about: showing people how to appreciate what they have, shock them into appreciation . . . or a submission of sorts? Isn't that the mission of organized religion?"

Tripsy pulled back, walked around the office, gently stroked my high priestess in the bronze bust on the pedestal to my right, still looking rather regal and all-knowing. As Tripsy's fingers moved slowly over her head, I thought I saw Zxta smile. When I blinked, she was all regal and composed again.

"I guess. Yeah, that sounds okay. You need to shake people up sometimes, especially most people who just follow all the rules. Most people do that, follow what a few tell 'em to do. It's pathetic. These people could think for themselves if they just thought about it. But they don't wanna, 'cos they don't trust their own knowledge and experience. They always need some kinda validation from others. So, I'll give 'em something to think about: what lies on the other side . . . death. It's a wake-up call for the population. Wake up and see that life is precious." She wrapped her scarf around the bronzed bust, sculpted the ends of it with a flourish, a lovely finishing touch.

"That's so contradictory, Tripsy. I don't get you. On one hand you tell me that life is precious. On the other, you tell me how you're gonna kill yourself and broadcast it to a voyeuristic public. I just don't get it." Nervous, I fingered my gorgeous tie again, this time with both hands. The pigs had quieted down.

"It's not for you to get. Just write it all down and tell others. Someone smarter'n you will get it."

"What's your message?"

"I dunno. Maybe it's that I wanna wake people up and see that there's a lot more to life than just listening to authority, 'cos those in so-called power are usually wrong and they want the worst for us. Just look all around you, dorkus. You don't need to know everything. Look at the sorry state of things. They suck. And it's 'cos someone plans it this way. That's all."

"Why suicide?"

"I'm a martyr of sorts, dorkus."

"Ah, I see: you need to kill yourself to get people's attention. Is that

it? Death is the medium for your message?"

She did a few yoga poses on the floor, then hopped up and sat down next to me, put her feet on my chair. "I like how you grasp difficult subjects. You musta been something in medical school. Pride of all your professors. All those awards and stuff," she said, waving her arm around the wall with my diplomas and certificates.

Getting up, I turned to her: "For the record, Tripsy, I never thought of myself as an overachiever." That contemplative look: my eyes now focused on the ceiling near my diaries, just like she did so often. "And as far as I can recall, I was never the apple of anyone's eye, either."

Her toes moved over the seat of my chair. "You ever put that in writing?"

"You mean, in my diaries?"

"What else?"

I moved back to my seat, removed her feet from my chair, sat down, spun around to face her. "Just like your diary is none of my business, Tripsy, the contents of mine are of no concern to you. Now, are we done here today?"

Her eyes sparkled slightly, her mouth turned up in a slight smile. Very slight. "Maybe someday, like I said before, you'll read my stuff. So tell me, dorkus, why were you so willing recently to share your diaries with me? Now you're blowing me off."

As she got up, she removed the scarf from the bronzed bust, wrapped it around the arm of my chair, tied a lovely knot, pick up her things and left without further word.

I was alone once again, massaging my soft and supple tie with the pink pigs in a field of rich, delicious green pasture, and staring down in disbelief at the beautiful soft-sculpture she'd gifted me. There was a message in there somewhere and, as usual, it eluded my grasp.

My subconscious had begun to decode some of my doodles, especially the little tome I created some time back: a small elegance among randomness. Elegance? Yes. Little artful patterns set against a field of mush. One had to study the scenes carefully to discern them.

I've found the best way to study something or discover a pattern among background noise is to feed as much of it as possible into your subconscious so your CHILD can savor it and come up with an answer to share with you. If you simply drip-feed your subconscious every now and then, it will get pouty. No one wants a pissed-off inner CHILD. I took in as much as I could right there. When I stared at it long enough, the little patterns started moving against the background.

I swear I saw the palm trees dancing around this little tiki hut at sunset, Zxta crooking her finger, beckoning me to join her at the bar. . . .

Session #39

I absently touched the scarf she had tied to the arm of my chair, as she walked into my office and lay down on the floor, threw her high-heeled legs on a chair and lit up a hooter.

"Call the cops and challenge 'em to get there before I off myself!"

"Now I've heard it all," I said. Not too sarcastically, I hoped.

"No, you haven't, dorkus. And you never will. I'm just educatin' you on some of the basics before I go."

"Morbid comes to mind." More sarcasm? To what end?

"And what the flip is suicide, dorkus!?"

By now, I had habituated to her name-calling. No, it was beyond that, something bordering on endearing, some lame acceptance or resignation. It was more than just my being lazy, trust me. I truly appreciated how she saw me. There was no contempt in her delivery, thank goodness, although her voice did occasionally rise an octave and shatter a few wine glasses.

"It's just that I feel some of your methods are—"

"What? Unconventional? Immoral? What!? Suicide is all those things, and more. Maybe by the end of our sessions you'll wake up and see what I see."

"I'd like to see what you see right now, Tripsy." I could picture those elegant doodles, dancing about like Tripsy often did, imparting her wisdom to a rockodon shrink.

"You can't. Trust me. Let's just hit the subject, okay?"

"Fine."

"Let's say you're not gonna video or shoot or do a death blog, but you want something. Set up the suicide day, place and time, and get everything ready first."

"Like?"

"Well, if you're gonna shoot yourself, all you need is a pistol. If it's a drug OD, then the tools and drug of choice. If it's more complicated than that, then you need to plan more. Like if you're gonna jump off a highway overpass into zippy traffic at night. These things take coordination, dorkus. You gotta be a good manager here. Forget that, ya gotta be a producer, like in Hollywood. Get all those talented people together and make 'em do what you want. Takes planning. Hell, I coulda done up Gettysburg or the Battle of the Bulge pretty nicely. All it takes is a little planning."

"So you say, Tripsy. Something tells me you see things a bit simpler than they truly are. The Battle of the Bul—"

"Stop! Let's not go there. I see things like I see 'em. At Gettysburg, I woulda gotten a thousand terrorist Rebel-Yellers and made 'em low-crawl at two in the mornin' over the battlefield right up to those Union boys, and jumped 'em while the assholes were snoozin'. Hardly anyone played by dirty rules back then, except the French and Indians. It was all, like, get in two single lines, face each other like dumb little schoolboys, and march into battle. Gimme a break. That's all soooooo old-school British."

"We're getting too far off the subject of alerting the police before your suicide, Tripsy."

"Yeah, I know. I get all worked up when I think about how stupid people are, how they feel some need to do what the so-called authorities tell 'em. March 'em off to their deaths like in World War II. Makes me chunk to think of such beautiful people giving in to assholes."

"Chunk?"

"Puke, dorkus. Yeah, you're right, I got way off course here. So, let's just say I'm gonna put a bullet through my brain pan. All I need is a pistol and a couple bullets."

"In case you miss the first time?"

She acted like she didn't hear me, continued on: "Like I said before, one is for you. So, go to some nice place for dyin', like maybe a Southern Baptist church. They love daily sufferin' and sacrifice, all that

Catholic pain. Sit in a nice comfy chair inside the church, get the gun ready—maybe tape it to your hand so it can't fall to the floor and go off accidentally—and call the cops. When they bust in like SWAT with Dudley Dooright leadin' the charge, point the gun at your head, say, 'Surprise, Five-OH, you're late!' and pull the trigger."

"Gone in a flash, huh?"

"Is there a better way?"

"I dunno about better, Tripsy. But it would throw some cops into therapy for years. They say one law-enforcement officer dies every two days. Imagine how many live through those experiences but are traumatized for life."

"You study teen suicide and you haven't thought about all the thousands of ways to go? You kiddin' me? Dorkus, you mos def need to get your head outta your books. There's a real world out there and you should check it out sometime before your clock winds down."

"Where does this anger come from?"

"What the flip, dorkus! I don't need a middle-aged teleprompter!"

"You're damned good at avoiding what's important, I'll give you that, Tripsy."

"Important? To you, maybe."

I pulled a chair up to the couch, leaned forward. "It should also be important to you, Tripsy. I'm not the one who has to live with your anger, your distrust of adults, especially men. You do. I'm just trying to draw out the roots so we can figure out what to do with them, maybe alter the colors of the flowers, change the beauty of the plant."

"If ya see a weed, doc, pull it out."

"You're just talking in circles. Why don't we cut this short today? I've got a lot to do—"

In a whirlwind of pillows and blanket and clothes, she spun around the room, yelling: "Dammit, dorkus! You don't care about me! If you did, you'd listen to me! All you do—"

In a desperate act, I jumped in her face: "I do listen to you! That's really all I've been doing for ten months! You rebuff my every attempt to understand you! I don't know what the hell to do with you! One moment, you're an angry teenager! The next, you're a charming young woman! There's no behavioral continuity here, Tripsy!" I loosed one of my famous 130-dB atavistic screams, too. Didn't shatter any wine glasses.

Father would have said, "You really hammered that chick, son! Bet you can't do it twice!"

A loud knock at the door, my assistant entered. "Sir, is everything all right?" She was visibly concerned although not the least bit embarrassed coming in to check on me.

I turned and raised my palms to her: "I'm sorry, Mary. Everything's fine. Please close the door. We'll be okay. Thank you." As I turned back to Tripsy, she was gathering her things. "So that's it? No clever retort?"

Without looking at me: "Listen, dorkus, I don't need a half-ass shrink tellin' me how to live my life." She then faced me, said, "But someone really needs to tell you how to live yours, cuz you're a loser."

Maybe a part-time loser. Not looking at her, I said, "I'm not telling you how to do anything! Maybe your parents should find someone else to help you." Damn, was that the wrong thing to say! I looked around the room for some kind of sign, a talisman of support.

The bronze bust to my right stared blankly toward the center of the room where Tripsy stood, preparing her things for imminent departure. If only my high priestess could talk. My fear was that she would say my dear old father was right.

Not feeling a whole lot of support coming from anyone or anything in my own office, I poured myself some tea, half the tea spilling onto the table, my hands shaking; so unlike me. Bracing the table for my inevitable crashing to the floor, I forced myself to look directly into her eyes, painful as it was. Was I embarrassed? Ashamed? Confused?

Considering those three options, my father would have said, "All the above, son. Congratulations on yet another, ah, perfect score."

Tripsy looked at me once more: "Yeah, maybe you're right." She walked around to my desk, untied her scarf from my chair, stuffed it in the trash can, turned to me again, said, "See ya," and did what she did best: sauntered out with the flair of an Italian runway model, leaving behind a slowly diffusing wake of mysterious perfume, antiperspirant and pissed-off teen.

The bus had pulled up just before she got there, then suddenly departed. Tripsy walked down the street a ways and greeted Jimi Hendrix's old chief roadie, the now-decrepit Henry, with a warm hug and kiss. Wide-eyed and beaming, Henry stood from his wheelchair, handed an old guitar to her. It had an otherworldly luminescence.

Even that far away, I saw it clearly: a bright-red Fender Stratocaster. Didn't Jimi used to—

Session #40

When a patient missed a session, it was for one of two reasons: death or a failed attempt at suicide. If the former, I usually received a phone call: a parent, member of the clergy, or the police. In failed suicides, a parent or guardian always rang me, followed immediately by an emergency-room physician, usually yelling at me about how stupid I was for not preventing this in the first place and where the heck did I go to medical school—Madagascar State University?

For the record, "regular" doctors have little respect for psychiatrists or psychologists, and I can see where their mistrust lies: our work is usually inaccurate and most patients do not get better without the aid of BigPharma intervention or surgery, which only masks the underlying neurochemical problems. But it surely makes BigPharma trillions of dollars richer each year.

I'll admit it: some of us shrinks simply stink at what we do, violating the Hippocratic oath by first doing harm—and lots of it—to patients. Most shrinks go into the profession to escape the real world where all normal humans play and prosper. Others, too, enter the profession to figure out how they're so screwed up. And some even love to research the brain's chemistry. Somewhere along the way, though, they manage to treat patients and prevent them, at least temporarily, from killing themselves.

I said treat, not heal. When I thought of that insult, the image of my father always came to mind. He spent more time with his personal banker than his patients, and knew more about how French cologne por homme mixed with various natural body scents than he did the pharmacology of those epileptic drugs that caused suicidal behavior in teens.

I'm sorry, was I criticizing my father? I promised you honesty here.

Worst of all, perhaps, is the sad realization that we psychiatrists are just middlemen who are attempting to determine the underlying neurochemical and neuroanatomical problems that result from a patient's behavior. Many shrinks and psychs will disagree with me. I'm fine with that. I know what I know, and that's that.

Father would say, "Atta boy. You tell 'em, son."

As I was saying, before the rude interruption by my father, their disagreement lies in the fact that there are neurologists and neurosurgeons who deal directly with the diseases of the brain, and all my kind do is, as stated earlier, act as middlemen. The "real" doctors call us quacks in many cases, much like MDs call PhDs "pseudodoctors." Personally, I've always felt that MDs are arrogant and narcissistic, having few good things to say about anyone, including their own peers. When we are finally able to reveal what's inside the gray matter of MDs, they may not like what we find. . . .

In fifty or maybe a hundred years, when high-technology, science and medicine have enabled us to know what makes the brain function as it does, we will have no need for my profession. For example, a normal person suddenly commits a rash of crimes, culminating in murder. Of course, the police get their man, arrest him, and drag him to the nearest NeuroScan clinic, a futuristic facility where a specialist will visualize both the neurochemistry and anatomy of a person's brain, using a noninvasive technique. They'll be able to "see" aneurisms, tumors, clots, etc., plus abnormalities well below the atomic level, where any kind of DNA mutation may be seen. And they'll see them with striking nanoscopic accuracy and clarity from simple blood and urine scans, plus high-resolution regional and whole-body scans.

Science fiction now, reality later. That's how science and technology work.

Anyway, once at the NeuroScan clinic, the new patient—no longer murderous, of course, having been shackled to the bed in medieval irons—undergoes a highly detailed brain scan that reveals the underlying cause of his abnormal behavior: a microscopic tumor in his amygdala, a region of cells in both medial temporal lobes of the brain. The amygdala is responsible, in part, for modulating emotional states, including sudden-onset rage. I won't go into significant detail here, so please don't ask.

I could hear my father: "You're keeping it simple because you don't know anything, son. A wise move, indeed."

Just so you know: I excelled at math, physics and chemistry in college, and was one of the few medical students who understood biophysics and biochemistry in med school. Most med students don't know diddly about the physical sciences, nor did they wish to learn. Sad but true.

Just so you know. . . .

Anyway, with the advent of the NeuroScan clinic business model, there will be no need for us intermediaries—the psychiatrist, psychologist, social worker or any other mental health professional. For now, we are just temporary caretakers of human behavior.

Temporary.

Instead of shrinks in the future, we'll have experts in neurothis, neurothat who will analyze behaviors via their neurochemical and neuroanatomical correlates, and not the behaviors themselves. The study of what we now know as human behavior will be obsolete. Behaviors then will be seen as actions and side effects of neurochemical and neuroanatomical processes. To change a behavior, the neurogeeks will accurately tweak the delicate chemistry and anatomy of the brain and nervous system.

How did I get onto these subjects? Was I trying to distract myself from the fact Tripsy was not here today? Instead of calling in another patient to fill the void left by Tripsy—in my schedule, I mean—I chose to read her file again and take more notes, do more doodles. Again.

I called Tripsy's mother to see what happened. She'd not seen her in several days, and provided a lukewarm apology for not alerting me sooner. She said Tripsy had called her to say she was staying with a friend for a few days. She seemed not to care much, and that bothered me. A lot. Perhaps she was used to Tripsy's absences. Not much relief at that. I felt even more lousy at her not being here.

Tripsy's mother had no issue paying the bills, even when her daughter was a no-show. So many parents out there are absent from their child's life. They only provide the bare necessities so they don't get thrown in jail. No wonder our world is in such misery. Quickly dismissed that thought and got back to Tripsy. . . .

Weren't we making progress, Tripsy? You were opening up to me in new ways, it seemed. Did I miss something?

Father: "I'm sure you missed a lot of things, son. Keep up the good work."

Session #43

Call me an idiot but, for a fourth straight week, I left Tripsy's usual time slot open. Just in case. I know what you're thinking: I really am a dorkus. Right on both charges, and I know it, okay? No need to rub my nose in it.

Pu'er was brewing in a quart-size pot on my hotplate, diffusing tendrils of—how to put it?—a lovely bouquet of earthy tea leaves and detritus throughout my office. Beyond that, a cool northerly breeze on which rode delicate puffs of fresh lavender and sage and oranges was drifting in through my open windows, and a large garlicky Caesar salad was resting quietly on my desk, beckoning my limited palate.

Even if she didn't show, I would be fine. Fine, I tell you.

Father: "Fine is the Great American Euphemism, son. It can mean a multitude of things. In your case, however, it's an acronym: forgetful, incompetent, namby-pamby and empty-headed."

At that, I sat at my desk and prepared to relax. Closed my eyes for what seemed like a long minute, felt the air in the room shift imperceptibly, then raised my nose to sniff the air. . . .

"Call the local radio and tv stations and tell them the good news!" The scream lodged in my right ear, now legally deaf because of Tripsy's repeated assaults.

My hand accidentally hit the salad dish, upending the garlicky concoction just about everywhere within a two-foot radius, and I jumped up and came down hard in my seat, which shot backward and into the table with my boiling tea pot, now a spreading stain on my tiles. My only thought at that moment was whether the grout around all the tiles had been properly sealed from hot, stinky liquids with a long history of staining things permanently.

"Smells like piss and poo in here, dorkus. This a pig farm or a shrink's office?" She lay down on the couch, pulled the blanket over her, rolled slightly to face me. " 'Sides, I wanted to tell you you're wrong."

I was feverishly mopping up the pu'er behind my desk. "About . . . what?"

Do you know how far a quart of spilled tea spreads out on an expensive Italian-tiled floor? My desk's legs at the bottom were now stained lightly with the stuff.

"Me," she said.

"Please . . . tell . . . me," I said, almost out of breath from grabbing paper towels and throwing them down onto the floor, hoping to corral the tea that was making a mad break for the door.

"Nothing's wrong with me, dorkus. I'm just going through some late post-puberty stuff we girls feel sometimes. Maybe it's hormonal. I dunno. I do know I have nothing on my mind, and nothing bothers me. Not even you."

I looked up, said, "Okay, then why don't we just get back to our discussion? I believe you were talking about calling in the media, yes?"

"Shut up and listen, dorkus. It's not that diff from callin' the cops. This time, though, it might be good to get some national coverage, maybe HBO."

"HBO doesn't have a news service," I said, throwing a soaking-wet towel into my trashcan.

She pulled off the blanket, sat up. "Oh, honey, when I call 'em and tell 'em this, they'll make one just for me. In the least, they'll get some dude with a videocam to cover it for some reality show later on. Something. I know Fox'd eat this like ice cream. I can see it now: I'm sittin' in my little pew at the church, while the place is fillin' up with morbid assholes who wanna see some chick, flat-out bent on suicide, blow her last thoughts all over this dinky little place of worship."

"Maybe you could choose another venue?"

"Why? Hell, it doesn't really matter. I think stickin' it to those evangelical Southern Baptists or Dallas Christians would shake 'em outta their cages. I'll stick to my little church, thank you. You're all like, spare the civilians. Me, I'm goin', forget everybody and their noise. Bring the kids, the dog, some popcorn. This is real life in modern America, dude. Welcome to it."

"Okay, so you've got the cameras all there, then what?"

"I'd make a little speech about what brought me there, let some people try to talk me outta the deed, then when they felt like they were gettin' to me, pull the trigger and check out. I only wish I could see all their reactions and laugh at 'em."

"You're into pain. Creating it, I mean." My horrified look was one to behold: the tea had made an intricate pattern of impressionistic swirls and smudges in my precious tile. The effect, perhaps informative in some arcane fashion, appeared permanent. I sat up on my knees, surveyed the damage, and sighed. Rather loudly.

Tripsy got up and came around my desk, looked down at the newly created "Rorschach meets Pollack" installation, with a few loaded pistols painted in. "I'd call it . . . mmm . . . tranquil impressionism."

"Very clever. Thank you." When I looked at it again, I couldn't help but agree.

"Making people feel my pain is my thing. If they get it, then I've accomplished something." Her smirk spoke volumes about the stained tile. "If not, drop it. Someone or something else hopefully will get through to 'em. I'm not being sadistic here, dorkus. You don't get it. Man, if that stuff didn't smell so bad, dorkus, I'd do the whole floor in it."

My face in my hands: "You're right, I really don't understand, Tripsy."

She patted my head like a dog: "The point is not to inflict pain for the sake of inflicting pain. I'm not tryin' to be mean here. Pain's a great motivator, stud. You can get people to do whatever you want with the right kind and amount and frequency of pain. You should know that. The Jesuits been doin' it for like, 500 years."

How'd she know about the Jesuits? "I agree," I said, rocking back on my heels and jerking myself upright. I looked around for what to do next, couldn't think of the right thing. Get some bleach and remove that hideous stain from the floor? Forget the mess and give Tripsy a proper welcome home? *Home?*

My father would say something like, "Son, you should take up finger painting for a living. After all, six year olds can do it."

"So, if I show people all the horrors of suicide, maybe some of 'em'll understand what it really is, how it starts, and maybe how to stop it before they do it themselves or maybe before their kid does herself in."

"It's a noble cause, yours. I just disagree with your approach." After ten months, what the heck did I know about her approach?

"Hey, I'm no fuckin' genius here, dorkus. And from what I've seen so far, neither are you."

"Genius is not what makes the world go 'round, Tripsy."

"Then what does?"

"People who *think*. Those who find clever solutions quickly and efficiently, regardless of the naysayers and failures."

"Yeah, you've said that before. You dig thinkers, huh?" She bent down, pushed some paper towels under each of the desk legs.

"Yes, I do. They think things through, come up with plans, and carry them out according to their plans, more or less. And they're flexible when they need to change direction on a dime."

"Got any hydrogen peroxide?"

I picked up my phone and asked Mary to get some. Less than five seconds later, it seemed like, she knocked and then entered, and handed me the bottle.

Tripsy grabbed it out of her hand, not acknowledging her: "Good, stud, cuz you just defined me and my methods, so shut up and listen." She then turned to Mary, said, "Need somethin', sister?"

Mary looked at her with a pained expression, then over at me, smirked, and left without a word.

"Like I said, I don't do this to be sadistic. I'm not a sadist. And I hate doling out pain like some concentration-camp doctor. All I wanna do is make people aware of what us teeny tots go through, and what makes some of us kill ourselves, even though there seems to be so much hope for us. Let's move on, okay?"

Was she asking my permission? "Okay."

We both moved from my desk. She took her perch on the couch, and I sat in a chair next to her.

She appeared not to notice or even care that I was now a couple of feet from her. "Before I offed myself on camera, I'd tell 'em to come read my little diary, which I'd have on me when I died."

Did I hear her correctly? "What's the purpose?" I felt like a fisherman who'd just netted a big catch—something bigger than my boat—and was now delicately trying to sink in the hook, careful not to lose my grand prize. At that moment, I had an evil thought about an old man, the sea, a huge marlin, and a bunch of ravenous sharks that reduced his prize to bits of tissue and bones.

"It'd be my last will and testament. In it I'd pretty much tell people all the things I don't have the patience to say all in one mouthful. I'd say I'm sorry, too." She looked away, thoughtful.

Be careful what you say, Dr. Moore. She's on the edge now, and could reveal more, or. . . . "Why?"

"Because most people are really like you: they would think the worst of me before they'd allow me to say anything that might be of some value to 'em."

"So they're instantly prejudiced against you?"

"Of course. Aren't you? Look at me, dorkus: people tell me I have these gifts of beauty and brains. Most people aren't physically beautiful or smart in any way. They hate people like me . . . or secretly wanna be me. So hypocritical and judgmental, know what I mean, dorkus?"

"I'm not judgmental, if that's what you mean." That's a big pile of poop, and I knew it. In every human I'd ever met, I immediately sensed their chemistry, judged them to be right or wrong, good or bad, kind or cruel, compassionate or cold. I was as judgmental as they came, and I'm sure she sensed it. Tripsy had that same unique sense of interpersonal and cross-species chemistry. "I assess things, try to figure them out, Tripsy. Judgments need moral terms to describe them, and they're always unfair and inaccurate. When we assess something, we try to do it without the morals injected, using only pure objectivity. That line of inquiry leads to more accurate analysis."

"Oh, baloney, dorkus. We won't go there right now, though. Anyway, I'd write it all down and ask that it be published or printed somewhere, so people could read it."

"Why don't you just do it now, Tripsy?" I said, looking up at my own diaries, then down at my precious manuscript. My beautiful dust-covered—except for the unmistakable swirl made by Tripsy's fingertip—manuscript on suicide in teens.

"No one'd read it. I guess."

"How could you possibly know that?" I noticed she followed my gaze, all the way up the bookshelves. I chanced this: "I would. In fact, I'd be honored, Tripsy."

Her sad smile was the only thing I noticed as she got up and left me there alone. Again. After she'd gone, I wasn't sure whether to be angry at her for causing me to spill that pu'er all over my tiled floor. Or whether to castigate her for not showing up these past three sessions and not alerting me. Whether to be angry at myself for not responding appropriately to her during the session. Or whether to be angry at the awful-smelling tea that grew little tea legs and tried to invade the rest of my office space.

Father: "Son, you need to take full responsibility here: you're an idiot and it's all your fault, whatever the tea started."

My own wisdom on extended holiday, my father actually sounded like the voice of reason this afternoon. . . .

Session #44

Now that she had returned, I was making every effort to understand the miasma of emotions I was feeling: anger, fear, empathy, love. I'm sure you've got this all figured out. Makes me wish I were blessed with such clarity and intellect. Unfortunately, I am not, so I struggle each day to make sense of my surroundings. Please forgive my shortcomings.

Like I said, I was examining what I was feeling with her coming back after nearly a month without even contacting me, and found myself too confused to untangle the threads. Maybe the time wasn't right for me to discover this just yet? When would be?

By the time I looked up, Tripsy had already sat down. On the chair by my desk. Next to me. A foot away. "Yes?" Sounded like I was taking someone's drink order.

"Email DeathLeakage and tell them to pick up the video I'm gonna make of my death."

"I've seen that website. Disgusting." I tried to keep working, but having her that close to me was still unsettling. I could see the distinct shape of the tip of her nose . . . the delicate blonde down that covered her arms and legs . . . her perfect fingers the nails of which were painted a beautiful turquoise, with swirly flourishes . . . those well-worn jungle boots with no socks.

"Why? Can't handle reality?"

Straining to listen to her every word, I finally got it: "Images of death aren't reality to me, Tripsy."

"Ever been out in the wild, doc? Seen how animals treat each other? Seen 'em when they're hungry and desperate, injured yet they still have to go out and kill to survive? Ever seen that sorta stuff?"

"Yeah, on Discovery Channel."

"You and your Apple TV and newspapers. I'll bet you dust off and polish your remote, don't you? Pro'ly iron the Sunday paper before readin' it, too."

"Actually, Tripsy, I download all my news on my computer."

"Cool iMac. How much?"

"I don't recall. I think my assistant ordered it for me."

"You do anything on your own, dorkus?"

Ah, a challenge. "Yes, Tripsy, I do most things on my own, including ordering things online. Sometimes I have my assistant—"

"Assist you," she interrupted. "Got it . . . pay attention here, dorkus: our society's tried to tame the wild. We have these pathetic zoos with animals that eat 'food' in buckets. Not like in the wild, where a lion has to run down its prey and suffocate it, then eat it. No one delivers that lion's meal."

"Unless some hapless gazelle walks up to the lion."

"Like I was sayin', I'd call this website and let 'em know I'd be videoin' my suicide, then at least they'd put it out there for the world to see. You know how many people'd watch that?"

"And then some other news usurped it. People have a short attention span, so you have to give them new thoughts and ideas every so often, Tripsy. Especially with the growing population of ADHDers. That's why you're better off sticking around and educating people for many years, instead of in one fell swoop with a one-hit, in-your-face death video. Why would anyone want to tune in to you and your thoughts?"

Ignored me again. "So you don't think my video'd make Sundance?"

"I'd keep my day job, quite honestly," I said, getting up for a glass of water, anything to get away from her intensity. She radiated heat like the afternoon sun.

"Well, that's you. Me, I like shock treatment better."

"No one likes old news, Tripsy. You need to keep it fresh."

"Like I said, at least my death'd be on the web for people to see. Like goin' to a library and readin' an old classic."

"Classics have timeless messages in them. What would yours be?"

"That's what I've been tryin' to tell you, dorkus! I'm tryin' to educate people about suicide, what it is, what causes it, and what makes a teenager take her life. Isn't there something in that?"

"Yes, I just meant that there has to be some good reason, some lesson for people to want to revisit it. Classics remain in people's minds because of their timeless nature, their elegance, their unique messages. Again, people need a reason to see your work, let alone revisit it from time to time."

"Yeah, and I'm givin' 'em a reason: this is me and I'm suicidal. Wanna know why?"

"That's what I've been trying to figure out all these months."

"Sounds like you're giving up on me, dorkus."

Was I? Did I shoot off some "piss-off" pheromone she could detect? I sat at my desk again, drank the water in one long gulp, wishing it were something stronger. Much stronger. Didn't I have a bottle of Stoli around here somewhere?

"Well, are you?"

Not sure what to say, I muttered: "For someone else to give a shit about you, Tripsy, you first must give a shit about yourself." With that, I rose and moved to the door, opened it for her.

"And this means what to me, dorkus?"

"Like I said, Tripsy—"

"I know, I know: first I have to give a shit about myself. You realize you said the s-word, dorkus? Have a good week. See ya!" she said, bumping into me as she breezed past.

Session #45

"Do a podcast of my suicide!" she yelled from the large sitting area outside my office.

Little Tyra looked at Tripsy and smiled, clapped her hands and yelled, "Tripsy!" And, no, it wasn't because Tyra looked forward to hearing the podcast.

After careful thought, I decided that I needed to hire Tripsy to look after Tyra. After all, she was the only human Tyra had ever reacted to, except the occasional "Hi" she said to me. I found myself wishing I could be more like Tripsy. Or more like my father. Or more like—

"Yeah, just something a little more hip, even though podcasts've been around like, forever. Actually, come to think of it, I'd do all the stuff we've talked about over the past coupla weeks. Why not? Get the best coverage, get my message out there for as many people as possible to hear it, and then let the spaghetti hit the wall wherever the hell it hits the wall."

"I agree. So why not write a book?"

"Maybe I already am."

Her comment made me notice something about her scarf: it had a repeating pattern of beautiful palm trees painted ever so delicately on it. Was that batik?

Palm trees. Palm trees. PALM TREES!

Okay, I understand. Thank you. Was there some relationship between her comment about maybe writing a book and my palm-tree doodles? Probably not. She and her behaviors were too complex for my simple readings of tea leaves. Ah, forget it, there were coincidences everywhere in my life, but I had no idea what they meant or what the hell to do with them. What the hell was the point in receiving a message from The Universe if I didn't have the skills to decipher it. What the fuck, indeed.

Father: "Good on ya, son; you used the h-word. Welcome to manhood."

"Anyway, the point's that I put my suicide and all the stuff that goes with it in as many diff things as possible: radio, tv, book, web, podcast, dating sites. I figure if you're right and my news becomes old news right quick, then I best get out there in as many ways as I can. I do have a message and it's important."

"Everyone thinks their message is important. It's—"

"Heck with that! I know most people have something to say about everything, but most of the time it's crap. It's not useful at all, cuz they've not thought it through. It's just some rehash of their history, something they read or heard somewhere then filtered through their little brain."

"Yours is different, of course."

"My message and my brain, yes. If you didn't think so, you wouldn't be writing all this stuff down all the time, would you?"

"I'm doodling, Tripsy. The recorder takes it all in, though."

"At least somethin's paying attention! Yeah, the podcast is pretty cool, cuz I could make a video of it and then live-stream it."

Ah, yet another clever medium to show off your suicide skills. "After you've killed yourself?"

"Yeah."

"So this kid would just walk into wherever your dead body lies, and take the video of your death, and not somehow be moved by what he or she sees, namely your dead and decaying body?"

"Right."

"Okay, I was just checking. I don't know of many kids who could do that without being traumatized by the scene."

"I'll hire a pro. Don't worry about it. Thing is, it gets out. You've seen the snuff films on the web, so you know they somehow have gotten out. Mine's gonna get out, too. You can't stop this. Authority can't sanitize my death in any way. My thoughts and feelings will get out, and they will help somebody someday. 'Sides, I read somewhere the words of smart people aren't appreciated until a hundred years after their death. Maybe mine will be appreciated now, though."

"So you hope."

"So do you, dorkus. That's why you listen to me."

"Is there any other medium you plan on using to broadcast this event?"

"For now, no. Wait! I'll send out invitations to all the kids and tell 'em to bring their phones, so they can all shoot it at the same time. Cool! Like a buncha Japanese tourists shootin' shots of some dumb parkin' lot in Topeka."

I bent down to fetch something from a bottom drawer, and when I raised my head, she was gone.

At the street, she reached into her bag and found a book that hadn't been there before. "What the—!?" Reached in and pulled it out. One of my diaries. "Holy flippin' hooters!" I thought I heard her yell, as she looked back at me, standing at the window and mouthing the words, "What the fu-fu-fu-fuuuuuu, indeed."

7

Famous Last Words:
What to Tell the World Before You Die

What do you say to someone, anyone, knowing it's the last thing you'll ever share? Ever. How do you tell your mother you've lost all hope and, through the impossibly dense neural fog, can't see any other way out except that great leap into total and infinite darkness?

Where do you summon just the right words to shape into an apology to those you've known all your life, to those who surely will not understand your pain? How do you teach the world that, even though this is your chosen route, it is and should never be the path taken by anyone else?

Somehow, we manage to forgive the apparent hypocrisy of young suicides. We forgive their arrogance. Cast aside their pontificating. And society chooses to forget that . . . they . . . gave . . . up. Experiencing pain for an infinity was just too much for them, and that light at the end of the long, dark tunnel was just as I said before: the oncoming headlight of a freight train.

Not their parents, though; they didn't give up. Nor did anyone else left behind. It's always some reflection of a failure to mom and dad, brother and sister. They're the ones who continue to suffer, long after their loved one takes her own life. Some suicides want the living to suffer greater and longer than a suicide did.

And to learn how and why, we focus on the underlying current of pain and sorrow, despair and depression that brought them to a state of suicide. My job is to study this current—swift and churning, perilous and severe—as it courses through the lives of many young children. Often I wish for fifty or a hundred years to travel by in an instant, leaving me standing in the midst of a new age of understanding the human brain, a time when my profession is long gone, absorbed by a much leaner medical science.

Yes, I see myself standing inside one of those futuristic NeuroScan clinics, awaiting the emergence of one of my young patients from a recent scan. When the technician appears, he hands me the results of her scan: 42% decrease in volume of her right hippocampus; 33% decrease in activity of her nucleus accumbens. The course of action is stated in bold at the bottom. They suggest administering a cocktail of nanosomething molecules that will repair the damage. Without any side effects.

That is the future I dream of, especially for young people in the throes of suicidal thoughts and behaviors.

Some years ago, a friend sent me a copy of a suicide letter, written by a fourteen-year-old girl who shot herself on a scorching, humid Texas Saturday at exactly high noon. We know this exact time, because there was one eyewitness to her suicide, the family's maid.

When I first read the girl's letter, I was riveted by its clarity, calmness of tone, a detached coolness about it.

She wasn't crying out for help or blaming anyone. In fact, she said it was all her fault. This girl was simply saying goodbye . . . to everyone.

And this is what intrigued me the most, her writing not a suicide note—a letter of death—but a final goodbye to her lovely family. What is so bitterly ironic is that she looked at the whole affair with such intellectual clarity, yet she failed to grasp that this may have been only a temporary state for her. She couldn't see into the future far enough and witness a different life, one of pleasure and purpose and happiness.

When Tripsy brought up the subject of saying goodbye to loved ones, I was again mortified and deeply saddened by the mere thought, and I felt it important to share it with others, these farewell thoughts.

So, now you know: I got into this business because I wanted to help people relive horrors.

Sadistic as that sounds, my aim was to meet them head on and to work through them, rather than forget them as my father had continually preached. His method of shoving dreadful memories deeper and deeper into the human mind—read: repression—seemed to have worked for his patients, although I argue that they may have been better off facing their fears in therapy.

I believe that people should not repeat mistakes, although it seems that is exactly what people do: repeat mistakes with striking similarity with each successive generation, if not more frequently on many smaller fronts.

I wanted to tell Tripsy more about this, as I felt she would somehow see things in her life differently, but I know that she's on her own track and must continue traveling down it to the end. I'm sorry that her chosen end is suicide. I'm obligated as a healthcare professional to intervene to protect Tripsy. No, it's not the law in some areas of our country, but it is a moral assignment no one should ignore.

So, I am doing what I can to help her. I realize it may be unconventional to some practitioners, but I feel we must use what works in a given situation. Besides, many mental-health professionals ultimately end up failing their patients, so how could my approach be viewed as worse? And those very professionals will castigate me for my views, and all I would say is this: "People, just examine the results: kids are committing suicide at an alarming rate, so whatever it is you're doing is not helping in any way. Except maybe to kill them faster and sooner."

Young kids like Tripsy lack the experiential experience to appreciate the gift of life, in general. They're preoccupied with reality shows, their iPad or iSomething, texting to their friends, experimenting with the latest designer drug, skipping school to go to ditch parties that promise sex, drugs and alcohol—a great escape from their own reality. You name it, they're addicted to it and will spend more time at it than in a history book. They live in the here and now, and now means in the next five minutes and has nothing but passion and energy in it. I do admire the energy and free spirit of young kids, but I feel it's often misdirected.

More kids today are engaging in illegal and dangerous activities, something we would've shunned in my time. As I listened more and more to Tripsy, I felt deeply saddened. A part of me also felt a sense of hope, as she spoke her words of teen wisdom. If she could, in fact, reach people with her passion, then perhaps her paucity of experience in real life doesn't mean a thing. Whsat she lacks in real-life experience, she more than makes up for in raw passion. We should all be so fortunate to feel and experience the great passionate wisdom of an *Indigo Child*.

While I have seemingly allowed Tripsy to do as she pleases, there's much more to this therapy than you may glean from these pages.

How do we teach a child and prepare her to face the challenging realities of life? In the animal kingdom, young animals are given harsh treatments under real-world conditions. Some succeed and go on to become adult animals. Those who fail die quickly and are recycled. I feel that we are just animals that must be trained with a large-size fear factor. Without it, we never learn proper balance or respect for the greater world around us.

Tripsy clearly needed some balance. What puzzled me most of all was how she could have so much at her disposal and not take an interest in anything. Her parents were wealthy, even though they seemingly took little interest in her. Perhaps this stemmed from Tripsy's continually crying wolf? She had all the money a young woman could want. She had resources that other kids would kill for.

Poor choice of words. Sorry.

My point is, Tripsy had it all. She doesn't know what to do with it. Or genuinely doesn't care about any of it. Or does she?

Session #46

This very moment, I was preoccupied with the young woman sitting in my favorite chair behind my favorite desk. My desk. More accurately, I was preoccupied with how to eject her from my chair, without causing her to throw a hissy fit.

She simply looked up at me and shot a bolus of this into my face: "G'bye, everyone, I love you!"

Knowing I should've been writing or doodling all this, I took relief knowing my recorder was always recording. Everything. I even had hidden video cameras installed up by the uppermost shelves of my bookcases. Why? To document any untoward activity by a patient, anything that may be construed as immoral or illegal or felonious. Since I was the only one who has ever seen the videos, most of which have been transferred to DVDs, I wasn't too concerned about anyone witnessing Tripsy lighting up another one of her hooters.

I really should mention this, in my defense: I ensured that Tripsy had a medical marijuana card, so she could legally smoke inside the confines of my professional practice, under my supervision. That also meant outside in the safety of my section of the expansive yard. So there.

Blew a few smoke rings in my face, said, "Don't try to make me cry today, you weenie."

"Do I ever?" I asked, gently touching her arm and lifting her up and out of my chair, then guiding her over to her couch.

Yes, it really was *her* couch. It had her scent on it, her essence. Yes, one could argue that others had lain on that couch, deposited their own DNA, but Tripsy's rose to the top, erased all traces of the others, and simply dominated. . . .

"This is not one of my fave subjects," she said, rearranging the pillows around her.

"What about it?" I took my seat. And, no, my seat was not Tripsy's seat. She could have the couch. I wasn't yielding on matters of that chair. No way. That was *my* chair.

If you must know, I got it at a garage sale in Asheville, North Carolina. It once belonged to Zelda Fitzgerald, who sat in it every day she was in residence at the hospital where she was treated for schizophrenia, and was one of the few items that escaped the horrible fire that took Zelda's life. Funny thing: I had a predilection for objects once touched by such special creatures. Secretly, too, I often dreamed of traveling back in time and having long chats with Zelda, perhaps even discovering what ailed her delicate and brilliant mind. My pet hypothesis: Zelda was actually not schizophrenic or depressed. She was perfectly fine, according to some people who witnessed her before she was committed. Some entity placed her in a padded cell against her will, and medicated her so she could not speak out against those who committed her. Yes, her chair continually told me this.

"Telling someone I love 'em."

It took me a couple of seconds to focus on Tripsy again: "How is that so hard?"

Not missing a beat: "I never got it. Why should I dish it out?"

"Why should you dish out destructiveness, you mean to say?"

"Now you're talkin' like a shrink. That's my boy."

"This is what I do, Tripsy."

"Not lately. You're a lazy thing nowadays. Shut up and listen."

"All ears." Lazy? I thought I'd made some improvement over the past ten or so months.

"I figure one way to calm down the 'rents from the ultimate eff-you might be to tell 'em all goodbye and how much I love them. I mean, really love them."

"Do you?"

"What did I tell you!? Dayum, dorkus. Of course I feel something for

them. I'm just a scared kid who wants to be loved. Isn't everybody? Don't answer that. I don't wanna hear your noise right now. Yeah, I'd love to tell my 'rents how I really feel. I dunno if it'd change the way I feel about offin' myself, but at least I could say to 'em what's on my mind. I think you should be able to spill your good side before you go, to tell people all the great thoughts and feelings you have inside yourself, mostly to let others know you weren't this random person who decided on some messed-up whim to kill herself. Personally, I'd tell the weenies how I loved 'em for burning me so badly."

"You don't really mean that."

"Okay, maybe not. They did some good things: taught me how to go potty without doin' a stinky Jackson Pollack on the carpet . . . showed me how to tie my laces so I wouldn't fall on my face . . . showed me what to eat and which fork to use. Let's see if I remember this right: one of the forks impales the salad and the other one stabs the cheeseburger."

"Oookay."

"I just made a funny. You should support me when I make a funny, dorkus."

"I do support you, Tripsy. What else would you tell those you love?"

"Since I really can't think of much, based on my messed-up life, I'd rather preach to people what they should do instead. That cool with you?"

"You're asking for my permission?"

"Take it or leave it. Kids should be grateful that they even have 'rents. I mean, when I was in New York last year with my friends, they all told me about their screwed-up childhood. No one could remember what their father looked like or what his name was. They didn't even know what he did for work all day to pay the bills, school, clothing, vacations and the pretty rooms with all the entertainment they could ingest, not to mention, it doesn't cost those kids anything! So, what should I tell them?"

"This is *your* commentary."

"To be grateful that the one 'rent left didn't beat the crap out of you too much or too often? Listen, dorkus, 'rents are the big reason we're all so unhinged to begin with. And to think that out of all the thousands of schools in this great big nation of ours, there are none that specialize in teaching people how to be 'rents. Can you believe this? The most important job in the world has no training whatsooooever! And it's designed that way! Doesn't that blow your teeny mind!? Okay, maybe not. Your 'rents were probably good little taxpayers."

"That is correct, Tripsy, but you are also an instigator."

"Yes, and it's us 'gators who start revolutions, dorkus. Behind every revolution in history has always been a smart-as-hell female."

"Didn't know that."

"It's true. We always got the men to do the dirty stuff, but we're the brains behind 'em all."

"I now wonder if Napoleon knew his boss was a girl?"

"Most men are too dumb to know their boss is a girl, dude. They're all pussy-whipped. I could get just about any guy I wanted just by spreadin' my thighs a few inches. They'd fall all over me, do whatever I said. Now that's power, dorkus."

She had a point, you know. "And the point of this is?"

"Girls rule. Remember it."

"With you here, how could I not?"

"I'm trainin' you up pretty well, dorkus. Now, back to what to tell your sweetums . . . this ain't the place to lie, either. I'd be real honest here. Ya wanna leave something behind they'll think about all the time."

"It's hard to associate good memories and pleasantries with death, Tripsy."

"You're right. Maybe we should just say piss on it and wait 'til next week."

"What's next week?"

"What to really tell your 'rents. Stay tuned. . . ."

"Did you do any reading over the weekend?"

That one stopped her cold, paused for a good ten seconds, then: "Yeah, this great story about a little kid who gets bossed around by his dad all the time. And all he wants to do is kick the old man's ass."

"There must be more to this little kid than that." Did I sound disappointed? Maybe she didn't get it? Something told me she was just being coy. The truth would emerge another time.

"Maybe. Sounds to me like he was really weak minded, couldn't stick up for himself."

"So who should care for those who can't care for themselves, Tripsy?"

Silence again. She fidgeted some, stroked her hair. "His 'rents shoulda done something! Assholes."

"What if his parents were the root of it all? Especially the male figure in his house?"

"Why didn't the little boy kill himself then?"

"In spite of his lot, he was always optimistic about the future, which is where he spent most of his time."

"Doing what?"

"Getting lost in it."

She sat next to me. "What happened to this little boy?"

A hint of smile on my face, which I intentionally directed to the floor. For dramatic effect, of course. "I guess you'll have to stay tuned." Raised my eyes to meet hers.

"What I say is diff from what you say, dorkus! What you're tellin' me now is like mixin' apples and—"

"Oranges, I know," I interjected, thinking I knew exactly where she was coming from.

"Forget oranges and piss on you, dorkus." She was standing at the door before I could open my mouth to say something else as equally clever.

"More like jalapeños," she added. And, in a flash, she was off. . . .

8

The Famous Political Statement

How many more martyrs do we need on this planet? A thousand years ago, history recorded very few people who willingly gave their lives for a cause. Any cause. When people went to war, it was to kill the enemy, and hopefully not lose their precious lives during the process. It took significant brainwashing of populations with clever and deceptive propaganda to convince people to kill themselves for a cause. Sadly, that same brainwashing goes on to this very day. . . .

Ten years after the Summer of Love fizzled out, I fled the pretentious shoppers and wannabe gawkers of Worth Avenue to spend summers in Europe, where the biggest threat wasn't that the Soviets would send a dozen heavily armed divisions of well-trained soldiers over that imaginary line somewhere between eastern and western Europe. It was the irrational thought of sitting outside some quaint café in Paris in one moment of bliss, then suddenly being blown into a pink cloud by a member of some overzealous anti-Everything gang.

Nowadays, this irrational thought is a common occurrence, especially in the Middle East and a few lawless dictatorships in the lower Americas. While religious fanatics appear more the rule than the exception, the end result of their handiwork always has a political bent, even though martyrs wish for a divine outcome with so many virgins. This seemingly double-edged sword produces the same result as I saw in the '70s: fear. Perhaps worst of all is that terrorism requires so little funding to pull off a horrendous act.

It costs less than $25 to make a nice big IED that goes BOOM! All you need add is one madrassa grad with a low double-digit IQ, who majored in Terrorism Against the West 101, and who has but one life to give for Allah. Or is it Mohammed?

I'm with you: thank goodness it's only one life to give. . . .

The internet and worldwide web have virtually closed the gaps among most places on the globe, except the Congo, delivering terrorist propaganda from one little room in downtown Baghdad to millions of kids' computer screens across the world. This simple coalescing of like-minded idiots draws many non-thinking fanatics to regions of terrorist activities, making it easy to recruit would-be bombers and snipers and other fools who generally raise hell in the name of some god simply because some seemingly illiterate, yet very passionate, mullah rewrote passages in the *Koran* in his own ghastly image.

Point is, Tripsy brought up so many possibilities for making her political statements that I had to stop doodling and take notes like a real shrink—uh, I mean, psychiatrist. While I secretly consider myself a deep thinker on many levels, I hadn't considered how a young girl might conjure up reasons to kill herself in the name of some political cause. American girls just don't do this. The ones who fall in the middle of The Great Bell Curve are the so-called average girls who wake up more or less on time each school day, more or less mind their parents, more or less watch way too much tv, carry an iPad instead of books, think more about cute boys with tight butts than chemistry or English literature, talk incessantly on their iPhones, make amateur sex videos with their boyfriends, among various other more-or-less teen duties.

Did you see anything in the above description about plotting terrorist acts?

Neither did I.

Which is how I was so shocked to hear of Tripsy's elaborate plans to kill herself to make a political statement. I've mentioned this on more than one occasion: Tripsy's IQ (should be labeled *Indigo Quotient*) resides far to the right of The Great Bell Curve, beyond nearly all others of our species. While her peers are rushing to watch the latest episode of *Pretty Little Liars*, she sits under a tree in the park at night and, flashlight in hand, reads Kierkegaard. And the occasional graphic novel. They used to call the latter comic books, mind you. Now they're more sophisticated. And some are even considered literature, if you wish to believe that, and Tripsy devoured them in one sitting.

Ah, I get so far off track these days, thinking about Tripsy and her various intriguing points of view. I often wonder if I should hire her as a consultant and have her present during some of my sessions with other troubled girls, especially Tyra, who is now doing remarkably better. She now speaks in short sentences, all beginning with "Tripsy." I wanted you to hear the good news.

Where was I? While I'm reasonably well trained in the neural and behavioral sciences, Tripsy is trained in something far more valuable: everyday teenage life. And her take on it is unique, to be sure, because of her *Indigo* chemistry.

This is not to say I'm not good at what I do; sometimes I am, even though I admit to a nagging, deep-seated insecurity that isn't likely to dissipate anytime soon. Anyway, I'm certainly not one to over-prescribe any type of medication, even though I freely admitted to being lazy in my approach to treating suicides. It's just that this young girl seems to have the wisdom of an age-old soul who has seen it all and made some good sense of it. Someone whose neural wiring is such that she just gets it. I wish I were of the same cloth. Wait a minute: if I know she gets it, then doesn't that mean I get it, too?

Back to suicide and the political statement. What's tragic is that not a single suicide for politics changes anything. Anything. If these people would actually consult a scholarly treatise on the subject, they may think twice about giving their lives for some political cause. Okay, the religious fanatics probably would do it anyway.

What their public suicide does is scare the heck out of a few local people for a few days, until the next great headline comes along and tops theirs. Poof! One day they're big news; the next, they're an insignificant link on someone's blog, if even that.

The lingering sorrow of their families is perhaps one of the most devastating consequences. And it's a wound that never really heals: the death of a child by suicide. I get calls each month from parents who are still grieving over the loss of their lovely child. They have yet to let go. And they never really do . . . until their own death.

Was I going somewhere with this? Ah, yes. My point is that killing yourself to make a political statement is a waste of flesh and energy. I think Tripsy paints a better picture of it than I do. I'm sure you'll concur, because none of you are running red lights and speeding down to my office, begging me to continue.

Session #48

"Make a political statement!"

"You're kidding me, right?" I said, standing next to the couch, holding the blanket out for her.

She yanked it from me, plopped down, lit up a hooter.

I looked up in the direction of each hidden video camera, shrugging my shoulders, mumbling, "Don't blame me, I'm not in charge here."

"I'm not sure I follow, Tripsy."

She blew out a huge python, sent it my way. "I'll use small words: everything we do could be thought of as a political game, even on a tiny scale. Politics is all about interrelationships and manipulating those involved to get what you want. It ain't necessarily about government."

I raised my eyebrows, smirked a bit. "A bit simplistic, but yes." Actually, she was spot on. After Kierkegaard, sounds like she devoured Machiavelli's *The Prince*.

"Don't you see? Everything we do is about getting what we want, dorkus. Duh. And how do we get what we want? We manipulate someone else to give it to us. Even if I ask my mom for ten bucks to see a movie, I have to snuggle up to her like I'm her stupid poodle and practically beg for it."

"When you want your ten dollars," I added quickly.

"Just so you know, dorkus, I'd kiss her fat tush for twenty."

"And for a hundred?" I secretly wished she'd put out that hooter. What if Mary or one of my other staff came in? Mary had been giving me funny looks lately, either because she too was stoned or she was letting me know she knew. What was I worried about? It was actually legal within the confines of my practice. Anyway, I hate it when my staff knows stuff and casually drops an innuendo, that mutual knowledge, you know. Maybe I should talk to them and clue them in about my new technique for treating patients.

"Hell, I'd kill the next-door neighbor's kid and all his gerbils."

"That's a bit over the top." I finally took my seat in the chair next to her.

"You're missing the point!" Flicked the ashes on my dear floor.

At first, I was mortified, until I saw the pattern developing on the tiles: her ashes sprinkled down unevenly like gray and black snowflakes over a section of pu'er-stained tiles. The rendering reminded me of a field of wheat, waving violently under a summer tornado, dirt and debris scattered as far as my mind's eye could see. The only thing I could think of was to run for cover and hope that tornado didn't suck me up and deposit me in little pieces somewhere over Nebraska. . . .

"Did you hear what I just said, dorkus!?" She flicked the lit hooter my way.

It bounced off my forehead, bright red and orange fireworks bursting in front of my eyes. On impact, I was still staring at the image on the tiles: the tornado dissolved and was quickly replaced by a volcano erupting. My goodness, this would surely require considerable analysis and careful interpretation this evening. I'd never get to sleep.

I looked up at her. "Yes, I heard you, Tripsy! You almost burned my head!" In one motion, I'd gotten a moist cloth from the sink and dabbed my forehead, more for effect. Truth? It didn't hurt at all, but she scared the heck out of me.

"I get it, I understand it, and I agree with you. Yes, it's conceivable that everything we do is political. I'd even say we have it written in our genes. The natural pressures on humans to cooperate with others to get what they want probably didn't have the term politics in mind when they evolved." Wiped my head again, this time moaning a little. Hey, it complemented the theatrics, hers and mine.

"Ahhhh, I was hoping you'd say something like that, grasshoppa!"

"Why?"

"Because it paves the way for my argument about killing myself for some political cause."

"Geezus."

"Do you now get my point?"

"Yes, as I said before. So why don't you elaborate on this political cause. I presume it's only one, yes? And don't ever do that again. It's very dangerous and disrespectful. Anyway, about this single political cause of yours."

"Does it have to be only one?"

"Are you a fanatic for more than one cause?"

"Could be. I'm passionate about a lot of things. You should know that by now, dorkus."

"I do. It's impressive. It's just that when some young person finds a cause that appeals to them, they jump into it with all they have. I can't imagine someone doing that with more than one cause. After all, you can only die once."

"You need to sit back and take a listen, schoolboy. Dig this: the sole reason for my killing myself for some political cause is to get someone's attention. Could be the 'rents, my neighbors, people in this town of soft bananas, or that idiot in the White House. Could also be other people or organizations, especially some big corporation or religion. If I wanna wake up my 'rents, I could do something local like go up to the Santa Barbara Courthouse tower, light myself up with unleaded, and then do a flaming somersault onto the gardens below."

"You might get a front-pager with the local press."

"I know. Big deal. That's my point: small statements call for small suicides. Hell, I'd rather bring attention to all our soldiers who're dying for nothing in Afghanistan and Syria. I mean, they're getting blown up every week, seems like! And for what?" She looked out the window behind her, moved to it. "Look, dorkus, it's really cool outside. Let's go out." Without waiting for me to respond, she was off.

I did the only thing I could do: sighed, put on a jacket and followed her.

Before we even sat down, I said, "So how would you raise someone's awareness? After all, most people love their small lives: hot coffee and reality tv in the morning, yoga, dinner and reality tv to wind down the evening. Anything outside that little sphere doesn't even put a dent in their bubble."

She turned around as she walked onto the lawn. "If some cute-ass chick like me'uns walked completely nude in the middle of Ragheadville or Goatfuckistan, then shot up like a Roman candle, I think I'd raise a little awareness."

I cleaned both chairs, put towels on the seats. "You'd raise holy hell and blood pressure in Islam is what you'd raise, Tripsy. You'd probably be shot for not wearing a burkha, then they'd stone you to death for not being castrated. And after that, they'd lop off your pretty head for stealing their headline that day. You'd be screaming for your life, rather than yelling out your dying political statement."

"Stop being a realist, will you, goober?" Smoked her hooter, looked up at the tree.

"I call them like I see them, Tripsy."

"Put on a new pair of glasses. Don't comment on that, either. Just shut up and listen. I'd love to show the world how loopy it is to send out a bunch of great American guys my age to walk around a desert in heavy gear and carry weapons made by the lowest bidder, all to teach these people some kinda democracy. Gimme a break. Even dumbass me knows you can't just force a new ideal on people who've grown up differently for thousands of years, and who've known nothing but killing neighbors in the name of some dead religious dude. You're about to say something. Shut up."

I obeyed, of course.

"Like I was sayin', I'd love to show everyone how dumb this is by first callin' all the media about my impending doom, without givin' up the exact site. Then I'd fly over there to Dubai, take a cab to Iraq, find the most public place in the desert, and do myself. All on a hundred different cameras. And, no, the Army wouldn't arrest me and ship me home. I'd really pull this off, doofus. Really. I think it's a cool way to off myself, plus I become a martyr for my own cause, the very same cause that all these lazy Americans should be takin' up and aren't 'cos they're too busy hittin' each other up for easy sex. Pisses me off we do that, too. I mean, fu-fu-fu-fuuuuu! You see why I'm so mad, don't you?"

"Yes. I just don't understand it all. You seem to be mad about

everyone and everything. You certainly don't discriminate, Tripsy. I'll give
you that."

"You don't have to understand right now. It'll come to you. Someday.
I hope." She looked up and blew a bolus of smoke into the tree, making
the birds tweet off key.

I listened intently as the stoney birds belted out a new song. I actually
liked those new crazy harmonics, I did. "Right. I guess you know all the
criteria for a successful political statement?"

"Lemme see: it's gotta be seen by a lotta people at once . . . it's gotta
be visually stunning and memorable . . . gotta be sticky—"

"Sticky?"

"Gotta stick in people's minds, dorkus."

"Got it."

"So, gotta be sticky . . . gotta have some duration so it doesn't lose
balance to the next up-and-coming headline . . . and it's gotta force
people to think about the meaning behind the actual act."

"Moly hoses. People aren't thinkers like you, Tripsy."

"I shock you sometimes, don't I, dorkus?"

"You . . . give me pause, Miss South. Let's just say that, okay?"

"Sometimes you say the sweetest things, dorkus. Most of the time,
though, you're an uptight dorkus who thinks he actually understands

girls like me. You're more dangerous than I am."

"Some part of me feels you're right, Tripsy. We all evolve in our own ways." Sometimes, I wish I could wring her beautiful neck. Yes, indeed.

"You're not tellin' me you're actually evolving, are you?"

"Maybe."

"I may stick around for another year if that were true, dorkus, or come back as a tall, gorgeous, thirty-six-year-old hottie with a PhD in Psychology, someone who can figure you out and put you back together. Course, there'd pro'ly be some leftover parts."

My smile said it all: this kid was funny at times. When she wasn't being a brat. "Why thirty-six?"

"You need someone your age, but a little younger, dorkus. Shut up and relax. Besides, my time on this planet's almost up."

"When you first walked into my office, you stated clearly that you only had one year left in you. I was . . . deeply concerned."

"You were strangely attracted to me, as most males are."

"Not every man sees you as a prospective lover, Tripsy. I think you fail to recognize how much I devote to helping patients. I don't sleep with them, even though some of them happen to be beautiful young girls who are extremely vulnerable to external stimulation. I purposefully do not engage in lascivious behavior with my patients. Something tells me you know this." I paused a moment, then: "And I do admonish myself for allowing you to smoke in my office, even though it is legal inside my practice and under my supervision."

"Yeah, shame on you, doc." Lit up another hooter, took a looooong drag, blew it up into the tree again. The little birds came down a few branches to inspect the source of their sudden euphoria.

Who said birds have little bird-brains?

"I hit a nerve, I see, dorkus."

"No, you shocked my whole CNS. Forget a nerve, young lady. Yes, I was offended by your remark. We've been meeting for, what, almost an entire year?"

She looked away, hurt. "I guess."

"You think you know me, Tripsy? You don't, although you do make me think differently about various situations we discuss. Thing is, you seem to always want to gore me with both horns."

Still not looking at me: "Just keeping you awake, Freud." Several of the birds fluttered down to her, perched on her shoulders, chirping away.

I looked on, surprised. "Believe me, Tripsy, I've never been more awake."

"About this political statement thingee?"

"Fire away," I said, knowing both horns were being racked onto their missile rails, ready for combat.

"All things considered, it's probably the best way to off myself. I'd not only be doing what's best for me at the time, I'd be raising awareness about a cause I'm passionate about."

She pulled out a cracker from her bag, held it to the little birds. "I'm severely pissed about runaway immigration in this country. Here's what's gonna happen: when you call some company, any company, you're gonna get, 'For English, please press one . . . for Español, please press two . . . and for Chinese, please press three, four, five, six, seven, eight or nine.' "

And here I thought they were launching an all-out attack in 2047.

"I'm really pissed about that, but I'm most passionate about females being mistreated by men across the globe. It's a pandemic."

"Didn't know a seventeen year old understood what that really was, a pandemic." Wrong thing to say. Again.

"Hey, dorkus, I'm not just a pretty face, you know?"

"I understood that the moment you walked in here twelve months ago, Tripsy."

"It helps that your behaviors reflect what you say, Dr. Moore."

I was still staring at her, as she fed her entourage of very happy tweets. "That's one of the very few times you've called me that." My face blank, it spilled out absently.

"Your ego gets in the way a lot. Shut up and listen . . . I'd deploy all my resources to inflict the greatest damage here. I know how to do it, where to go, who to call, when to do it, and how it will turn out. Period. It'd be a long-lasting sting to many people. Something that'd give them more than pause, as you've said."

"Not what I was talking about—"

She waved her hand dismissively: "I'd give 'em a means to change their thoughts and behaviors, 'cos that's what it takes sometimes, a shock to the system that forces people to shift their thinking, their way of life. It'd be a revolution. And, as you know, dorkus, revolutions are dreamed up and planned not by men, but by women."

"I'd heard that one before."

She perked up. "What'd you think?"

"Well, I didn't actually research each and every war, every revolution, but I saw anecdotally that there were women who were deeply involved behind the scenes."

"Behind the scenes. Do you realize, dorkus, that most of the action happens behind the scenes? And men have little or nothing to do with it? How ironic that it's the men who then flip on the very women who dreamed up their whole revolution, and then persecute them. Baffles me, dude."

She inhaled a lungful of hooter, then blew it out slowly all around her, moving her head side to side, up and down. The entire living contents of the tree, and a few neighboring ones, were descending on her.

"I can appreciate it."

"Why do you think that is?"

"Evolutionarily speaking, men are the worker bees. They do the bidding of the queen bee. And sometimes their chemistry changes for the worse and they kill the queen, then later find a new one to lead them. If not, they all die."

"No kiddin'. It's always a female that drives evolution. People say that males and testosterone drive evolution by sheer aggressiveness, but it's really estrogen and progesterone that conjure up these ideas and formulate the means to carry them out. Estrogen's the engine; testosterone's only one of the fuels. Thank goodness we girls also run on unleaded, diesel and rocket fuel."

"Again, I can appreciate that."

"You're backpedallin', dorkus. You truly have no idea what drives change, do you?"

"Evidently not." The wind shifted and wafted her smoke into my face. Mmm-mmm.

"Keep something in mind, dorkus: Pussy drives evolution."

Had to turn away from her, stop and think about that one for a minute, I must admit.

"That's why my killing myself would raise such awareness, regardless of the political cause. When some guy offs himself, no one bats a lash; they just dig another grave. When a female dies, people stop and ask why. It's mandated somewhere in our faded genes that people shalt feel shitty when a girl dies. Period. 'Nuf said about that one. And don't try to rationalize it all, either, 'cos I'll chop off Mr. C.O. Jones."

"C.O. Jones? Who's he?" I felt dumb for not knowing this one.

"Cojones. Bollocks. Stones. Balls. Nuts. Testicles!" She pulled out something from her purse.

"What're those?" I asked, feeling a little euphoric, not unlike those tweets, now buzzing around us like flies.

"These? They're my little baby-blue bullets. Earplugs. I'm tunin' you out."

I looked down at my watch, frowned. "We still have twenty-four minutes."

"I have a month. Right now, I'm gonna listen to my own breath leave my body, one molecule at a time."

"And I suppose that thing there—"

"Eye shades. For the next . . ." Checked her watch. "Twenty-three minutes, I don't wanna see you or hear you. Wake me when we're done."

The birds looked a lot more loopy now, trying desperately to maintain their perch atop her shoulders, on her legs, around her feet. One on her head fell to the grass, peeping something unintelligible. Several others followed, stoned on Tripsy's wicked weed.

If I stayed in my seat, I knew I would surely follow, so I walked back to my office and fell fast asleep on my couch.

Going to Hell

My idea of heaven and hell is simple: they exist only as constructs in the minds of humans. They were conjured up by controlling people to keep us in line. Not unlike God, that fictional character invented by certain grownups as an imaginary friend who will be there when things become impossible for us lowly humans. And Satan? He's the character who prevents our doing evil to one another. Or maybe the guy who instigates evil deeds.

Oh, boy.

Tripsy put forth the ideas of heaven and hell as if they were real entities. While I disagreed with her approach, I did go along with how she preached about the possibility of such heavenly or hellish regions that drove people to do different actions. She felt that the very thought of there being heaven gave the majority of people hope, something good beyond the randomness and disappointment of reality.

Her notion of hell was reality itself.

Part of me agrees, although I try to see the goodness in all things, especially in reality. You'll need to read deep between the lines to get that one.

The brevity of my introduction to this chapter reflects not my laziness as a compiler of these sessions, or as a psychiatrist, but my true thoughts about heaven and hell.

Let's just listen to Tripsy's viewpoint. When we're done, I'd like to hear your thoughts on the subject. Thank you in advance. . . .

Session #49

I watched her saunter in from the street, a casual look on her face, as if proclaiming: What, me a suicidal kid? I'm more normal than all you normals.

"No screaming entrance? If it's strep throat, don't even breathe in here." I think I was smiling.

She swept past me. "I kinda dig hell."

"Good way to start a meeting."

"Jeeez, dorkus. All I said was, I like hell." Dropped her bag on the floor, fell on the couch in a perfect recline, gathered her pillows.

"So reality is the real hell for you?" I took my seat behind my desk.

"Everything's an illusion. My eyes see only what they're programmed to see, with filters that take in visible light. I wish I could see in the infrared part."

"You'd like to see into the darkness?"

Rolled over on her side, faced me. "The abyss isn't so bad, you know? If you stare long enough into it, you begin to see strange patterns of light dance all over the place like a violet aurora."

"Borealis?"

"Is there another aurora out there, dorkus?"

"There are many, Tripsy."

"Coupla years back I was checkin' out the radio and heard this caller, some young chick asked the dumbest question I'd ever heard: 'Who the hell's aurora borealis anyway?' Clearly a product of the California public school system."

"Don't tell me: you called in and gave her both horns."

She rolled back over, closed her eyes. "Nope. Just walked back to my room and lit up a hooter." Absently pulled out a hooter. . . .

"Do you have to light another one of those things?" Actually, I was looking forward to it, something to numb my thoughts about her leaving soon. Leaving. I was still in a quandary about that term, leaving. What did it really mean?

Lit it, exhaled in my direction. "C'mon, doc, I thought you were getting used to my hooters."

"I wasn't—"

"Shut up. 'Sides, Mary Jane slows my thinking down to a soft roar."

I peeped an eye open. "You have sensory overload, you're anxious about everything."

"Lemme finish my story, dorkus."

"I'm sorry, ma'am." I sat back, put my hands behind my head.

"Don't be. Just shut up and get me some tea and cookies. Where was I? The abyss. The eyes always like some kinda input from the so-called real world. When we're asleep, those jelly marbles rock back and forth, trying to wake you up. Annoying, aren't they? Like they got a mind o' their own. In fact, they do. When you ignore 'em long enough, they make stuff up. I stare into darkness for about thirty minutes, and allow my eyes to adjust to it, then the purple aurora appears. At first, it floats around in front of me slowly, changing shape like the clouds do on windy days. If you see a cool pattern up there in the sky, you lose it with the next blink. That kinda thing. Can never pin down one real image like a snapshot, 'cos there's always a newer and more beautiful one the next second. I just look and look, without really moving my eyes around. The images then dance faster and change shapes more and more until real images start to appear. Stuff I'm familiar with. It's like my eyes have tested me to see if I'm paying attention, and after an hour of this nonsense, they give me the real show."

"A show? Of what?" I sat up a little straighter now, more interested.

"Reality. The future, I think. Hell, I dunno. I forgot what this session was about."

"Hell. Suicide. You seem subdued today, Tripsy."

"Just a few weeks left in me."

"I still don't get that. Maybe I should check you in to the hospital for thirty days of observation, plus suicide watch." Something deep inside me screamed for me not even to consider that alternative. And I wondered why.

Rolled her eyes at that one. "Soooo, about the thing called hell. And where are my milk and cookies?"

"Hey, I thought you ordered tea?" I hopped up like an eager schoolboy and poured tea for both of us, got a bowl of cookies for Tripsy, handed them to her.

"Thank you . . . I'm a woman. I reserve the right to change my mind at any moment. Just think of me as frogleg-eatin' French poodle with a huge bank account. You're a man. You have no rights, so just do as I tell you and get me my rum and Coke."

"Uh, we have a rule about alcohol here."

"Uhhhh, you mean a rule like the one about Mary Jane? I bent that one into a pretzel on Day One, so just get me a piña colada, and go light on the colada.

"Technically, marijuana is legal in my office, as I got you that medical marijuana card, remember?" I ignored the request, sat down again, sipped my tea.

"Yeah yeah yeah. Meantime, I'll tell ya all about hell. We're all just these little sacks of about a thousand different chemicals that bang into each other every few nanoseconds, like you've told me on more than one occasion. I'm amazed more stuff doesn't go wrong with us every day. Billions of reactions all go right. How can people say that some dude called God made all this up? I could see it if God were a woman, but crikey, a guy invented all that? No way. Anyway, all this chemistry makes us who we are. Just a few reactions short and you're an alcoholic. A few more and you're a beauty queen. Too much o' this, you write symphonies. Too little o' that, you're a prisoner in your own body, doomed to schiz all your life. Gotta cold? Pop some echinacea and vitamin C. See? It's all chemistry! Dayum, how come people can't get that? Idiot shrinks like you tell us behaviors are independent events, and can be cured with therapy. Maybe so. Behavioral modification changes chemistry. Maybe even anatomy in the brain somewhere."

"You've read this?" I walked over to the club chair next to the couch, sat down, took one of her cookies. Mmm-mmm, what kind of cookies were those? I made a mental note to have Mary buy some more.

"Like I said, I got it from you, mostly. I'm a lazy girl, dorkus. All I do is look at the results all around me: chemicals change our behaviors. End of discussion."

"I wish it were that simple, Tripsy." Yum. Did Mary accidentally give me pot cookies?

"C'mon, dorkus, this is your idea. The only things we don't know yet are exactly how chemistry changes our behaviors. Mark my words, dude: in a hundred years, science'll uncover these mysteries. In fact, you'll probably be assigned these ID cards that have all your chemistry and behaviors listed like on the back of a Betty Crocker cake-mix box."

"Human behavior, demystified." Got up and poured myself more tea.

She must have recalled something I said in one of our sessions, because those sentiments are distinctly my own, right down to the prediction of the future in fifty or a hundred years.

"Yuuuuuup."

"You sound wise and all-knowing, well beyond your years, Tripsy."

"Some people grow up fast, learn a lot, then flame out early. Shut up and lemme talk. I've seen all these lousy behaviors, especially with men, that are killin' us all. If women weren't around, the world'd be a giant hole. I mean, you guys love to shoot each other and blow stuff up. Not a day goes by without some dude loppin' off another dude's head, or blowin' up a bunch o' innocent people. We dump this stuff in all the water sources we have. It's no wonder the fish're tryin' to crawl up onto land again, so they can kick some ass. 'Magine that: walkin' out to your car and havin' to dodge land sharks. This place is so messed up right now, it's no wonder it resembles all ideas about hell. It is hell. Did evolution do that to us? I don't think so. When I stay with my friends' families, I see everyone laughin' and smilin' and havin' a good time. When the number of buttheads gets past five, then stupid stuff starts to happen. Group chemistry brings out the weenies who want all the power, all the money, and all us cute-ass girls with tight pussies who say yes to everything. That's a by-product of human behaviors, all that group behavior that leads to no good. If we were actually thinkers who wanted to save our human existence, wanted to evolve into higher bein's, we'd outlaw any group, company or corporation over five people."

I shifted uncomfortably in my chair. "I'm not sure the Defense Department would go along with your proposal."

She glanced at me, smirked. "Anyone who shows any signs of power-mongerin', castrate 'im and send 'im to the boys choir."

"So this is all hell? Worth dying for?"

"Certainly not worth livin' for. I don't think I'd even tell anyone or try to broadcast it. I'd just walk off a high mountain cliff at midnight."

"Into that deep, dark abyss?"

She got up, walked around the office, stared absently at all the books. "It calls to me, dorkus. It calls to me and says: I got somethin' better down here than what you got up there, honey."

"You'd rather not make an attempt to change the world? You'd rather kill yourself and leave us behind to fend for ourselves?"

"What's one less chick in a world where men don't listen anyway? 'Sides, I'm only worth as much as men want to imagine."

"That statement bears further thought, Tripsy, Why don't we—"

Walked in front of me, faced me directly: "Know somethin'? I should off myself and not have to listen to your nonsense anymore. Hell, yeah. Way I see it, this is the Golden Age of Civilization, dorkus. Enjoy it while you can, 'cos unless there's a quantum leap in technology that lifts us stupid-ass humans outta this hell, we're doomed."

At this point, I was trying to recall how I previously had been so impressed with this young woman. "How long do you give us?"

Just smiled at me, reached out as if to tousle my hair, pulled her hand back. "Seventy-five, a hundred years, max."

"Where'd you read that? Why don't you sit down, Tripsy?"

She moved back to the floor, stretched out. "You must think I'm a real non-thinker, huh?"

"I didn't say that. I just—"

"You just . . . think of me like all men do. I saw you checkin' me out back there. Duh. Like I said, I'm a lazy girl. All I do is look around me at what's goin' on. Oil's not runnin' out but they tell us it is; what a lie. We've built an entire civilization around oil. Every damn thing is made up of it, runs on it, needs it to survive. Man has built a whole business model on a product they tell us is nonrenewable. What happens when that product is withheld by those in power? The world model collapses."

"I agree."

"Soooo, dorkus, hell is only gonna get worse for those who stick around longer'n fifty or so years. It already has. I'm no statistics guru, but I get numbers. And the numbers tell me crap is happenin' now all over.

You know what drives the atmosphere?"

"I don't understand the question."

"The atmosphere has an engine. Differences in temperature and molecules drive it. It's what moves the oceans, the winds, starts hurricanes and cyclones and other nasties."

"I think it's a little more complicated than that, Tripsy." I sat back down in the club chair, reached out for another delicious cookie.

She handed me the bowl. "Maybe. But when you change the temperature drastically, like we're doin' by shootin' CO_2 into the sky, let's say, some of those temperature-driven things break down. It won't take much to change ocean currents. That happens and the northern hemisphere chills like a freezer. No more headin' south for the winter, 'cos the south'll be deep into a winter of its own. Like I said, unless there's some quantum leap in technology, or we stop what we're doin' cold turkey, crap will roll downhill fast. That, my Dr. Dorkus, is hell to me."

"So you'd just kill yourself and expect to go to . . . where?" Mary definitely dropped in a few buds in these cookies. Wow!

"If there really is an afterlife, I guess I'd stay in hell. Who gives a flip anyway? I was born and raised in hell, spent seventeen years there, vacationed there, lost my cherry there. Why would I wanna be anywhere else? Hell's all I know."

"I don't know if this is a good time to ask, but where did the name Tripsy come from?"

"The things you shrinks think about. My great-great grandmother was a full-blooded Cherokee squaw. Her name was Trip-something. I added the 's' and 'y.' "

She finished off the cookies, handed me the bowl, got up and gathered her things. "Better watch the sarcasm, dorkus, I was nursed on hot peppers, and I'm a mean thing when aroused."

Don't engage her on that one, Dr. Moore! "So that's all there is to know about hell?"

Feeling my challenge, she stopped at the door, turned around. "For kids in the middle of a crisis like mine, Dr. Moore, life is hell. Everything is hell. I could talk to you all day about my life and the reality all around me. And it would seem redundant as hell. Pun intended! But I have a better plan!" With that, she sprinted off. . . .

Looked up at this obscure passage I'd framed and placed on a shelf, a small reminder of what to do in situations like this one.

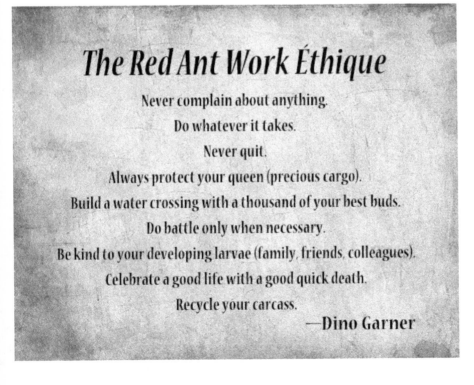

The Red Ant Work Éthique

Never complain about anything.

Do whatever it takes.

Never quit.

Always protect your queen (precious cargo).

Build a water crossing with a thousand of your best buds.

Do battle only when necessary.

Be kind to your developing larvae (family, friends, colleagues).

Celebrate a good life with a good quick death.

Recycle your carcass.

—Dino Garner

Heaven

Tripsy redefined hell pretty well, far better than I ever wanted to. While her explanations seemed simplistic at first glance, they had a certain weight to them. A person's lot in life, their place, is defined by them and them alone. She was right: she had been born and raised into what she called a living hell. The most difficult part was that she felt she belonged there. I hoped that was an inaccurate interpretation on my part.

The biggest part of me wanted to see her climb out and find a new place for herself. Some people just can't be helped, though, even if we fill them to the eyeballs with chemicals from BigPharma and chain them to the floor. . . .

Was I giving up on her? After all, she had shaped and encouraged me to conduct the most unconventional therapy—if you wish to call it that—I've ever used with a suicide patient. So far, I'd been flying blind, with a great part of me wishing to medicate and hospitalize her long term. Another part of me, that nagging little voice waaay up and back in the attic of my subconscious, ordered me to maintain course. What's the worst that could happen? Simple: she kills herself and I go to prison on numerous charges, including professional negligence.

Here's something else: I had a dream last night about my being in a car with Tripsy and we were driving on a one-lane bridge over an impossibly deep abyss . . . in the dark. The only lights anywhere came from my little car. I had three choices: go forward, fall off and die, or do nothing. When I analyzed it this morning, I used my inner six year old to interpret it. He said that Tripsy's presence meant that I felt responsible for her. Being on a one-lane bridge meant I felt obligated to continue on a very narrow and prescribed path. Having no other paths to take meant I confined myself to only one choice: moving forward along that one path. Being over a deep abyss meant that I was deathly afraid of anything other than that one, narrow path.

I do apologize for writing such a short chapter, but I feel I have finally run out of relevant comments. As I approach the one-year anniversary of Tripsy's first barging into my office and upending my dull, boring and listless life, I feel a tinge of sadness, and I'm winding down to. . . .

In times like these, when I feel totally lost and without a compass, much less an azimuth to follow, I think about the young lives that are no longer, those who left us far too early.

Here I am, reasonably educated, even in my own profession, and I can't interpret the words and behaviors of a tortured child. I find myself wishing for a hundred years to go by, so I can look inside this young woman's brain, discover accurately what ails her, and cure her with some kind of futuristic pill-treatment, something that reverses the bad chemistry and makes her the healthy . . . kind . . . decent . . . intelligent . . . thinking young woman she was born to be.

And when I wrote those words, "born to be," I struggled with the realization that some of us simply are born with a certain chemistry that predisposes us to the greatest of happiness . . . or the deepest abyss in hell.

"All that college and no knowledge" is a rebuke I earned in my late teens when I worked at a moving company instead of taking a school internship with a shrink-friend of my father's—just to piss him off. I honestly thought I knew it all, would show those rednecks a thing or two about how to load a truck, and sometimes made my thoughts known to the driver of our van.

One day they stood back and let me do it my way. One mile into our trip, the contents of the moving van shifted dangerously, and caused the van to swerve to the left, cutting off a Cadillac in the next lane and nearly causing an accident.

The driver of our van was actually cool about it all, given I thought he was going to drag me out and beat me senseless. He was clearly fuming, but he took a deep breath, maybe a few minutes' worth of heavy Florida air, and told me, calmly, "All that college and no knowledge'll get you or someone else killed someday. If I's you, I'd shut up and pay more attention to guys who know what they're doin'."

Then he turned around and repacked the van, and afterward approached me and added, "You was right about packin', son. Damned good job. Thing is, you left out one little detail: the last tie-down strap." He held it up to my face.

Where the blazes was I going with that one? You're smarter than I am, so you figure it out.

Session #50

"On second thought, I'd like to see what heaven's like," she said, standing at my door, licking a popsicle.

"I thought you were resigned to staying on earth, so no suicide, Tripsy? What flavor?"

"Orange-banana. Still, dorkus, I've always wondered what it'd be like to see this place everyone's been ravin' about for two thousand years. And that brings up a good point: has heaven only been around for two grand?"

She leaned against the doorway, downing the rest of the popsicle, then came in.

"If not, how is it that Neanderthals and Homo you-know-whats never mentioned the place? I mean, look at the 20,000-year-old artwork from Central Asia: not a damn thing about this heaven. It's all about music, dude!"

"You're talking over my head now, Tripsy. I don't know a thing about Asia." Except that I breathed in their dust every day.

"Sure you do, Dr. Moore: you said Asian dust falls all over Santa Barbara, right?"

"That's about the extent of my knowledge of Asia, I'm afraid . . . anyway, if you kill yourself, won't you be relegated to—"

"If there is a heaven, everyone should be able to go there and get repaired."

After her treatise on hell, I wondered where this would go. "How so?"

"Start over from scratch, make a new me."

"So you think there're no rules to get in?"

"Yeah, right. The most exclusive club on the planet. And they have a one-time, million-dollar membership fee, plus a passport with a special visa only stupid white dudes like you can get. Way I see it, all I do is off myself, grab a one-way ticket to heaven, and play tourist for the rest of my new life. I know what you're thinkin', dorkus: something dumb, so don't even say it. Worst-case scenario: I put a bullet through my brain pan, get cremated, then cuz I killed myself instead of dyin' by 'natural causes,' i.e. other than by my own hand, they gimme a coach-class seat on some junk steered by some blind dude who makes all the wrong turns, runs outta gas and takes a hundred years to get there cuz we all had to get out and push the thing up a tall-ass mountain like Sisyphus. Big deal. Doesn't matter how ya get to the party, long as you show up."

"A hundred years late."

"What difference does it make? In heaven, the keg's always half full. Anyway, you'll be up there makin' me more piña coladas."

"Sorry, water or tea will have to do."

"No biggee. I'll just light another one o' these . . . Mmmm-mmm! So, once I get there, I sit down with one o' Saint Pete's buddies, some gatekeeper who asks me all kindsa stuff and passes me onto the next judge. Long story short: I get in."

"Bravo!" I said, opera-clapping.

"Sekir baschka, dorkus, I was a shoo-in."

"What?"

"Ukranian battle cry, you moron. Means off with your head."

"Oookay, Tripsy, so once you're in, then what?"

"See what grandma's up to."

"You think you'll actually make contact with people you've known?"

"Dude, get this: when you get there, they hand you a little black book with names and addresses of everyone who's there. First thing I do is see the old relatives, pro'ly punch out my grandpa 'cos he messed up so royally with my dad, then go visit Jimi."

"Jimi?"

"Hendrix, you moron. His pic is right on your precious shelf up there! You secretly wanna be Jimi and Brian Johnson, don'tcha, dorkus?"

"No comment."

"Anyway, I'll bet he's got, like, twenty new albums out. Dude's had forty years to jam with Jesus hisself! Think of all the other dudes up there to session with! I mean, he's pro'ly turned Mozart onto acid and Molly and Mary Jane by now! Way cool."

"Your imagination knows no bounds, Tripsy."

"Shut up. I've always wanted to ask Roosevelt if he really knew about Pearl Harbor before the Japanese dropped in and bought all the golf courses and land for hotels."

"And if he did?"

"Methinks he'll get a slappin'. My great-grandfather was at Pearl Harbor. That's where he met my great-grandmother."

"You're going to slap a former president of the United States?"

"Yuuuuuup, even if he is responsible for my greats hookin' up. After he gives me the ditty, then I'll smack 'im around some. Be nice to talk trash with Ghandi and Ghengis Khan, see what the hell they were thinkin' in between all those centuries of war and one week of peace. Nope, make that one week of blast-out partyin'!"

"I can only imagine what you'll do to Mr. Ghengis after he reveals his track record to you."

"Hey, this guy was righteous! See? I could spend a hundred lifetimes up there just having long conversations with cool people who made history, instead of sittin' here on this lame-ass couch, monologuing with a dorkus."

"I must admit, Tripsy, my person pales in comparison to those historical figures. Besides, don't you think there'll be long lines to visit with these people?"

"Tell me something: if George Washington saw me in the nude, walkin' up to the front of the line, you think he'll wanna chat with King George about how poorly Geo treated the colonies, or have a nice sit-down with—"

"He'll either have a myocardial infarc or swallow his teeth."

"See? C'mon. What would you give to have a sit-down with Freud?"

"I'm not going to kill myself to have it, if that's what you mean."

"You're scared of dyin'. I know it, so don't say it. Thing is, I'm not. In fact, I'm lookin' forward to it. Now that I think about it, I'll get me a three-day pass to hell, too, so I can see what Nixon's up to. Bet he's still tryin' to recruit demons to the Republican Party. Who else? Man, there're sooooooo many cool musicians to hook up with! Kurt Cobain, Terry Kath, Jimi, Keith Moon. It's gotta be one big-ass block party every day and night. No need to sleep, so they just party down 24/7."

"You paint an . . . unusual portrait of heaven, Tripsy, especially wanting to see those classic rockers. That's way before your time. Still, I don't think—"

"I'll bet sex is awesome."

"That's something you haven't spoken much about."

"Don't go there. Ain't my thing right now, especially with all this work I gotta do. I already told ya I had a boyfriend once. Like babysittin' a four year old. With a big dick that always pointed north. Jeezus. No diseases in heaven or hell, dorkus! I could, like, go bi and do 'em all!"

"I thought you'd be preoccupied with talking with interesting people."

"Eff that, dude. I'll majorly need some sex."

"You mentioned bisexuality? Is this a norm for you?"

"Think of it! I can do whatever I want, up or down. Take a tram to hell for a few days, see the sights, sex my brains out, then cruise back home for some serious face-time with dignitaries. I . . . am . . . so . . . stoked."

Low whisper: "I . . . am . . . so . . . fucking . . . worried."

She heard that one: "Easy, Doc, the f-word doesn't flow trippingly off

your tongue. I'd stick with fiddlesticks or fudge."

Somewhere along the way, I had grown tired. Not so much of listening to Tripsy rant. My real peeve was how she hit upon so many relevant subjects on teen suicide, things I never considered. I was almost envious. Did she plan this whole event, to "monologue with a dorkus for a year" and then produce something useful? If so, what was it? If you know, please share it with me, because I'm still at a loss here for how to explain a year with this *Indigo Child* of fiery wisdom.

Was it really wisdom or was I just going nuts? Had I descended into my own private state of mental illness? A small contingent of voices in my head begged me not to think so poorly of it all. After all, I was a hero with Little Tyra's parents, who were now conversing with her daily, albeit in very simple language. Tripsy did all the work there with Tyra, but I felt a small part of it. The parents loved me for it, even though I tried to explain to them that their mute daughter was cured by an *Indigo Child* who acts like a schizy, nutty suicide.

Maybe it takes bad chemistry to heal bad chemistry.

Made me wonder how I would end up after Tripsy had departed. In that moment, I wished she would read my diaries. Don't ask why, though. Another irrational thought. . . .

11

What If There Is No Heaven Or Hell?

I must admit that I don't understand The Universe. I did struggle through a quantum mechanics course while in medical school, mostly because the med-school classes were so downright mundane at times and I needed to get off campus.

Don't get me wrong, I loved learning about medicine, but I needed variety outside that medium. I was looking for additional stimulation, something I could bring to medicine, I felt.

Point is, even though I learned a lot about how The Universe works, albeit in strange, cosmological constants and variables, it made me think even deeper about the possibility of there being multiverses and alternate realities and such. I know it sounds off the wall, but what if there really were heaven and hell? What if all those writings about Jesus and God were based solely on truth, something established thousands of years ago? What if. . . .?

My goodness, I can't believe I'm saying this. As I see my own words in print, I sit here, aghast, the closet atheist who thinks he knows everything.

Anyway, and what if there weren't a heaven and hell? What if we just die and turn to dust, replenishing the earth with our "previously owned" molecules?

I was surprised to see Tripsy light up when discussing heaven and hell. Her reaction to their possibly not existing was equally surprising, but I need you to decide for yourself.

Sorry to be so short here, but she's much better at this than I am. I'm sure you agree, since her off-planet wisdom and my sandbox mini-thoughts are often insoluble and most of the time barely miscible. . . .

Session #51

Today was one of those days when one could not possibly remain indoors. I dismissed my staff early—uncharacteristically very early—and strolled outside for my last session of the day, with Tripsy. Since she always arrived at the bus stop across the street, I sat in patient wait, one of those predatorial cats on the African savanna. I know you know I'm far from that image, a predatorial anything, but it sounded cool when I first wrote it, lifted my spirits a bit.

"Limbo: are you kiddin' me!?" she screamed in my ear.

I jumped out of my chair, looking around for the foghorn that just blasted me.

Tripsy deftly descended from the highest reaches of one of the oak trees, under which we have sat during outdoor sessions. I swear that woman looked like Tarzan's sister, loin cloth and all.

Following her down, I yelled, "Where the—!"

She lowered herself from the last branch and took a seat next to me. "When you go, dorkus, you just . . . disappear forever. The only thing left is a memory of you in each person you touched. When I think about it, I haven't touched as many people as I'd hoped. I need to go out and touch many more. Need to be a hyperkinetic multiplexer."

Hyperkinetic multiplexer. Where'd that one come from? "You're only seventeen, Tripsy. You have a lifetime ahead of you," I said, regaining some measure of composure.

"Don't try to talk me outta killin' myself."

"Why would I do that?" Some deep inner voice told me she would never waste her own life. Never. Was I safe in this assertion? Should I medicate her immediately and place her in a hospital for her own well-being? Or mine? 5150 sounded like a good number right about now.

"It's your job."

"My job is to listen. Sometimes there's not a darned thing I can do for people like you." For people like you? And this means what, Dr. Moore? Who on earth was ever like this kid?

"Like me?"

I was backpedaling, as Tripsy would say: "People whose sole wish is to kill themselves."

"It's not my sole wish. I also wish that you'd stop wearin' those dorky ties."

"What about my dorky ties?"

"Oh, never mind. Sooo, what were we chattin' about? Limbo! Okay, I'll buy the possibility that when we kick, we just . . . kick. Nothin' happens after that. Bugs invade me and eat me from inside out, then crap me all over the countryside. Part of me'll become a flower, other parts a grasshopper, some others a new tree. My luck, though, I'll be the anus on some incontinent skunk. Be eatin' and drinkin' skunk juice day and night."

"Guess you'd better touch a few more souls, then. C'mon, Tripsy, you have to. You have this magical touch with people."

"How do you know?"

"I sense it. Plus, I've seen you with Tyra. She talks with her parents now, and it's all your doing."

She stopped at the mention of Little Tyra. "I'm just a kid, dorkus. I haven't lived, like you've said before. And I need to get out in the real world and—"

"Experience it!" I interjected.

She took out her diary, opened it.

"What's that?" At that moment, I felt she was about to reveal the key to Tripsy and what made her tick. I was certain that I could heal her at this very moment, if I could only understand what she entrusted only to her precious diary. It just felt right. Know what I mean?

Holding it up to my face, she said, "This diary belonged to a ten-year-old girl, Constance Templeton. She killed herself in her parent's barn in the dead of winter, in 1799. Hanged herself from the rafters. This is what she left. I've read it a thousand times and I still don't get it."

I knew what she meant. Believe me, I knew. Still, I was in mild shock at hearing about the author of "Tripsy's" diary. My momentum and spirits were now crushed. Again.

"Constance was the smartest person I've never met." Her voice broke and she wiped the tears from her face, looked at me. "Little girl half my age was more articulate than almost anyone I'd ever read before, like she was from some other world or universe. An *Indigo Child*, dorkus. She wrote about the stages of sorrow long before Kübler-Ross did. She wrote stories about her life after death. She wrote long goodbye letters to her parents, her brothers and sisters, her friends, even the guy who owned the feed store down the road."

Indigo Child. "I'm sorry, Tripsy, I always assumed it was yours. Your mom said—"

"The bitch always assumed I was writing in this diary, but I was just tracing the words Constance had written, hoping they'd somehow give me . . . something!" She cried now, not looking up.

Nothing I said would soothe her, I knew, so I tried the dumb

approach: "It's a technique that some writers use: they pick a favorite novel or nonfiction book and rewrite it as if it were their own. Pretty effective, you ask me." I was so full of it. Who cared about this technique right now? Fact is, I didn't know what I was talking about.

Tripsy characteristically ignored me: "I was hoping to understand what she'd written, maybe put it in a book someday. I was hoping you would be able to help me comprehend her pain."

I sighed: "Tripsy, I'm sorry, but I can't. I'm more than happy to take a look at her thoughts, maybe interpret them in my terms. I'm not sure that's what you're looking for." My goodness, I was such an asshole. And I was clueless about how to proceed here. All that college and no knowledge, indeed. . . .

"I'm leaving it with you. Read it, will you?"

I took it in my hands, held it reverently, not knowing what to say. What else was new? Tears flooded my eyes until they became a molten crystal that fell and rolled slowly down my face, hot to the touch, calling to me somehow. Words still wouldn't surface. I had read years ago that tears contained specialized proteins that, when secreted by the glands in the eyes, brought on an amazing sense of relief. I wished desperately to feel this right now, but it never came.

Tripsy reached out and held my hand, then put her head in my hands and cried and cried for long minutes. I don't know, maybe it was an hour. The little birds above us were silent, a sort of honor to the solemn moment in their realm.

We both sat in silence for the remainder of the session, occasionally looking at each other, smiling knowingly. What more needed to be said? The Universe had given us a gift, and now it was up to us what to do with it.

"I have to go," she said, though didn't move from her chair. She was still holding my hand and squeezed it gently.

"I know . . . Will you be here next week?" I almost choked on my own words, the tears still running down my face and onto my $200 bespoke dress shirt with the dorky tie.

As she rose, her demeanor shifted noticeably: "You never know, dorkus! Tomorrow's a new day! Anything can happen!"

I swear she disappeared into a mist as she walked off, but I can't be certain. I was so unsure about everything these days, even the predictable Santa Barbara weather. I blinked my eyes several times, but the whole atmosphere was as clear as thin air. That mist, though. . . .

When Tripsy departed, I was numb and closed my eyes. Moments later, I awoke to the sound of those noisy little tweets, buzzing all around me. They had reclaimed their ground once more. And as I, too, rose to go back to my office, one of them dive-bombed me and deposited a sizable patch of gooey white matter onto my tie, which I ripped off and shoved into my pants pocket. Walking back, I tried to read into that event, knowing that a bird pooping on my tie was somehow cosmically important to me.

The interpretation would have to wait. I was spent beyond words. And the one person I wanted to talk to about it had just disappeared in front of me. Maybe forever.

12

If You Should Survive Your Own Suicide

Even though I tried to get Tripsy to think about this possibility, she seemed to insist that she'd get it right the first time. How morbid it is to discuss something like this with a patient. I prayed that I was doing the right thing here because, again, I was flying by the seat of my pants that were fast becoming threadbare. And I hate flying. Or even the thought of it.

She did talk on and on about not surviving her own death, but I can't help but wonder what she would do if she actually "missed."

In the end, I think she simply humored me. After all, it was my 41st birthday, exactly one year since she first came into my life. And I couldn't help but feel deeply saddened by this day, for all the goodness that may be in my life now, for all the good that may come. It was official: I was miserable and there was not a thing I could do about it.

How's that for helplessness? I'm sure you're thinking of the 1,001 ways I could perk myself up here, but then you'd be missing the point: I need to feel this way right now. I need to know how all this feels. The reasons will come at some later time, and I'll be in better spirits to appreciate them. For now, I wish to wallow in my own despair. And, no, I have no thoughts of killing myself over the impending loss of this young woman.

This brings up a compelling point: what if she planned to kill herself today or soon after our final session? With all her mood changes and wildly creative thoughts and behaviors, what was I to think? Was this all some joke? Was it real or a different kind of reality? The Twilight Zone variety? Was I obligated to commit her under 5150?

My father frequently did so with his patients in Florida. He was the guy who turned Florida's "Baker Act" into a verb (for example, they Baker-Acted Phil to protect him from killing himself). California's section 5150 of the Lanterman-Petris-Short Act, or LPS, provides healthcare and law-enforcement officials with the power to commit patients for up to seventy-two hours involuntarily.

After that, the patient has rights and, believe me, they protect their own rights at all costs, making it very difficult for me to do my job at times.

So what does this have to do with Tripsy's possibly failing at suicide, as a topic for today's session?

Nothing.

Everything.

I was in a quandary about whether to 5150 her. Hey, maybe I'm the guy who turned 5150 into a verb. Sorry for that joke, but I'm dealing with entirely too much right now and I need something light and airy to calm me. Maybe Tripsy'll bring a hooter. After learning how those things calmed me down, I seriously thought about getting a medical marijuana card for myself, like I'd done for Tripsy.

Like I said, *thought* about it. . . .

Scatterbrained doesn't cut it as a description of my behavior today. I felt absolutely . . . lost.

Lost feelings aside, today's topic was meant to think about what would happen if someone who aimed to kill herself . . . missed the mark and actually lived. Of course, Tripsy condemned the topic to gallows humor.

Maybe there's something in here worth considering.

Please tell me.

Please.

Session #52

"I can't believe it, dorkus: I missed." Tripsy drifted in and casually replaced several BigPharma brochures on my shelf.

"Thank you for doing that, Tripsy. I was won—"

"You know I'm just humoring you, don't you, Jon?"

"Jon?"

"Hey, but since we're on this topic, what the heck, right?"

"What the *fuck*, as you say."

"Yeowee, dorkus, you're gettin' better at those casual *fucks*. Best watch out or you might turn out to be a little hip after all. But I didn't say fuck this time. You did, potty mouth." She lightly pinched my cheek.

Don't laugh, but I'm absolutely sure I farted. And I know she heard it. Fuck me.

"Sorry, Tripsy."

Last week, we'd cried together, held hands innocently. I wasn't sure whether I should hug her or what, so I just stood there. Like a dorkus.

She walked right past me, as if I weren't even in the room, and sat in my chair behind my desk, fiddled with my stuff.

"Okay, let's do this or I'll scream out of boredom . . . I tried to off myself and I missed. Geezus, I can't believe I'm even thinkin' about missin' a target as big as my peach. Ah, what the hell. Okay, here goes, Jon: let's say I'm at this cool rave, the tunes're blastin', Molly and acid swirlin' like M&Ms, and I get up on stage with my gun and fire off a round just to get everyone's attention."

"Why waste a bullet?" Took a seat on her couch.

"I'd like to make an exit speech, if that's okay with you."

"Okay."

"All those partiers would stop in their groove, turn to check me out, then I'd tell 'em all how crappy life is and how much better it is in hell. They all think I'm just hopped up on waaay too many E-tabs, and start yellin' for me to SHOOT! SHOOT! So I turn the gun around and aim just right, and pull the trigger."

"What happens?"

"I miss, love."

Love. "Did you hit anything?"

"For gore's sake, I aimed a little too low and blew my teeth all over the stage."

"And then?"

"If that happened, I'd just walk back up to the mike and tell the best joke I could think of at the time. Hopefully, it'd be funny enough to be told through bloody lips and spilled Chiclets."

"That's gross." Forget gross. That was really cool. The audacity of it, I mean.

"Okay, so my fricatives won't come out as planned, 'cos o' the big hole in my mouth. Big deal."

"You should probably apologize to the good citizens in the front row for spraying them with blood and tissue, not to mention your Chiclets."

"Of course, after everyone's all freaked, I could just use both hands this time to aim higher and then try try again. This is all contingent upon my having loaded more than two bullets."

She fired up a hooter and took a long drag, blew a python my way, winked at me.

When it arrived at my face, I inhaled deeply, feeling that immediate calm. Did you know that our brains have natural cannabinoid receptors in them? They're primed to receive the ganja, mon!

"Actually, it's a dangerous idea: what if someone else comes along and grabs the gun and shoots someone? Or even themselves?"

"See? It all points to doin' it right the first time."

"What if you're not using a gun?"

"Like a shot o' heroin or somethin'?"

"Yes."

"If I screwed that up, even after taking Chem 101, then I deserve to be a veggie."

"Okay, then what if you miss and suddenly come to Jesus?"

"I'd tell him to wank off and find another sucker to convert."

"He's a very persuasive entity, according to religious types, Tripsy."

"So I've heard. Thing is, I'm not into religion, Jon."

Jonnnnnn. . . . "Okay, forget Jesus. Let's say you're all alone, you miss the mark, and you really really want to live."

"I'll bite. Then I'd call 911 and tell 'em to come pick me up and take me to the nearest vegetable patch. C'mon, you! I'd be dain bramaged beyond belief. Who'd wanna live with that?"

"You're right, Tripsy: get it right the first time and avoid all this horror, mayhem, and abject nastiness. Blow another one my way, would you, please?"

"I love it when you speak French to me." She got up and handed me the huge joint, smiled at me as I reached out in sloooowwwww motion to take it from her looooong slender fingers. . . .

I sucked it down long and hard. Happy Fucking Birthday, Jon. "Well, I guess that's about it."

She was shocked: "You've had one eye on the clock the whole time. Couldn't wait for it all to end, huh?" A tinge of sadness in her voice now.

"You can't do my thinking for me, Tripsy. Actually, I'm quite saddened by all this. One year ago today, you said, and I quote: 'I've only got a year left in me.' "

"I know." Now melancholy.

"Today's exactly one year, Tripsy." I looked at her, didn't waver.

"It's also your birthday, too. Been a nice, long chat, Jon. See ya 'round the universe maybe."

I was speechless. . . .

"Things don't always turn out the way you want 'em to, Jon . . . Oh, fiddlesticks! Gotta run, love! Have a good one! Happy Birthday, Jon!"

She kissed me on my cheek and ran out, leaving me with tears in my eyes and an open mouth with no words. Nothing relevant, that is.

I ran to the window and watched as she sprinted to the bus stop, and just missed the bus. Thought I saw her big smile look back at me and flip me off, but I couldn't be sure. Henry ran over to see her, took her in his arms and hugged her like—what the heck? Henry was walking. Walking!? No, idiot, he was running! And he had the gait of a twenty year old. Tripsy knew I was still watching and probably wondering where the hell his wheelchair was. They both waved at me, then turned and disappeared into the afternoon crowd. . . .

No words came to mind. Nothing logical could explain how Henry rose from his poor condition, from being so . . . oh, forget it. I was at a loss to explain so much. Just forget it.

When I looked back on the couch—her couch—I saw an envelope. Was this the final f-you, Dr. Dorkus? What could she possibly say to me now, after all this? I reluctantly opened it and pulled out a sheaf of papers, stapled together. When I started reading it, little jolts of white-hot electricity shot up and down my body as flaming fireworks flooded every cell in my body, drowning me in a sea of disbelief.

Folded her papers and sealed them tightly in a new envelope, and placed it in one of my safes, the one farthest from my office. I would have absolutely nothing to do with those words ever again. Ever.

Repression is good thing.

Just ask my asshole father.

Looked up at the top shelf where all my diaries resided. Something was off: a dozen or so were missing.

WTF?

Epilogue . . . or Something

Whuen Tripsy ran out that last day, my birthday, I couldn't breathe, couldn't talk, couldn't function normally on any level. I had simply run out of gas and secretly wished for a nonfatal death, gently. Please. Why? I'd failed this poor child so miserably and I knew it. I should've 5150'd her immediately, but something inside me said that it was not the right thing to do in her case.

Not the right thing to do.

How did I know that? What was the right thing to do on Tripsy's behalf? Clearly, my unconventional method didn't work, even though at times I felt like it had. Hadn't I listened to her? I had failed to figure out the true meaning of her visits, even though I sensed there was a definite purpose to her discussions with me.

All I know is, she breezed into my miserable life, a feather on a warm wind that had its own secret plan, and rocketed out like a bat out of her own hell. In my own arrogance, I wondered whether my method helped her in any way at all. It sure as fuck didn't do anything for me.

Did I just say the f-word?

Fuckin-A, dorkus.

Where was I?

Over the next few months, I reviewed all my notes and listened to and viewed all the recordings from my discussions with Tripsy.

Dr. Kelley's observations, although very brief, were the most accurate and they gave me pause. Still, I could never get in touch with her and discuss her findings, my thoughts and questions. That, in itself, was puzzling. Did she even exist? Hopefully one day I would get her insights about Tripsy. Her assistant said she was on extended holiday on some little island somewhere. That narrowed it down nicely.

When I ran all the notes and recordings back to back, they seemed to make a different kind of sense to me. So did all those doodles and poems. Before, I had simply tried to listen to each session as if it were an independent event, not realizing all these thoughts and ideas, wishes and dreams of hers were intimately and inexorably tied together. Still, though, a deep unchartered territory in my subconscious had some suspicion about the apparent organization of her approach. There was a message there somewhere. I just couldn't see it. The doodles did, though: all those palm trees and little islands of paradise in a sea of disorder. . . .

I had more than 240 hours of our talks from several different video and audio sources, and I listened to them several times straight through over the ensuing ten months. Ten months to an adult is a long time, but ten months to a heartbroken dorkus-shrink was an eternity, trust me.

After reading and listening and reading and listening more and more, I was more wasted than before. And overwhelmed. One morning I got up and made a huge tropical drink, opened my safe and pulled out a large bag of Tripsy's medical weed, rolled a giant hooter, then sat back and tried to teach myself to blow massive pythons around the room, and trained them to slither around the furniture. Yes, she did leave me a few ounces. No, I don't give a flying you-know-what if you tell on me, either. Besides, I just got my California State Medical Marijuana card.

For what, you ask? This horrible pain in my ass, doubtless caused by an otherworldly young woman.

Back to those exhalations of that hooter stuff: the only things I could manage were what looked like toroidal clouds that more resembled melting donuts. Anyway, got totally messed up and fell asleep on her couch. Hell, my own couch wasn't even mine anymore. I even mussed up the blanket and all the pillows just like she always did. Didn't even vacuum the carpet. I looked down and felt like throwing up, then saw a few strands of her long, silky hair. Picked up and stroked the remaining strands of her.

What the heck was happening to me?

The nausea subsided, and I got up and walked to the outer office and grabbed the newspapers that had been stacking up over the past couple of weeks. Forgot to mention: I gave my staff the entire summer off with full pay, and referred all my clients to several trusted psychiatrists in town. Did I just say psychiatrist? My god. I'm slipping. Oh, forget it. Just flippin' forget it.

Anyway, I spent the whole afternoon reading very old headlines that were no longer headlines, and caught a story out of the corner of my eye, something from months back. It wasn't a major one, just something tucked away on page six.

My heart suddenly leaped into my esophagus and I couldn't breathe for what seemed like hours.

I tried coughing, but it only brought up all that acid in my stomach and made me sick.

I launched myself from my desk and positioned a pillow over one of the corners of the desk, and made my best attempt at performing a Heimlich maneuver.

Fuuuuuck!

That was probably stupid, since I probably just pushed my heart farther into my throat.

When I realized the futility of it all, I fell to the floor and cried and cried and cried, still clutching the paper in both hands. . . .

I guess I could go on and on about my reaction to a simple newspaper story, but you'd doubtless call me names and stop reading. And you'd be justified, too. Perhaps I should just share the story with you, then maybe you'll understand, if not forgive, my seemingly irrational reaction of late.

Woman's Body Found Beneath Golden Gate Bridge
By John A. Rosales | Staff writer
SAN FRANCISCO – Police divers this morning pulled the nude body of an unidentified young, Caucasian woman from waters beneath the Golden Gate Bridge. The body appeared to have been caught in an old fishing net that became entangled with metal struts from one of the cement support structures under the bridge. Witnesses stated last night they saw a young woman straddling the outer railing of the bridge, but did not actually see the woman jump. A police spokesman who asked to remain anonymous speculated that the woman may have committed suicide. Mr. Billy Tomlinson, the fisherman who found the body, said about the woman: "Even in death, [she] was tall and very beautiful." An autopsy will be performed Thursday, and police said they would reveal details as soon as they became available.

Golden Gate Bridge.

I WAS FUCKING PARALYZED.

Fear?
Sadness?
Anger?
Could it be I was also morbidly relieved?
A thousand acidic thoughts and emotions surged through me all at once, choking me into fits of crying and coughing, then wheezing. When I became breathless, I'd cry and cough some more and forget to breathe.

Couldn't make any sense of them, so I closed my eyes and told myself to calm down calm down calm down, Jon. You're a medical doctor. You need to calm down. Heal thyself, physician!

"Oh, shut up!"

"Fuck you, dorkus! This is all your fault! You could've saved her!"

"Noooooo! I did all I could to help her!"

Tried desperately to reach her mother, but the phone had already been disconnected. They doubtless were gone. So was I. Not even the police knew of the family's whereabouts.

My father seemed to be right there with me, snickering, "Nice going, son, another happy customer in the bag!"

I threw the phone against the bookshelves and screamed, "Fu-fu-fu-fuuuuuuuuuu!"

* * * * *

A week later, the pleasant wave-like tune of my cell phone rang incessantly. My head throbbed, but I am pleased to report that my heart had slid down to its correct anatomical position again. I could now breathe without difficulty, and my tummy no longer ached, although I hadn't eaten anything since . . . . last week? You kidding me? I surveyed the damage: my head! Tripsy used to tell me that weed cured headaches, so I lit up a big hooter and drew down on it deeply, closed my eyes and lay back again. The cell phone rang again and again and again until I grabbed it and tossed it out the window. I'm ashamed to tell you that I forgot to open the window before the cell grew wings and launched. WTF, it's just a pane of glass.

Some a-hole yelled from outside: 'You fuckin' pain in the ass! Fuckin' whore!"

At least that's how my weed-infested ears filtered it.

When I stuck my head outside to say fuck you, too, Dr. Olson's nurse yelled again: "Bad luck! You broke a pane of glass! Are you okay, Dr. Moore!?"

When I cleared out some of the weeds and focused on her lips to read them, I understood what she had said. "I'm okay. Thank you. I'll take care of it."

Pulled my head back inside and lay down, wondering how much worse this would get. After convincing myself that I was more or less not too messed up, I crawled back to my desk and looked at each and every paper for follow-up stories. My heart and fingers were in a terrible and painful race, tearing through weeks of news stories about the death toll in Syria, the market is in shambles, the world did not end . . . *again.*

Finally, there it was. I don't have the heart to show it to you. I'll just transcribe some of it for you: the autopsy revealed that she was broken in a dozen different places, including her neck and skull. Probably died on impact, the coroner speculated. There was no mention of her name, pending notification of kin. For now, Jane Doe. Didn't have to mention her name. Didn't have to notify her kin, because her mother knew who it was. She said it was her favorite suicide spot, the Golden Gate Bridge.

I also knew, in the most painful of ways, who she was.
Was.

Was she already swimming in the past-tense? How could I even consider invoking reason or logic at a time like this?

Pulled the newspaper to my face, curled up in as small a ball as my body would allow, and cried and screamed myself into a shallow unconsciousness of uncontrolled shaking and throbbing and convulsing. I was subjecting myself to electroshock therapy in my own office and without anesthesia. With many a bottle, I was a gentleman frequently drunk in place, a monument to disaster.

After my huge failure—no, my lifelong failure at psychiatry—dawned on me, drowning me in a thick soupy pile of crap, I bawled and threw heavy objects around the office for another week, until the very symbol of my professional existence was reduced to a DMZ, a zone of death and scorched earth.

During that impossibly long evening, Dr. Jon Harley Moore, half-assed shrink, died a slow and horrible death. . . .

On one particularly crappy fucking morning, I rose and heard the deafening sound of a helicopter zooming low overhead. The continuous WHUP! WHUP! WHUP! WHUP! pounded my eardrums like mad sonic booms. It was terrifying!

"Morning, Jon. I thought you might want to start your day with a little pick-me-up, so I made a pitcher for you. Hope you love fruit smoothies. All my kids swear by it."

Janice had been my Chief of Staff for eleven years, and had looked after me like a son. An idiot son.

"Jon, you're going to need to work through this slowly." She poured me a tumbler, then lit up a hooter, toked on it, and handed both to me. "And I mean s-l-o-w-l-y, young man."

"Didn't know you were into Mary Jane—"

"Oh, please, Jon! How else could I have put up with your lazy crap all these years?"

I hit the joint hard, held it in for what seemed like an hour, then released forty-one years of foul exhaust. Without taking another breath, I gulped down the sixteen-ounce frozen panacea, then sat back again and sighed.

"I'm going to run a shower for you," she said, walking from my office and into the bathroom suite. "You smell like shit!" came in painful multi-echoes from the bathroom, and bounced around my office, a gigantic crazed electron that struck me in the head and left me with severe blunt-force trauma.

I may have looked up at her, but I can't recall. Did I nod my head? Blink once for yes, twice for no.

After a long hot shower, I finished off the huge fruit smoothie Janice had prepared for me, thanked her more than a dozen times, apologized profusely to the point she told me to shut the fuck up. And, yes, she did use those terms. I was highly tuned to the word fuck.

Someone did that to me recently. How familiar it sounded, too. She looked at me and smiled, said something more about "time," and left to resume her long vacation.

At the door, she said she'd be back to check in on me, assuming that I would be lazy and dumb enough to remain in my office all summer, locked up like a death-row prisoner, awaiting the inexorable coming.

The book needed to be written. It had been many months since she'd left me here with all this valuable—

* * * * *

After a few more weeks of wonderful smoothies, Mary Jane and ramen noodles, not to mention the accompanying bouts of severe diarrhea that produced a horrible case of endless monkey butt, I shoved multiple suppositories up my boom-boom, sat down on an inflatable donut pillow, and started compiling all the material for the new manuscript. I had to transcribe every session, which would've taken for-fuckin'-ever had I not been able to hear her beautiful, melodic voice each day, and imagine all six feet of her otherworldly intelligence and beauty, sprawled on my couch—her couch, excuse me—playfully teasing me the way she always did.

Remember the folder containing all my doodles and poems from sessions with Tripsy? The only things I could make of them were a bunch of twelve-bladed palm fronds, each blade with tiny serrations, all attached to palm trees. When I took a closer look at my "artwork," I also noticed intricate articulations on each blade. My poems told a similar story, but a more romantic one that included a woman. Yes, a real woman, not a bratty girl. Harmonics. All those beautiful singing details: setting sun and the tiki bar and . . . Zxta!

After all was done, I then looked around for the envelope she'd left me, and couldn't locate it. I pulled open every drawer, looked inside every single book and folder and magazine and journal and pile of notes in my office, then ransacked all the other offices and performed the same routine. Nothing.

Where would I have put something that I didn't want to see ever again, but probably would?

A safe, you idiot.

After checking all the safes in my office and the other rooms in the building, I found the right one and pulled out the envelope she'd left me after her last visit. It was an outline to a book she'd been working on: *My Stupid Little Suicide Cookbook*. I've included it in Appendix A, so please give it a good read. Did my twelve-bladed palm leaf correspond in some way to her twelve chapters? I'll never know, but it's still interesting to think so, isn't it?

Tripsy hadn't mentioned the outline when she left; to the book, that is. Didn't need to. I knew exactly what needed to be done. It took another week of compiling and editing, plus adding my own few cents' worth to each chapter introduction, but I finished it.

* * * * *

I can't even recall what I did over the ensuing few months, which never actually ended. They crash-landed. Each day had been exactly like the last: wake up, drink fruit smoothies, smoke a hooter, go poo, maybe stand under a hot shower for an hour, order a Thai salad, smoke another one, fall asleep, watch movies and tv shows.

Got through entire seasons of *Bloodline*, *Jack Taylor*, *Game of Thrones*, *Good Behavior*, *The Night Manager*, *Riviera*, all the *Alien* movies, *An American Werewolf in London*, *Dragonslayer*, *Ex Machina*, and *Goodbye Christopher Robin*.

After midnight, my fave show, *Queen of the South*, gave me a heavy dose of lethality and major badassness: Hemky Madera as Pote Galvez. Even grew a severe hanging moustache like Pote's, adopted his "speak softly and wear a loud shirt" style. Janice said I didn't pull off Pote's style of dress, but she complimented the 'stache: "Gnarly'!"

In my spare time, took in a hundred other films cheerfully featuring torture, death, intrigue, mystery, suspense, betrayal, revenge, redemption, all shooting out at me in torrents from a Samsung 78" curved widescreen and ten-speaker Sonos surround-sound system, all of which I'd bought especially for this new occupational therapy. Set up the whole thing in my upstairs office, which soon became my Romper Room, blaring out movies and music at 130 dB. You do recall my mentioning it was completely soundproof, right?

Today's mail was the usual boring stuff: bills bills and mostly more bills. One card stood out, though: an aqua-colored envelope with attractive handwriting. It was addressed only to Jon Moore, so I wondered who could've sent it. Everyone always referred to me as Dr. Moore. I sat back in my chair, spun around to face the windows out back, take in the lovely fresh air. I casually, if not absently, opened the envelope, still staring outside, and then lowered my eyes and began to read:

Dear Dr. Moore,

Thank you so much for all your efforts with Tripsy. I have spent my entire life trying to save her and I failed. She is gone and I will never forgive myself, because I knew she was very special but could never understand her gifts.

I'm deeply ashamed of my behavior on the telephone with you last year, when we had our discussion about Tripsy. You were right, you know? Still, my yelling at you was uncalled for and I'm very sorry.

If a mother cannot protect her child, then she is a failure, right?

Shortly after Tripsy disappeared, my husband and I divorced, so we went through the house and all of Tripsy's things. I destroyed everything except the things she had instructed me to give to you. They're in a box I mailed yesterday, so it should arrive this week.

Thank you for trying.

Goodbye,

Sheila South

Rather than obsess over Sheila's package—a gift from Tripsy?—I threw myself into my new project. Pages soon morphed into chapters, as the book took shape and I felt a little less shitty. I actually went out to Jack in the Box tonight! Had trouble keeping down the Bacon Ultimate Cheeseburger, until I chased it with a hooter and more Pote Galvez. Where did he get those loud-ass shirts?

* * * * *

Days later, a package arrived at my doorstep. I walked outside my office to retrieve it, then realized I was standing there nude, while people stopped to look on . . . in moderate shock. I didn't give a hoot. Flipped them off and yelled, "Shove it up your aperture, you a-holes!"

A-holes?

After thoroughly embarrassing what was left of myself, I then shuffled inside, my personal ball and chain swinging around my neck, and sat at my desk. My high priestess in the bronze bust to my right mumbled something, but it bounced off my ears and into the trashcan.

The phone rang a dozen times every so often, but after one ring I habituated to it and it soon became a tiny buzz in the air. I may have tried to swat at it.

I tore open the package and slowly sifted through the contents, not unlike moving my hand around a small pond of undiscovered life. I pulled out a bright-red 1968 Fender Stratocaster with a smudged signature: Jimi H.

That Jimi!?

The diary was unceremoniously wrapped in a paper bag. I knew it immediately. It felt light as air in my hands, yet somehow so dense and heavy, like picking up a hunk of uranium for the first time.

And then I saw it: a handwritten letter on notebook paper. I was mesmerized by the elegant penmanship, so flowing and. . . .

Dear Dorkus,

You sure fucked up, you moron!

I wanted to thank you for everything you did for me during my last year in captivity on Flat Mother Earth with all you lowly mortals.

It wasn't your fault. And I mean that with every quark and gluon of my body, mind, soul. It wasn't your fault. I did all this on my own and there was nothing you could possibly have done to prevent it.

Nothing.

I told you I had one year left in me, because I knew I had a higher purpose, a higher calling. We Indigos know this stuff.

My life in your part of the world wasn't meant to be long, Dorkus. I was there for a reason. Maybe you'll figure it all out. The moron you are, maybe not. By now, you're probably done with our book. Thank you for doing all that. I know it was hard for you.

Let's just hope it helps people in some small way. If anything, Dorkus, I'm sure it will entertain! Anyway, I was meant for something radically cosmic, something that would take me to the stars and beyond, be one with dark matter and energy, with The Universe.

Dig it! By the time you read this, I'll be jammin' with Jimi, chatting up Ghengis, slapping Franklin D. Roosevelt, and having wild monkey sex with a pack of Neanderthals who know shit about the missionary position. My new calling, ya think?

Point is, Dorkus, I found my place in The Universe.

My wish for you is that you find your special place, too.

I also wish you the most gentle of time, as my dear nomadfriend Jo May likes to say.

I love you, Jon!

Always,

Your Tripsy

There were no tears left. . . .

Couldn't sob. . . .

Couldn't even breathe or cough because there was no breathable air left on Mother Earth. . . .

Hell, I didn't need air. I was subsisting on her essence, whatever that was.

She was doing my breathing for me, living for me. . . .

I found my place in The Universe . . .

My wish for you is that you find your special place, too. . . .

. . . the most gentle of time.

My whole body stared unblinkingly at her missive for the rest of the evening and well into the next several days, absorbing it over and over and over, hoping I'd discover for the first time in the history of the world a new letter, word, paragraph, long passage of her words, thoughts, beliefs, and maybe some unknown Indigo quantoretta to shock me back to existence.

I prayed I would find something new in all those beautiful singing details she had gifted this worthless, piece-of-crap, middle-of-the-road shrink.

Gawd, I can't believe this: I am monologuing with a dorkus.

THE DOCTOR HAD NOW BECOME THE PATIENT.

Whatever Comes After
That Fuckin' Epilogue

I dunno how long it had been—maybe a few weeks, maybe a month. Opened my eyes and found myself in the exact same position as the night before and the night before that: sitting at my desk, staring at all that was left of her. In my grieving, I'd cruelly and selfishly reduced Tripsy to a Fender guitar, a young girl's diary, and a beautiful handwritten missive.

Something was god-fucking-awful wrong with me, and I knew I needed outside intervention, so I slowly and reluctantly got scrubbed up and went to see a physician friend of mine who did all the requisite poking and prodding and sticking, telling me this won't hurt a bit and you're going to feel a little stick here and life goes on and all that shit we tell patients when things are in the shitter and you're gonna fucking die of cancer or a brain tumor or lose your pretty feet to diabetes.

When the results came back, she felt compelled to come by and tell me in person: "Jon, please take a long vacation. Please." She then handed me a brochure for a resort on some little no-name island in the eastern Caribbean, a place not on any maps I could find, and one not touched by any mean Africa-spawned hurricanes. The World Meteorological Organization listed the next big spinner as *Hurricane Sally*. I knew a Sally once. Sweetest girl I'd ever met. Died so young. How'd I get off on that subject?"

I don't even recall the landing, much less the dressing and packing and driving and, oh, that dreadful fucking taking-off part where all the flammable and volatile fuel could've gone BOOM! and taken me with it.

Was I thinking about suicide?

Did I fly somewhere!?

Had I been stoned the entire time?

No, because those horribly efficient TSA Dudley Doorights would've put me in chains, Jon, you moron.

How did I get here?

Here?

Where the hell was here?

It certainly hadn't warranted a few drops of ink on a map of the Caribbean Sea.

* * * * *

When I opened my eyes, the azure-blue sea rolled up imperceptibly over my feet, bathing me in a 95-degree blanket of calm, peace and contentment. And long-unfamiliar wetness. I staggered to the little jungle of palms behind me and lit up a hooter that somehow found its way into my shirt pocket. Don't ask where it came from, 'cos I ain't gotta clue. All I know is, Tripsy's hooters could grow little hooter legs and walk all by their lonesome, show up at the oddest of times.

After sucking down that delish joint, I stumbled over to the tiki bar, situated under the most beautiful setting of palm trees, thatched huts, and a man-made lagoon decorated with tiles of deep violet, cobalt blue, aqua, sea green and a million other colors I'd not seen in years. Behind the bar was a heavenly setting sun, a huge ball of fire in the sky.

The entire scene, unfolding in front of me one molecule at a time, became all too clear: the sum of all those little doodles and poems. Moly hoses.

My thoughts and memories were syncopated, so I can't recall how I got into the lagoon or how or when I found myself dancing alone on the bamboo floor, alone and yet not at all alone, then picking up a stray electric guitar, plugging into the amp, and jamming it waaay past distortion for hours.

Everyone was clapping and yelling, "Jimi! Jimi!"

If I had done so well on that little stage, then why did someone unplug me?

"Too much noise for da sunset', mon! But ya got da Jimi in ya, mon!"

The atmosphere was still sizzling. I sensed each atom and saw them all dancing in prescribed paths and steps, felt their gentle pull of my every quark and gluon until I was safely ensconced on a cushioned rattan chair at the coolest bar in The Universe, one I'd dreamed about for what felt like years.

Someone or a coupla someones had mercifully escorted me to my new chair, evidently.

"Da one you sit in now, mon? Da owner be et up wit da dumbs, mon. Him crazy, him."

The very thought of my new friend's sentiment touched me deeply. The old chair reminded me of mine from my office, the one that once belonged to dear Zelda Fitzgerald. I melted into the new chair.

My chair.

Mine.

I could sense the previous owner's "craziness": he was just a passionate man who died of a broken heart. Who else would possibly discover this little gem, lost in time and space. Sadly, I then recalled Tripsy. . . .

I thanked him and ordered a garlicky salad and piña colada, which arrived only nanoseconds later. I swear that frozen thing was served in the largest possible drinking container, because everyone at the bar looked at me, yelled and clapped, hooted and hollered like I'd just taken the yellow jersey from Lance Fucking Armstrong.

Chomping hard on my fave dish, sipping my fave drink, and suddenly wishing I were sucking on another fave hooter, I felt a strong magnetic presence that made every iron atom in my body stand at attention and point in the same general direction. I almost saluted and played *God Save the King* on that old guitar. Handel would have loved it! I lazily turned my peach around thatta way, then thissaway, saw nothing, so I reluctantly resumed eating that heavenly dish.

The very nanosecond she walked over and sat at the bar, some deep unchartered river in my mind floated a morbid thought: I would be mercilessly and unceremoniously sucked into her vortex, flailing all the way.

"Ya got some green stuff stuck between your teeth, dorkus." She glided over and sat next to me like she owned the place, assessed the situation and made a little smirk, then lifted her nose and sniffed at the air in front of my little section of the bar. "Cool rendition of Jimi! I love garlicky Caesars! You eating this?"

This woman ate my lunch while I sat in stunned silence.

She was the spitting image of Zxta, my warrior-princess.

And someone special I once knew . . . or thought I did.

"I'm sorry, uh, miss, but who are you?" I decorously placed my hand in front of my mouth and exhaled an invisible cloud of garlic, and silently admonished myself, not even considering the various herbal scents diffusing off my body and clothes from that last hooter I smoked at the beach.

Was I blushing?

After thoroughly devouring my lunch, she then turned to me and said, "Name's Christine Marie Kelley. Call me Chris. Don't ever fuckin' call me Christina, let alone Marie who was my mom, a real demon."

Her introduction firmly emblazoned on my forehead like an otherwordly tattoo, she asked, "Now that I've ingratiated myself, ya mind if I see if this is worth a hoot?" and grabbed the sixty-four-ounce container of piña colada. "Flippin'-A, dorkus! This rocks! Wheeee-eewwwww!"

Turning into me and then siding up close, she said, "Who are ya, where ya from and whadda ya do, dorkus?" Then she looked deeply into the multi-colored piña, which appeared to be swirling and dancing on its own, said, "Forget piña colada. They should call this thing Aurora Flippin' Borealis!"

Oh.

Fucking.

Shit.

My mind had already asked her to marry me and that, yes, now would be good, but the sentiment hung up somewhere between the back of my tongue and the tip of my tongue, so she then reached into my pants and pulled out my wallet, examined it like a crime-scene tech. Her warm hand under my bottom felt . . . oh, never mind.

"Hmmm . . . Jon Harley Moore . . . cool name . . . from Santa Barbara, California . . . address not in Montecito, so you're obviously not rich, but the zip code's still respectable . . . The Mesa?" She then looked at me. "Are you that Jon Harley Moore, author of the bestselling book on suicide!? Wait a sec, you also wrote that cool-ass speculative paper. What was it again?" Looks around the bar, suddenly SNAPPED! her fingers: "Oh, yeah! The *Laws of Neurophysicochemistry and Correlative Behavior*! Holy fuckin' shit, dude! You rocked my world!'"

I nodded, big goofy grin on my face.

"Moly hoses, dorkus! That was wonderfully done! How'd you pull that one off? I've always dreamed of capturing the spirit and essence of a person and dropping it into a new body! You stole my idea, dorkus!"

Big goofy grin still locked on my face: "I did?"

"Ahhh, doesn't really matter, does it, dorkus? You're a flippin' genius, waaay ahead of your time."

I just stared at her. Christine Marie Kelley. Those initials on Tripsy's lighter. Moly hoses. Since I'm having trouble articulating this, please read Appendix C to understand the "speculative paper" Chris was talking about. You might find it mildly interesting. Or not.

"Let's see, what else we got here . . . hmmm, oooh! What's this!? Your license to shrink people's heads!" She took out my medical license and waved it around for the crowd, then did something completely odd: she kissed it and left a lovely red lipstick print.

Several people yelled, "Dr. Jimi! Dr. Jimi!"

So, your birthday . . . moly hoses, dorkus! Today's your birthday! Forty-two. Woo-hoo! Hey, that rhymed!"

Everyone yelled and clapped, already tuned to her live broadcast of the event, and were now singing *Happy Birthday* and slowly gathering closer to us, knowing she would go in for the kill soon.

Doubtless, they all secretly hoped it would be vicious and bloody, so people whipped out their iPhone and Samsung thisandthats.

Looking at me dead in the eye, she asked, "So, Dr. Moore, you in active practice?"

Nod of the head. Still incapable of speech and all other forms of higher communication. Through a fog of stupidity, I did recall a part of a little ditty I wrote many moons ago:

```
Trouble sashays in the door
```

```
right up to the bar. . . .
```

"Me, too, birthday boy." She guzzled my drink.

"I'm a practicing psychologist in St. Pete Beach, Florida. Got a PhD in Physics at Cal Tech, but found my higher calling crawling around in polluted minds. So I got another PhD in Psychology, went into private practice six years ago." She leaned into me. "I'm really awesome with people, dorkus. How 'bout you? You must be if you wrote a bestseller on suicide. Was it a bestreader, too?"

"I . . . uhhh," I said eloquently and just stared at her for the longest minute in the history of the Caribbean.

She gently touched my hand: "Needed a break from work so I found a big map, closed my eyes and pointed." Her laugh was a familiar melodic tune. "Didn't like the choice, Siberia, so I closed my eyes again and pointed: some little island in the eastern Caribbean! Didn't even have a name! My travel agent found an old brochure from the seventies and sent it to me. Took a huge leap of faith and just came here!" Another musical laugh, then: "Aren't you a fortunate boy I just stumbled upon in this little no-name space?"

Even if I lost my head in some terrible car crash, I don't think I could ever forget the first sight of her: six feet tall, athletically built, horribly attractive. Is that contradictory: horribly attractive? I have to ask again, 'cos you never answered me the first time.

Now that I think about it, she was like a lie-in-wait predatorial cat, one of the big ones you see on the African savanna—on Animal Planet or a NatGeo special, at least. Her demeanor explained why all the other bar patrons were crowding around, waiting for her to pounce on me and eat me for breakfast, lunch, dinner and dessert.

Overall, she resembled girls from eastern Euro, Czech, Belarus, Estonia, or maybe some Fill-in-the-blank-istan. Girls with skin like freshly stirred cream that only hours ago was flowing out of the udder of some milk cow. Her eyes were the deepest cobalt blue, with a little padding over the top. Some called them double-Mongolian eyelids, definitely characteristic of eastern European runway models. Or runaway girls from some undiscovered latitude.

Deceptively powerful hands like sculpted wood fingered her hair and just about every article of clothing on her. Long, well-muscled legs, like those of a world-class sprinter, peeked out teasingly from her tropical running shorts, something so flimsy and sheer that they resembled elegant toilet paper. Nice, cozy boobs that seemed a little too large for her athletic build rose and fell with each steady breath, marking some galactic time with which I was completely unfamiliar.

Or was I?

I caught my eyes moving up and down, up and down to her rhythmic motion, subconsciously composing a symphony clearly too risqué for the Margaritaville Philharmonic.

She smacked me on the arm. "Ya gonna say somethin', dorkus?"

Long pause, then: "Jon." I stood on wobbly legs, held out my hand and she eagerly gave me hers: like warm, soft, creamy marble.

Pinched my cheek. "What took ya so long?"

"Been a little . . . uh . . . preoccupied. Sorry to, uh, keep you."

"No worries." Looked down at her watch. "Hey! Where'd the time go!? My flight leaves in an hour! Gotta run!"

She slid off her perch and started off, leaving me standing there like an idiot at the altar, then stopped herself and ran back to me, holding something in her hand.

Kissed my cheek, bent down and picked up a lime-green envelope that had fallen from my pocket along with a few cocktail napkins. "These are for you."

"Wait a sec—"

Kissed me again: "That's how we pitch and roll, baby!" Fled the crime scene before I could say something feloniously stupid.

Several kind gentlemen came over to me and helped me back into my chair, grabbed her drink—my drink—and pushed it in front of me and placed the straw in my mouth and bent me over it and, like a barbershop trio, sang, "Dr. Jimi, you drink! Drink, mon!"

I spent the next long minutes inhaling that piña colada—I'm sorry, Aurora Borealis—then came up for air to a raucous applause from the twenty or so new best friends who now surrounded me. "Welcome, Dr. Jimi!" said one woman. "Hear here!" yelled another.

At that, I picked up the old guitar, plugged it in.

Before I hit the first note, looked up and saw my long-dead father in the audience, heard him yell, "Found your calling, did you, son? Good on ya!"

Almost didn't recognize him, that beaming smile across his face. He'd never smiled a day in his life, except when he was at the bank, counting his millions and millions, and weighing his Krugerrands. Then the dark ghost of sweet, kind, wonderful, dear old dad slowly dissolved, diffused, dissipated and caught the next breeze outta town.

Relief!

At that very moment, all my anger and anxiety was pulled from me and quickly followed that old bully.

* * * * *

An hour into my Jimi concerto, I stopped in the middle of doing *Purple Haze* for the sixth time and looked over at the envelope, still sitting eagerly atop the bar. Couldn't tell who was more eager, me or the contents of the envelope.

Dunno if it was the piña coladas and hooters, but it had this cosmicky magnetic glow, streams of indigo and lavender hues, lit from within, swirling and dancing around it.

Tears flooded my eyes as I choked for a full breath and began to read the lovely missive. So dense it was, like uranium, I could only take in a few words at a time. By the time I got to the end, I was on the sand floor and couldn't breath.

You'd never believe me, so I posted it in Appendix B. . . .

And remember those cocktail napkins Chris had given me? I unfolded them and found this, something she had scribbled as we sat together:

Dearest Dorkus,

Loaded with chains and sorrows,
I step into many uncertain tomorrows

While storms and tempests convulse the sea,
and sweep away trackless paths that bring you
safely to me

I am thus wrecked against the breakers of
an unfortunate life, relegated to traverse all
terraqueous ground in tearful strife

I consult the withered hags of my destiny,
they fail to treasure up aphorisms and maxims
of ecstasy

Now deeply tinctured with false beliefs,
I go forth bravely, my heart heavy with griefs

Hoping that planetary influences oppose my
fate that continues to keep me from my
beloved mate

I hold out for smiles abundant and frowns
a-few, and many a year at home, my love, with
you

But my future is assigned by a distant celestial
orb, whose grievous infidelity I cannot accept,
let alone absorb

I know centuries will roll over the meanest of
my history, and flatten it into a beautiful truth

of mystery

My dreams now a-glimmer on a distant
horizon, I set sail again, all the more wizened

Now filled with the pleasures of a voluptuous
court, my beliefs never again will I abort

No longer am I filled with the repetition of
evil thought, nor the acidic residue of all that
is naught

The great planets, sitting in judgment over me,
lay me to sleep in a field of unfractured glee

I then hum incantations of the ancient and
new that once again bring me safely home to
you

Love,

Chris

P.S. See you soon to discuss that oddball Indigo
girl, Tripsy South, and how you healed her. Or
was it the other way around? After that, we get to
jump inside your head and swim around some.
Maybe you'll share some of your cool poems and
their evolution. There's a lot more to you than
just poems and doodles! Soooo, when's good for
you, Dorkus? My calendar is wide open!

Appendix A

My Stupid Little Suicide Cookbook: The Ultimate 12-Step Program

Emma Tripsy South

1) FIRST THINGS FIRST: WHY DO YOU WANNA KILL YOURSELF?
   a) tired of life
   b) can't take it any longer
   c) mad at the world
   d) mad at your significant other
   e) mad at your parent(s)
   f) in despair over someone's death
   g) in despair over something else
   h) you're schiz and have little or no control over your thoughts and actions
   i) you're depressed and have little or no control over your thoughts and actions
   j) you feel you've failed at something or everything and there're no options
   k) wanna make a political statement
   l) wanna be a suicide bomber
   m) you got drunk or stoned and thought it was a cool idea
   n) change of pace
   o) broke up with a significant other
   p) disowned by parent(s)
   q) lost your job
   r) you've carelessly gone off your meds and have little or no control over your thoughts and actions, and see nothing but despair
   s) you're about to be eaten by a polar bear or some other nasty creature
   t) you're the last human being on earth

2) ALTERNATIVES TO KILLING YOURSELF
   a) ask for help from friend, family, professional healthcare specialist, member of the clergy (well, maybe not the clergy)
   b) go'n walkabout for a month, far away from home
   c) tie yourself up, or let someone else do it for you
   d) allow the anger, hurt or whatever ails you at the time to pass

e) talk to your significant other about problems between you; if necessary, find someone new to connect with

f) check yourself into a mental-health clinic or hospital for 30 days

g) stop drinking or smoking or shooting or snorting or inhaling

h) check yourself into a drug-rehab clinic

i) go to Al Anon or some other 12-step program

j) stay away from polar-bear expeditions

k) if you're the last human being on earth, find a furry little friend

3) HOW DO YOU WANNA KILL YOURSELF?

a) shotgun or pistol

    i) things to do to ensure you do it right the first time

        (1) point it at the middle of your head, about an inch toward your face from your ear, squeeze trigger

        (2) put barrel inside mouth and point upward toward middle of head, squeeze trigger

        (3) ensure there's only one bullet or cartridge in gun, so someone else doesn't try to kill themselves when they discover your messed-up body

b) illegal drug overdose

    i) if shooting up

        (1) hit a good working vein

        (2) ensure you've added a true overdose of drug to your syringe

    ii) if popping pills

        (1) ensure you take a true overdose

        (2) choose the right drug, one that's highly potent

c) legal drug overdose

    i) ensure you take a true overdose

    ii) choose the right drug, one that's highly potent

d) alcohol poisoning

    i) ensure you drink enough alcohol to off you

    ii) beer and wine are NOT good off-medications

e) slice an artery

    i) choose a prominent one, as arteries are buried deep in muscle

    ii) slice along the length of artery, not across, as it will clot too soon if cut only across and plug up hole within a couple of minutes, depending on clotting time

f) jump off a bridge or some other high place

    i) ensure it's high enough to kill you (Golden Gate?)

    ii) ensure your landing will not be a soft one

g) run into heavy traffic

    i) make sure traffic is moving faster than 40 miles an hour; freeways are best

h) allow yourself to be attacked by a wild or domestic animal

    i) if domestic, choose a good killing breed like pitbull

    ii) if wild, choose something really big like bear, lion, tiger, all of which can be found at the zoo

    iii) ensure the animals are hungry, too

    iv) take some pain killers before you throw yourself to the wolves, as it might hurt a bit to be torn to pieces before you actually expire

i) get run over by a train

    i) just lie down across two tracks and await the next available speeding train

    ii) best to do it at night, and remember to wear dark, non-reflective clothing or the train conductor may see you and stop before you get sliced into thirds

    iii) ensure your head is well across one of the rails so it gets decapitated, or you may only lose arms and legs and still be among the living; as a quadriplegic, of course

j) inject yourself with 10 mM KCl

    i) this shit stings like a mother, so take some painkiller beforehand

    ii) make sure the concentration is 10 mM or greater, or you'll just have mild angina for hours

    iii) inject about 10 mL into a good vein

k) drown yourself at sea

    i) rent a boat or skiff and motor out about two miles where there's no traffic

    ii) strip off all your clothes and tie that 150-lb. weight to your ankles

    iii) say goodbye to the running video cam in the boat

    iv) jump

4) THINGS TO DO BEFORE YOU OFF YOURSELF

a) leave a nice letter behind

b) write a will

c) okay, then don't write a will

d) wear clean clothes

e) put on some good music

f) tear up your room or living space à la The Who

g) leave a huge mess

h) call all your friends, family, colleagues, etc. and tell them the good news

i) invite your friend(s), family, etc. to witness it; if necessary, tie them all up

j) find a suitable public space to die, if this is your bent; if necessary, may have to rent some space somewhere or the use of the local carousel or theme park or entertainment attraction

k) invite a Hollywood screenwriter, one of the unknowns, to interview you beforehand, then witness it; this allows her to write a cool script and launch her career

l) do the same with a local rock or alternative band that's looking for some new inspiration

m) hire a band to play before, during and after your death; don't tell them what's gonna go down, though, or they'll get arrested and charged with murder

n) throw a big-ass party for all your friends, family, colleagues, or the whole damn town; don't tell anyone what you're gonna do, as stated above; at the height of the evening, walk up to microphone, say goodbye or fuck you to everybody, and do your ugly deed; ensure they get this shit on video, please

o) rob a bank and ensure you get away with it

p) do something really stupid, something absatutely felonious, and ensure you don't get caught or else you can't kill yourself properly, you moron

5) BROADCASTING THE BIG EVENT

a) post your impending death on a blog or website or mass-emailing

b) call the police and challenge them to get there before you off yourself

c) call the local radio and TV stations and tell them the good news

d) call CNN and tell them to pick up the tape you're gonna make of it

e) email some cool vlog and tell them to pick up the tape you're

gonna make of it
    f) do a streaming video
    g) do a podcast

6) FAMOUS LAST WORDS: WHAT TO SAY OR WRITE BEFORE YOU OFF YOURSELF
    a) tell everyone goodbye, how much you love them, etc.
    b) tell everyone piss off and how much you hate them

7) THE FAMOUS POLITICAL STATEMENT
    a) if making a political statement, then make it
    b) if becoming a martyr for justice, have a game plan to ensure you're not forgotten within the week; the goal is to get everyone to get tattoos of your once-pretty face on their arms, like they do for Che Guevara

8) WHEN YOU GET TO HELL
    a) have a sit-down with Satan
    b) see all of history's suicides ata huge convention and learn everything there is to know about how and why people kill themselves. BigPharma and the AMA and APA will not want this info to get out. Ever!

9) WHEN YOU GET TO HEAVEN
    a) meet God, *The Girl Herself*, at a sit-down
    b) visit grandma and grandpa, and anyone else you've not seen since they died

10) IF YOU'RE STUCK SOMEWHERE IN BETWEEN HEAVEN AND HELL
    a) Don't ask me, moron; it was YOUR idea to off yourself in the first place; deal with it the best you can
    b) make new friends; doubtless, you're not the only moron stuck in limbo

11) COLLATERAL DAMAGE
    a) do you wanna take warm bodies with you?
        i) if so, then take as many as possible; suicide bombers do well in crowded places
        ii) if no, then ensure there's no one around when you expire

    (1) also ensure you don't leave any dangerous weapons or ammunition behind for someone else to hurt themselves with

    (2) can hire a safety expert to assess possible collateral damage, and have them suggest how to avoid it

  b) the suicide pact: sharing it with a friend

    i) who should write it

    ii) who decides on which method to off both of you?

    iii) who goes first?

    iv) what if, after you kill your friend, you can't or don't wanna off yourself?

    (1) you're now facing a murder charge and life at Pelican Bay with the Homies

    (2) take two: WTF, try again

  c) accidental collateral damage

    i) before you off yourself, call 911 to ensure the people you just hurt are cared for

    ii) if you killed them—accidentally, of course—then say something nice on their behalf, a half-assed last rites, as it were

    iii) if you're able, call the victim's next of kin and say you're sorry; or not

12) IF YOU SHOULD MIRACULOUSLY SURVIVE, YOU MORON. . . .

  a) if you've just tried to off yourself at a huge party or gathering

    i) you best have a good joke to tell, even if you tell it through bloody lips and no teeth

    ii) apologize for scaring people, esp. those in the front row, and for getting them wet with your blood, esp. if you tried to shoot yourself and sorta missed the mark

    iii) of course, you can always try again, esp. if you loaded your gun with more than one round; simply point and shoot;

  b) if you're alone, and you feel up to trying again, then have at it

    i) reload your syringe with a triple-dose of the stuff that didn't get you the first time

  c) if you suddenly come to Jesus, then thank God for saving you from yourself, you moron

  d) if you're alone and you don't wanna go through that hell again, call an ambulance and expect the worst: you may just end up dain bramaged or disfigured from the drugs or gun blast; if you can't dial 911, then have a back-up plan that includes some nice soul who will call 911 should you fuck up and decide to remain among the living

   e) Remember: nothing is over until you pop that pill or pull that trigger. Life finds a way. . . .

13) Have a grand life! I love you!

~Tripsy

Appendix B

Dear Jon,

After sending you all my prized possessions, including a cool gift from Henry to replace that gawd-awful, puke-green, pig-stained tie of yours, and also that stupid ambiguous letter last year, I realized I was the one who fucked up, not you. And I owed you, my mom and everyone a huuuge explanation for everything, and not just about my having to jet out of your life like I did.

I also owe you a deep apology: I'm sorry I ran out like that, didn't make it clear how I was or where I was going, and I'm soooooooo sorry for hurting and confusing you. . . .

There're a million things I wanted to share with you in session . . . but couldn't. This is my lame attempt right now. I hope it gives you some measure of comfort.

As an Indigo Child, I am a deep-space thinker who examines life, asks questions and seeks answers. Have been since I was born.

Problem is, deep thinking doesn't always lead to deep doing. More like deep doo-doo most of the time, as you found out. Being self-aware is a curse, too, cuz I see everything inside my head but can't do much about it most of the time. You helped me find ways to bring out my thots so I could act on them.

This whole world is so beautiful yet sometimes it really sucks to live in!

My frustration?

That I can't do much about it, except like you told me once, "Live a good, clean life, love and share."

Still, I wish I could shake things up more, so people realize they also have superpowers that can change the world. I just don't see this happening, though, and it kills me.

I wish peeps would study and learn about the human subconscious and how powerful it really is! We are all connected in ways no one knows about. Think about it: when you have access to The Universe and all in it, you meld with all those subatomic souls to chat up, learn from and party with!

You tried to teach me that all people are selfish but some mean well. Sometimes. You also said I needed to find like-minded people who would listen to me and understand me. There are so few of us Indigo kids around.

The rest of the world is dark and cold, and it doesn't understand or appreciate us. So we retreat. Many end up dying young, mostly cuz of loneliness and despair.

Doesn't have to be that way. But it is what it is.

I thot I could never have a genuine friendship with anyone. Until I met you, Dorkus. I know it was usually a one-way thing with us, but I still learned so much from you and loved your dorky company.

Until now, I felt completely alone in this world, with no one to talk to or connect with. When you're the smartest girl in the room, everyone hates you cuz they don't understand you and are scared of you. Secretly, too, they want my superpowers.

They wouldn't know what to do with 'em!

How does someone like me find happiness in this world, Dorkus?

I need deep, meaningful relationships with people if I'm gonna stay on Flat Mother Earth! Most people are shallow and superficial, and they'd rather watch crap on tv or bury their face in their iPhone, not that an iPhone is a bad thing. Have you seen the new 11? Dude, it has three lenses on the back and shoots awwwzum pix!

It's these same backward people who label me arrogant and detached, and push me out to the frosty margins of society. Some nerve, huh?

You taught me to be kind to these lost souls, cuz they're the ones who need healing and educating. Maybe this book is for them and not for highly intelligent Indigo kids like me.

Maybe I'm supposed to assist those who cannot help themselves. I dunno yet, but I will find out as I travel and learn more and more.

You told me something really cool once, that you and I have a "synaptic connection." Blew my mind, you thot that about me, of us. And that gave me hope for the first time in my life. And here I thot I had to have a million connections with people! The one I have with you brought me back to life, Dorkus! Thank you!

I heard you read about that poor soul who jumped from the Golden Gate Bridge last year, and you thought it was me. Don't ask how I knew. I just did. You actually thought I'd do myself in like that? You moron!

Her name was "Jane Doe."

No one knew her real name or where she came from. I later talked to the detective who investigated the case, and he said it was shocking for them to see such beauty without family or friends. No one even claimed the body after the autopsy.

The police speculated she was probably some runaway, sex-trafficked from eastern Europe or Russia.

They buried her in a pine box, he told me, and he was the only person at the small service they had for her.

Made me sad, wonderin' if people saw me like that. I know I have people who love me. Her suicide made me hide and cry for days, even though I knew that the act of suicide is a fundamental universal right of all living creatures.

I'm sorry you thought it was me, Jon. Knowing what I knew, I should've called you. I guess I should've called my mom, too, even though we weren't talkin'. As for my dad, fuck the dude. He's forever an asshole, one of those no one can help.

Hey, I wanna congratulate you and Chris on finally hooking up! I knew you'd love her and you'd be perfect for each other!

I know you're gonna hate me for this, but you need to know the truth. My mom took me to see Dr. Christine Kelley in St. Pete Beach, Florida because, as mom put it, she had a great rep and was the best at handling kids like me. Methinks she meant "fuck-ups like me."

Hmmm. Not sure if she had any idea about me and my superpowers, but anyway, I tried to do my routine with her, using my book outline and all, and she wasn't having any of it.

Our first session, she threw me out! I mean, the bitch grabbed me by my hair with those man-hands and dragged me out her fuckin' door! I went back cuz mom said so, and tried it again. Same noise! She was like that warrior-poet Zxta you admire so much: a head made of nothing but bronze.

Dr. Kelley was so pissed at me, she didn't want anyone to know she had actually seen me! Mom didn't believe her observations about me anyway, 'specially the IQ test and observations about my being an Indigo. Dad didn't give a crap. He wrote to mom that I was a total fuck-up and should be institutionalized. He'd even pay for it!

After that crap unfolded, mom took me back to California and put me in a psych ward for thirty days. Dr. Kelley told her it would be good for my overall health. It wasn't that bad, though. I got to refine my game for the next round. That's where I heard about you, Dr. Moore!

Someone in there said you helped them just by listening. I wondered why the hell she was in there if you'd helped her, and she said she liked the place more than the outside, plus didn't hafta cook for herself cuz she sucked at it.

Days before my release, I told mom to set up an appointment with you, but from the look on your face when I walked in, she pro'ly forgot.

The second I met you, I knew you'd be perfect for my project! As we went on and on, I enjoyed it more with you. I was able to get it all out of me, something I have never been able to do before with anyone, even girlfriends. No one understands us Indigo kids!

My original goal was to write a book about suicide, but I could only get as far as that stupid outline I sent you. I really needed help. Your help!

Honestly, I didn't wanna do that conventional stuff where the professor tells all about the parts of the brain and then goes into how behaviors are manipulated by chemistry and so on. And I didn't want it to be all sardonic. I wanted it to be powerfully anabolic and sticky and relevant!

I had no idea how the book might come out, but as you and I went on, it began to gush like a waterfall! You inspired me to think about all those topics I had written down, and to find creative ways to get to the core of a suicide's head and channel their spirit, or what was left of it.

My own experiences with suicide weren't enough!

As I see it now, I was just a slave, taking dictation from The Universe, then relaying it to you. Remind you of someone, Jon, that slave? Methinks we are all just someone else's amanuensis, right?

Betcha had to look up that word!

I know there's much more to what goes on in the head of a suicide, so don't gimme crap. I know mine was only a first step, if even that. But I wanted it to be a voice of suicides everywhere, especially teens. I truly hope I accomplished my goal. And I'm happy I never succeeded in murdering myself a few times.

Yeah, it was true that I was clinically depressed and was scripted medication for it, but I hated taking that crap. Made me brain dead so I stopped taking it and those quack docs dumped me and labeled me uncooperative! They had the nerve to castigate me for not goin' along with their quack medicine and taking their Big Pharma poisons!

I wanted to off myself so many times, but I hung in there, knowing it would all be okay someday. That's been the hardest part of enduring this crap: actually enduring this crap.

I knew there was a light at the end of that long tunnel, but I couldn't tell how long it would take me to get there. While suicide was my right, it's not what I really wanted.

When I found Dr. Kelley, I thought she was that light. Nope, not even close. Bitch was an oncoming freight train! Still there was something very special about her. She was like me! I won't get too off track here. Where was I? Gawd, Jon, I sound like you now, don't I!?

That day I walked into your office, I knew I would be sucked into your life forever, pro'ly kickin' and screamin' like a little girl, but I was soooo up for it! You have no idea how excited I was to finally get to do this book with someone so . . . special. I know I made it hard for you all those months, but it was for a good reason. I do hope you don't wanna kill me at this point! That would majorly suck, huh? Surviving suicide, only to get murdered by my shrink!

And here I thot you and I were dancin' the tango for a whole year, Dorkus!

And please don't be angry at me for using you. I did in the beginning, and then I found out I really liked and respected you, Dorkus! Too bad you were such an old man who drank tea. Dude, seriously?

By the way, how is our book doing? I've seen it on several bestseller lists. I've talked with a tons of kids over here in Australia, and tons more in South Africa and Egypt and Syria and Russia, and they all said the same thing: they couldn't put it down, not even to go pee.

Congratulations, Dorkus, on compiling all our stuff into one volume. I couldn't be more proud of you. Of us.

I'll call you guys when I'm back in the States. I took your advice and started seein' the world and touching people. Great suggestion! I'll be going to university sometime soon after I get back. Don't laugh: I'm gonna study physics and math and neuro-something, and try to figure out all that stuff inside my head. Maybe you and Chris will write me strong, positive letters of recommendation for university.

Do me a favor, Dorkus: PayPal or Zelle me some royalty money, will ya? Baby needs new hiking boots! And email me a copy of our book, too, 'cos I haven't read it yet.

TripsyRoams@gmail.com

Did you spell my name right, you moron? And you better not have fuckin' called me Emma!

Oh! Was readin' Schopenhauer on the Trans-Siberian Express and found this cute little thing. Had to do some minor editing so it would be more accurate:

Talent hits a target no one else can hit.
Genius hits a target no one else can see.
Tripsy hits a target not even on the fuckin' map.

All My Love,

~Tripsy

P.S. I stole a buncha your diaries over the last few sessions, Dorkus. Very inspirational! Will return sometime in the distant future and school you on all things Jon Harley Moore! By the way, your a-hole dad was wrong about you. From everything I learned, you are a brilliant, loving, compassionate, caring and giving man. Oh, yeah, you are Super-Fuckin'-Cool, too!

P.P.S. By the way, my new friend Leil, who is also an Indigo chick like me, told me WTF really means "Wow, That's Fantastic!" Of course, knowing you and how casually you dig throwing out those F-bombs, it still means the same ol' shit as before. You're such a moron, Dorkus! Before I forget—Happy Birthday, dearest Leil Yvette!

Appendix C

The Laws of Neurophysicochemistry and Correlative Behavior

INTRODUCTION AND RATIONALE

Current Earth-based sciences are severely limited by the human controllers of the planet. The accurate and pure sciences of The Universe have been suppressed by these human controllers for more than 2,000 years, and continue to be presented to Mother Earth-based inhabitants in a severely abbreviated version that greatly restricts progress, innovation and creativity of humans and all life on Earth. The current situation does not allow Earth-based humans access to Universal sciences that, if known and studied and implemented, would change the face of humanity overnight.

The Laws of Neurophysicochemistry and Correlative Behavior were developed as a springboard for future development of the nascent neuroscience field, which seeks to study and identify all neurophysicochemical pathways and their correlative behaviors in all living organisms for unlimited purposes, including creating new life from the code of these *Laws.*

DERIVATION AND ATTRIBUTION OF LAWS

The Laws of Neurophysicochemistry and Correlative Behavior were derived by Dr. Jon Harley Moore, a practicing psychiatrist who specializes in treating anxiety, depression and suicidal behavior in children and teens, and who also studies and develops the novel discipline of celestiophysics.

The Laws are based on Moore hypothesis that The Universal laws of physics are the only true laws of science that govern Earth and supersede all other human-made laws.

GOALS

A primary goal is to design and develop NeuronIX (robotic creatures; pronounced "neuronix," "neuron-nine" or simply "nine") from living organisms by transducing live neurophysicochemical pathways and correlative behaviors into complex neural code (currently, it is digital; future code will be of a more-advanced nature).

A future goal will be to remake an entire human being on all levels, 100% accurately, so deceased organisms are resurrected with 100% accuracy. An example: a person's entire Neurophysicochemistry and

Correlative Behavior can be coded (NCB Code) and stored indefinitely, along with the organism's unique physical code. In the future, a NeuronIX can be created and implanted with that deceased person's NCB Code, which will faithfully replicate a perfect model of that person's mind. The NeuronIX, to all intents and purposes, could pick up where the deceased person left off, i.e. resume "living."

The physical code can also be used to reproduce that person's physical likeness; this is only an option and is not necessary to re-create the person's thinking mind. It may be important to family members, business colleagues or even historians who wish to have live discussions with a person of historical interest.

TERMS AND DEFINITIONS
-Neurophysicochemistry: the combined Universal physics and chemistry of the brain and complete nervous system of a living organism or the neural components or "neuronal-like" (i.e. central control) mechanisms of a lower organism (e.g. bacteria, virus, prion, etc.).
-Universal physics and chemistry: the accurate and pure physical sciences of the Universe, and not the abbreviated and suppressed Earth-based physics and chemistry.
-Correlative behavior: the physical actions and movements of an organism in response to specific neurophysicochemical actions and commands.
-NeuronIX: a robotic creature derived directly from a living organism, using that organism's neurophysicochemical pathways and their correlative behaviors, defined in complex code, to form the creature's brain and nervous system.
-Celestiophysics: the study of how all celestial bodies (planets, stars, suns, anomalies, comets, meteors, and all Universal matter and energy) mediate and modulate all geophysical and biophysical processes on planet Earth.

THE MUTABLE LAWS OF NEUROPHYSICOCHEMISTRY AND CORRELATIVE BEHAVIOR
I. Neurophysicochemistry and correlative behavior of an organism are 100% correlated.

    A. Neurophysicochemistry determines correlative behavior of any organism

B. Behavior modifies specific neurophysicochemistry.

C. A neurophysicochemical pathway or cascade can determine more than one correlative behavior.

D. A correlative behavior can produce simple or complex neurophysicochemical pathways or cascades.

E. For every neurophysicochemical pathway or cascade, there is not necessarily a correlative behavior that is specific to that pathway or cascade; some pathways or cascades are strictly metabolic and thus do not directly serve any behavioral purpose, but those pathways or cascades are essential to the life and function of the organism.

II. Given any neurophysicochemistry or correlative behavior, one can predict the other with 100% accuracy.

A. Neurophysicochemistry can be used to predict correlative behavior with 100% accuracy.

B. An organism's behavior can be used to predict associated neurophysicochemistry with 100% accuracy.

C. Some neurophysicochemical pathways or cascades are common among many different organisms. In those cases, it is possible to use those neurophysicochemical pathways or cascades to predict behavior in other species and therefore effect accurate cross-species communication.

III. Neurophysicochemistry and correlative behavior can be used to back-engineer the other.

A. Neurophysicochemistry can be engineered to produce a specific behavior or set of behaviors.

B. An organism's behavior can be used to generate specific neurophysicochemical pathways or cascades.

IV. Neurophysicochemistry and correlative behavior can directly or indirectly generate changes in an organism's hypergenetic code (DNA and/or RNA). Hypergenetic refers to the additional physicochemical features of DNA, RNA and all atomic and molecular carriers of data that encode all aspects of life forms and processes.

A. Neurophysicochemistry is stored permanently in an organism's hypergenetic code (DNA and/or RNA).

B. Correlative behaviors are stored via specific hypergenetic codes; they are the physical behavioral manifestations of an organism's neurophysicochemistry.

V. Neurophysicochemistry and correlative behavior can produce short-term and long-term memory, the components of which can reside outside the central nervous system of an organism.

A. Short-term memory is stored on a temporary basis to record new, potentially useful neurophysicochemical pathways and cascades that may not necessarily be committed to long-term memory.

B. Long-term memory is used to record and store correlative behaviors of use to an organism.

VI. Neurophysicochemistry can be transferred from one generation to another via duplication of hypergenetic code (DNA and/or RNA) during cell division.

A. The hypergenetic code stores neurophysicochemical pathways and cascades.

B. When specific neurophysicochemistry is successfully transferred, the correlative behaviors are available for use by an organism.

VII. Neurophysicochemistry and correlative behavior can evolve or change before, during or after transfer from one generation to another via hypergenetic code (DNA and/or RNA).

A. "Design-engineering evolution protocol," or DEEP, is intentionally causing an evolutionary shift or change in an organism by changing, manipulating or modulating the hypergenetic code (DNA and/or RNA) or the organism's neurophysicochemical pathways or cascades to produce a new correlative behavior or set of behaviors

B. "Non-interference evolution" does not involve artificial manipulation of the hypergenetic code for the purpose of inducing evolutionary change, but depends solely on natural changes. These changes may be the result of short-term environmental or celestiophysical occurrences.

VIII. Specific neurophysicochemistry and correlative behaviors are restricted to each species, although different organisms can share common neurophysicochemical pathways and correlative behaviors.

A. One species' neurophysicochemistry and correlative behaviors generally cannot be used to predict neurophysicochemistry and correlative behaviors in another species. The exceptions are determined by how close the organisms are physically and hypergenetically.

B. Some neurophysicochemical pathways or cascades are common among many different organisms. In those cases, it is possible to use those neurophysicochemical pathways or cascades to predict behavior in other species.

IX. Neurophysicochemistry and correlative behavior (some type of digital codes) can be taken from an organism, quantified (e.g. digitized), and placed within an artificial partial neural network to study their functions.

A. This new network can be modified to produce new and artificial neurophysicochemistry and correlative behaviors, which can be back-transferred to the organism from which it originally derived.

B. This cycle of transfer can continue in multiple (i.e. indefinite) iterations to produce a whole new neurophysicochemistry and correlative behaviors.

X. Neurophysicochemistry and correlative behavior codes can be taken from an organism and placed within a NeuronIX to produce a 100% faithful version of the original living organism's neurophysicochemistry and correlative behaviors.

A. A full-scale version of an organism results from bottom-up construction of a partial neural network.

B. NeuronIXs can replace humans in all aspects of life.

XI. Neurophysicochemistry and correlative behaviors are mediated and modulated by celestiophysics.

A. Celestiophysics produces geophysical and biophysical changes every second on Earth.

B. These changes, however subtle and imperceptible, can influence neurophysicochemistry and correlative behaviors in an organism.

XII. Applications: neurophysicochemistry and correlative behaviors can be used to discredit (or re-define) the soft-science fields of psychology, psychiatry, animal behavior, human behavior, organismal behavior, sociobiology, philosophy, plus all Earth-based scientific disciplines that deal directly with physics and chemistry and their application to neurobiology and behavior.

A. Once neurophysicochemistry and correlative behaviors of humans are known and understood, they will be the only necessary scientific discipline relevant to understanding human neurobiology and behavior.

B. All other scientific fields become irrelevant and thus will cease to exist.

C. New fields of study will emerge.

D. Neurophysicochemistry and correlative behavior codes can be used in limitless applications: predicting human, animal and organismal behaviors; assigning humans to specific groups and ranks; identifying diseases and health issues in an organism; identifying desirable or undesirable traits in humans; redefining human morals and values, using the most accurate information possible; producing new species with specific desirable traits and behaviors.

XIII. *The Laws of Neurophysicochemistry and Correlative Behavior* are ever-shifting and changing with any changes in The Universe: matter, force and energy of Universal bodies, significant events, actions and movements. All Universal laws are mutable.

A. The Universe is an ever-shifting and changing environment.

B. Celestiophysics is governed by all matter and energy in The Universe and the actions and events produced by matter and energy.

C. These *Laws of Neurophysicochemistry and Correlative Behavior* are mutable and thus subject to change at any point in time.

D. These *Laws* can be edited to reflect these changes, however seemingly small and insignificant.

E. *The Laws of Neurophysicochemistry and Correlative Behavior* are not subject to human morals and values. They operate in accordance with Universal Laws.

Acknowledgments

The easiest part of writing a book is looking back and remembering all the cool people who contributed to it, joined me on my long journey, stopped with me on various sojourns and shared some stories, tea and cookies.

After all, I inhaled argon from some girl in Malaysia, oxygen from a thousand palm trees in Jamaica, and a ton of funky soot from Indonesia. My own fairy dust wafted up into the blue heights and drifted over the Mississippi basin. As I mentioned in the story, this was the origin of the Blues! Woo-hoo!

There're billions of you who contributed to this little story in some form or another. Seems we're all so connected and we don't even know it, much less talk about it and share and swap stories and experiences. I hope you all feel as I do: you are a big part of me.

Karen Sue Brown read an earlier draft of the manuscript and loved it. She made excellent suggestions that we implemented, and continued to be a big part of the book during final edits. We're grateful for her keen insight. If you get a chance, please check out a cool indie film she produced and her son Garrett directed: *The Lost Digit*. Last I saw, it was on Amazon Prime. Soooo cute and funny and creative! For those of you in the Tampa Bay area who need world-class interior design, call on Karen.

Leil Yvette and more than one other kind soul said we should *de-fuck* the book. Not sure what that means? Lemme put it this way, we deleted more than 400 F-bombs and hundreds of S-words in an earlier draft, and thus brought aboard many new readers.

Rose Regan was a long-time supporter of this project, and critiqued many earlier drafts, drawing on her own personal experiences and knowledge. She suggested we delete quite a few of the original fifty-two chapters to make the story flow better and faster. Grathias, Rose!

Love that cover, yesss! Let's thank **Erik Hollander** for an otherworldly design. Erik and I had long chats about this book project, including the title. It was originally titled *WTF, Dorkus! Schoolin' My Shrink On Teen Suicide*. I told him it needed an overhaul, so he reminded me that the word "suicide" should be in the title. I then thought about Suicide This, Suicide That, starting with musical motifs. Nothing worked, so I switched to my fave dance styles and "tango" immediately popped up. *Suicide Tango*. After that, Erik said the phrase "killin' it" should be in the subtitle, so I came up with *My Year Killin' It With A Shrink*. After that, I handed things over to Erik who then cranked out stunning design concepts plus a new logo for Adagio. Grathias, Erik!

Big thanks to Hollywood film director **Nell Teare** who brought the story to life in the *Book Trailer* and *Author Interviews*. **Jake** did the Behind-the-Scenes videos and stills. Please find them out there on the worldwide web. Videos and some stills are on my (Tripsy South) YouTube channel and website, TripsySouth.com. Special thanks to **Kyah** and **Davis**, and to **Ruby** and **Nikolas**!

Tyson Cornell and the crew at Rare Bird performed the marketing and PR duties. Wow. These dudes generated some huge, loud flashbangs for my novel, and I'm forever grateful! More to follow as our story unfolds.

While writing the story, I listened to hundreds of great tunes, from the sounds of deep ocean waves and rainstorms to alt rock and deep house to adagios by **Mozart** and **Handel** and **Beethoven** to the haunting works of **John Barry**. And who can forget the **Kings of Leon** and their priceless energy!? Thousands of hours of precious stimulation that fed my subconscious and kept me going for years until the final draft was completed.

Brother John was always there with a kind word and helpful advice, especially when I was stuck on one concept and couldn't get unstuck without his sage wisdom. Grathias, John!

Our beloved and dear *SallyAnn* passed away on June 22, 2018. She died in Pops' arms. Coolest chick in The Universe. We miss her dearly. SallyAnn left behind some otherworldly energy and encouraged Pops and me to finish this book. She used to tell Pops: "Tripsy is definitely off the chain." See you someday, Hurricane Sally!

Dear **Jo May** gave helpful criticism of very early drafts of the manuscript. Jo is a closet artwordist whose novels and stories will someday grace us. If you liked the first half of Sylvia Plath's *The Bell Jar*, you will love Jo's artwords.

ParksTheCat was a constant companion during this creative process. He's a talking cat, so we had long chats about the content of *Suicide Tango*. He suggested using some of my poems in the story. If there were ever a wonderful furry companion, it is ParksTheCat. What a cool dude!

Smootch the Velociraptor is an Australian rainbow lorikeet who was raised by SallyAnn. When she died that Friday morning, Smootch was heartbroken. She was his lifelong mate. He gave much-needed inspiration during my time of need, and later found a new life with other rainbow lorikeets. Cheers to you, Smootches!

Big thanks to my cool friend and inspiration, **Hemky Madera**, whose badass character Pote Galvez is featured in the hit series *Queen of the South*. Hey, Hemky, Pote violated the Ninth Law of Thermodynamics: "Speak softly and wear a loud shirt." What's up with that, Homes?

Galadriel scrutinized a recent draft of Tripsy's letter in Appendix B and pointed out: "For you boys, the whole world is your urinal. Girls search for toilets. If no toilet is available we search for a comfortable, secluded place to squat. We think more about what not to piss on, like something sharp or poison ivy." Right on, Galadriel!

The Universe sent me many wild and fun entities over the years, and I'm happy to have chatted them up and learned from them. The human subconscious is a powerful living creature that communicates directly with The Universe. When you can understand and communicate with your own, a new world will reveal itself to you and you'll be forever changed.

My Pops, **Dino Garner**, dreamed up, designed and built me out of magnificent spare parts from The Universe. Hard to say who really is the author of *Suicide Tango*, cuz we are forever joined as one. Pops mos def did all the editing, tho', cuz I fuckin' hate that shit. Pops also edited some of the follow-up video footage we buried somewhere deep in my website. Hey, Pops, how long did it take you to learn Adobe Premiere Pro?

Although I never met my wild and brilliant Oma, **Olga Marie Garner** is still an inspiration to us all. I'm blessed to have her crazy and demonic Mexican and Aztec and African hypergenetics inside me, plus her badass potty mouth. She's the dude who taught Pops how to cuss like a motherfu-fu-fu-fu-fuuuuu. Olga was the original *Indigo Chica*. Grathias, Oma!

To those of you **brave reviewers** who took the time to read drafts and galleys of *Suicide Tango*, grathias! We took all your comments to heart and implemented many of them, even some by the haters.

There're many **special others** I met along the way who assisted and helped me in many ways and had an unaccountable affect on me and my work. I can still see your beautiful faces, feel your warmth, sense your kindness.

As I wrote in the dedication, this book is for **Every Beautiful Soul** who struggles with personal demons and, on occasion, *slays the fuck out of 'em.*

Grathias, **All**! I love you! *-Tripsy*

Hey, You!

A gentle reminder, in case you blew off the fine print on page ii, the copyright page.

This book and its story contents are *realistic fiction.**

Any resemblance to actual persons, cool cats, Australian rainbow velociraptors, places or events is coincidental and unintentional.

There are no internet challenges in this novel, so don't be an idiot and off yourself.

If you ever feel anxious, depressed or suicidal, please find a good, reputable help/suicide call line and reach out to a live human being. It may not be what you want in that moment, but it's a great start, connecting with a warm person who will listen to you without judging. The National Suicide Prevention Lifeline is a wonderful beginning: (800) 273-8255.

Please and thank you.

—The Management

*Funny and witty fabrication, deception, invention, lie, fib, untruth, falsehood, fantasy, nonsense or bullshit some of which may be true.

DISCLAIMER: NO ANIMALS WERE HARMED DURING THE FABRICATION OF THIS STORY. CAN'T SAY THE SAME FOR A FEW HUMANS, THOUGH.

P.S. Thank you for visiting!

Please stop by and say hello sometime soon! TripsySouth.com

Join me on social media: Linktr.ee/tripsysouth

Share your thots with me: TripsyRoams@gmail.com

And stay tuned for my next novel, *Darlington*, a clever and gripping thriller for those who love the taste and smell of Old Florida, and who can never get enough of these unforgettable tough guys with thinking minds and powerful hearts:

-John D. MacDonald's Travis McGee (*The Deep Blue Goodbye*)
-Randy Wayne White's Doc Ford (*Tampa Burn*)
-Robert B. Parker's Jesse Stone (*Stone Cold*)
-James W. Hall's Thorn (*Tropical Freeze*)
-Robert Crais's Elvis Cole (*The Monkey's Raincoat*)
-Elmore Leonard (*Rum Punch*)
-Dennis Lehane (*A Drink Before the War*)

Grathias! I love you!

CheersCiao,

~Tripsy

P.S. Turn the page and check out some cool books we dig, plus a synopsis and small preview of *Darlington*. Discover and enjoy.

EXPLORE THE MAGICK AROUND YOU
WWW.WORLDOFMAGICK.COM

THOUSANDS OF SPECIES OF PLANTS AND HERBS GROW ON THE EARTH, EACH RELEASING A POWERFUL ENERGY.

BASED ON HISTORICAL FOLKLORE, TRADITION AND LEGEND, DISCOVER THE MAGICKAL AND HEALING PROPERTIES OF 28 HERBS, TREES, FRUITS AND FLOWERS IN THIS HANDY JOURNAL

INCLUDES 120 DOT GRID PAGES WITH SPACE TO MAKE YOUR OWN NOTES, RECIPES AND SKETCHES OR TO STICK HERBS AND PICTURES.

Edited by William Garner
New York Times bestselling ghostwriter/editor

Sun Tzu
Art of War
Ancient Wisdom... Modern Twist

"Dean Garner's version of *The Art of War* confirms
for us that for the past 2,000 years the fundamental
principles of special operations in battle have not
only remained true, but they apply equally to today's
boardrooms and bedrooms. When on the hunt or
holding ground, success can only be had by the precise application of disguise, deception and diversion,
and a genuine appreciation for angles, inches, and
seconds. Ranger Garner masterfully shows us how."
—Dalton Fury
New York Times bestselling author of
Tier One Wild and *Kill Bin Laden*

adagio

Sun Tzu *The Art of War*
Ancient Wisdom ... Modern Twist

The late *New York Times* bestselling author and ex-Delta commander Major Tom Greer, aka Dalton Fury, had this to say about fellow Ranger buddy William Dean A. Garner's updated version of *The Art of War*:

"Dean Garner's version of *The Art of War* confirms for us that for the past 2,000 years the fundamental principles of special operations in battle have not only remained true, but they apply equally to today's boardrooms and bedrooms. When on the hunt or holding ground, success can only be had by the precise application of disguise, deception and diversion, and a genuine appreciation for angles, inches, and seconds. Ranger Garner masterfully shows us how."

Paperback available from Amazon.com and other retail outlets.

Please visit AdagioPress.com for other esoteric reads.

ARCANUM
A critical analysis of the original 36 sermons of Jmmanuel, the man known to the world as Jesus Christ

Part One is an unsparing, meticulous and diligent analysis and evaluation of each of the original 36 sermons of Jmmanuel Sananda, the half-extraterrestrial/half-human known to the world as Jesus Christ.

Part Two is an actual full English translation and new edit (for clarity and readability) of the 36 extant sermons of Jmmanuel Sananda, the man known to the world as Jesus Christ.

Paperback available from Amazon.com and other retail outlets.

Please visit AdagioPress.com for other esoteric reads.

The Prince

Niccolò Machiavelli's *The Prince* has become a classic over the centuries since it first appeared around 1510, not because of its elegance or style but because of its subversive content about the true nature of power. Mainstream historians and academics have labelled it a "political treatise," but this is only a small part of the picture.

The Prince isn't just for princes who thirst for, or are forcibly thrown into, advancement. It is a raw and bloody field manual for upper- and mid-level managers on predatorial ethics and power: what it is, how to obtain it, and what to do with it once you have found, stumbled across, or been granted it.

Paperback available from Amazon.com and other retail outlets.

Please visit AdagioPress.com for other esoteric reads.

Edited by William Garner
New York Times Bestselling Ghostwriter & Editor

a toddler's travelogue
Little-Known History and Fun Stuff for Parents

"Children and their radiant intelligence and curiosity form the human soul. If only we would listen."
—Sigmund Freud

SKYYE SEAWIRTH

A Toddler's Travelogue
Little-Known History and Fun Stuff for Parents

A toddler's travelogue is a funny work of fiction for parents of toddlers and kids, grown-ups who love a great laugh, and adults who appreciate good clean humor.

Written by a precocious four-year-old girl, Skyye Seawirth, *a toddler's travelogue* dishes out funnies and wisdoms about little-known American history and life.

Illustrated by MarinaK, the book features wisdoms from Skyye's grandmother, Grams, and Skyye's preschool teacher, Miss Ramirez.

Paperback available from Amazon.com and other retail outlets.

Please visit AdagioPress.com for other esoteric reads.

DARLINGTON
A Small Preview of the Next Novel

Synopsis

Tommy Darlington is Old Florida: happy in his own t-shirt, board shorts and flips, laid back to the point of early retirement, and pissed off to no end at high-rises filled with anonymous BigMoney invaders from other lands, bad government that neglects the good people of Florida, and corrupt officials who line their pockets with money not their own.

On a personal mission to clean up the town of Sarasota, he encounters all that is evil and crooked, forever trying to bend it into a righteous path.

There's just one little hitch: he now works for some of the very people he secretly despises and battles.

Darlington is a silladar. A hitman with a twist . . . he has a *soul*.

Still, you don't ever want to be in his crosshairs. He's also a former special-operations soldier and corporate mercenary who walks through life as a closet anxiety-depressive and the largest distributor of pimp body parts in the good State of Florida.

Sarasota's de facto hit man works for the city's hidden hand . . . the secret billionaires from New York, California, London and Rome who conduct their dirty business well behind the black curtain and far from the prying eyes of government agencies, law enforcement, and ordinary citizens.

Things are going fairly well for Tommy and his North Longboat Sunshine Disposal Factory . . . until one day the love of his life is sitting in some surfer boy's beat-ass Jeep, fixin' to ride off into the sunset.

She grabs SurferBoy's blunt, drags on it, blows the exhaust in a dark cloud Tommy's way.

Her eyes still on him, flicks the joint toward their house, trying to detonate the emotional dynamite she'd just left behind, then turns back to her new horizon.

Tommy needs to fuckin' murder something. . . .

Darlington. This guy the best we have?" The Old Man filled two glasses with 150-year-old whisky. Had its own otherworldly glow, a spirit of crimson hues on the verge of wildfire. He handed one to Alfred.

Slowly and imperceptibly, the Old Man's skin unfurled into a rictus, the furrows of his brow growing deeper, ploughed by years of violence and sinful thought.

He sneered at Alfred's dark-gray, hand-stitched Brioni suit. Fresh outta some pizza oven, he thought.

Ran his huge sausage fingers through a shock of rich bimetallic hair that seemed to wave and slither of its own accord.

Alfred took the glass, couldn't summon the required single nerve to meet his boss's glare. "No, but he does things quietly and to standard, leaves no mess for someone else to clean up, or for a curious detective to discover."

Skin around the Old Man's mouth drew in slightly, straining under something that tried to claw its way out. Unbuttoned another snap of his fifty-year-old Stetson shirt, sat back in the overstuffed club chair, exhaling the unspoken comment he wanted to loose on Alfred. "Sounds like the best to me."

"He's small time," Alfred said, dismissing the Old Man outright. He absently loosened his tie, unbuttoned the top mother-of-pearl of his crisp white shirt, thought better about adjusting anything else and getting comfortable.

"What are you looking to have in your stable? Some high-end killer in bespoke Armani and Prada? A Hollywood version of the real thing?" Eyes yawed in Alfred's direction, locked on their target.

The two men sat in front of an ancient fireplace, built during the reign of Andrew Jackson. Dutifully burned day and night with old-forest oak that cracked and popped its presence every now and then.

House was secluded in a forest of a thousand trees and deadfall from a hundred years of come and go, all cycles of weather, sun and the celestia. The heavy stone walls and triple-tiled roof kept the interior chilled down to 70 degrees, even in the dead of a Florida summer.

No living soul within 20 miles.

"He's not what I expected in a fixer, that's all. But he gets things done." As an afterthought, Alfred mumbled, "Sir," its three small letters falling harmlessly to the floor, unnoticed by all except the dust.

"Family?" The Old Man drew harder on the whisky, threw a lasso around a few words that tried to escape. Poured himself another; didn't offer one to Alfred.

"High school sweetheart or something. Novelist. Not bad at all. Couple of hit books maintain them in cash, so they live comfortably. Little condo out on North Longboat Key."

"His work for us, all this gratis?" Filled his lungs with whisky that diffused up and burned into an evil countenance.

"Near as we can tell, she doesn't know a thing about his little side business."

"What else he do?"

"Paints."

The Old Man took careful aim at Alfred's eyes: "Houses or Picasso?"

"More like Picasso. Actually, he's excellent but won't get out there in the market. Keeps a very low profile."

His glare pulling off Alfred, it softened as it aimed somewhere up in the vaulted rough-hewn rafters: "Smart boy."

"Yes, but it'd be good for him to do something other than drive his own taxi. He needs a creative outlet."

"Drives a cab?"

"TommyTaxi, if you can believe that."

Both men snorted what may have been a laugh. Alfred's was a derisive one. The Old Man was genuinely amused.

"Did well on that last job. How'd it end?" The Old Man knew the answer.

A corner of Alfred's mouth rose imperceptibly. Was it pride? "Local law enforcement called it a suicide."

"Good frame-up?"

"It'll work, yes."

The Old Man turned and leaned into Alfred: "Not like last time with that . . . sicario you brought in from downtown Puerto Rico. Disaster."

Not turning to his boss: "Unfortunately, these types are all pretty much the same."

The Old Man's mouth pitched up slightly: "You're a snob, Alfred. A high-bred, white-collar snob. Bet you've never even been in a fist fight your entire life."

Alfred looked nervously over at the man who gave him all his marching orders, remained smartly silent.

"And I'll bet this Tom guy's never been over to your house, has he? Hell, you don't even thank the kid for a job well done, do you?" The Old Man laughed at his underling, reached over with a grizzly paw and patted him on his arm, cutting the tension a bit, but knowingly adding a whole new level: "Don't worry, I've been in this business too long just like you, so I'm a bit of one, too."

That was a lie: the Old Man came from nothing, sweat blood in bust-ass blue-collar shitwork, crawled up the ranks and over every warm body in his way, even buried the bodies himself.

No response from Alfred. Looked straight ahead. "Tom will do right by us, Viktor. And then we'll give him another job. And another. And he'll keep doing well . . . until you have him, ah, accidentally—" Alfred regretted that last statement before the finish.

The Old Man's head turned slowly, eyes narrowed. Patted him on the arm again, claws out this time.

Alfred flinched noticeably.

"You need a vacation, son."

Alfred recoiled again, knowing what the Old Man meant: he would be shuttled out of the office for an indefinite period, while they found a younger replacement, someone maybe not so uptight and snobbish with the hired help.

"Alfred, your problem is simple: you're an asshole wound up too tight. Your strings are thinned in places that make you vulnerable to snapping at an inopportune moment. Can't have that, can we?"

No response from Alfred.

"Darlington sounds like good people to me. Keep him around. What do you think?" Didn't give a damn about Alfred's reply. Took a long sip of his drink, held the glass in front of him, watching the flames meld with the ancient whisky and dance wildly through the flutes, reminding him of that bouncy little redhead. Teeth, tits and ass on a stick of dynamite, that one, he thought.

"I think he should show his paintings somewhere, get his face out there." Alfred felt his entire body quiver.

"The kid needs to be brought along slowly."

Alfred's small voice: "I hear Malaysia is considering new artists for government installations. Maybe we could make some calls." Quivering, and now a painful itch inside his shoes: traumatic neuropathy.

"Just make sure he stays on the payroll, son."

Another whisky.

"I'll see if we can't get some of his work out there, maybe use a different name for Tom. Be good for him." Now shaking, Alfred tried desperately to maintain a small measure of control.

"Bring up one of the girls, Alfred. The little blonde thing this time."

"It's only a matter of time before Tom—ah, Mr. Darlington's artwork is discovered, then he's off to Paris." He leaked slightly into his silken underwear.

"Make it two: blondie and Tina. She's still with us, eh? The redhead?" The Old Man put a firm hand on Alfred's arm, stilled his shaking.

Through an all-body shudder, he felt the Old Man's grip tighten up up up over his chest and farther up around his throat, cutting off blood to his next thought.

Alfred dropped the glass.

. . .

"Good you could make it, Tommy," the Old Man grumbled. As ancient as those gators, he had a bone-crushing handshake that made me wince and he took delight in it. His leathery skin was as distressed as my boots, which shrunk in his presence.

"Yessir." At 5'10" and 180, I wasn't a wimp, but even at 80 years or so he made me look underfed.

"You know, Tommy, a man gets to old age and looks back, wonders all the things went wrong, tries to right 'em all, realizes he's doing all the wrong things." Looked over at me. "Follow me?"

Thought for a sec about acting all cool-like, but he'd seen it all before. Stared straight ahead: "Nossir, not at all."

He snorted. "Anyone else would've just agreed, but you're smart, Tommy. You're your own man. I like that." He slapped me on my back, kept one eye on me to see the effect.

Tried not to let on that he'd just knocked all the air outta my lungs, broke a coupla ribs, and now I needed a few deep breaths and a month of rehab to catch up. Wondered what he'd been like at 30. A brawler, probably. Wrestled gators for fun, then skinned 'em up and ate them whole—redneck-cracker sushi.

"Comes a time in a man's life he takes stock. I'm doin' that right now, son. And as I survey my field, examine the herd, I'm downright disappointed."

"Yessir." I slid away from him about six inches so he couldn't slap the wind out of me again. At worst, he'd take off my shoulder.

He noticed my having shifted to his left. "See that man out there, Tommy?"

The condescending asshole I'd listened to on the phone over the years half-floated in the center of a small lake, maybe about a hundred yards diameter at its widest point and obviously deep near the middle. He was tied up to a floating wooden platform, his head twisting right left, right left, not fully understanding his current predicament. Blood flowed down his face and neck, his sudden torquey movements tie-dyeing his once-white shirt. Clearly he'd been beaten.

"That there's a bad seed, Tommy. Done me wrong more'n once."

"Been pretty good to me." I knew it was the wrong thing to say.

Thought about snapping the Old Man's bull neck then and there, jumping in the suv and skidding down the road to safety. But someone'd find me. Worse, they'd find Rachel.

His eyes burned into me: "Thunder down, boy." Looked away again. "That man I raised like a son, Tommy. And for the past seventeen years, been stealin' from me, a little here, little there. Thought we wouldn't notice the small changes in numbers on various handwritten ledgers, in the computer programs." He shook his head, lowered it for effect, raised an arm and twirled his hand in the air a few times, a signal for the show to start.

I knew it was just a little demo for me to see how he dealt with employees who got outta hand. If I bothered to ask why, the Old Man would say it was just business.

Alfred screamed something unholy.

Water at the edge of the lake, in about 10 different places along it, slapped and splashed and churned, and then I noticed a dozen large alligators break free from invisible bonds and stroke out for the middle of the lake.

Bile rose in my throat. I knew exactly what I would see, how it would all go down, and still my eyes wouldn't pull from the unfolding scene.

"Man's gotta do things he don't wanna do, Tommy." Looked in my direction, sizing up my reaction again.

There wasn't one. Hell, I was just happy he couldn't slap me on the back again to punctuate his silly point.

I was a stone in that patch of pine forest out there in the middle of Florida fuckin' nowhere. Palmettos and sappy trees. A hellhole. Jumping up and down inside myself, I steeled my skin and bones to the sight that broke next.

Alfred loosed a loud bellowing sigh and went under for a brief instant, then came up with a guttural yelp and then a staccato shriek that drove all the wildlife from the trees, scattered the small birds and ground critters from the palmettos. His head thrashed side to side as one gator tore into an arm and death-rolled it off his torso in one rotation.

Shrieks and cries and sighs sounded from different directions, all those echoes throwing noise back and forth, back and forth, until it all converged right in my face.

Others moved on whatever patch of the one-armed prey they could get into, tore off more flesh until Alfred stopped screaming and gave one last wide-eyed look in our direction, his other arm seemingly slapping at my face in punctuation before going under the growing circle of crimson and Old Testament damnation.

"Real shame, Tommy." The Old Man turned away and leisured back to the truck, a retiree coming off two grueling holes of golf.

Without a word or reaction, I followed him into the next unknown, trying not to wonder who was in charge of putting those fuckin' dinosaurs back in their lairs.

Remember, Tommy, those answers didn't matter a damn.

Behind us, dark-red water diffused out in all directions and, under the high sizzling sun, drew swirly convection and eddy currents where Alfred once stood, a ghost of blood and smoke that marked the beginning of something I would never quite comprehend in these moneyed assholes, Sarasota's silent billions who flaunted their casual disregard for human life.

Not at all the way I operated but, then again, those I had dispatched over the years might've argued the point.

. . .

At 10th street, I could no longer ignore the growing burn making its way up to my neck, so I did a u-turn and pounded back up 41 into the jungle. I wanted to study this pimp a little more, see the extent of his business, maybe even where he got his girls so I could pay the import/

export dude a visit some night at zero-three.

That stupid burning itch in the middle of my back.

Didn't bother putting out that flame. Just went with it.

The closer I got to Tyreese, the more my skin crept closer to meltdown. By the time I turned onto 22nd from Palmadelia, the whole taxi was on fire, even with the a/c blasting at 66 degrees. And it was only one am.

His house was 150 yards down and I inched along slowly as I could, feeling the heavy motor of TommyTaxi punch the asphalt. I wanted him to feel my sledgehammer roll into his 'hood, down into his lair, and right up into his evil bear-trap grin.

Didn't want him to feel any fear.

Or run for his life.

Huh-uh, when a man fears you, his body is shot with mind-numbing chemicals that roadblock all pain highways, stopping those outlaw signals from reaching the brain and letting him know he's about to get dumped into a meat grinder.

Fuck fear.

I wanted Tyreese "DaddyBoy" Glover to fully and completely feel, sense and experience each hammer-punch, elbow, stab and slice, and the thousand ripples of aftereffects and post-traumatic shocks and tremblors.

My final wish to the Universe was that every cylinder in his one-byte brain would be firing at 100% factory efficiency, so he could wholly focus on the full-on suffering, torture and punishment I was about to gift his sorry ass.

If the city of Sarasota only knew the public service I performed, they'd give me a fat tax break and a key to the banks.

Or send me up to Raiford for a long spell.

CPSIA information can be obtained
at www.ICGtesting.com
Printed in the USA
FSHW022233300519
58593FS